RUST & SALT

BY

EVAN BRANDON BRUNO

TELEMACHUS
PRESS

This book is a work of fiction. Names, characters, places and incidents are either the product of the author's imagination or are used fictitiously. Any resemblance to actual persons, living or dead, or to actual events or locales is entirely coincidental.

The publisher does not have any control over and does not assume any responsibility for author or third-party websites or their content.

Cover art and design by Scott Harshbarger

Published by Telemachus Press, LLC
http://www.telemachuspress.com

ISBN# 978-1-937387-86-0 (eBook)
ISBN# 978-1-937387-87-7 (paperback)

Version 2011.12.10

Printed in the United States of America

10 9 8 7 6 5 4 3 2 1

Dedication

For my longsuffering wife, Meme,
My longersuffering parents, Debbie and Randy,
My brother, Weston, who strengthens me,
And my friend, Greg, who is a loyal and good example.

These remain my steadfast co-authors all,
and may God bless them bountifully forever.

When the Devil comes,
To steal your day,
Just hit your knees,
And start to pray.

—Frank Rust 1959

RUST & SALT

Prologue

AS WIND RUSHED over the plains outside my window, blowing gusts of exhaled dirt and clod, I had dreamt nothing but the cautious sleep of a guilty conscious. I drifted away sometime in the endless nighttime hours to sounds of a Panhandle summer as the farmhouse was pelted like a wayward vessel in a meteor's wake.

Then the digital pattern roused me from another despondent, dreamless slumber. The telephone came into focus. Its red light fluttered. I picked up the handset and listened, salivating for intel like a some rabid coyote roving the plains.

"Raining here," the voice said, and I could hear he was telling the truth. It wasn't a bad connection at all, just rain, hard rain. Fella on the other end must be outside on a pay phone or something.

"Who you trying to call, friend?" I asked, but something distant registered a familiarity on the other end.

"You."

"Well, do me a kindness and tell me who I'm speaking with," I said back, nearly ready to hang up, but that voice....

"I've—uh—I've just. I've got to see you, Amarillo," the voice said. He knew me, knew my first name, my number, where I could be reached. I can count on one hand the number of people in this world who know either one of those bits of intel or even how to find them. The nature of my business keeps information like that confidential to say the least. "I know it's a haul," the voice continues. "I know it is, but... There's nobody left to talk to and I'm seein' all these things and... I swear I don't know what's real anymore and—"

"Whoa, let's just take it down a little. I—I'm not sure I can place who this is. You got a name for me, or—"

The voice stopped. All I could hear were crackles from rain patting the receiver. I began evaluating what little I'd learned so far: it's raining, and he said it was a haul, so whoever it was isn't close enough to be dangerous. Far as I knew, my team hadn't crossed anyone from the south, and the voice was decidedly older than mine, putting him around mid-sixties or seventies? Maybe even older? And the biggest piece: he knew my first name. Job calls don't come in like that. Isn't protocol. Isn't done. Still, there was something so familiar.

"Please, son. Please, Amarillo. You're granddaddy isn't around anymore, and well, he was so dear—and if he were still with us I'd call him—but he's not and I feel like I'm cracking up and I know they're gonna get me—I know they are—they're everywhere all the time looking at me leering and—"

That's when it hit me. I knew this man. Sure, his tone had dropped, become more gravelly, but I think I'd placed it. Connor Weekly, the music director at the church my granddaddy pastored. But that was so many decades ago. I hadn't seen him since—.

"Please, son. You're all that's left," Weekly pled into the phone with an anguish and fear I couldn't shrug off. I spent several weeks under Weekly's care after what happened in Wylie, Texas. I was just a kid then, but he and his wife had helped me when my parents dealt with the aftermath.

"Mr. Weekly—I"

"Please."

I sat there for a minute, weighing it all out. The man was so old, I remember thinking, he's probably strayed out from his nursing home and just wandering around confused. But then I thought maybe I owe a small debt to him and to my granddaddy, too as they were very close friends. After all, it was either go and help Weekly or spend one more day in a fog working at the Tahoka cotton gin.

I drove three hours through early morning darkness west on 82, then highway 380 until it turned into 70 across the New Mexico border, and took that all the way to Roswell. There was a little Mexican diner then, one of the only things that wasn't alien-themed. La Posta, I think it was called, a couple miles from the main drag and away from all the little-green tourists. Didn't matter much though. I got there before the roosters sounded morning. The rain kept it dark, so when I pulled up to the curb, my headlights painted the large window out front. La Posta was small, but it was nearly full of people, mostly men, mostly Hispanic, sipping coffee over their cigarettes and *migas*.

I didn't spot Weekly when I first went in, kicking the mud off the bottoms of my boots, my jacket and wranglers wet from the rain that still battered the New Mexican landscape. Someone had dumped a line of white granules at the doorstep of the diner. Looked like salt, but it was too warm outside to worry about ice. I surveyed the diner through the smells of mildew mixed with chorizo and smoke. Then I spotted a man that I would have never taken as Connor Weekly. This man was thin, gaunt even, hunched over from many difficult years and dirty as all get out. He was one of the only Caucasians in the place, and the only one alone, so it had to be him. I registered a hint of gratefulness that I never had to see my granddaddy that way.

"Mr. Weekly? Connor Weekly?" I said to the man seated in the booth staring into a dingy, white mug of coffee. He looked up sheepishly, noticeably afraid of something.

"My word, boy. You got old; didn't we get old? You favor him. He had a mustache too, you know. Bigger than yours, but he had one. Sit down—yeah—sit down. Had lots of coffee. Had to stay awake—yep—alert."

I sat slowly. Something was very wrong with this man. I looked around the room to see if anyone else was paying attention. They weren't.

"Any follow you?" he asked, "What am I saying—of course they did—they always do. They're everywhere? All around? Do you see them? Ever seen one? What am I asking?"

"I'm not quite sure what you mean, Mr. Weekly," I said. "Listen, do you know where you are? Where you came from? Is there someone I can call? Children—"

"I put some across the foot of the door there, but you stepped in it," he pointed to the entrance. "I did it several times, but they just keep sweeping it up and yelling at me in Mexican—it's from the table anyway, but I just kind of hope it works. I hope, you know, just—just hoping for something that isn't going to work," he said, beginning to break down, his eyes red and swollen. I could tell he had been crying, but I had no idea what to do.

"Please, Mr. Weekly... I think you're confused. But I can help if you just—"

"Help me, Amarillo? I can feel them. I can *feel* them all around me. Everywhere. I can't even move anymore. It's like—it's like a pressure, you know? They're always around me. Pushing in. Crouching next to me. I can almost feel their breath on my neck."

"Who? These people?" I asked, looking around the diner.

"How are *you* going to help me with *them* when you can't *see* them? When you can't *hurt* them? I've run out. I've run out of everything and I can't see them anymore. But you know what, boy?" he says, eyes blazing at me as he lifts a trembling, boney finger. "They can see you. See us. Right now. They're always here, and they bite. They bite, and they tear, and they rip us open. And they... hurt us... I can't take anymore. I can't."

"Who? Mr. Weekly, who are you talking about? What—"I raised my voice, and the rest of the diner started to take notice.

"If the old man comes to you, do yourself a favor and spit in his face before you tell him no. Spit in his face, Amarillo."

I remember seeing something glint from under his tattered coat. I knew what it was, I can always spot one, but I don't know why I didn't react. It was all so strange. This man was in agony, and I had either lost the means, or lost the capacity to know how to help. Even when he brought the muzzle of that pistol to his temple, I did nothing, didn't even flinch. I just watched it like a movie, like it was happening on a screen. I even caught myself thinking maybe it was better this way.

And just before he pulled the trigger, he said, "Why did it have to be us? Why did He do this?"

I remember the only thought going through my head was how I would get out of there without my license plate being copied down. All I thought about were the possibilities, and the strategic evaluations for any eventuality, any obstacle, any objective. When would the next call come in? When would we earn the next paycheck? When would my team be set into play once again? It was like staring at the ceiling above my bed as death once again surrounded me.

But, it wasn't the blood spray on the walls, or the panic his suicide caused in La Posta that proved to be the scariest thing about that dull, wet, New Mexican morning. No, the scariest thing was that all these years later I know Connor Weekly was right. He was telling the truth when at the time I dismissed him as old, tired, and crazy. They *are* always here, always around, sometimes so close you could swear you feel their acrid breath on your neck. And you know what? They do bite, they do hurt, and they sure as hell can rip you open. While part of me wishes with everything that I had never picked up the phone so many restless years ago, that I never had gotten in my truck and drove through the night to Roswell, another part of me wishes for divine ignorance, that Connor Weekly had only been old, and tired, and crazy, and that now, years later, I wasn't exactly the same. Old and tired, yes, but crazy? Nope. Not crazy. Just awake. Just certain.

Chapter 1

THESE GERMANS WE'RE meeting, the ones with the rocket launcher and the heat-seeking stinger missile we need for the next job are as good a reason as any to try out the new recruits. These particular Germans aren't sophisticated or very well organized, so it shouldn't be a tough scrape if the deal goes sour. Not that I want it to go sour, but you won't see me crying if it does.

One of my new guys sits in the back seat of our Mercedes drawing breath like there's not enough of it, mumbling to himself with itchy nerves. It takes two cars to get all of us to the meet. A moderate rain comes down in sheets before we make it to the bridge. I lose sight of my men in the other car a beat longer than I want. Some—maybe most— would say that if you're team can't fit in the same vehicle, your team is too big. May be right, but I've got recruits to audition.

"Mr. Rust, sir?" the new kid says to me from the backseat. I think his name is McGinnely. Fought in the latest Iraq dust-up and thinks it prepared him for our line of work. We'll see.

"Call me Amarillo, son. We're not in the service anymore," I say.

He pauses for a thoughtful moment.

"We gonna make it out of this one, Amarillo?"

I can't help but laugh. So does Park, a long time team member we picked up in South Korea while on a corporate security detail. Our job was to escort Park's brother safely to the U.K. A lot of people back then wanted him dead for whistle blowing on a tech firm for secretly trading info with the country's northern adversaries. We got the whistle-blowing brother to London. Park saw how we worked and wanted to come with us. That's the way it's been for a long while.

"*This* one?" Park asks McGinnely, smiling. "Have you ever been on *another* one?"

"No, sir. I jus—"

"Then how about you just stay calm, son," I say. "Check your corners. Steady finger on the trigger. Follow my instruction. All that stuff they taught you in the Corps. You haven't seen a tough action—this—this is nothing. Cake. We get in, make the deal, walk out with the stinger, and that's that. Calm is all I need from you. You want to work for me, you just stay calm."

Horrace, another team member from way back, smart like Walt Whitman with the heavy beard and receding hairline to match, slips our car off the main street just before we enter the bridge. We're headed under it. Our meet happens on a forgotten dock next to the Spree River. Berlin is full of narrow side streets that jump out at you like lions in wait if you aren't ready for them. It's a good place to do business. The city's infrastructure remains so convoluted from hundreds of years of tumult and transition that finding somewhere quiet, some dark alcove tucked away from the prying eyes of German police or responsible citizenry proves easier than most other European locales. Trust me, I've been to them all, and Berlin makes our job easy.

We pull to a stop after winding under the bridge that now shields our car from the rain. Soon my other car pulls up even with us and shuts off its headlights too. I lean forward in the passenger seat and try to catch a glimpse of my partner, Bock, in the next car through the beads of rain on our windows. He's got a couple of new prospects with him as well. Our man, Everly, almost blends in with them. He's young and thin with long features that most take for weakness. Everly's in the back seat with another new kid, Taz, I think he said his name was, certainly some ridiculous Marine nickname that makes him feel tough. I can nearly guarantee he's the one that won't make the cut. The meatheads with big names are almost always the first to wash out.

Bock's window rolls down. Horrace lowers ours. Rainwater squeegees from the rubber window seal and spills down the side of the car.

"Where did you find these tossers, mate?" Bock says in that deep, gravelly Scottish brogue I've come to expect. It contrasts with his well-manicured, Wall Street appearance. He's always tailored in fine Italian suits and glossy patent leather shoes that cost more than most people's cars. "They arsk some right stupid questions," he tacks on.

"It's what we got, podnuh," I say, almost calling attention to our paradoxical partnership that I often can't believe has lasted so long. He's in Canali and Farragamo; I do Wranglers and Laramies. I've got a Carhart coat and a handlebar mustache; Bock's got a black Am Ex and a manicure. Don't exactly know how we linked up, but that's just the way it's been since the way back days, since the old team.

"Fine," Bock says. "Let's just get in there and take this bleeding missile so we can go home."

Horrace points down the darkened dockyard further obscured by wave after wave of pelting rain. I look and see a pair of headlights flash on and off quickly in two strobes. Bock sees the lights and rolls up his window.

"Okay, that's them, let's pull up," I say, but Horrace shakes his head.

"Wasn't pointing at those lights," he says.

"What then?"

"The other ones. There was a signal before the signal."

"Means they've spread out then, taken positions. They smell something," I say. "Okay, Park, keep the doors shut, call Bock on your cell and tell him to dump the newbies here. We've got a tactical change. Horrace—"

"Mr. Amarillo, sir?" the kid in the back tries to cut in.

"Horrace," I ignore the recruit and continue, "you'll need to go up to the meet with me since you're the only one they trust. Bock can stay behind with Park. Everly will—"

"Amarillo? Sir?" the kid asks again in a scared, chirpy voice.

"What?" I ask, annoyed.

"Is there going to be trouble, sir?"

"Shut up, kid," I say even more annoyed, realizing he's going to be dead weight no matter what. I turn my attention back to Park. "This one isn't even close to ready for this, so keep him down and alive." Now back to the kid, "Listen to me, McGinnely. You stay close to my man Park. He'll try and make sure your momma has a pretty little forehead to kiss on Christmas Morning, okay? Go back to Missouri and cook sausage. This ain't your bag."

I instruct the three new fellas to leave the car doors open for cover once they exit and keep their weapons trained on the periphery. My team can take care of any primary threat, but if they've got snipers or hidden bogies ready to pop out and fire point blank, we're in big trouble. Visibility's just too low. Bock insists on going with Horrace and I up to the meet, so Everly volunteers to hang back with Park and the newbies. With little light present, and not much fear of being monitored through night vision because of the storm, we all step out, some switching cars, some loading weapons and sighting-in just in case under shadowed cover of the bridge. The Germans will wait because we're the ones they think have the money.

"Sgt. Major Rust?" the only prospect I actually know, a kid named Haim, asks. Back straight. Chin high.

"I told you, Haim, I'm not your instructor anymore. Cut the rank-busting. It's just Amarillo Rust out here, got it?"

"Sir," he says, unable to drop the whole soldier act. "Sir—uh—Amarillo, sir, I just—we don't—it's just that I didn't see anyone back at the rally-point actually pack the suitcase in the trunk with money, sir."

"Just because they think we're here to buy something doesn't mean we're actually here to buy something," I say, patting Haim on the shoulder. "Why pay for what you can steal?" He couldn't be more than twenty-seven or twenty-eight now. Haim was part of the last platoon I ever instructed out of Ft. Sill in Oklahoma. I sure hope he works out.

See, we have a paying job coming up that necessitates a little boom-boom bigger than we usually have the equipment for. So naturally, rather than getting ourselves on some watch list by purchasing black market

arms, we just did a little light recon, found out who's currently in possession of a stinger missile launcher, and decided to borrow it for the next
couple weeks. That easy. You wouldn't steal from the military, because
well, they're the military, and you wouldn't go soliciting interest because
that turns out bad for you just about as often as it turns out good, so the
easiest thing to do was send Park and Horrace into the field, give them an
expense account, and tell them what to look for. Those two are good at
finding anything we need. They ingratiate themselves to the proper par-
ties just to find out what they've got in their toolbox, in this case a group
of Germans who like to dress up like the Third Reich is still full steam
ahead.

Now, Park's not exactly Arian enough for these yay-hoos, so he
hung back and pulled recon—watched, recorded, snapped Polaroids, and
listened to a mountain of phone calls. It was Horrace that did the heavy
lifting. Horrace looks German, even has the bald head groups like these
covet, so it was he who got in good with the skin heads. First part was
the hardest. Park found out where the group met up to talk business and
fraternize, play dress-up, whatever. Turned out to be a pub not far from
the Spree. Horrace showed up, started hanging around, began talking to
the right people and such. It all culminated in he dragging some poor son
of a gun in front of the pub and beating him within an inch of it, shouting
all kinds of racist business and yapping about the degradation of the
country, all in a perfectly executed south Berlin accent. And just like
that, Horrace was in. Clockwork.

Forget what you've seen in the movies. Criminals are generally not
criminals because they're misunderstood geniuses of aristocratic lineage.
Criminals are—for the most part—stupid, sometimes fantastically so. It's
another thing that sets my team apart. Get rich quick is the mantra of
most in this business, and so it draws the shortsighted and short-tem-
pered. Both of these attributes cloud judgment and render decisions to
the tactical at best. Strategic, deliberate thinking is almost never
employed, and when it is, it's like monkeys trying to play chess with
Kasparov.

Yeah, Horrace got in with no problem. That single act set him apart and put him in the advantageous position of not only being sympathetic to the cause—whatever the hell that was to these goofballs—but also as a brazen and particularly dangerous individual. For some reason, criminals love that too. Even the big bad boys like to have a bodyguard who's even crazier than they are. To the skinheads, that was Horrace, a bad man without the fear or consideration to beat a fella nearly to death in front of a Berlin pub at high noon.

Took only two days for Horrace to confirm the group possessed a cache of weapons that would make just about any mid-level Mexican drug cartel jealous. And our way in was that the Germans were looking to expand their arsenal all the time. Horrace offered this information to Park who, through phone and email, pretended to be a Chinese arms dealer with an unmarked shipment of seven Spatz semi-auto street-sweepers fresh off the line and burning holes in his hot little hands. The lead skinhead set up a meet at the shady end of the Spree.

So here we are to get the stinger. Of course, they only have one rocket. We were expecting two since that's usually how they come, but Horrace told us the fools went into the Fichtelgebirge mountains one weekend and shot one at the side of a barn, just to see what it'd do. The business is full of these silly costume gangs who want to play rough. Bock and I have gone up against plenty, and most of them fold like the Republican Guard in the first Gulf War.

We're gearing up and switching cars, Haim to one side of me, against the wet brick bridge wall, storm picking up just feet from us, when I see the first flash of lightning. I feel rain splash my face even though we're protected under the bridge overhang. Then I see another flash of lightning. Shards of brick pepper my face. That's when I know the lightning is muzzle-flash, and the rain on my face is what used to be Haim's head. The poor kid's body slaps the ground like raw meat on a butcher block. The Germans have a sniper stationed somewhere high on our three or four. We've got to nullify him and get to those flashing headlights before they take off.

Only the Taz kid stays out of cover too long. He saw his fellow recruit take one and zero out, so he's hyped and firing blind as soon as he can rack his snub-nosed HK MP7A1 sub machine gun. The rain and dark absorb his rounds like rolling dough. His screaming makes him another easy target. We try to call him back to cover, but he's out in wasteland, overwhelmed by everything and unable to hear a word. Too green. Another washout. We can only wait for him to die out there, but the silver lining is when he bites it, we'll see the sniper's position once and for all. We keep our eyes to the dark while Everly helps Bock snap a night vision attachment onto the gas-pistoned AUG in his hands. We would have had Park bring a sniper rifle to the meet, but I never thought the skinheads would smell a rat. Best we've got is the AUG assault rifle, and Bock's the one to man it since he learned to shoot back in Scotland where rain is just the way it is most days.

The first shot from the sniper fizzes through the rain so hot I can almost see its steam through the droplets. It plunks through Taz's gut, causing him to instantly drop his weapon and crease over like a helluva stomach ache. The second shot's gonna shatter through the top of that melon head of his if Bock doesn't spot the muzzle-flash quick enough. We all see the flash. Got to be a roof. Everly points over the hood most of us crouch behind for cover. Bock pops up, and brings the sight to his eye.

"Got him," he says deep and calm.

I try one more time to call for the Taz kid to drop and roll to cover, but no deal. He's too busy trying to pack his guts back into the wound in his abdomen, the rain washing red waves of whatever's left of his life down the dock into the Spree. By the time the second shot flashes like a distant lighthouse, we hear an engine rev and tires squeal. The sniper erases Taz's head a millisecond before Bock cracks off a well-trained shot with the AUG. The rest of us don't have to wait to pile into one of the cars. We all know—save our only remaining recruit, the little weenie McGinnely—that Bock hole-punched the sniper. Now we've got to stop the skinheads from getting away with the stinger launcher. It's the key to our next job, and while we aren't getting paid for this one, the next job,

the one Park set up with some strange old man I've never seen or even
spoken to, that pay is said to be extremely generous.

We leave Bock with McGinnely at the bridge. They have use of the
other car. Whether Bock decides to break down the AUG and help us
chase the skinheads through the streets of Berlin, or just yank McGinnely
to the airport and send him home next-day-air is up for speculation. All I
know is Horrace has his foot pinning the go pedal to the floor. The
shocks are getting some workout as we hop and push, roll and slide our
way behind the road-water spray that is the skinheads' sedan, frantically
tearing away from us. Their turns are sharp and wreckless; they've
clipped half-a-dozen parked cars already. That brings lots of attention we
don't need. You'd think it's a good thing we're doing this so late at
night, but all that means is that the only other people on the road are
cops. We slide around Kunzweg Platz, sloshing drunks and storefront
windows with oily street water. The skinheads are heading toward the
Mitte district, the once eastern bloc slum turned pub and club hotspot.

"They're gonna try and lose us in the people," Everly says.

"Look for them to bail when the crowds thicken up, Horrace," I say.
"Mitte starts at Hauptbahnhof. Right there," I point at the hulking train
station just ahead of us, its bright, polished metal skeleton gleaming
through a thousand panes of crystalline glass.

The target sedan blows through a light, taking a hard right off
Steintordamm to Kirchenalle running parallel to the station. We narrowly
miss a van in pursuit, then a green utility truck. The undercarriage of our
Mercedes groans under the burden of our turn. I fight to stay in the passenger seat, digging my fingers hard into the armrest. The skinheads fail
to yield at the Bremer intersection. Horrace locks up the brakes as I brace
my palms on the dashboard. We have no choice but to screech to a stop
as a procession of short-skirted university students stumble along the
crosswalk with predictably salivating males in tow. I shoot a look at my
driver, but Horrace just shrugs. The skinheads are gaining valuable yard-
age. When the gaggle passes, our Mercedes squeals alive, leaving heavy
black tracks and acrid smoke behind.

Just as the skinheads attempt to run another stop sign at Kirchenalle and Ellmenreichstrabe, the other Mercedes we stole from the Nocti Vagus parking lot a couple of days prior enters view from the right at high speed and slams into the passenger door of the their sedan. A hurricane throwing pieces of both cars into the air like Mardi Gras beads. Looks like Bock didn't make it to the airport with the recruit after all. Don't know why I ever had a doubt he'd show up for us. Bock bagged the sniper, the rest of the skinheads, and now the missile too. Virtually a one-man job. If we were getting paid for this, it wouldn't be an even split.

"We're on double time, boys," I say as we pull up to the crash scene. "Keep it running," I say to Horrace, then to Everly and Park, "Check on Bock and the kid. Get them in here. I'll get the stinger."

"If they even brought it," Everly says.

"Oh, they have it," I respond. "Too stupid to bluff."

I jog over patches of shattered safety glass: glinting snow on the pavement, around hunks and twists of metal and dodging looks from witnesses that amass from houses and pubs by the second. Bock slaps away the hand Everly offers him and emerges from the Mercedes seemingly unscathed but for a thin trickle of blood down the bridge of his nose. He stands and stares down onlookers while straightening his coat and tie. McGinnely didn't fair as well. Park's torso is deep into the car trying with everything to pry the kid out. He's a frightened cat with claws firmly affixed to the ceiling.

"Go on, get!" I yell at some passers by. "*Raus hier! Raus hier!*"

None of the skinheads made it. Can't say I'm too choked up. Bock slammed them hard. Sardines in a can rolled over by a cement truck. Surprised the stinger didn't go off and send us and a nice chunk of this Berlin intersection sky high. I find a decent hunk of wreckage, part of the door-frame I think, and shove it between the trunk lid and frame. I shimmy it down the mangled slot until it's wedged with a good hold just beneath the latch. Making sure it's secure, I take a step back and bring up my right boot as high as I can, then let loose all my force and stomp down on the piece of metal hoping to pop the latch open and retrieve the case with our missile launcher inside. No luck, the piece of doorframe I used bends like chewing gum. That's when I hear the sirens. I unholster my rubber-gripped .44 revolver and blast three rounds as close to the trunk latch as I can. Probably not the smartest idea, but I haven't got time. I'll be seeing the swirling blue lights on those green and white compact law cruisers coming around the corner any second. Besides, the stinger isn't armed, so the charge should be benign. My pistol trick works, the trunk flies open, people are screaming, or running, or both; my team is packed tightly in the car, ready to get out of Dodge. I snatch the heavy case and slowly haul it to the Mercedes. Park darts out and helps me walk the case to the car while Horrace pops the trunk.

"They're here," Horrace says, adjusting the rearview, emergency lights reflecting off his eyes.

"We're not," I say slamming the trunk as Park and I squeeze into the car.

Chapter 2

"WELL FIND SOMETHING else, Everly. Nobody said you have to flip burgers," I say, taking a swig of whiskey.

I look at him the way my granddaddy used to when I told him I wasn't going to split one more log. Bock's in the corner cleaning that .45 of his with a stained handkerchief, and a frothy pint of Guinness on the table within arm's reach. He glances up at me and I just shake my head with a petulant smile on my face. He rolls his eyes and goes back to polishing.

The bar's been closed for us. Amazing what a few dollars in a sleazy part of Berlin can get you. Only my team is allowed in. We bought the keys for the night and sent the owner to bed. Said we'd bartend for ourselves and lock up when we're finished. Everly's in front of me, complaining as always. Park and Horrace are adjacent us at their own table, laughing and drinking themselves into a well-deserved stupor. To no one's surprise, McGinnely's gone. He should be halfway over Ireland by now.

"I'm just saying—" Everly says, taking a drink and looking away.

"Oh, I know what you're saying," I tell him between sips. "You say it every stinking time you get a chance. You know the deal. I've explained it to you over and over and over. This team? This team, you work a day job. This team, you're accountable. No heat. No excuses. This team has a system."

"I know."

"No, no you don't know, Everly, if you *did* know, you'd stop bothering me with this trash all the time. Now, there are a hundred other teams you can join up with and they won't ask anything more of you than your scalp and a steady hand, but this one? This one we work safe. Alibis. Clean records. Low key until we're ready to pop."

"Under the radar," Everly says, swigging his beer again.

"Under the radar, that's right," I say, "and why is that boys?" I call to the other table.

"Cause we hide in plain sight, Rust." Horrace yells with his drink in the air, hooting and hollering like some bum at a horse track.

I take a drink, just grinning at Everly. "We hide in plain sight, son. Plain sight. That's how we work so well. That's how come you ain't never heard a siren one coming down your street when you sleep, and that's how I aim to keep it."

Then Bock pipes up from across the pub. "So you get yourself another bleeding day job and stop whinging away like a fud."

Horrace and Park go real quiet. It's not like Bock to speak much after an action. Anything out of that mouth, and you'd be lucky to be across the pub.

"I don't want to hear another bloody word about you and work, Everly. Not once more. If I do, I'll come wherever you are and slice your tongue out with a length of piano wire."

"Oooo," I say looking back at Everly whose beer trembles in his glass. "I wouldn't push that one, son. Sounds serious to me. And on that note, gentlemen," I say to the rest of them, "I don't know how you got here, where you're staying, or how you're getting back home—and I don't want to—but I'd say it's just about time to do it."

I stand and raise my glass for the last swallow. "Nice work. Bock and me'll lock up. Thank you for your continued service. We'll be in touch. Check the sim."

The boys gather their coats and adjust themselves, taking their last gulps of beer and whatnot. They stagger to the door, Park and Horrace bracing each other so as not to topple. Everly doesn't take another drink.

He gets up, shakes my hand, and takes a nervous glance over to Bock who doesn't return the nod Everly gives him. I note the discomfort and pull him into the handshake.

"Don't you go worrying too much about old Bock, Everly. I'm in charge here. He knows it. You get yourself stateside and put in applications at one of those big electronics stores or something. Hear they're nice places to work. Had a couple that used them before. Decent pay. Low hours. You'll be fine. As for him," I gesture to Bock, "wish I could say his bark was worse than his bite, but you know just as well as me, don't you?"

Everly tries his best to smile. I release his hand and he slips on his jacket real quiet like and takes off out the door into the rain. Then it's just Bock and me and a bar-load of dirty glasses.

"You're the one in charge are you, Rust?" Bock says, standing up and shoulder holstering his gleaming .45.

"That's right, Bock. Least as a formality," I say. "Didn't think you much as the jealous type."

He pulls on his gloves and that long navy pea coat. "Last of the auld team you and me," he says, staring. "Started out just around the same time if I recall correctly."

"That we did," I say.

"So how's that make you the one in charge?" Bock says standing stoic in the low amber light.

"Cause you would've discharged that pretty gun of yours right between Everly's eyes if he'd have come to you, I suppose."

"You're probably right," Bock says walking to the door. "I'm not one for civil administration."

"Guess we got it figured out then," I say.

I see a grin creep across Bock's face. "Be seeing you, Captain," he says giving a quick mock salute before disappearing into the storm. "Have fun with the dishes."

The next job is for an unspecified palate of considerable value—possibly gold—held at a makeshift installation in remote Albania. Northern Pogradec, next to the lake of Ohrid and the Macedonian border.

Rumor is, there's an old AH-1 Cobra attack helicopter watching over the area, hence our need for the stinger launcher. This action ups the ante. We're not a Seal team. We're not organized paramilitary. But the pay-load is big, real big, and the place is away from prying eyes too since the group we're up against is based in Pogradec proper, several hours away. We don't even have to enter the site and move the palette. Our clients are sending their own team along with a truck and forklift for that.

I don't like outside people and I don't like explosives, but I do like money. Plus, I've got Bock next to me and the boys behind. All goes well and we'll be all the way gone before Pogradec proper even hears a whisper. Should be a Merry Christmas.

Chapter 3

MOST DAYS I'M asleep, even though I'm walking. This particular one started with gunfire, thankfully it wasn't directed at me for a change. When I figured that out, I took the time to shower and get dressed for work at the cotton gin. The sound of discharged buckshot travels a long way on the Texas plains, and I knew just who was shooting so early in the morning. The game warden called me and asked that I go tell old Teasel to kill his chickens the way everybody else does, by twisting their necks. I agreed, but telling Teasel to do something today meant that he'd forget all about it the next.

I pulled my '93 Dodge up to the old man's house, noticing the rapid weathering that had occurred since the last time I had come by. The harsh, sandy winds of the plains would swallow up the old farmhouse yet, and Teasel was too run-down to stop it. Most of the time he sat on his porch all day, hoping, I'm sure, that the postman would come by with something, anything providing some interest for the day. Most times that didn't' happen, and because of it, Teasel resorted to other strange amusements, like blowing the heads off his chickens. He didn't think far enough ahead to realize that there weren't many left for him to shoot, and killing them meant no eggs. Since the game warden made Teasel promise not to drive anymore after he scared the young Ramis girl off the road as she was walking to school one morning; he had quite literally nothing to do all day.

I get out of the truck cautiously as the last shot echoed across the fields only moments ago. I stand next to the truck with the cool, dry morning breeze passing my face. Teasel was libel to slip into full dementia any time now, judging by the poor condition of the farmhouse. I hear some pots or pans or something clambering inside. I wait and hear another gunshot.

"Holy s—Teasel!" I call out. "It's Rust. Come on out of there."

I hear nothing at first, like he's heard me but doesn't know what to make of it.

"Teasel," I say again. "It's just me, Teasel, now come on out."

"Get on out yourself," I hear in a muffled, tired voice from just the other side of the door.

"I'm not coming up there, Teasel," I say, doing exactly the opposite, cautiously moving to the side of the house and skirting toward the door with my back to the wall.

"I ain't gonna shoot you, Rust," he says in an almost apologetic way.

"I know you ain't, but you got the game warden on you again. I come to get you to stop that shooting."

"I can shoot whenever I damn well want too."

I keep moving down the wall until I'm just right of the door.

"He ain't taking that away too. It's my damn house and they're my damn chickens."

"Nobody arguing it," I say slowly pushing the cracked door open and peering inside.

The place is a mess. He's certainly lost it now. The living room is strewn with all sorts of garbage: old newspapers, clothes, the odd used spittoon cup or plate smeared with the dried remnants of a bygone meal. Looks like he drug his bed into the room too.

"It's making me old," Teasel says, and from the sound of it I judge he's in the kitchen.

I slide through the cracked door, checking each doorway with a glance and slowly move across the living room. I notice blood and feathers on the floor in streaks. He's lost it for sure.

"I'm inside, Teasel. Now you be good now."

"I said I wasn't gonna shoot you, you stupid son of a bitch."

I poke my head around the corner into the kitchen and see more mess. Nothing is clean. Nothing put away. Filth everywhere you look, and more feathers, more blood. Teasel's got the shotgun at his side and they're both leaning against the sink. He's staring off to nothingness.

"I can't farm. I can't drive. I can't screw," he says and just then he seemed the saddest man in the world. "I can't even kill my own chickens."

I move over to him, still a bit cautious and gently take the shotgun away. Two live rounds in the over and under. He turns to me, almost like he's staring through me. I've seen the look several times. Some call it the thousand-yard stare, but that's not right. That's not what it is. When somebody looks at you like that, they're inside. They're thinking about what they've done and why, and what they could have done differently if they had the time. Most often they don't have the time, and that's what hurts. It's that brick wall. It's death, and it's waiting. All your life it waits, and even while you know it, you don't really. It's so far away, just standing there and watching you and all you do. And every day, every year it gets closer. Might just move a step toward you, but usually you don't notice until you're staring it square in the face. That's when you know there's no more time, and what you had, you wonder about how you used it, and the futility of trying to figure a way to get it back. Teasel has that look, and it haunts me because one day I'll have it, too.

"Your daughter tells me she'd like you to stay with her in town. Told you that last time. She'd be real happy to have you, Teasel. Saw her at the grocery a while back and she told me so herself."

He just looks to the floor and shakes his head.

"Come on now. You're going to go down with this old house if you don't. Tahoka ain't so bad," I say quietly removing the shells from the barrel and resting the shotgun on the opposite wall.

"Ain't the same," he says. "Tahoka's a big city now."

"Shoot, Teasel, you can't find a town small as Tahoka anymore."

"Feels big to me."

If my granddaddy were still around, I'd have wanted to hug him. The way I saw it, death was inches from Teasel's face, and he was fighting with whatever was left. I've been there. I've seen men fighting for their lives even though the grip around their necks was impossible to break. I had been the agent of it, and I had watched. I never savor it. It is ugly. Physical or emotional, the death of a man is difficult to watch. With time and practice, one can dull himself to its effects on the psyche, but it's much easier when it's someone you've made yourself hate. Teasel was as close a friend as I'd had next to Bock, but in my line of work, you try real hard to segregate your day life from the other. I guess I've done a pretty good job of it.

I put my hand on Teasel's shoulder and just sit there for a while. He doesn't break, but it is close to the surface, or maybe the ability has left him altogether.

"I don't want to go there, Rust," he says, not looking up. "I've lived here most of my life. Addy's buried out under some tree out there, but I can't find it anymore. I can't talk to her anymore. Almost can't remember what she looked like."

I remember a boy I had in my crew for only two weeks. We had an action in Los Angeles. It was the first and last time we dealt in trafficking narcotics. It was for a Mexican outfit a few miles away from Tijuana. A competing L.A. gang was tipped off to the truck. When we drove through their neighborhood, they got us in a bottleneck. The lead car took most of the hit. We managed to make it out. Bock brought along a couple of phosphorus grenades. The gang had never seen them before. Didn't know how to react. Burned them all to a crisp. The boy drove the lead car. He managed to drive out of the crossfire, even ran one of the tangos under the grill, but he didn't make it home. His wounds were deep in the abdomen. Painful. Bock said he'd do it, but the boy didn't know him like he knew me. I told him I would do it. I cupped his cheek with one hand, and told him he did a great job. I shot him in the temple. He wouldn't have made it anyway, and we couldn't take him to a hospital.

Teasel has the look that boy did, just on the verge of tears, but maybe because his body won't let him, he doesn't cry. Teasel didn't see me take the shotgun from the wall or drop a shell into the bottom barrel. I don't know why, but I hug him tight with one arm. I let it sit for a minute, and I think I can feel Teasel giving in, just about to heave. Before he can do it, I lift the shotgun with my other hand just under his chin, careful not to touch it so he doesn't know what's about to come. I back away a split second before I pull the trigger. He saw death coming, that much I knew, but he didn't see it coming from me. It was quick and it was painless, and while I couldn't cry over Teasel, I felt it heavily, but not for what I'd done. What I just did saved him from a far worse death, a languishing one that would drain further and further away until no part of the man remained. He would sit until his heart gave out, even if he felt like it already had. A person can live a long time without even being there, and Teasel was too much of a friend for me to allow it.

I stage the scene quickly, almost without thinking. I wipe the gun down and trade my prints on the handle for his. I pick up his phone and do my best to sound shocked at what I'd found only moments ago, the old man on the floor, dead by his own hand. His daughter wouldn't like it, but she wouldn't understand anyway. Not yet at least. But everyone will in their own time. Trust me, it's much better to call your own time of death than for death to call it on his.

Chapter 4

BOCK SITS NEXT to me in the passenger seat of a tinted Chevy
Suburban staring out at morning mountain fog. Both Everly and Park are
in the back seat. We're north of Pogradec proper, tens of miles from the
last house or farm. I thought we'd stick out like a sore thumb in the SUV
idling on the side of a dirt road, but besides there being no one out here
to stick out to, turns out that Pogradec is a fairly well-visited tourist
haven because of the nearby lake. It makes sense why the organization
we're stealing the palette from operates from there. Unbeknownst to
most, tourist spots are some of the greatest places to base a team. We use
them all the time. Vegas of course is wonderful, but it's nearly impossible to stay off camera. That would worry most teams, but it doesn't
bother me all that much because we would never pull an action there
anyway. It's a place to meet. A place to plan. You use it like hornets use
a nest. Converge. Talk to all the other hornets. Grab some shut-eye. Plan
the next day's routes over a nice meal etc. Then you go out and start the
stinging. You don't blow up your own nest. That's for the half-wits, and
trust me—there are plenty of those out there to keep my team completely
anonymous. We call them chaff. A camera's got to catch you doing
something suspicious in order to be a danger. So, my rule is this: Don't
do anything suspicious in front of a camera. And in the case you must
carry out suspicious deeds finding yourself unsure as to whether there are
cameras in the immediate vicinity? Always assume there are and commit

your suspicious deeds elsewhere or until you are positive you can disable them.

This is why a place like Aspen, Colorado or Windemere of Yorkshire, or even Pogradec, Albania are always great places out of which to base your team. These tourist cities are better than Vegas because there's a constant flow of fresh, transient faces. They come. They mill around town. They go. Just like we do. It's a little school of perch inside a great big school of perch. Virtually undetectable. And the best part: almost no cameras. Once you pull some heavy recon on a team and find out they operate like this as well, you'd be good to alter your strategy, because a team that operates like we do is a smart team, one that might take a little more planning than first thought.

"Sure you and Horrace vet these guys, Park?" I say, craning my head back to look at him.

"Which ones?" he says back. "Targets or clients."

"Well both, man."

Park said he did. He tells me that the client is far more difficult to dig anything up on. He contacted us through the proper channels, and the deposit went though decryption just fine. The money's good and safe, but the client is quite the mystery. This should bother me more than it does. Bock's just being polite not to second guess me on this one. It isn't everyday a client asks you to lift a palette of "extremely valuable material" and load it on a truck that someone else is going to haul off for you, and oh yeah, one other thing, you might have to blow up an attack chopper when you get there. A client asks that much of your team and they should be an open book. Not this client. But in times like these, when times are tough, some people, people like me, just have to take bigger risks. Money doesn't grow on trees, it grows at the end of a gun barrel.

As the fog begins to burn off, we finally see why the client gave us this exact position to set up. The installation sits down in an open valley of brilliantly silken grass, free from trees for 360 degrees. We're sur-prised to discover that the narrow dirt road our SUV sits on is about seven inches from a steep drop-off leading to another small hump of a hill with the valley below it. The structure in the valley looks concrete. Looks decommissioned or abandoned military. You never know in this part of the world. Crow's nest formation. Narrow slits in small rotundas on either side of the large warehouse door standing like a steel Atlas in the middle, intimidating anyone stupid enough to approach. Right then and there I know what Bock knows. This job is way above our pay grade. Our only solace is the stinger missile sitting in the case behind Park and Everly. But we've only got one rocket, and that's supposed to be for the chopper. Maybe god's light would shine down and we wouldn't see any helicopter today, in which case we'd improvise use of the stinger and blast the door with it. Of course that would possibly jeopardize the palette inside, but we'd worry about that later. Main question is—

"Where the bloody hell are these fuds?," Bock hisses.

Park checks his watch. "Should have been here an hour ago."

"That's enough for me to call this thing off," Bock says. "We're sitting ducks out here."

"We got decent cover up here, Bock," I say. "Way that place is positioned, I don't think they could see us if we wanted them to. See the curve of this tree-line? The way we're nestled between that hill there and the mountain in front? If there's a chopper buzzing around up there, it's not gonna see us before we see it. Only one way in, but only one way out too."

Bock huffs.

"If this were some kind of ambush, I'd say they made it pretty difficult on themselves. Let's give 'em a few more minutes. Maybe they had car trouble," I say winking and smiling at Bock.

"Got movement," Everly says, staring down at the smart phone we outfitted with surveillance software to monitor the sensors we slyly placed on either side of the road a mile or so back.

"See?" I smile at Bock again who unholsters that .45 of his, racks one into the chamber, and lays it softly on his right thigh. I hear Park pull the hammer back on his sidearm as well. I just sit pretty and listen to Everly read me the distance.

"Calm, boys," I say.

"Forty yards," Everly says.

"I see them."

A white late-model European flatbed truck comes into view around the bend of the hill behind us. It travels slowly as not to kick up dust. Just then my sat. phone rings. I pick up to an older man's voice. Sounds middle-eastern.

"Mr. Rust," the voice says.

"That's correct. I assume you're in the approaching vehicle?"

"I am not."

I motion for the boys to have their weapons ready to go. Starting to look like an ambush after all.

"But no cause for alarm, Mr. Rust. I am under the employ of your client."

"Yeah? How do we know that? Have you spoken with Mr. Park? You his contact?" I ask with one eye on the truck stopped twenty yards behind us.

Bock sits like a Rodin in the seat next to me, his stolid finger on the trigger of that .45 and his unblinking eyes on the truck in the side view mirror. Everly puts away the smart phone and trades it for a Steyr machine pistol.

"I have not had the pleasure, but we *have* communicated," the voice on the phone says.

"Prove it."

"I sense some hostility, Mr. Rust. I know my men ran a bit late, but this happens in the business from time to time, does it not?"

"Let's just say your outfit is too secretive even for our tastes, mister vaporware. Now, what I'm looking at down in that valley was expressly what Park told me that you promised him it was not."

"And what would that be, Mr. Rust?"

"It looks Albanian military, and Mr. Park was instructed to tell you that we do not have the—"

"Mr. Park did a fine job communicating with me," the voice says. "This operation is just going to have to proceed on a little…faith I suppose you'd say."

"Well you call it faith and I call it trust, and as far as I'm concerned, you haven't given us any reason to proceed in any other way than with extreme caution or maybe even not at all."

"Mr. Rust, you arrived this morning under a complete shroud of protective fog on a road nearly as wide as your axels. If I wanted you killed I would not have orchestrated the former. If I wanted to kill you myself, I would have simply run you seven inches to the left. Where you sit is the only obfuscated advantageous position above the installation. If I wanted you to fail, you would have already."

"Good points," I say feeling like a novice.

"I'm gonna smash that feckin' phone, mate," Bock says, eyes blaring at the truck still idling in the side-view.

I nod and continue. "Ok, listen here. I don't know who you are, but your money's good. We're gonna continue on this little charade up until we feel you're not on the level. That happens and you're burnt toast, my friend. You get me?"

"Trust that I have done my research, Mr. Rust. Not only do you come highly recommended, but you come highly feared as well. Especially that one beside you. Mr. Bock, I believe."

"Yeah, he's a real go-getter."

"Indeed," the voice says. "Please forgive me all the same if my call set you and your men on edge. This was not my intention. I only wanted to wish you luck, and to let you know that the attack helicopter is indeed in the air today not three miles from your current location."

"If you've got the scratch to know a thing like that, why the hell do you need us? Been scoping your boys in the truck behind us. They don't look like lightweights to me. Why don't you just go fetch this gold yourselves?" I ask.

"I am a resourceful man, Mr. Rust, but even I cannot contend with an attack helicopter."

"Another good point," I say. Everything's starting to check out. "Okay. We're a go, so leave the breach and the chopper to us."

"I fully intend to," says the voice.

"And I assume that the men behind us will follow and load up the gold when we're done?"

"They will take care of the palette. You need only locate it. At that point, your part will be complete, and you will have free will to do as you wish."

"Sounds good. Let's do this deal."

I hang up the phone and tell the boys that everything seems on the up and up. Park and Everly step out and raise the back gate on the SUV to ready the stinger. Bock and I lock and load our P90 subs while keeping an eye on the still men in the truck. When I finish, I step up to their driver's side door. At first the driver just stares at me, then I make the roll down sign with an obstinate grin.

"You two *habla ingles*?" I ask.

"What you want?" the passenger says.

"Normally I'd give you a walkie, but how about you just roll yourselves up to the building when you hear a great big boom. Think you can handle that?" I glance at each of them.

The big one in the driver's seat never registers a response. However the equally imposing passenger nods and slaps his buddy on the arm to roll the window back up.

I hop down and notice that the boys have already put the stinger together. It's resting on Park's shoulder. Everly's at the edge of the road affixing cables for us to repel down to the valley floor. Bock's got his ACOG sighted P90 pointed toward the tree line at the bottom where we'll end up.

"That'll be the place to fire," Bock says. "Right next to the outcropping. Got the Mountain to shield any strafing. Large trees to slip into on the left and back if need be."

"Sounds good," I say, taking hold of a hook and cable. I pack my gloves down on my fingers and turn in, ready for the drop.

"I hear something," Everly says.

"That's the chopper. Let's do it," I say, and the four of us repel in unison down the side of the hill, each fast on our own cable.

Park hits the bottom first due to the weight of the stinger on his back. He's already making for the edge of the tree line. I'm close behind. The sound of an AH-1 Cobra is heavier and thicker than you'd imagine. It's a two-person craft, no cargo capability whatsoever, just a couple of pilots and a boatload of firepower. Missiles, Gatlings, seekers. Could be anything on the chopper arms, so the idea is to be quick about taking it out. The second we see kabloom, Bock, Everly, and I will take out across the open area toward the building. Park will hang back and hit the floor with a Turkish JNG-90 MKEK sniper rifle to cover us. I have complete confidence in Park's eye. We'll get to that building just fine.

After hearing it chup down the valley for what seems like several minutes, we finally see it. The Cobra is a low flying chopper that likes to get down and dirty when it comes to combat. I've seen several of these in action both in Iraq and Afghanistan. It's still the preferred attack copter to accompany troops on patrol due to its low-flying, hands-on approach. The Apache might be newer, but Apaches hang way up high and rely on electronic lock-ons and video optics. Those can and do fail. The Cobra is a flying gun, a flying missile launcher, guided by human hands on tactile triggers. It is perhaps the most dangerous flying machine in existence against infantry in particular, and since Bock, Everly, Park and I have our boots firmly planted on Albanian soil? That makes us infantry.

"See anything yet?" Everly asks.

Bock's staring down his scope again, this time in the direction of the thupping. Park quickly releases a few latches on his back and swings the stinger to his shoulder, flipping switches and arming the locking device. We wait, and I know all four of us are trying our darndest not to let all the adrenaline get the best of us. I recheck my P90 sub and look for movement at the building. Nothing. I'm relatively convinced those turret slits are vacant.

The chupping becomes deafening, the Cobra definitely above our position, though due to the mountain's cover, we won't see it but a milli-second before we need to fire. I can feel the air displacement of the swirling rotors in my chest. They compete with my heartbeat. I look over at Everly who's sweating and mouthing something.

"There she is!" Bock says. "Park! Fire!"

The Cobra breaks into the clearing about two hundred feet and change in the air. Without the mountain to shield the sound, the force hits us full on as we watch the Cobra prowl slowly over the concrete installation. I can't help but think about how out of our league this operation is, but that's all taken away when I hear three dull beeps followed by a shorter, higher pitched one. Park grunts to brace himself as the stinger locks on to the chopper, and with the trigger pulled, the high hiss of the missile flaring and combusting, shooting a plume of fire and smoke behind us takes off for the Cobra.

Park immediately drops the launcher as we watch, slack-jawed at the rocket heading for the chopper. Just when we think the Cobra is toast, the helicopter banks hard to the left, the rocket whizzes by, but curls around for another go. For the next couple of seconds, the Cobra and the missile perform an awkward kind of heat seeking dance in the sky with harsh moves forward and back, to and from each side as the rocket twists and curves. Then I realize it. That chopper's not going down.

"It's eluded the missile," I scream. "Open fire!"

Bock, Everly, and I burst from the tree line unleashing full clips on the chopper still wavering in an unstable fashion in the air. The rocket curls around one last time and takes off behind us, slamming into the mountain, spraying debris to our heels.

"Park, break out the JNG rifle and take out the pilots!" I say, still firing into the hull of the chopper.

The helicopter gains its composure and turns to the side. I stop and squint to see what I think I see. I note the weapon bays. I look into the cockpit, and I can't believe it.

"Bock! There's nobody—"

A streak of fire erupts from the opposite tree line three or four football fields to the north. Another stinger missile fired from someone else's launcher plows into the side of the attack chopper sending it reeling across the clearing in a hail of smoke, metal and flame. The Cobra arcs down in a shower of debris, the rotors rip into the ground, shattering them and reducing the rest of the vehicle to a fireball of scorching jet-sam.

"What the—what in the hell was that?" I scream, realizing that we're all the way out in the clearing, all the way in out in the open.

Bock grabs my arm and pulls me to start running again for the installation. He's blindly firing the sub-machine gun with one hand, as Everly has already made it to the door. There's been no resistance yet. Maybe we were just that fast, but I doubt it. How long could it possibly take someone on the inside to pick up a gun after hearing an explosion like that? Two explosions like that? Who shot that Cobra down because it sure as heck wasn't us.

"Breach it, Everly," Bock says as we reach the installation wall.

"Done," he says, holding a detonator. He's good. Didn't even see him slap a four-point hinge configuration of C4 on the door until it was already done. Everly moves to the side and goes flat against the wall. "3. 2. 1."

The metal door explodes off its hinges. I've got my wits about me again, so Bock and I take point to clear the entry room, guns at the ready.

"Clear to go," Everly says while Bock and I enter the installation bathed in its swirling red emergency lights.

The first room is a concrete box, nothing more. We move into systematic breach and clear formation, slicing the pie with each new room, scanning the doors with our P90s, Bock gritting his teeth hard, aching for contact.

"Clear," Bock says from across the room, almost disappointed.

I respond with an all-clear of my own.

"Clear," he says in the next room.

I respond in kind again, and start to think that this is all some kind of setup. No resistance. None whatsoever. The Cobra never fired a shot, and there was clearly no one here to protect the gold. But why? And who shot down the Cobra? Most likely it was the client's men. But not being sure is just as good as knowing nothing at all. Maybe the client was a disgruntled party from some other action. We may have signed away our lives by chasing the money on this one. I would blame Bock for not stopping me, for not offering a difference of opinion on agreeing to take this action, but then, he was most likely thinking the way I did. That many dollar signs can inspire a whole new level of greed where greed already grows.

Pretty soon, Bock and Everly figure it out too. There's nobody here. We still clear the rooms, though with less and less cautious fervor, that is until we get to the hangar with the giant steel cargo door leading outside. We're flat against wall to an interior entryway to the hangar. Bock peers inside quickly and judges it empty also, except of course for the prized palette sitting dead center on the glazed concrete floor. Alone.

"Aye," Bock says lowering his weapon and stepping into the hangar. "Least something goes as we suspect. There she is."

Bock walks up to the palette and pats the top of it. Whatever's inside is wrapped up tightly with layer upon layer of thick, industrial grade plastic wrap. Doesn't look like gold. My partner doesn't seem concerned or even mildly inquisitive about what happened outside with that mystery rocket from across our position. Even Everly know something's not right.

"Okay, great, we've got the package," Everly asks nervously, "but what exactly is going on here? Why isn't anyone guarding this?"

I take the walkie from my back pocket. "Park, come in," I say into it.

"And who took out that chopper?" Everly asks louder this time.

"Who gives a shite," Bock says, running his hands across the palette, studying it closely.

"This is Park," scratches through the walkie speaker.

"Who gives a—?" Everly says in disbelief.

"Park is there anyone out there at all?" I ask.

"You don't want to know, Rust," Park says back.

That's when I start to piece it together. I grit my teeth and make a break for Bock. He's caught off guard for once as I knock the P90 from his hand and tackle him to the floor. He's left me open guard. I take the position and straddle him, slamming a hand around his throat.

"You son of a bitch. You went over my head," I say through my teeth, spraying spittle on him.

Bock doesn't struggle. "What's the matter, auld boy? Out of sorts that I think more than one move ahead?"

"What the crap is going on here?" Everly says.

"What's going on here, Everly," I say, sweat starting to break over my forehead.

"It's that Bock brought along his own team and didn't tell us. That's what's going on."

Just then, Bock pulls a move out of nowhere, quickly sliding my shoulder up and dislodging my hand from his throat. He then slides out from under me, grabs my kneecap and reverses position until I'm vulnerable on my back. The cold concrete floor knocks the wind out of me. I struggle for air. It's hard to breathe with Bock's hand around my neck.

"The other team is backup, you tosser. I covered our hinds," Bock says, having that incredible control to seem calm though he's boiling inside. "I'll take a thank you. If it weren't for my planning a 'B' team, we'd be piles of chuck in that clearing."

"No, we wouldn't," I struggle to get out as Bock tightens his grip.

"What's that, you arrogant sod?" Bock asks.

"Get your stinkin' hand off my throat and I'll tell you," I let out in a hoarse whisper.

Bock looks like he just realized he almost killed me. His cold stare breaks, he takes his hand from my neck and pops up off the ground, walking away and wiping his brow with the sleeve of his coat. I stay on the floor, slowly regaining my breath and voice.

"There wasn't anyone piloting that Cobra," I force out, massaging feeling back into my throat.

Bock looks at me like I'm a fool. He then takes a walkie from his back pocket. He switches the channel and brings it to his mouth.

"Horrace, take the team and search the wreckage for bodies. Positive ID at least one pilot."

"Sir," comes back through the walkie.

"Won't do any good," I say, sitting up, still rubbing my neck. "I said there weren't any pilots. You see any pilots, Everly?"

"Didn't have time to notice."

"Well I *did* have time and there weren't. Weren't any weapons on the arm brackets either."

"Are you completely mental?" Bock says, visibly irritated. "No pilots. No weapons. I suppose it was a child's toy, yes? Some snotty wee one chasing behind with his bicycle, aye?"

I stand up and pick up Bock's P90. I walk over and hand it back to him.

"Don't know. But I ain't lying either."

"We'll see," Bock says. "Boys are checking up on it right now. There's got to be a boot, a foot, a finger, something out there."

All three of us wander the room, still heaving and trying to slow our pulses. I've got my hands on my head, breathing deeply.

Everly's on the walkie with Park. "You see the other team?"

"Yeah. I see their position," Park says.

"Who'd you bring on this deal?" I ask Bock from across the room.

"Only see Horrace. Think I see Dresden though. I've got a bead on them," Park says.

"You brought Dresden in on this?" I ask Bock in disbelief.

"Short notice," Bock says, moving back to the plastic-wrapped palette.

"Short notice, my ass, Bock," I say. "That was stupid. Very stupid, and that's why you aren't in charge."

"I'm in charge just as much as you are, you redneck twit," Bock snaps back.

"I think I see Dresden out here. I count four. They're rifling through the downed chopper. Could be sabotage, right? How much resistance did you run into inside?"

"Nothing. No resistance here," Everly says back.

"Tell him to get in here. Tell them all to get in here," I say to Everly. "You screwed up, Bock. Bringing him, you fouled up and you know it. Everly, go out there, get Park and help the rest of 'em look for body parts or whatever the heck's out there."

I look over to Bock. "You won't find a thing, but go on and try. And figure out where that truck is. I want the hell out of Albania."

Everly turns and leaves. Bock and I just stare at each other in silence for a spell. The room is ice cold and quiet. Only the palette stands between us.

"We made a deal, Bock."

"We made a deal?"

"You've got a hair trigger. I don't. We agreed that I call the shots, especially after what went down after your old girlfri—"

"Even though my calling a shot kept us alive and possibly made this action a success, you still want to push this '*I'm in charge*' bit? Spare me. And when are you going to drop that shite about the girl, mate? How long until I live it down? You think I haven't paid for it in full yet, do you? Paid for it myself?"

"Could you not both be correct?" says a voice that echoes through the hangar, making it nearly impossible to get a fix on.

I snap the P90 to my shoulder and check my corners. Bock does the same with his .45. We move to each other, back to back until we both notice an old man lurking in a shadowed corner of the hangar. He moves and he's dead.

"The feck are you?" Bock yells.

"He's the guy on the phone," I say.

"Correct again, Mr. Rust. Mr. Bock, I presume. You are a nasty one, aren't you?" the man asks with a strangely genuine smile.

"Maybe," I say, "but he's my partner, so answer the question or we're gonna light you up good."

"My name is Elijah Tishbe. I am your client, and you have done well."

Chapter 5

FINALLY EVERYONE IS assembled in the hangar. I've got
Everly and Park on my six and Bock's moved away from me. His "b"
team, the one I didn't know anything about or authorize consists of that
sick son of a bitch Dresden, Henry Knapp the former FBI man, Horrace,
and a new fella I've never seen before, bald, black, and absolutely
gigantic. Bock calls him "The Yak." Nobody found anything in the
wreckage, a fact Bock didn't like much. Each team stands at an uncomfortable distance from the other. Park's glaring at Horrace. They were
close and worked together on most actions. Dresden's his usual unset-
tlingly anxious version of himself. He's looking at me with his best
antagonistic grin. Henry Knapp's staring at the ground, noting the
uncomfortable mood in the room. I don't think he was in on the score.
And as for the big one, this Yak, well, he's making me seven kinds of
nervous with that giant gleaming smile that's obviously directed at me.
As far away as we are, I still have to look up to see it.

"You got a name, big Yak?" I ask, trying anything to get him to stop
smiling at me.

He nods, even his smile has muscles.

"Got some reason why you're smiling at me like a water-head?"

The smile fades. He gets serious. "My name is Toure' Yakubu of
Rwanda. I have heard many stories about you. I am excited to finally
meet you."

"Well I don't know a thing about you, big man," I say, glaring at Bock. "I usually interview potentials myself."

"Then I am sorry we meet like this, but it is a pleasure all the same," Yakubu says, nearly bowing.

"Fair enough. And you," I say pointing to Dresden. "You, I know. And you were instructed to screw off in a permanent fashion."

Dresden chuckles. "Why, Rust, I'm not working for you. So, I suppose you're the one that should 'screw off,' as you tactfully say."

I turn to Bock and shake my head. "Why, Bock? You saw what he did in Chicago."

"I told you it was short notice. I needed four men."

"Then you should have come to me!"

"Gentlemen," the old man with the shoulder length grey hair at the front of the hangar says. He calmly walks toward us with his dress shoes clapping crisply on the concrete floor. That finely tailored navy suit he's in gives Bock's a run for its money. "It seems the situation has been altered on all sides."

The man walks like an aristocrat with proud persistent steps that stop in front of me. He rolls on the balls of his feet almost comically and onces me over like some kind of investment. His face is too close. I notice a long, jagged scar across the old man's left eye, down to mid-cheek. The eyeball itself is glazed over, a dull, hazy green. He's probably half blind.

"So you are the infamous Amarillo Rust," the old man says, smiling inquisitively. "Sergeant Major Amarillo Rust, formerly of—"

"Of the United States Army, that's right," I say. "Look here, I generally don't entertain all the pleasantry dung. I'm not with that outfit anymore, so how bout you just get to telling us what's happening on your end. As you can see, I've got a few administrative problems of my own."

"You certainly look the part, Mr. Rust. The crew-cut and manicured mustache in a time when most men prefer a clean-shaven face. You must admit, you've not strayed far from your former self, as is often the case with most men," he says.

"The feck is he talking about?" Bock says, exasperated. "Maybe we can kiss and make up by shooting this old bugger together, Rust. Call it male-bonding."

I look past the old man, still inches from my face and grin at Bock. I know he isn't joking. The old Tishbe fella swings around and gives Bock the same treatment, and that's when I feel everyone in the room tense up. I, for one, can handle a little awkwardness, even some hazing. I was in the military after all. I can keep my head, but not Bock. Bock's in this line of work because he can't much function doing anything else. While his appearance is one of a slicked back, mannered, finely dressed London high-financier, what bubbles beneath the surface is anything but. That's not to say Bock's not a good guy, even a friend, he just never got taught the way to behave in polite society. It's no B.S. all the time with Bock, and while I trusted him without reservation—before today at least—this was exactly the reason I insisted on running the day-to-day operations of team admin. myself. This business is chock full of jokers and mad men. Their teams never last because rather than plotting and planning about what to do "in case," they just haul off and trade it all for extra fire-power. There's not enough Semtex in the world to blow the doors off a well-crafted plan. It isn't that Bock doesn't understand, or even agree on this point, it's just that he can't help himself.

"Thomas Bock," Elijah Tishbe says, smiling admirably, so close to the Scotsman's face he could smell yesterday's breakfast. "Not much to find out about you, yes? Your reputation not only precedes you, it completely supplants all else. You are known in circles as a wild and sometimes even cruel man, though you would never describe yourself as such. In your mind, you are a man of obligation and completion, almost obsessively so. All loose ends must be tied. All payment only deposited after all objectives have been reached, the proverbial fat lady having sung her last."

Bock grits his teeth, nearly snarling. Bock's going to put his fist through the man's cranium. All the way through.

"But your remarkable effectiveness in these and other areas stems from pain and agony of a loss so terrible that most should fall to their

knees that they never experience it," he says. "And this is why you will
not strike out against me, Thomas Bock. Because above all things that
which you hold onto with a grasp stronger than death, a place where you
hold your faith and allegiance is in the idea of truth. Truth and currency.
These are of the few principles for which you care any longer, and I have
spoken both to you here today."

Bock closes his mouth and takes deep, measured breaths, but his
eyes still dart around the room nervously. I've never seen this. Bock does
not back down. While Tishbe does allow Bock some room by taking a
step back, he still speaks with a confidence and unwavering eye contact
displaying absolutely no subservience or fear.

"In this, you are now certain that I mean you no harm or ill will," he
says looking around the room and spreading his arms. "To any of you."

The hangar remains silent for a moment. I look at Bock staring at
the floor. Tishbe really struck a chord. I can't believe the old guy's still
vertical. But then, Bock looks up slowly to Tishbe.

"You had better be glad I don't give a piss for who you are or where
you come from, auld man. I've killed several for much less. It's your
money I'm after. If I could get it without you breathing, trust me, I'd do
it," Bock says. Then he glares at me. "This is your bloody team, mate?
Then run the fecking thing and get us our payment. I want out of
Albania." He then storms out of the hangar through the doorway we
breached to get in.

I stand there at a loss for words. There's no precedent for what I just
witnessed. I once saw Bock literally shoot a fella in the privates for calling his mother a pig-whore in Portuguese, and I'm not sure Bock even
met his own mother.

"Look what you done, Tishbe," I say, trying very hard to lighten the
mood. "Okay, boys, I'd say we're pretty much done doing whatever it
was this old man wanted us to do here, so how about you all disperse. I'll
get your cuts to you as usual. Even you fellas," I say to the Bock's "b"
team. "After all, you guys took down the Cobra, and I can appreciate
that. The old man and I need to have a word."

The men begin to file out without ceremony. Dresden didn't even need me to finish. Horrace and Park approach each other slowly and give an uneasy handshake to each other as they walk out. Yakubu was the last to leave. He gives me a polite nod and smile, which I return, well, the nod at least. The man is so large he nearly has to crouch and turn sideways to get through the doorway.

The old man and I are alone in the hangar now, standing several feet apart. The only other thing in the room is that plastic-wrapped palette sitting like an albatross in the middle of the hangar. We stare at each other for a moment, not quite angrily, but more cautious than anything. Some of the heaviness has dissipated, but what remains is just odd. Even I see the comedy in it.

"Okay, I'll start," I say. "I don't usually do much questioning of my client's interests, and I don't reckon I'll do too much of that now. We all deal with secrets in this line of work just as much as anything else, and while I can respect your privacy, I'm afraid I'm gonna need some answers. Just what are you jerking me and my team around for? Trying to get yourself killed?"

"Your request is understandable, Mr. Rust," Tishbe says. "But you must trust that my motivations were completely forthright. However, I must ask you to respect that those motivations are mine alone. And while there is information I would very much like to disclose, due to the unfortunate convolution of the action today regarding your team's unauthorized division of duties, now I regret, is not the time to have the discussion. I hired you to negotiate a series of actions, which, however unorthodox your methods, you did achieve. Therefore, payment is indeed due. And payment you will have. It sits before you now." Tishbe extends a hand to the palette.

"Thought that was yours."

"Quite the contrary. The contents are yours. They always were. If I may offer a suggestion: there were two teams in operation today. Split the palette down the middle. Offer one half to your partner, Mr. Bock, so that he may distribute the contents among his secondary team. I suggest you distribute your half to your men."

Just then a deep rattling echoes through the hangar. The massive steel hangar door begins to shutter and lift, revealing Tishbe's two men standing next to the white cargo truck.

"How the hell am I supposed to get that palette back to the States?" I ask.

Tishbe turns and walks casually toward the truck, the two men open up the doors and the driver gets inside. The other man holds the door open for the old man.

"You are a man of resources, Mr. Rust. More than you know. Transportation of the palette will be of little difficulty for a man of your talents. You will hear from me again in exactly one year's time."

Tishbe steps into the passenger seat, and offers a casual wave. His man closes the door when Tishbe's inside and hops into the bed of the truck. I rest the P90 on my shoulder in total confusion and watch the truck back away from the building and disappear down the valley road.

Chapter 6

THREE MONTHS AND no word from any of the boys. Nobody's tried to contact me for their fees on the Albanian job. Nobody's given me a heads up on any wet work. Nothing. I'm at the cotton gin back in Tahoka working the bale press. Usually I'm outside directing the trucks in and out of the loading bays, but Harper McGee's kid, the one who officially works the press, has gone home sick again. The kid claimed pig flu, but since it's Monday, I'm going with a pretty standard residual hangover from the weekend. I see the kid and his high school dropout buddies down at *Sharkey's* on weekends when I'm not away on real business. I note their beat up pickups parked out front most nights I drive past on my way home. The McGee kid's okay, but he's got a mouth on him. There's not much future for a boy like that outside of radio or cable news, and judging by this one's command of the English vernacular, or distinct lack thereof, don't think show business will be calling.

I have been judged for the way I speak as well, I suppose, though falsely in my case. With a first name like Amarillo, which I know will be a shock to learn is also where I was born, it's difficult to find soap strong enough to wash the Texan out of one's mouth.

The Texan accent is not a southern accent. It is a Texan sound alone, and a West Texan accent is an even different animal. It is as lyrical as the Irish, but not soft and mellifluous as the French. A West Texas sentence unfurls like a rolled up rug. The pace of words always constant, never jerky. No stops and starts. A West Texan sentence flows either slowly or quickly depending on the speaker, not at all like water bubbling over stones in a clear, shallow creek, but instead the well-paced deeper stretches, straight, brown, and thick like milk chocolate. It is the lemon twist in a glass of heavy sweet tea, the dab of horseradish atop an ice-cold gulf oyster, that bite of cilantro in salsa freshly prepared. It is as much a part of me as my eyes that see the splendors of my state, or my ears that can instantly recognize another from my geography across a bustling hall a world away.

This is all to say, I am proud of my accent, and it isn't just because of Texas pride. Twice in my life I had worked to stamp out the uniqueness of my voice. Both were gratuitous failures, even if I didn't recognize them as such at the time. It is the stereotypical lack of intelligence that travels along with those sharing my accent that serves as both my greatest detriment, but also perhaps my most discrete advantage.

You hear a guy like me coming and ninety-nine people out of a hundred are going to think you a fool before you answer their first question. This is why I make a point to be out in front of my team. I like to make contact when I can. I like to negotiate price. I like to be the first to greet a potential client, or be the first to engage a threat. Why? Because at those moments of first contact, I am instantly underestimated. I am taken as a redneck fool, and so their mental game adjusts, lowers. That shaves a little off their stack, and puts it into mine. This is an advantage, one that costs nothing more than a year's subscription to The New Yorker magazine. Those pretentious peacocks can have my money. I'd say they did me a favor. And this doesn't just work in the states. When I'm abroad, I sometimes lay it on even thicker.

I've been thinking a lot about old Teasel lately. Not so much feeling guilty, but just running the day through my head over and over, wondering if I had done the right thing by him. I missed the funeral, heard most did, but ran into his daughter in town. I offered my condolences. We lazily shot a game of pool over a pitcher of beer at *Sharkey's*. She didn't seem all that upset really. Maybe she thought the same way I did, and had she been in my line of work, she very well may have done the same.

See, while many think life is too short, as the saying goes, I beg to differ. I see life as excruciatingly long. My days at the gin tell me it's true, and the last three uneventful months have solidified it. Most people don't have anything to compare their lives to. Work. Sleep. Work. Bar. Sleep. Work. Movie. Sleep. It goes on and on until one day—snip—blackness. But don't think I'm talking down on anyone. Only thing different with my real line of work is that the real line of work's more interesting. Goodness knows I sleep. I wake up. I go to bars, have holidays, and even watch movies. In fact, I happen to enjoy romantic comedies most of all. There is a sweetness to them, like a slice of cherry pie for your brain before bedtime.

But if you want to know what I share most with every other person in the world, it's the black snip of death. Nobody escapes it. Nobody enjoys it. Where most people go wrong is thinking that someone can go calmly or die slowly or simply drift off, cross over, or pass away. Nonsense. Death is immediate. One second you're here and the next you are not. You exist. You existed. A person "dying of cancer" is not dying. They are living in a real bad situation. Dying is a split second event, and I've seen enough of that to make me respect it. If the choice is "quietly passing" during the horrific throes of cancer eating your insides as you sleep, or a .220 *Swift* slug between the eyebrows, mark me down for the *Swift*. It's twenty-one, and the dealer's got blackjack every time. Point is, why not live all the way? I thought my stint in the forces would be that, but found the service to be about as boring and mundane as Teasel's last days. Going out on my own and teaming up with Bock and the boys on actions insured that every time I went out there was real work to be done, and real living to be had. Sure, the dealer still always holds a blackjack, but at least I can push him every now and then. Can't do that at some cotton gin in Tahoka, Texas.

I leave the gin at quitting time and head for *Sharkey's* in my pickup. There is a relaxation in not having to look over my shoulder all the way there. Sometimes the adrenaline surges produced by scoping for tails in exotic international locales is fun, but even I need a rest every once in a while. I beat most of the work crowd to the bar, so I easily get my beer and choice of table. I choose the one in the back corner closest to the TV so I can hear the news over the old juke that they refuse to change the music out of. I pop my quarters into one of the billiard tables and hear the balls release. I choose a cue and wipe the lager froth from my mustache. The barflies from the bank downtown file in first, still looking for a husband like somebody new is gonna wash in. They don't come to me anymore because they know not to. I suspected the painters would be in next, and they were. They usually beat me here, but not today. Seems the Chavaroo rig needed a fresh coat because the roughnecks are right on their heels. I don't play pool with painters. They couldn't give you a decent game if their lives hung in the balance. Too high from locking themselves in with the fumes all day. But the roughnecks are always good sports. The fact they often get violent puts most people off, but they know better than to bring all that around my table. Their taunts fail to affect my shots. Besides, their spoils depend on their manners if they come around looking for a game with me. I had to crack a roughneck's femur a few months ago for insinuating I was trying to hustle him. I'm just that good at pool.

There's a story on the news about another bombing in Israel. A bus. Fifty-three dead including the Palestinian jihadist. It's the only way they know how to actually score a kill. They are without a doubt the poorest shots on the planet. I welcome actions in that region. Their training is sloppy, their gear pathetically antiquated, and their singularly fervent mindset renders them almost completely inept on the field of combat. No creativity. Fish in a barrel. The Israelis' approach is completely the opposite, and that is why they are feared. This is why a mercenary out of Israel is a highly coveted prospect in my line of work. You'll be hard-pressed to find anyone better, and I always have my eye open for fresh Israeli recruits.

"Fancy a game, mate?" I hear behind me.

I grin and take pull on my beer, not turning around. I know exactly who's on my six. "Don't know. Got money?"

"I can spare a few for a beggar like you."

I turn and can't hide my pleasure at seeing Bock again. He smiles, and we shake hands. I look him over and laugh out loud at his getup. He's tucked one of his French-cut button-downs into a pair of brand new Wranglers that are a bit too big for him. And those boots look like some dandy come out of a Fort Worth honky-tonk on Saturday night.

The bar has filled in, so I don't worry about anyone listening in on us. "What in the world are you wearing, boy?"

He chuckles and pushes my shoulder. "Eat shite, mate. I've never been to this godforsaken heap before."

"Cufflinks?"

Bock just shakes his head and laughs. "Didn't know what to expect the way you talk about this part of Texas, you twit. Thought I'd see dragons and fairies the way you prat on."

We just stand there for a short while, both getting the picture that there's no hard feelings.

"Good to see you, Bock. Took a chance in coming here though."

"Got business to tidy up."

"Suppose we do. Reckon your boys are sniffing around for their piece of Albania."

"Yours aren't?" he asks.

I shake my head. "Hadn't heard a word. Figure they'd try to get in touch when they did."

"Probably waiting to collect on the next one," he says, checking out the barflies who are eyeing him like a grilled T-bone. "And stop calling them 'my boys.' They're ours. We're partners in all of it."

"You sure about that, Bock?"

He looks off like he's agitated.

"No, no, I don't mean it like that," I say. "I mean is that really what you're saying? Are we partners? Are we gonna operate on the level now and hash out all the BS ahead of time?"

"You going to listen and stop calling all the shots like some autocratic arse?"

"Reckon I can give it a try."

"Well then, it's sorted."

We have a beer and a game. Bock doesn't interact with any of the locals because he knows the rules. I know the rules too, and since we wouldn't allow any of the other boys to ever show up where we live our day lives, Bock and I don't spend too much time in the bar. I already noticed a few of the gin employees come in, and so a cover story would have to be concocted, even if I didn't need to use it. Bock shouldn't have shown up here, but I knew that if he ever did, it would be for a darn good reason. Getting yourself paid for an action is always reason enough to turn up anywhere, and so we finish our beers and head out for Teasel's place, and to the palette of our spoils.

Chapter 7

I CHECK MY rearview again to see Bock driving the rental SUV behind me as we kick up dust on the dirt road out to Teasel's. The Texas plains sit expansive and empty before us. When we left the bar, Bock asked me whether I looked inside at the contents of the palette. It was rhetorical, just trying to judge my reaction. I didn't let on, and I've spent the last half hour trying to figure out how he's going to take it. I imagine he'll want to tear the limbs off of one Elijah Tishbe, that is if we ever find him again. He seems like the type of man who can stay under for as long as he feels the need. Though, even having seen our "payment," some part of me still believes he will make contact in a year just as he said he would. Eight months and change to go. Not sure how I'll feel about it from day to day. Today I don't hate the man. Somehow I see something more in all this. It's too elaborate for a crazy person. I know that chopper in Albania was controlled remotely, and I'll bet anything the installation was his to begin with. Tishbe's not crazy, he's setting something up, but for the life of me, I can't figure what.

I pull to a stop in front of the farmhouse. When I had the conversation with Teasel's daughter, I told her I'd look after the place. Told her I was the closest thing to a friend the old man had, and so I'd put the house back in some kind of order so the family could put it on the market later. Least I could do, I told her. She was only too happy to hear it, and agreed quickly. I saw that woman drive past my house three times in so many years to see her father. She couldn't care less. I could do whatever I wanted with Teasel's and I'd be libel not to hear a peep from her for the rest of my days. So, I cleaned up the inside as much as I could. Made it a safe-house that I probably wouldn't need. I set up a bed in one of the back rooms, and an encrypted terminal with rations in the kitchen. It was mostly reflex. Always have a second place when and if the first gets burned. But like I said, I didn't think I'd ever need it. Then Albania happened and all the sudden I had a palette of garbage that needed somewhere to stay. I got my hands on an eighteen-wheeler from a fella I know in San Antonio and drove it down to the port in Corpus Christi where I picked up the palette from a cargo container I had Park procure from Singapore. I drove it back Tahoka way myself. Gave me all sorts of time to think about what went down, but like I said, the answers just didn't come. The whole thing's still a mystery.

I still remember when I first pierced the plastic with my seven-inch tactical *Spyderco* and started hauling in heavy wooden crates through the front door. Took all afternoon, and I didn't open a single one until I was finished. I did it carefully, considering the possibility that this was some elaborate hit job and Tishbe rigged the boxes with explosives. In fact, judging from the contents of the first one I opened, I suspected a bio agent. Didn't take long to dispel that notion.

I get out of the pickup just as Bock pulls up and does the same.

"Welcome to my home away from home," I say, walking to the door and I can tell that old Bock is full of nerves. He smells bad news, and I can't say I blame him.

Inside I had already halved the crates from the palette into two stacks at opposite sides of the room, one stack for my team and the other for Bock's. All contain one of three contents, and so I set out three representative crates neatly in the middle of the room.

Bock looks at them, then at me. "What's it all about then?" he asks.

"Well, I checked and seems like all the boxes have one of three things in them, and you ain't gonna like any of it."

"No gold, I take it."

"Nope. No gold."

"Figured as much. How bad did we get buggered?"

"Pretty bad. Pretty bad. Darned entertaining though. Wish you could've been here when I tried to figure out what all this stuff was. You'd have had a hoot."

"Think so do you?" he says. "Which should I look in first?"

"That one on the left is pretty good," I say.

Bock grimaces. "What's that bloody putrid smell?"

"The crate on the left."

Bock walks to the wooden crate that sits before us about the size of a standard kitchen trashcan. He snaps open his knife and kneels down, sliding the top over with the blade.

"Powder," he says under his breath.

"Yep," I say.

"Coarse. Clumpy. Kind of greenish yellow."

"Yep."

"Stinks to hell, mate."

"That's because it's sulfur," I say, watching a loose clump of it crumble between his fingers.

"There's more of these?"

"Many more just like it."

He shakes his head. "Okay, what's in the others?"

"See for yourself."

Bock opens the crate in the middle with his knife the way he did the first one.

"More powder," he says, exasperated.

"Well, not exactly," I say, watching him like you would a baby with a strange new toy.

"Safe?" he asks, stopping himself from delving his hand into the white granules.

"Oh it's safe," I nod, almost grinning.

Bock shoves his hand in and brings up a handful. It runs through his fingers like an hourglass. "This is salt," he says.

"Bingo," I say.

He slings what's left of it back into the box. He's more confounded than angry, but this is Bock we're talking about, so I need to try and keep him cool. You never know when it's coming. The last one he opens with his hands.

"Now this one's fun," I say.

The contents of the last box are in protective wrap, just not like we're used to. No bubble wrap or foam peanuts here, just what seem like very old rags, browned from time, and impossibly fragile. The item Bock picks up just fits in the box along with the protective wraps: about sixteen inches tall, and as wide around as the grip on a Desert Eagle. Bock starts unwinding the rags like a mummy until the item is completely exposed.

"Bloody hell is this?" Bock says. "A cross?"

"Looks that way."

"Ornate. Carved. What's this metal?"

"I'm guessing its iron, maybe some copper around the bottom there," I say. "Catholic probably. Early though. You know those long cross things priests walk down the aisle with during Mass?"

"Don't know, mate, I'm Scottish, but I like these jewels. Rubies here. Topaz, emeralds, gilt silver." he says carefully inspecting the artifact. "Looks so old. What do you think it's worth?"

"Don't have the slightest idea. It's shorter than those things that priests carry in, but the bottom shaft seems like a handle of some kind."

"It does," Bock says without looking up, still inspecting. "Bloody beautiful. How many of these are there?"

"Not many. Only twelve total. The rest is, well…"

"Crap," he says.

"Reckon so."

"Well they've got to be worth something. Maybe this is the real payment. Maybe all the rest is for throwing off port inspectors, you know. To hide these crosses."

"I don't know, Bock. How do twenty-four crates filled with white powdery substances *repel* attention exactly?"

"Fair point," he says, standing, still holding the cross. He stares at me for a long minute. "I'm almost too confused to be angry with the auld tosser."

I chuckle. "Know what you mean."

"Not to say we shouldn't hunt him down like the dodgy son of a monkey's arse he is."

That's when I tell him what Tishbe said, that he'd make contact in one year from that day in Albania. Bock didn't take it well, probably like I should have. He said the man was playing us for fools, that we'd never see hide nor hair of him again. I didn't argue. I told Bock that he could take his share of the crosses and I'd deal with the crates of sulfur and salt if he wanted, but surprisingly Bock said he'd take his half in full.

"If I'm to be paid in table salt and fart powder," he says, "then by George, so will the rest of 'em."

I help Bock load up crates into his rental SUV. We shake hands like we've never been cross, and he takes off down the road. I watch until the dust trails melt seamlessly into the sky. Guess old Bock thinks pretty much like I do. Time to get back to work. Time to make some real money.

Chapter 8

ONCE KNEW A fella named Toby Dennis. First met him in junior high school back in Amarillo. We became friends, and when we graduated high school, I went into the Army. Toby decided he wanted to be a pilot like his daddy and entered the USAF. We kept in touch for the first couple years. Met up on bases when we could, even took a wild trip to Mexico once when we were both on leave for margaritas and senoritas. We lost touch around the first Gulf war. One day, years later, after I had quit the military and gone out on my own, I thought of him, and that gave me an idea.

Private contractors need a way to communicate with their people. Most run roughshod, thinking no one's listening in on their cell and landline calls. They do business right out in the open and then wonder how, by some miraculous turn of chance, heat comes their way. This usually results in they being driven even further undercover. Sometimes they have to take months or even years off until one day they find out they can't get work and their money well has run dry as the Monahans sand hills. Most of these types are too stupid to trace it back to the obvious: compromised communications. In a post 9/11 world, one must always assume someone else is listening.

I've heard some teams use what's called a draft method for getting intel and orders to their team undetected. The plan calls for each member of a team to have a second email account and password. The designated communicator of the team holds with him the username and password for all team-members' accounts. When a communication needs sending, the point man goes to an encrypted terminal, a library, or an Internet café and opens each team member's account, using his list of passwords. He or she then creates a new email, and types the communication which could consist of meet locations, targets of opportunity, or payment drop locales, etc. But, instead of sending the communication, they simply save the email as a draft in each member's outgoing box, thus giving the appearance that the person who's name is on the account typed up an email, but either wasn't finished with it, or for whatever reason just hasn't sent it yet. And so, the next time the user logs in to their account, they check their outbox drafts, read the communication, and all is right with the world because nothing ever really got sent over the Internet. That's the theory at least, but there is a flaw in that system.

Most email clients are based in the cloud now, the software is held on servers somewhere out in cyberspace, remotely. And since the communicator is using a "borrowed" terminal for all intents and purposes, it follows that the *saved* draft, by definition of being saved, is transmitted to the cloud, or Internet, to *be* saved. Therefore, by saving the draft, you are saving it on the Internet, and so the information is being transmitted anyway.

Well that day, thinking on my childhood friend, I remedied that problem. Flying is an expensive hobby, well out of reach for most, but today, computers have gotten cheap and powerful enough to allow any Tom, Dick or Harry with the desire to pretend they're a bonafide Howard Hughes. Flight simulators have gone mainstream, anyone can purchase one at their local big box electronics retailer, and though their popularity has waned considerably over the years, the remaining enthusiasts are just that, almost disturbingly loyal and obsessed with the precision of avionics and its vernacular. There are websites that cater to flight sim enthusiasts. Most have forums where they get together and share stories of piloting their little fake Cessnas with custom liveries and their phony flight plans for fantasy Boeing 727's. Often they get together via these forums and plan virtual "fly-ins" where they all agree to network over broadband each weekend and fly in formation to agreed upon exotic locales, negotiating arrival times and even runway designations. I find the whole thing strange and silly, but in it, I also saw opportunity.

The first thing I needed was a website, so I did some research and set my sights on one of the less popular flight sim forum links. Fewer than fifty registered users frequented the site anymore. The web is riddled with forums like these. I contacted the person listed as owner of the domain name of msflighsimjunkie.com. Turns out it was a twenty-four year old kid out of Flagstaff, Arizona. I gave him a load of dung about my love for the sim, and the site, and offered him just under nine grand for the full setup, domain, architecture, etc. He knew the site was dead, but he didn't think I did. So, thinking himself a sharp little bandit, he took my offer. I now owned the site, and as it turned out, the very best system for communicating with a team I could have ever devised.

When I met up with the team a month or so later for a security action in Cupertino, CA, I told them about how I had found a new way to get messages out to them. I gave them a crash course in flight sim speak. I told them to all set up forum accounts, obviously under assumed names and locations. I said that they should check in on the site and post at least once a week to populate forum traffic, even copy and paste other entries from other forums if they had to. The only important forum topic would be entitled, "Weekly Fly-Ins." If I had an action planned, I would create a post something like this:

"Ok, about Saturday, are we still set for the Caribbean? maybe meet in TNCM, Princess Julliana Int. in St. Maartin...the scenery is floating around, Hogster, if you could point out where you got it that would help people who dont have it very fun place to fly...and you make sure you have some reggae playin, dis is da caribean! ETA 12:30 CMT."

It was that simple. Anyone looking for work that I had approved would simply respond if they were available. Depending on who and how many boys I needed, I would simply post the following:

"Be grate to see you omniroxx, toucan15, Hogstar!"

No one with an account was being cut out of anything other than the parameters of the given job. If I had a problem with anybody, I'd let them know up close and personal. Of course, Bock usually took care of that before I had to. And speaking of Bock, this is something he never would have come up with. Bock loves the action, and he's darn good at it, but he needed a deliberative mind to complement his wet work acumen. It is true that this form of communication had its limitations as usually we did meet, at least originally at an airport, but I could always throw into the post that we were simply performing a "fly-over" of, say, Rockefeller Center, and we'd meet up there. In the event we needed more specificity than the sim would generally allow, I'd tag on: "We'll pick up brochures," and since we always met for briefings in well-populated tourist locations, the phrase was a code for the operative to find the bank of tourist brochures nearest the airport's main entrance and meet up at the location of the second brochure on the rack. This was a technique we rarely had to employ, as I've said, there is no substitute for a well-crafted plan. Only when both of these techniques fail would my employee be authorized to use a landline to contact me directly on my satellite phone.

So it seems we'd do it again. I just got word of some work in Lithuania running arms across the Russian border. Working in Russia and its bordering countries used to be easy since most of the population was either starving or on the take, but since gaining membership in the European Union, all that's changed. Money still talks, and we've got plenty of that, so I rarely anticipate much resistance moving the guns. I post an entry on the flight sim forum. Heard back from Bock, Everly, Park, and Horrace. We meet at Kaunas International Airport in a week. Maybe we'll take in a museum or two. I know just the place.

Chapter 9

PLEASE BE UNDER no false assertions that geography all over the world is all that unique. There are five basic forms of terrain: mountains, desert, forest, plains, and jungle. Mountains can be thickly forested, or rocky and desolate like a desert. In terms of weather, you've got clear, wet, hot, and cold. It's all just a mix of these, but you can pretty much anticipate what you're going to run into and choose your gear accordingly. The only things that differ are the people and architecture. Architecture may or may not play a part in how you're going to carry out an action, but one thing is for sure, the people of a given location will most certainly become a major factor in how it all plays out. Therefore, it behooves one to learn what makes people tick.

The Lithuanian people are among the most homogeneous on the planet. You can find some Poles and some Russians, maybe a few Belarusians, but on the whole, Lithuanians have stayed put. Of course, there are the exceptions. Fierce haggling for control over the country in the twentieth-century primarily between the Nazis and later the Soviet Union did cause some dispersion across the globe. A million or so Lithuanians made their way to America, but a surprisingly healthy pocket emigrated to Ireland, making up roughly a little over one percent of their total population. This is mostly due to Lithuania and Ireland sharing a very large and devout Catholic majority.

Upon my arrival at Kaunas International Airport in neighboring Karmelava, I make it quickly through customs thanks mostly to my accent and expensive passport I actually purchased from a talented fella not far from here in Jonava nearly a decade ago. I head to baggage claim and almost run right smack into Horrace, who furiously rolls himself a cigarette while licking his lips somewhere under that heavy beard of his, not paying attention. He jolts when he sees me, his eyes perk up, but then he fights the urge to acknowledge me with more than a nod and a curt apology in Lithuanian, a language I know virtually nothing of. Horrace speaks it fluently, that and about ever other language we've ever needed him to. Horrace loves being abroad. I suspect mostly because his favorite thing in the world is smoking, well, that and not being in the States. He's an intelligent man who can handle himself, and often says that few countries in the world are as restrictive as the United States. Most countries are socially quite liberal, an assertion Horrace fervently and sometimes argumentatively holds. He says that as long as you don't publicly say anything negative about most governments, you can pretty much get away with murder.

I nod back to Horrace and stand several yards away at the baggage claim. I see him light the cigarette and take a deep drag from the corner of my eye. Horrace's bag drops down the chute and takes a pass around the carousel. He takes the bag, flips up the handle and rolls it over to a bank of uncomfortable seats along the wall where he sits and smokes. I'll never get over how pleased he looks getting to smoke in public buildings. My bags are next. I take them and do the same as Horrace, but sit along the opposite wall. From here it's a waiting game. Tardiness is ill advised in this business. Punctuality is key, and lack of it often results in your replacement. No job means no pay, so I'm not surprised to see Park show up, then Bock, and finally Everly, who's treading on thin ice with Bock already. He would do well to arrive first for a meet, but its hard to tell Everly anything. Truth be told, I'd probably cut him loose if I had my better judgment about me, but there's a kindness in Everly that I find comforting, I suppose. He's young, never had a father, that whole deal. Everly picks up on things quickly, especially his surroundings. He notices entrances and exits, unorthodox points of entry and escape faster than most. It's innate, a preternatural knowledge of where you are and how to get out. You don't find that often, and when you do, it's a trained, rote type skill that easily falls back on textbook theory rather than gut instinct. Bock doesn't see much value in it since he's more of a run-and-gun type guy, and truth is, Bock usually doesn't move quietly anywhere, but I've noticed Everly in action plenty of times. He's gotten us out of many a sticky situation whether Bock wants to admit it or not.

With all the boys in attendance, each pretending not to know one another, I stand up and pretend to fiddle with my Blackberry. I grab the handle of my suitcase and make off toward the exit. I sense the boys discretely getting up and following me, one by one in measured increments of thirty seconds or so. I stop at the tourist info booth and slowly select the brochure for the restaurant *Perkuno Namai* on the top row. The team member behind me will note this and either grab the same brochure or at least glance at it and remember the name. The man after him will do the same, and the one after him until we all know where we're meeting. The men book their own rooms wherever they like, get there however they choose, but know that two hours from the time I touch that brochure, they are to meet at the designated spot. At 20:53 Eastern European Time, we plan the Lithuanian action.

Chapter 10

THE HOTEL RESTAURANT at *Perkuno Namai* has a private room downstairs called the "library," complete with stocked bookshelves, wood paneled walls, and low lighting. Bock and I enjoy pints of local Utenos grinning at the story Everly tells as smoke from Horrace's cigarette curls above the table. Horrace steeps himself in some intellectual conversation with Park. I'm still not sure what business Park took up in his day life after leaving Korea, but Bock and I are fairly sure that Horrace is a professor. He's always engaging Park. Maybe he thinks Park's the smartest of us. I don't know about that, but he's certainly the most secretive. One thing I've learned is that the most secretive man in the room is usually the one with the most to lose.

"So you dinnae know who she was?" Bock asks, spurring Everly on after becoming sidetracked by an outburst of laughter from Horrace and Park's conversation.

"Yeah, okay, so this chick is standing down next to her car by the entrance. She's woken up half the apartment complex. It's four in the morning and she doesn't give a rip, man. Not a care in hell."

"Wait, so now it's four in the morning?" I ask, missing that part.

"Four. Around then. So she says, at the top of her lungs mind you, 'It's goin' down, Paul! I'll make it all come down!' So doors are opening, windows are sliding open, but I've had mine cracked since the beginning. Front row seat. I mean, this guy is getting the reaming of his life. But this Paul, whoever he is, isn't claiming this chick. She's screaming at a wall."

"And her car is still halfway in the grass?" Bock asks, chuckling and taking a swig of beer.

"Absolutely," Everly says. "Curb jumped, doors open, stereo blasting. Lights, the whole thing. And I'm just waiting for the pigs to show. So, then, she starts grabbing at her chest, and—! pulling at her clothes. 'Is this what you want, Paul? You want this again you son of a—'"

"No," I say.

"She starts tearing her clothes off, and let me tell you, this is not something you want to see. This chick is hefty. Hefty. She's ripping at her clothes, they're flying all over the place. She works off her pants, kicks off her shoes, and now the rest comes off. Buck naked from the waist down."

"And this is in January," Bock says.

"Winter. Frigid. And I'm not kidding, guys," Everly says dramatically. "Audible groans. They come from everywhere. It's like a play. Groans from down the hall on my floor, from the windows down below, above. Everyone's up, and everyone's watching the show."

"So what now?" I ask, fumbling for a cigar in my jacket pocket. I notice that Park has become distracted and turns his attention to Everly. Horrace keeps on with his diatribe, staring at the table and using his hands to make a point. Pretty soon he looks up at Park, who's smiling at our conversation prompting him to sigh.

"Well this Paul guy still isn't taking the bait from whatever apartment he's in. Who even knows if she's got the right complex, you know? But either way, she ups the ante. She goes to rip off that horrible tracksuit jacket, except the zipper gets stuck. This frustrates the fire out of her and she starts wrestling with it, stumbling around in circles and spitting and cursing up a storm."

The table laughs. Even Horrace cracks a smile.

"Well I guess then it hits her that it's about three degrees outside, so she stops, and she's huffing and puffing. People all around are laughing from their windows like it's a sitcom or something, but she's focused, boy. She's not hearing any of us."

"The cops still haven't shown?" Bock asks.

"Not yet. But she starts trembling because of the cold and all the sudden she lets out this tired scream and bolts back to her car and shuts the door."

"She's heating up," I say.

"Oh, that's bloody brilliant," Bock says, and for the first time in a while, I hear that deep guttural laugh come out of him.

"Come on Everly," Park says. "I call BS. *'The cops don't show.'*"

"Park, I'm being straight with you, man," Everly says. "Don't know if there was an orphanage on fire or if Oprah got stuck between her couch cushions or what, but no cops, man. No cops."

"She doesn't leave does she?" I ask, jovially lighting a stogie.

"Nope. There's a couple seconds of quiet except for some people still laughing from their windows, but then she bolts back out like the Hulk and starts right back up again, and this time she's worked her way out of everything. Birthday suit naked. Big, pasty, undulating, naked, and all the sudden nobody's laughing," Everly says. "I've seen some things, guys, but this? This is a whole different kind of ugly."

"I get you," I say.

"Think so?" he asks with disbelief.

"I've had some awful bad days."

"So now? Sirens. Four cars blazing. Seven of them jump out and tackle this thing to the ground. Worst part was seeing her cuffed and bent over the hood of a squad car. Last thing she screamed out was: 'Paul Nelson Herman! Why have you forsaken me?'"

"Bloody hell, mate," Bock says laughing and pounding his pint glass on the table. They rest of the boys are laughing it up too, including myself. Everly always had a knack for storytelling. To tell you the truth, we all need a little levity here and there.

Everyone's having a good old time, but business needs addressing. We've all worked together long enough to strike up some pretty good common friendships but at the same time, we've all got to be careful.

Nobody knows one another outside of the action, except for Bock and me. The less we know about the real Horrace or Park or Everly or any of them, the safer they are. We all know that, and the integrity of that discretion serves as proof that we *are* friends.

Everyone at the table quiets down, ready to talk. I start by letting them know why we're here. Running guns. Eastern European borders can be tricky places to negotiate. You gotta know when your papers are enough, when time for greasing the right palms is at hand, and in extreme cases, when to blow the lid off the whole deal.

First order of business is to get our hands on a couple of cargo trucks. Then we outfit them with legit cargo in order to negotiate checkpoints and any other scrutiny we might run into. With his societal knowledge of just about anywhere, Horrace suggests we steal some paper trucks, but that cargo would be too light. We need something heavier in the back, preferably metal just in case they're scanned. Heavy cargo would deter an unloading investigation by authorities if for no other reason than because it's too much of a pain. If they scan the trucks and get metallic signatures from the guns, we can always point to the decoy cargo. The construction business is booming in this part of the world. We're picking up the guns from Russian syndicate contacts about twelve miles north of the Latvian town of Rezekne, a place where the government is converting an old Soviet air base into a cargo and passenger airport. Some kind of metal construction equipment would be optimal cargo. The airport will be bustling with workers and trucks as it is. We'll blend in with no problem. Yeah, so sheet metal would work just fine.

Rather than spend our time scoping for trucks and possibly compromising the entire operation with unnecessary risk, Bock suggests we bring in outside help with truck procurement. He said he would contact Henry Knapp, Dresden, and the big African he called The Yak to deliver trucks to Rezenkne. I okayed Henry Knapp and Yakubu, but Dresden, I told him, was out of the question. A third man would be needed though, and so I asked Horrace if he wouldn't mind going along. With Horrace on truck detail, he might be able to buy a couple or at least negotiate with the locals. The less mess the better. Horrace said he'd go with the truck team. Park knows enough Russian to get us most of the way through to Daugavpils, Lithuania and the Baltic coast. That's where our involvement ends even though the guns are supposed to go on to Ireland.

"Who in Ireland needs this many guns?" Horrace asks.

"Guns are going to Northern Ireland. Probably wind up in Belfast," I say.

"IRA?" Everly asks.

I nod. "Seems like they're open for business again."

"Aye. Heard about this. Didn't get the mileage they were hoping from the cease-fire with the Brits," Bock says, leaning back in his chair and gnashing on a cigar. "Ready to light it up again for the auld Republic."

"They usually deal in explosives. C4, *Semtex*, crude IED's in subway trashcans, that type of thing," Horrace says.

"Guess not anymore," I say. "Not really our concern, interesting as it all may be. What I'm interested in are trucks, what kind and how we're going to get them. The rest is standard gun running we've done a hundred times. We'll use the false walls and a center cage for our gear. Fabrication has got to be done before we get to the Rezekne airport site.

"We've used Henry Knapp before, and Horrace, I know you're good, but Bock, how about this Yakubu fella you're all the way into? He know his way around an arc welder and a rivet gun?"

"Don't know exactly. But he can certainly lift the feckin' trucks over his head if the boys should need to change the oil."

Got a good laugh out of that, but there was no doubt that the most important part of this action going off without a bang would be the trucks, not weapon malfunctions, not dialectical issues, and not hot tempers. The trucks. The trucks have to be believable. To achieve this, I've pieced together a system that I can't believe more teams haven't figured out yet. Guess that's why we get so much business, and it goes a little something like this:

First, we putty the guns like wallpaper to each interior wall of the truck, including the ceiling, muzzle to stock, clip to sight, until the inside of that truck is covered with PP-19 "bison" subs. Then over the guns we build a false wall in the cargo area of the delivery truck all the way around. A box within a box, close and tight to the guns so shifting during travel is virtually nil. We build two trim casings to go around the exposed edges of the false walls, near the cargo doors. Both are metal. One we stuff trim pieces between the false wall and the actual interior about two to three inches back, butted up against the first column of guns. The second piece we place over that and rivet it down good. If authorities suspect a false wall, they might spend the time to take apart the first casing, only to reveal a second. The search usually stops there. We had checkpoint officers pry off the first casing once while gun-running in Laos, but nobody's ever suspected enough to try and pry through the second; of course, this time we're in the Balkans, so you never know.

With the guns puttied in neatly rowed columns inside those false walls, the second part of the plan is constructing a steel metal cage about the length of your average coffin and about twice the height. The cage is more like a steel mesh tunnel than anything, open on both ends. It rests in the middle of the truck's cargo area. We pack the cage with our gear and munitions, along with one team member who rides inside. Gear, guns, and our merc packed away, we then load our decoy cargo all around the outer walls of the cage, behind it, and lastly in front, completing the appearance of a non-descript cargo truck loaded with standard construction materials. Using this technique, the driver and passenger up front will only need to carry a knife or maybe a small pistol if he's really good at hiding it. All the gear's in the back with our man in the cage. Now the driver has a walkie-talkie channel open at all times so the man in the cage can monitor for any sign of the authorities. If there's trouble, our man in the cage detonates small squib-like charges planted on the hinges of the cargo doors, popping them open. The palette of sheet metal blocking the cage's exit is on casters hidden beneath its wood-molded base. All the man in the cage needs to do in order to hop out with guns blazing is give the palette a good kick, sending it rolling off the back of the truck. From there he can toss a piece to the driver, one to the passenger if necessary, and everybody can go to town.

Problem is, the man comes out of the cage and the mission is as good as toast. It's a last resort. You might get away with it at a remote border checkpoint, but if anyone, and I mean anyone else is left alive, that mission is burned. Might as well cut and run. That means leave the trucks, leave the guns, leave everything and get the hell out of Dodge, because they're coming. Icing on the cake is the putty we use to stick guns to the interior walls of the trucks is explosive. I'll have a cell phone that rings the detonators. Be fine as long as I'm at least ninety yards away when I make the call. The trucks go kabloowee and there's no guns, no fingerprints, no DNA or hair, absolutely nothing left. Only thing we lose is a boat load of cash and the cost of the guns. But, we get out with our lives, and let's not forget about our anonymity. Anyone on the team will tell you, both are worth far more than cash.

With the boys clear on the mission, we're scheduled to meet up in two weeks. Horrace, The Yak, and Henry Knapp will be sent ahead to get the trucks ready. I hope Bock has time to get the job done.

Chapter 11

A HEAVY GREY front wipes the Rezekne sky by the time I leave
Kolonna Hotel. I take a cab to the airport construction site where a small
fuel depot sits, bustling with construction workers grabbing coffee and
exchanging stories. Three old men are parked at a small bistro table outside, sitting on folding chairs, and playing some kind of Latvian domino
variant. Everly leans against the wall next to them in a hard hat looking
cold and sullen like all the other workers, a cup of black coffee steaming
in his hand. I enter the fuel depot to find Bock and Park chatting with
each other. As I get closer, I realize that Park's the only one speaking in
Russian, just loud enough for everyone else in the place to hear. Bock
just nods his head every so often pretending to understand as Park estab-
lishes a loose alibi for the other workers to overhear. Bock gets sight of
me and nudges Park. I motion for them to meet me outside.

We convene around Everly, each wearing the hard-hats and construction gear we lifted from a Polish contractor's site a couple of weeks
ago before we left Rezekne. We're on the lookout for our trucks. Nothing
yet. I take care to notice whether the old men at the folding table can
hear, but even at this time of morning they look so old and drunk that I
doubt they realize we're standing next to them.

"Should've beaten us here," I say softly.

"Trouble with the trucks perhaps," Bock says. "They'll be here.
Henry Knapp is good with a wrench."

"Henry Knapp doesn't speak Latvian," I say.

"Horrace does," Park says. "Be fine."

"Two trucks, right?" I ask Park.

"Two." He nods.

"Little ancy, brother," Bock not so much asks, but cautions me.

I shake my head and glance at my watch again. I don't tell them the Russians haven't contacted me for a week, not since they said they'd have the guns ready for pickup in a grove behind the airport at precisely 8:25 EET. I didn't count on a checkpoint to enter the construction site. Civil, non-military regulations are usually far more lax in this part of the world. It's 8:15 EET now. Unless Horrace and the trucks show up in the next couple of minutes, someone would need to enter the construction site and head over to the grove to assure the Russians that the deal's still on. However, if the Russian outfit is worth their weight, they would have someone milling around here to monitor *our* progress. I've been in the game long enough not to expect that from the Russians anymore. Russia is the Wild West now. Anyone can stumble upon a load of guns and offer them to market. There's almost no one watching, and if there is, they're more than happy to look the other way for a cut.

"Park," I say. "Snoop around here for someone who doesn't know what they're doing or look like they belong. We're cutting it too close on time."

"And do what?" Park asks.

"Look for someone hanging off to the side away from everyone else. Somebody with a walkie or on a cell phone. I don't know, somebody who keeps looking over at us or maybe off to the northwest: that patch of trees beyond the site. You find somebody like that and real gently figure out if he's with the Russians. You know how to do it."

"They'll be here, Rust. Back it down," Bock whispers.

"Can't risk it," I say. "I don't think the trucks are going to make it. We have to keep the Russians calm. Park, you find him and tell him we're still on. Just to wait. We'll be there."

"Think we need to keep you calm, mate."

"Go on, Park," I say.

He walks away, smiling to the table of old men and pointing at one of their stacks of dominos. "*Vins ir jums!*"

The old men at the table explode into laughter as Park disappears around the corner.

"Come on, boys. Come on," I whisper under my breath, hoping desperately to see the trucks come down the street, that or Park come back with a contact.

"Don't worry," Everly says. "We'll just send Park through the checkpoint and he can make contact with the Russians to tell them himself."

"They aren't going to listen to him. They've only spoken to me. I've got to go."

"You don't know Russian," Bock says.

"I know."

Just then I catch one of the old men eyeing me. He turns in his seat toward me. I break his glance and chuckle like one of the boys made a joke, but I can see in my periphery that he's still looking at me.

"*Idi syuda, paren,*" the old man says.

"For the love of—" I whisper.

Bock looks over at the old man and says sorry in Russian as best as he can. We slowly move away as if we've got purpose, but the man seems adamant.

"*Paren, Idi syuda,*" he says again.

Our backs are to them now. Everly peeks around us. The old man won't be deterred. Bock tells me to go over and laugh at whatever the guy says, that they're all drunk and probably just want to break our castanets or say something funny. Either way, my not responding will eventually set off all kinds of suspicion. Bock's right. It's the safest plan, so I turn around and craft my building angst into some sort of smile. I say one of the few Russian words I know as I approach the card table.

"*Privet,*" I say.

When I get to the table, the two other men continue to play dominos. The one that called me over motions for me to lean down and come in close.

"Calm yourself, American," he says. "Your men are not a kilometer down the road. We will wait."

I nod. Inside I'm completely rattled and a little embarrassed. The old man pulls me closer.

"Next time you decide to travel so far from your country, perhaps you should learn the language. It would save us all much trouble. I suggest you get your other man before we are *all* in much trouble."

I nod, about as mad at myself as I could be. I got jumpy and this old Russian contact noticed it. This was a monumental failing, and I had better get it together. I almost burned the action before it even started. As I walk back to the boys, I wave Everly over and tell him to go get Park.

"What was that all about?" Bock whispers.

"Tell you later. They're right up the road."

Bock makes a confused face then leans around me to take a look at the old man who has already turned back to continue drinking and play dominos.

Everly returns with Park just about the time the trucks pull up. Horrace drives the first. The Yak drives the one behind. Henry Knapp must already be inside one of the cargo cages. The rest of us walk up to the trucks as Horrace throws his into neutral at the checkpoint gate and steps out of the cab. We're saved.

"*Sveiki. Mēs esam no Grajewo Construction. Mēs esam no lokšņu metāla sūtījumu ziemeļu pūlis,*" Horrace says throwing on his hard hat and presenting a clip board to the gate foreman.

The foreman thumbs through the pages of his own clip board. I take the opportunity to quietly tell Bock and Park to ride shotgun with Yakubu. Obviously finding nothing about us in his notes, the foreman and Horrace bicker until both get flustered, resulting in Horrace turning around to slap Everly hard across the face with his clipboard, screaming something fierce and hateful at him in Latvian. The foreman tries to calm him down, but Horrace hauls off and strikes Everly again. I instinctively try to break it up, pulling my irate operative away and pushing Everly toward the truck. Everly throws up his hands and hops up into the cab of the truck.

"*Es saku tas idiots tūkstoš reizes, lai iegūtu uz sarakstu nosaukumiem pareizi, un viss, ko viņš var darīt, ir pievilt man,*" Horrace says to the foreman who chuckles and rests a calming hand on his shoulder.

Before long, the foreman waves us through the gate. I climb into the cab of the truck with Everly as Horrace grinds it into gear.

"Sorry," Horrace says to Everly as we drive past a myriad of workers, their heavy equipment growling and beeping. We weave through the construction site with Yakubu and the others close behind in their truck until we're around back, away from most of the bustling construction.

"What now?" Horrace asks.

"See those trees over there?" I ask. "They're in there somewhere. Should be a dirt road to the right of the fence."

"I see it."

Bock scratches through the truck's CB speaker. "We've got a few wankers near the north concourse making eyes at us."

I take the CB mic from the unit and open the channel. "Hang back. See if they care. If so drive over and have Park tell them we're laying cable for a comm. tower or something."

"Aye."

"Keep going," I say to Horrace as we continue toward the dirt road.

I see our other truck in the side mirror pull to a stop. One of the three construction workers way back by the concourse points at us. Yakubu's truck wastes no time in taking a broad turn around and heads back their way. I'd pay the workers off, but I'm not in the other truck, Bock is, and I doubt he'll be opening his wallet.

Pretty soon we're on the dirt road heading for a patch of trees. Latvia is a dull green, full of hills and forest next to its greyed out skies. The cold is coming fast. Snow will follow, making our job easier or more difficult depending on road conditions. I don't care where you're from, bitter cold doesn't inspire anyone to meticulously search anything. As long as we're not sliding all over the Eastern European roadways, a freeze could work in our favor. I know Horrace will know how to handle a truck in such conditions, but as for the African, I'm not so sure.

A clearing appears just beyond a thicket of trees. Twigs and branches crack and snap against our creeping cargo truck. When the clearing opens up, two black vans with five men in dark trench coats standing next to them wait for us. I tell Everly and Horrace to stay in the cab with the heat. I check my .38 special discretely, tuck it back into my boot, and get out to meet the Russians. One of them walks up to me and offers his hand. I shake it, but he holds it hard and doesn't let go.

"I was told there were two trucks," he says.

"The other one's coming. Just had to take care of some business."

"I will not ask if you were followed."

"Good."

"Until the other truck arrives, you will forgive us," the Russian says, motioning to the rest of his crew to draw their weapons. They do so arrogantly.

"Those look like the ones we're picking up," I say flatly. "The guns, that is."

The Russian nods. "Yours are in cases. In the vans."

"Okay," I say, grinning.

"Would you like to see one?"

"Well I see a whole bunch of 'em right now, character."

"For inspection."

"I don't really give a rip," I say. "We aren't the ones gonna be shooting them. Listen, this'd all go a lot faster if we could just start packing these into our truck. I don't like sitting around. The other truck will be here directly."

"And them?" the Russian asks about Horrace and Everly.

"They're cold," I say, "and I'm not going to load them myself."

"Okay-dookie, you can load."

"Okie-dokey. It's okie-dokey you mean to say."

"Whatever you say, American. We will watch you closely."

"You do that."

I call Horrace and Everly out. Horrace goes to open up the cargo doors in back. One of the Russian heavies follows him with gun drawn.

"You do understand that we're just transportation, don't you?" I ask.

"We do not care."

"Seems like you care enough about busting our chops, though. Open up the vans and let us get to work."

The three of us open our cargo doors. Palettes of sheet metal are in their places, giving us enough room to pull the false walls and casings out of the truck. Horrace attaches a hook and chain to the palette in front of the cage and pulls. The rollers do their job, and the palette comes thudding down to the ground. Everly hops into the cage and removes a couple boxes of putty, a small generator, and a toolbox with a rivet gun inside. Everything we need to get the job done

As soon as the Russians open up the first van, revealing several crates of PP-19 Bison subs, we hear the other truck pushing through the thicket. The Russians get jumpy and draw down. I hold out my arms and try to calm them. When they see that the second truck is identical to the first, they back off and lower their weapons. Everly goes to help Park and Yakubu open up the other truck just like ours, only this time, when the cargo doors open, Henry Knapp shoves the palette of sheet metal in front of his cage down with his legs and hops out. The Russians seem to get a great deal of pleasure from this, and as we putty the subs to the walls, we have what looks more like a crowd of adoring fans than the imposing, standoffish tuffs we'd rolled up on. They've clearly never seen this done, and the vocal Russian is visually envious.

"This is very ingenious, yes," he says, walking next to me as I carry a few more PP-19's to one of the trucks.

"Thanks," I say back.

"Leave it to the Americans."

"Why not? Everybody else does," I say dropping the guns in a pile at Everly's feet.

Everly's in charge of slapping putty to the sides of the guns. What follows is a virtual conveyor belt. Everly passes them to Henry Knapp who passes them either directly to Horrace and Park who stick them uniformly to the walls, or to Yakubu who works with Bock to do the same over in the other truck. When the process is finished, we slide the false walls in and over, then rivet them in securely before replacing the double casings and bingo: trucks are loaded. Only thing left is to decide who's riding in the cages. Bock enjoys laying in the cage. It's dark and quiet. He says he reads or dozes off. I'd say something about that, but it would fall on deaf ears. The walkie inside the cage is loud enough to wake him, I figure, and Bock doesn't strike me as a heavy sleeper. I don't like riding in it myself, it's like a coffin, and as team leader I guess I can exclude myself from the duty. I thought about Yakubu riding in the other cage, but he's too green, at least with us. We need Park and Horrace up front to speak if we get stopped anywhere along the way, and Henry Knapp already did his tour on the way here, so that leaves Everly.

"Rust, come on, no," he says, pleading.

"We're out of options, Everly."

"It's like a coffin in there," he says.

"Tell me about it, kid. I hate it too but there's nobody else."

"What about him?" Everly says pointing to Yakubu.

"That'd be like shoving a buffalo into a tuna can, Everly. Have a little compassion," I say.

"It is true, little man," Yakubu says. "I am quite large."

"Whatever," Everly says, rolling his eyes and hopping up into the back of the truck. "Nice knowing you," he says, then disappears into the dark cage.

Yakubu walks up and grabs the palette of sheet metal off the ground all by himself. Must weigh five hundred pounds. Usually takes all of us to lift it.

"Nice knowing you too, little man," he says before setting the heavy palette down in front of the cage without even breathing hard.

We all stand around like we'd seen Shiva or something, even the Russians.

"Holy knickers, Yak," Bock says. "Knew we kept your massive arse around for a reason. Think you could do that again?"

"Yes I do," the big man says.

With that, Bock gets inside his cage in the other truck. Yakubu lifts the second palette from the ground and rests it on the cargo floor just as effortlessly as the first.

"Happy dreams, Mr. Bock," Yakubu says, covering the cage opening.

I tell the rest of the boys to close the trucks and mount up.

"Now you glad you didn't shoot us?" I say to the Russian just before we leave.

"Very good."

"Guess that'll do it then. *Adios muchachos*. Tell Putin hello for me."

We watch the Russians in the rear view laughing and slapping each other as we pull away. Maybe this here Yak will work out after all. It's all highway from here to the Baltic sea.

Horrace salutes the gate foreman as we exit the site. I look for the table of old men playing dominos. The one who spoke to me is gone, probably making his way back to mother Russia with the rest of the arms team. But, then I see him. He's standing, hunched over from age at the back of the building like he's been there forever, like a tree. As we pass the fuel depot, I turn to look at him. He sees me. His head tilts up, eyes burning black with a smoldering look on his face. He slowly raises his right arm and points his finger and thumb at me like a gun. I can see him mouth the word "boom" and snap his thumb down to his index finger.

Chapter 12

WE'RE SILENT THE first several miles down southwest highway A13. I've got four boys in my truck. Horrace, Everly, and Henry Knapp ride next to me in the cab. Park drives the truck behind us with Yakubu next to him taking up all kinds of space, and Bock reading or sleeping or whatever the hell he does in the back. We're about an hour away from the Latvian university town of Daugavpils. Horrace listens to his mp3 player even though he should probably be listening to the Latvian police scanner we've got hooked up to the CB radio. I suppose he thinks Park has it covered, but his Latvian isn't nearly as good. I don't give Horrace a hard time about it. If it wasn't for him back at the gate, we probably wouldn't have gotten through in the first place. The old Russian contact helped us too, me most of all. I still can't believe I got so shook up. Maybe I'm just getting old. This work has a tendency to do that, like when a president goes into office with a full head of color and comes out the other end grey as Seattle skies.

Can't help but wonder what the old man was about behind that fuel depot. Was he just wishing me luck with all that "boom" business, or did he know something I didn't? I'm sure it's the former. He probably just needed to clear the table and get somewhere else so the Russians could swing around and pick him up without anyone seeing. Even in his attempt to calm me, there was a notable disdain underneath. But that's not uncommon either. Whatever goodwill America had banked after

WWII and later after September 11th was all the way gone now. In fact, the way things are headed back home, we're on course to becoming the slack-jawed red-headed step-child of the planet. We pretty much did it to ourselves, and I don't blame foreigners from gloating a little bit. We gave our share of grief to the Brits in the beginning, the Japanese during the war, to the Germans after the war, to the Viet Kong in the sixties, the Ruskies in the eighties. We've got the Muslims and the Mexicans now. People make their rounds of enemies. Everyone takes their turn on the bottom. Just makes sense that we have ours. Call it fate.

Take Henry Knapp for instance. As we drive, I think about him. At first glance it seems strange that an FBI man would break off and go into the private contracting business. But like everyone at some point in time, Henry Knapp got his turn to roll around under the life's bus. From what I hear, he was good at his job. He didn't mess around on both sides of the fence either. Straight arrow that Henry Knapp, the old team used to say. Except arrows don't always shoot straight, no matter how perfectly crafted or expertly shot. Every one of them takes a little curve sooner or later, and the potential of that arrow to stray increases with time, with wear, with how many flights off the bow it takes, and with how many lifts from the quill. Same went for Henry Knapp. He was part of an anti-mercenary and vigilantism initiative the agency put on a few years after the second Iraq war started. Seems that some of the *Blackwater* fellas decided to go into business for themselves and splinter off. They made a killing in Iraq, literally as well as figuratively. Siphoned off U.S. munitions, got into drug trafficking, and the human trade too they say. There was even a rumor a team of mercs took over a couple of oil platforms and started moving the black stuff to anyone who could pay. That included enemies of the United States.

The president at the time got the CIA involved. He had enough trouble keeping the natives in line. He didn't need an offshoot of their own private security force running haywire. Never mind that's what *Blackwater* was anyway, but I guess if a group of mercs have a CEO and an expensive looking web page, the U.S. will look the other way. Either that or hire them. The CIA did a fairly good job of disrupting para-military splinter operations overseas. I hear stories about some of them still being over there doing business, but nobody knows for sure. Most of them were driven back to the states. They became real teams when they got back, well trained, armed, and funded. Truth be told, it became increasingly tough for patchwork teams like ours to snag work. Since they were all trained together, their machine ran smoothly, and because their new base of ops was in the US, those teams became the FBI's problem.

That's where Henry Knapp came in. He didn't head up the crackdown initiative, but with a good deal of success bringing down some key figures in ex-*Blackwater* teams, he was right on track to inherit a decent position of bureau authority. Stand up guy though he was, the cops still showed up to his house one night to find his wife and two girls torn up dead at his home in East Jersey.

That's when Henry Knapp disappeared. He went underground. No one could find him. Guess he picked up a few things hunting those ex-*Blackwater* fellas. Of course they pinned the murders on him. Said he snapped under pressure. Said there was no reason for him to up and leave otherwise.

That was almost a decade ago. I've been working with Henry Knapp for the last seven years, give or take. He was under the mistaken impression that no one would know who he was when he started looking for work. Didn't count on private contractors like us being the same kind of gossipy sewing circle as anyone else. That's why everyone calls him by his full name. He's a company man, and once a company man, always a company man. Apparently he didn't expect folks in our business to harbor any deep-seeded hostility toward a guy who spent a good deal of his adult life hunting people like us down. Nearly got himself killed more than once hooking up with the wrong teams. Bock and I were the only ones who didn't want to suffocate him in his sleep. I always suspected the mercs killed his wife and girls. A lot of people did at first, but his disappearance didn't do much to support that theory. Funny thing is, Henry Knapp himself denies any merc involvement in the murders. He's got to know more, but if he does, he's not rattling any skeletons. Still, there's something honorable about Henry Knapp, not like that sick monster Dresden. Some of the boys try to equate the two, but I know better.

"So how you been?" I ask him. "Didn't get a chance to catch up yet."

"Okay," Henry Knapp says, lost in the road unfolding ahead of us as the first flakes of snow bounce off the windshield.

"Heard anything?" I ask.

He knows what I'm asking about. If he's the man I believe him to be, he'll never stop looking for who did it. I wouldn't. Horrace hits the wipers. The sky has ripped open now. Snow flushes down. Visibility rapidly degenerates to near whiteout conditions in a matter of minutes.

Henry Knapp shakes his head. "No. Haven't heard a thing."

I decide to ease up. I have never known a man more grieved. I rest my head against the passenger window. The boys will wake me if anything goes wrong.

Chapter 13

"WAKE UP, RUST," I hear Horrace say. "We've got a situation."

I shake the sleep out of my head and sit up. He and Henry Knapp are concentrating on the Latvian voices coming through the scanner.

"What is it?" I ask.

"They found bodies," Henry Knapp says.

"Shh," Horrace says as another garbled string of Latvian barks through the speaker. "Oh, man."

"Where?" I ask.

"Quiet!" Horrace says.

"Where, Horrace," I say back with authority.

"Rezekne. Construction site."

"The Russians pop off?"

"No," Horrace says, grinding the shifter into fifth and slamming on the gas pedal. "Bock did."

"The workers that saw us on the dirt road?" I ask.

"I was in the back," Henry Knapp says. "I didn't hear any shots."

"Bock's got a silencer on that forty-five of his," I say sharply. "We hit Daugavpils yet?"

"Already passed it. You were out for a while," Henry Knapp says.

"Tell me we're in Lithuania."

"The border's not five miles up the road," Horrace says.

"Okay. Alright." I say, anxiously pressing hard to think. "Turn off. We need to turn off. Find an alternate route."

"What? Go unpaved? With all the snow?" Horrace says in disbelief. "No, this is the route. We need to stay on the highway. We can get through."

"We will not get through, Horrace. Everyone saw us. We made a scene at the gate."

"We can get across the border," Horrace says insistently.

"We weren't on the manifests. They saw our trucks pass right by where the bodies were found. No, no. We'll find another route. I don't care if it's paved or not. We take our chances on another route," I say.

I tell Henry Knapp to find me a map in the glove box as I grab the walkie and switch it to the other truck's channel.

"Bock, you stupid son of a—" I bark into the walkie.

"I think he is asleep, Mr. Rust," Yakubu says back.

"Pound on the wall if you have too. You wake him up, Yakubu. We've got big problems."

"We heard." It was Park now.

"We're finding another route," I say wrestling to unfold the map with Henry Knapp. "You stand by and get me Bock. Now. Why didn't you idiots tell me what he did?"

"Didn't think it would be a problem. You know how he is," Park says over the walkie. "We couldn't tell him anything. We hid the bodies."

"What, did you run them up the flagpole? Get me Bock!"

"What's all the noise, mate?" Bock finally comes through, obviously roused from a nap.

"Bock. What did you do, Bock? I told you—"

"You told me to do what I had to," he says.

"You try anything else first? Before you canoed their friggin' heads?"

"Don't lecture me, Captain Rust. I took care of it the way I took care of it. Now what in the bloody hell is happening?"

"Well somebody found the bodies, Bock, and now we're all neck deep in it."

"It snowing yet?" he asks.

"I don't have time to give you the forecast, Bock."

"Did it start snowing?"

I grit my teeth and take a deep breath. "Yes. It's snowing. It's white. It's a winter wonderland. Why are you asking?"

"We'll be fine."

"Great. Terrific, Bock. Thank you. I'm sure you're right."

"He might be right, Rust," Horrace says. "Nobody's going to see us until they're right on our six."

"Yeah? And what about the border, genius? Last time I checked, radio waves travel a helluva lot faster than this piece of junk. The border on this highway is a major checkpoint. You suggest we up and throw down with fifteen or twenty armed uniforms? Think security at the port in Kedainiai might be stepped up just a bit?"

The walkies go quiet. Reality sinks in. We have to get off this highway and fast. The gate foreman at the construction site saw which way we were heading. It isn't rocket science.

"Here," Henry Knapp says, pointing at the map. "We make like we're heading into Medumi. It's small, and with the storm no one's likely to notice us. There should be a smaller road back behind it if we curve around the lake. We keep moving west to northwest. It's all forest and farmland. Might be a small town or two, but we'll blow right through them with the snow."

"There's a dirt road I've used before to cross the border close to Medumi," Bock says. "It's next to an old farm. Nothing out there but grass fields and trees. We'll be fine."

"Fine. We get stuck in the mud, you get out to push," I say.

"Relax, mate. We've got the Yak."

"I will push, Mr. Rust. All the way to the sea if I have to," Yakubu says over the walkie, laughing loudly.

"Thanks, Yak. Bock, screw you very much. We turn off to the right in three clicks, everyone."

Chapter 14

NO SIGN OF anything or anyone for several miles. The tiny farming towns we've passed through are barren. The few people we've seen who haven't taken shelter from the snow are certainly too drunk or too busy to notice us. We slip by completely undetected. Bock told us there would be a curve exactly 12.6 miles from the tiny village of Ilga, consisting of little more than a wool processing plant on the banks of a lake by the same name. A few houses shut tight from the cold mark the town as our tires grind deeper into the muddy snow with every measured mile past small outcroppings of rock surrounded by a thick blanket of towering Oak and Linden trees. We slug the final stretch toward the turn-off and pray the Lithuanian border is closer than we think.

We take the turn, Park's truck slogging close behind until we reach the farmhouse Bock told us about. It seems empty. I ponder whether to stop and wait the storm out.

"Anyone live here, Bock? We're at the farmhouse by the border." I ask into the walkie.

"Yes, and don't stop," Bock says. "There's no farmer living here."

I motion for Horrace to keep moving. "Well who is it then?"

"Doesn't matter. Just roll past."

"Well now you've got me curious."

"Move along, Rust. You don't want to know."

Horrace slugs the truck into gear. We feel the lurch; the back shim-
mies. Horrace gears down and slams on the gas, turning the wheel the
opposite direction. The truck slides off the ruts in the road. We're getting
stuck. This, of course, causes Park's truck behind us to slow to an
unfortunate stop and probably meet the same ends.

"Go around, Park!" I say into the walkie-talkie. "Do not stop—try to
go around. We might need you to pull us out. Do not stop."

"I can't see around you, Rust. There's nowhere to go," he says.

Sure enough, I look to both sides. Trees on the left, the farmhouse
on the right. Park can't move. He's got no choice. I would have him run
up on us, hit the back and push us through, but I can't risk damaging the
guns, the false walls, or my men in the cages.

"Park, are we stopping?" Bock says through the walkie. "Rust, I
said not to stop. Keep moving."

"We're stuck in the snow, Bock. No choice."

Silence on the other end. We hear only the wind trying its best to get
into the cabs, and the snow gently glancing off the windows. I look to the
farmhouse. There are two cars parked next to it. A sedan that looks far
nicer than what a Latvian farmer could afford, and a Jeep, a little older
than the sedan, but still not your typical farmer's fare.

"Who's in the farmhouse, Bock?" I ask, both of us knowing there's
no point in keeping it a secret anymore.

"It's Yuri Kostonov's sons, Rust. They run the show out of here.
We have to leave."

"Of all the places," I say to myself. "Horrace, we have to get this
truck out of here, right now."

"Who's Yuri Kostonov?" Horrace asks.

"He's from way back, and he's dead."

"So what?"

"His sons don't have fond memories of how he got that way."

"You killed their dad?" Horrace asks, grinding the gears again, trying to roll the truck from its rut.

"Well, technically," I say.

I see slivers of light flicker between the slats of the window and around the door casing. The front door opens. A man I've never seen, very large and very Russian emerges cautiously from the doorway. Two other men follow. Twins. Definitely Kostonovs. All are armed, but the twins hang back on the porch. I watch them closely. The first big Russian approaches our truck on my side.

"Bock. Everly. Rack 'em up and get ready. We've got company. On my mark," I say hurriedly into the walkie. Then I look to Horrace, "You're lost. You're taking a shipment to Medumi. Be humble. Kostonovs are barbarians. Be ready to draw down." Then I quickly lean over, away from the window, hiding my face, and pretend to be asleep.

I feel the big Russian step up on my side. He knocks arrogantly on the window. Horrace leans over and rolls it down just a sliver.

"*Кто вы? Чего вы делаете здесь?*" the big Russian asks.

"*Мы имеем отгрузку строительных поставок для Medumi. Я, кажется, становимся потерянным. Пожалуйста направьте меня назад к шоссе?*" Horrace says back.

I'm laying on the walkie with my heavy coat slung over me like a blanket, pretending to be passed out. Henry Knapp stares off in a masquerade stupor. With hands hidden, I'm turning the walkie volume way down, leaving the channel open so Park can translate for me from the other truck.

"Horrace just told him what you said," I hear Park say faintly through the walkie speaker pressed tightly to my unexposed ear.

I open the channel back up.

"*Ерунда. Вы лежащий свинья. Medumi - мили далеко с другой стороны реки,*" the Russian says.

"He doesn't believe us," Park says.

"*Я говорю правду. Пожалуйста. Мы так очень опаздываем. Будьте добры и направлять нас назад к проложенной дороге,*" Horrace says.

I close the channel and listen.

"He's pleading with the guy to show us back to the road. I don't think it's going to work, Rust."

I open the chancel back up and shift a little. I whisper into the mic. "Hang tight, Park."

"*Что не так с ним? Что это является легким? Кого он говорит, чтобы? Открыть дверь!*" The Russian says, beside himself.

I nervously close the channel having a fairly good idea of what's gone wrong, but just in case, I want to hear it from Park.

"He heard you. He wants inside the truck."

I cup my right fist with my left hand to brace the impact as I swing up and drive my right elbow through the crack in the window and into the bridge of the big Russian's nose. He flails back in an arc off the cab, instinctively pulling the trigger of the hidden pistol at his side. The report sounds through the snow as a round breaches the sidewall of the front passenger tire. Air hisses from the bullet hole. I see movement on the porch. The twins call someone out of the farmhouse. Must be more men inside. Henry Knapp tosses me the walkie-talkie and brandishes a knife from somewhere inside his trench coat.

"Bock, Everly. Wait for my mark. I want them close," I say.

Just then the big Russian leaps back up on the cab, this time shoving his pistol wrist deep into the window. He wants to get Horrace first. Henry Knapp grips his knife, reaches across me, and jams it all the way through, between the Russian's ulna and radius, pinning it securely to the roof of the truck. Again the Russian jolts into pulling the trigger, sending a deafening shot across the interior of the cab and shattering the small triangular window next to Horrace's ear. The Russian screams as I grab the door handle and throw all my weight against it. He drops the pistol and hangs in agony with his arm still pinned to the ceiling, bleeding, and he's screaming bloody murder.

I tumble to the ground, landing in a plume of fresh snow, still holding the walkie-talkie. I look to the porch. Four men armed with rifles take off toward us.

I raise the walkie to my lips. "Blow it, boys."

The squibs fizz and crack on the hinges of both trucks like dominos as the cargo doors blow open in unison, followed quickly by palettes of sheet metal blocking the men's cages thudding into the snow. Henry

Knapp has already recovered the big Russian's revolver and leapt out of the cab. He mechanically puts a hot one between the eyes of the screaming man hanging by one arm. His body swings limp and cold.

Bock and Everly, each weighted with extra weapons, burst out of their trucks, guns blazing. Bock drops a sawed-off 12 gauge and an MP-5 at the foot of his truck. Everly leaves a shoulder holster with two Baretta 9mms, another MP-5 on a sling, and my L1A1 FAL assault rifle next to ours.

Bock dispatches one man with that forty-five of his. Three rounds center-mass. Artful. The other man he sighted-in took one to the shoulder and still advances. Everly takes a different approach, sliding on one knee to narrowly avoid a three-round-burst while tearing up the offender's thighs with a Croatian Agram 2000 sub. The dead man slides a short distance in the snow.

Yakubu goes for the .12 gauge, pumping it once and unloading into the chest of the man Bock had wounded in the shoulder. With Horrace still in the cab and Henry Knapp preoccupied with the big dead Russian, the only quickly approaching offender was left to me. He opens fire. I roll to the left as the slugs punch through the snow. I scramble to my feet and sprint toward him, praying the move confuses him. I make it just in time, football tackling him to the ground. I grab the muzzle of his rifle and hurriedly pin it to the ground, leaving the man on his back with the other hand still on the trigger. I shimmy up to full mount, and towering over, clock him in the jaw with a right before uprooting the rifle from his grasp. His eyes go wide as the muzzle hovers an inch from his forehead.

Bock is already in the house going after the Kostonov twins. I see the boys following.

"No," I say, still on top of the attacker. "I'll go in after him. This doesn't involve you boys. You all stay out here and watch this one."

I get up, leaving the dazed man on his back. I pass the boys and head up the porch, leaning my FAL on the wall and pulling back the hammer on my Colt Anaconda .45 revolver.

"Yakubu," I say before entering the farmhouse.

"Yes, boss."

"Don't let any of them kill that fella."

Yakubu nods and smiles. I head inside.

Chapter 15

THE FARMHOUSE'S INTERIOR reeks. It's dingy and unkempt. A heavy coat of dust covers everything, twinkling in the air between slivers of light from outside. Empty liquor bottles riddle nearly every surface. Flies buzz around dirty plates of food. This was a flophouse. I move with caution, gun in both hands next to my ear. I hear scuffling down a darkened hall. I make my way slowly with dampened steps, rolling my heel softly to the ball of my foot, one after the next.

Just then, a gloved hand grabs my shirt and pulls me into a side room. It's Bock with that .45 at his side and a hushing finger to his lips. He ticks his head to the door at the end of the hall.

"House is clear," Bock whispers. "The twins are in that room. Somebody's in there with them. I think it's a girl."

"*Мы имеем заложника!*" comes from behind the door.

"In English, zipperheads," I say back.

There's a long silence. We can hear a girl crying. Sounds young. Bock and I trade disgusted looks.

"We have girl in here," comes back in broken English.

"Well, let her out," I say.

"No. You leave."

"You first," Bock says.

There's another pause. Then, "Who are you?" the other one says.

"We *know* who you are, brothers Kostonov," I say.

Another long pause between the girl's whimpers.

"I know this voice," comes from behind the door. "We'll kill the girl."

"Like we killed your daddy? Hell, we don't know her. Go ahead," I say. "Better'n what I suspect you been doing with her. We just want to get across the border."

"You did not come for us?" one of the brothers asks.

"Nope. Just a real freaky coincidence."

"Then go, American pigs."

"Okie-Dokey," I say slapping Bock on the shoulder and walking out.

Bock hangs back with a bewildered look on his face. Finally he meets me outside with the rest of the boys. I grab my FAL and holster the Colt. I tell the boys to pack up and get ready to go.

"You're just about to leave them in there?" Bock asks.

"Nah. I've got an idea. Hey, Yakubu."

"Yes, boss?" he says turning to me.

I look at the dead body of the man I told him to look after while we were inside. "Thought I told you not to kill him."

"He moved."

I shrug. "What part of Africa you from?" I ask after a pause.

"Rwanda, boss." He's not smiling anymore.

"Nasty place."

"Yes," he says, lowering his eyes to the ground.

"Lot of little babies killed over there during that thing with the Hutu in '94."

"Yes," Yakubu says.

"You're Tutsi, right?"

"I am."

"Well those two got a little girl in a room down the hall there. I don't think they've been treating her too nice."

Yakubu looks up at the farmhouse. He drops the .12 gauge as if in a trance and marches intently up the steps, muscles bulging and contracting, shoulders heaving until he disappears inside. I look at Bock who shakes his head at me and grins. We all watch the farmhouse and thank the good Lord we aren't in that room.

What follows must have been the most carnal and chaotic mess that nightmares are made of. We can hear the door to the room crack like a piece of balsa wood. A couple of gunshots follow, then terrible screams. Glass smashes and we hear what we think is a body hitting the ground at the back of the house. Another torturous scream rings out, and a muffled crack. Had to be someone's neck, though I've never heard one break so loudly. Then silence.

When Yakubu emerges from the house, I see his right hand covered in blood. In his left, he holds the hand of the little girl who wipes tears from her eyes. Yakubu kneels down to her and cups one of her cheeks.

"You are safe now. Go to that man with the mustache. We will take you home."

The little girl in the dirty floral patterned dress couldn't be more than eight or nine. She runs to me, her malnourished frame skinny and weak with fine blonde hair trailing like a mounded sedge. I look down at her and try to grin. She grabs tight around my leg, somehow knowing there's nothing to fear. We watch Yakubu walk to his shotgun, pick it up, and head around back.

"One of them is still alive," he says, pumping shell into the chamber.

It takes a while to hear a shot. No telling what he did to this other Kostonov brother, but I'm sure it wasn't any prettier than what he did to the first. We put the girl in the cab with Park so she could heat up while the rest of us wedge a couple sheets of metal under the back wheels of Horrace's truck. We manage to put everything back together by the time Yakubu shows. Bock's back in the cage, as is Everly, and we're ready to go. The border is only a half-mile down the dirt road somewhere. Looks like we'll slip into Lithuania unnoticed after all. Yakubu must have washed all the blood off of him with snow. When he gets in with Park and the little girl, he smiles and whispers something to her. I think she's actually smiling.

CHAPTER 16

SLEEP. WHEN I wake, I feel a little sorry for Horrace and Park. What should have been a seven or eight hour driving assignment turned into much more, and they were the only ones who haven't been afforded a wink of rest. We're still on some abandoned back road. The snow has let up. Only a slight dusting covers the forest on each side.

"Where are we?" I ask Horrace, noticing Henry Knapp still in dreams next to me.

"Shouldn't be far now. Maybe an hour. The Yak's directing Park with the map behind us. How about him, huh?"

"Yeah, how about him," I say.

"Gotta be some story."

"Reckon so," I say. "Any word on the scanner?"

Horrace shakes his head. "Think they've pretty much given up."

"Good deal. Still gonna have to watch the port in Klaipeda. I'm sure our meet will have security scoped out pretty well around the boat, but you can never be too careful."

Horrace nods. "What about the girl?"

"Don't know. You ask Park?"

"Yeah, but we don't know where to take her. He asked where she lived, but the only one she'll talk to is Yakubu now."

"Park can listen in. What did she say?"

"She's talking gibberish."

"Klaipeda's a big town. Might get you or Park to find her a place."

"Always us," Horrace says, sighing.

"We don't speak the language, Horrace. Besides, I'll give you overtime on it. I've always taken care of you boys."

"I know, just tired."

I pat his shoulder. "You done good. All of you. Just get us to the port and we'll think about the rest then."

Chapter 17

THE MILES STRETCH on. Once out of the snow, the rolling green of grasses, farmland, and thick trees twisting into each other continue. Henry Knapp wakes only to lull away again. Park told us through the radio that the little girl's name was Brigita, but not much more.

I see something off in the distance, on the side of the road. People. Men, but at the same time not men. Not exactly. Perhaps I'm still dreaming. Five of them appear at first, but as we drive closer, two more. Two are being beaten mercilessly by the others. One man, fair with large green eyes in a white shirt now stained with blood and dirt languishes on his knees. Another in a heavy navy blue winter vest holds the man from behind so he cannot fall, while one of the others pummels his ribcage with sharp white-knuckles. Blood expels in a spray from the beaten man. The other victim lies helplessly on his back slipping in and out of consciousness. I can't see his face, but three assailants crowd around furiously mauling him without restraint.

Among the myriad vexing characteristics of the sight are that none of the men pay so much as a glance in our direction. Our engines growl through the trees, now so close we see the pupils in their eyes. What's more, these forms appear in the literal middle of nowhere. No town sits close by, not a farmhouse, or even an automobile within visual proximity. The scene becomes more surreal as we pass. None of them, not one, ever seems to notice us. We might as well not even be here.

Our speed slows as we move past, our cabs silent as we watch the disturbing display. The air becomes thick, and then I begin to feel something—I'm not sure what. I hear something without my ears, a cry in my head. I have seen many men beaten and killed before. That's just part of the job. It's never fun, but inevitably we'll find ourselves on one end of a beating sometime or other. I've had to stand by and watch loss of life. Disconnection is a virtue in instances such as these. This time I can't shake it. In all my years, I'm not sure I've seen men beaten so badly, with such rage. To use a cliché, it's usually just business. Someone always has to move over for somebody else. That's the way of things, but this is something else altogether. All the sudden I feel a great sorrow for the kneeling man shooting blood from his mouth. I watch in the rear view. I take my Colt Anaconda and click back the hammer. Henry Knapp still rests asleep next to me, and Horrace remains transfixed in his mirror. We're slowly rolling away. I see the boys in the truck behind watching too. I roll my window down and pull myself up to a seated position on the edge of the window frame, steadying myself with one arm on the roof.

I bring up the Colt and raise sights to the one holding the broken heaving man from behind. I breathe deep and steady, training down on his forehead. Everyone deserves a fighting chance, I think to myself and squeeze the trigger. The hammer drops, igniting the cartridge and sending a .45 slug toward the man's head.

That's when it happens. I'm so focused I can almost track the very bullet. I've got him dead bang. The round enters on target, but then passes right through him like a ghost, only to slam into the ground behind him with a small kick of dust. No entry wound. No exit spatter. The man's forehead is completely intact. I did not miss, but the bullet simply passes through him like some kind of holograph, like some kind of ghost.

Just then, the man I thought I shot crooks his head and looks up at me. His grimace turns to surprise. The other five assailants stop immediately and do the same. All their mouths hang open. Black. Dead. Cavernous. They see me. All of them see me. But they do not move. They don't make a break for the truck or even run away. They just stare at me like I do them.

"What the hell?" Horrace says under his breath.

Each aggressor raises an arm and points at us in unison, eyes narrowing and glaring with admonishment, jaws still hanging open as if unhinged. They are silent, stoic even. Terrifying. Pointing. All I hear is breeze. I too feel unhinged, asleep, afraid.

I lower the Colt and then myself back inside the cab. I'm looking down at the floor of the truck. Horrace starts to say something else.

"Just drive," I say, and I can feel him slowly pick up speed.

The truck behind us follows. No one speaks when we reach the paved road to the port in Klaipeda.

Our meet unloads the guns and transfers them to the waiting boat. I send Horrace along with the little girl to find her someplace to stay. Everyone else goes home their separate ways except Bock who stands next to me, ready to torch the trucks.

"They helped themselves to the explosive putty," he says as we stare at the cargo boat pull away from the dock.

"I don't care."

"I heard a shot back on the road a bit. Just the one. What happened? Everyone's acting strange."

"I don't know," I say. "I really don't. Doubt any of us do."

"See a ghost did you, mate? A wee Casper floating above the road on his way to grandmother's house, aye?" Bock says sarcastically.

"Maybe. Like I said: I don't know. Be in touch a couple weeks down the line, partner. Take care getting home."

Chapter 18

TWO WEEKS BACK and I'm still not fully awake. I go to work at the gin quieter and more reserved. I can feel it. Everyone else can feel it too. I've stopped frequenting *Sharkey's* after work. I just go home and sit. I think, remember, and try to piece it all together over microwaved meals in cheap paper containers. I stare through the television and allow the cavalcade of robotic voices, impersonal laugh tracks, and indistinguishable music pass through me. I no longer hear anything but the repetition of the call I heard that day on the Lithuanian trail toward the docks. I see the beaten men. In my mind, they are beaten still: more blood, more anguish in their eyes, growing by every moment I think on it. The skin on the attackers' knuckles wear away with every strike, cracking, peeling back to expose ivory bone, but they just continue the beating: an unquantifiable hatred. The white of their shirts, and the navy of their jackets washes away to red, then to black as it soaks through, saturates everything, the ground rich with the dark spill.

I did not miss. I do not miss with that Colt. It's a heavy gun to use as a sidearm, cumbersome even. Bock gives me stick about it all the time, but I use it because I shoot it well. Very well. That gun chose me, and when I drop that hammer it hits exactly where I tell it to. No one can prove to me that bullet wasn't on target, but the target didn't fall. Wasn't even injured, not even grazed. Just went through like mist.

I would question whether I hallucinated the entire thing, but everyone else saw the men too. They had to see the shot. I know they did, and I know they witnessed the same thing. When the bullet passed through the man and hit the dirt, it was as if it had passed through them all. Why would they point like that? My boys saw that too, the pointing, the staring, those mouths open long like a choir sustaining a tone deep in their guts. Sure, the boys saw it. Only difference was those men weren't pointing at them. They were pointing at me. Only me, and I felt it. Physically, I felt it to the point that my sides ached, my ribs broken, a feeling of my mouth shooting blood like the ones they had at their mercy. It still hasn't let go.

I leave all the lights on now, and I don't know why. I go to the grocery during my lunch break, and try to make it home before nightfall. Something has changed. It is as if I've realized something that was never supposed to occur to me. Like it was off limits. No access. Like a door cracked open to a darkened room where a legion of voices whisper. I have peered in on something carnal, woeful, and more miserable than I'd ever seen or wanted to. I feel myself coming undone.

Chapter 19

THE DAYS DRAG on, until one night, after the gin grinds to a stop and the Tahoka winter rolls in on howling winds that break for nothing across their swept plains, I get a call. I almost don't answer. I almost don't even hear the ringing. The part of me that still holds some kind of discipline, the part struggling to wake up inches my hand closer to the receiver. I pick up the phone and try to clear my throat.

"Hello," I say in a crackle.

"Amarillo?"

"Yes."

"Terry Kerchow."

"Terry," I say like I'm asking him for a glass of milk.

Kerchow runs lines for Reliant Energy. I used to play pool with him up at *Sharkey's* every so often. He's a dull fella, but a true one: hard-working.

"Just wanted to give a shout," Kerchow says. I can hear the wind whistle over his voice. Sounds cold. "I'm over close to Teasel's old place. I know you're looking after it. The wind's taken down a couple of lines. I'm up in the bucket and I just thought you should know that there's somebody in the house. I can see their shadows milling around inside. Don't think they know I can see them from here, but thought you'd want to know, if you don't already."

"Terry. Thanks. I'll be over directly," I say. Then a pause. "Terry?"

"Yeah."

"You almost done over there?"

He's quiet for a second. Confused maybe. "I reckon I'm close to it."

"Good." I decide to lie to him. "Just saw on the news that there might be a twister headed our way. Maybe you should finish up and get on home to Regina and the kids, you know? I'm sure they're scared."

"Thanks for the heads up, man. Will do."

"Thanks, Terry."

I hang up the phone and instinct kicks in. I should at least allow for the possibility that it's nothing, maybe just some hobos or illegals looking to get out of the weather, but something tells me that's not the case. I go to my closet and push back a line of hung shirts, then give the wall behind it a good wrap. It jars loose and I remove the part that juts out. I modified the safe behind it with a fingerprint scanner I got from a guy in Milan. Call me paranoid, but if anyone ever traced me back to Tahoka, they'd find enough firepower to take on the Republican Guard single-handedly. I'd like to hold on to this stuff, keep it secret. Cotton gin workers don't usually have the money or use for much more than a hunting rifle and a pistol or shotgun for home-defense. Let's just say I've got a helluva lot more than that in here. I press my finger to the pad. I get an electronic chirp and a small green LED in return. The lock disengages and deactivates the detonator I've got wired to a nice sized chunk of c4 in the wall near the front door. Any unauthorized no-luck who puts their finger to this safe and isn't taken out by the initial blast will sure as heck burn to death in the fire that follows when their only exit has all but disappeared.

I haven't been able to touch my Colt since Lithuania, so I leave it hanging on the padded wall of the safe and choose the Benelli M4 combat shotgun instead. I've obviously lost my faith in slugs these days. The next thing I shoot at, I'm tearing up with buckshot, and if I have to get up close and personal, I might as well strap on a *Kevlar* vest and take along that MAC-SOG knife, our side used in Vietnam. Somebody's about to be real surprised, that or I'm about to be ambushed. Either way, I won't be showing up unprepared.

Chapter 20

THE WIND PUSHES my truck all over the road. Strong gusts from the west. I turn down the dirt road to Teasel's and shut off my lights. The moon peeks through the cloud-cover enough for me to stay on track, not that there's any worry about hitting anything out here. I could drive blindfolded in any direction for miles before coming across the slightest obstacle.

I put the truck in neutral before shutting off the ignition and coast the rest of the way. I see Teasel's place in the distance, about a quarter mile up the road. I pull the truck to the side and decide to hoof the remaining distance. Sure enough, the lights are on. Shadows dance inside. If it's Bock again, we'll need to have a talk, but the boys have all been paid for Lithuania. We're all square, so whoever's in there shouldn't be wearing my colors. I move diagonal toward the northwestern corner of the house, out of the line of sight from the windows. I hear a sound and stop, probably a varmint huddling deeper into a patch of grass or a quail jetting from low brush. When I'm sure it's not a threat, I continue stalking toward the house. I notice the shadows. Whoever's inside—at least two people from the look of it—just seem to pace back and forth. Then I think of the boxes inside. I almost laugh about the possibility of the people in there being burglars. Lot of good a bunch of salt and sulfur will do them. Then, of course, I'm reminded of the crosses.

Those might be worth taking, but who would know about them? Did someone talk?

I end up at the chicken coops next to the farmhouse. I move slowly in a crouch, measured breathing and M4 at the ready. I feel the heat of my breath filter through the hair on my upper lip. It trails into the air that drops colder by the second. I sit and wait for what seems like an eternity. Smarter to catch them on the way out, in the dark while their eyes are still adjusted to the indoor light.

"Be calm, Mr. Rust. You are among friends," comes off to the right.

I know that voice. I swing right and raise the shotgun. I drop to one knee and try to see who's there. From the shadows, he emerges. I see the small ember of his cigarette glowing orange, then the curling smoke, then the fine-tailored suit, scraggly shoulder length hair, and finally the man's face. Elijah Tishbe stands before me. I say nothing. I remain on one knee with my shotgun focused on center mass. I glance from side to side to see if his goons have been alerted.

"We mean you no harm. Merely fulfilling a promise."

"What are you talking about? How did you find me?" I finally say. The cold creeps through my clothing. My fingers want to tremble, but I hold steady.

"One year. I told you I would come to you in one year's time, and here I stand."

"Come to pick up that horse manure you left us in Albania? You're lucky—"

"You don't kill me?"

"No. You're lucky Bock's not here to kill you."

"Yes, Mr. Bock has spent a great deal of time and effort in pursuit of me. It's true."

"And money," I say. "Bock doesn't like to part with his money."

"Yes, and money. That is also true."

We stay locked-in to one another for a moment, though we can't see each other's eyes in the darkness. The wind whips around us.

"I had forgotten how cold Texas can be," Tishbe says.

"Uh huh," I say. Tishbe is testing me. He knows how heavy the M4 is in my arms with it raised the way it is.

"Lower the weapon, Mr. Rust. As I've told you—"

"Who's inside?" I ask through gritted teeth.

"Oh, you've been acquainted. They also mean you no ill will."

"Well, what are they doing?"

"Counting," Tishbe says, taking a drag off the cigarette. "Just counting."

"The boxes."

Tishbe nods. "That's right. Shall we go inside, Mr. Rust? You must be chilled to the bone."

"What about you?" I ask, noting that Tishbe doesn't even have an overcoat on. It must be approaching twenty degrees out here.

"There is cold, and then there is cold, Mr. Rust. Let us continue our conversation inside, yes?" Tishbe takes a final drag from the cigarette. Its orange light temporarily illuminates part of the man's face, and I am reminded of the scar down his left eye.

"You do something squirrely and I'll cut your head off and put it over my fireplace," I say.

Tishbe laughs out loud as he casts away the cigarette and turns, making his way to the front door. "I'm sure you'll try. I'm certain you would."

I follow Tishbe, but before going inside, check through one of the windows. It's just as he said, two men, I think the same drivers from Albania, stacking the boxes I had along the wall into three piles in the middle of the room. One of the men sweats as the other slides an arm through a coat with an unlit cigarette hanging from the corner of his mouth. He walks toward the front door and comes outside. He starts a little when he sees me standing there, and utters something in an eastern European language while digging in his pocket for a lighter.

I walk over to him, staring him dead in the eyes and pat him down. He shifts uneasily, but goes on lighting the cigarette as I feel for weapons around his waist and legs. Nothing. He's clean. The man says something else, but I walk off and enter the house.

"Okay, Tishbe. Your boy outside's clean. I don't get it. I'd tear your head off for stiffing us if I wasn't so interested in what you've got going on in that head of yours. So talk. I'm here, and as long as you keep your story interesting, I promise not to paint the walls with you."

"Ha. Yes. A way with words, Mr. Rust. Always a way with words. I *do* enjoy the American south. Such character!" Tishbe says clapping his hands with delight. "You know there are many places in this world without character. Without... color. Vibrancy. What richness you find in the south. Brazen? Perhaps. An underlying arrogance? Certainly, but also an earnestness. An assurance of capability. It is exciting, Mr. Rust. Really. So exciting. Even... refreshing."

"Well thank you for the happy feelings, Tishbe. I'm all flush," I say without returning a degree of his enthusiasm. "Talk."

Elijah Tishbe purses his lips and exhales audibly. He then brings his hands together and stares at the floor, deep in thought. "Simply to say, 'talk' is just too broad and voluminous, I'm afraid. We must start in microcosm." He brings his praying mantis hands to his mouth, looks to the three stacks of boxes, and points to them. "We can start with these. Perhaps questions and answers are the way to proceed?"

"Okay. What are they?"

"You didn't look inside?"

"Of course I looked inside."

"Then you know."

"Salt. Sulfur. Crosses. Go," I say with impatience.

"Not just any salt. Not just any crosses. And not sulfur, Mr. Rust."

"What then?"

"Brimstone."

"Is that supposed to be funny?"

"Not at all."

"Then tell me what it really is."

"It truly *is* brimstone, Mr. Rust."

"As in 'fire and brimstone?'"

"In a manner of speaking."

"Then get to the manner of speaking."

"Brimstone is not just a figure of speech, Mr. Rust. It exists as most any geologist or scientist will tell you. Brimstone is indeed sulfur, that much is true, but I ask you, is your American flag simply a piece of fabric? Is the earth outside this door only dirt or do you call it Texas? Is it property to be owned and traded? Is the human a mere animal or something more? This is brimstone. What you find in that stack of boxes is brimstone."

"Semantics," I say.

"To some. To some. Or perhaps objects and life of various configurations are often imbued, creating something else altogether. Something special, perhaps, and that uniqueness of the imbued commonality requires further classification."

"Is it worth anything?" I ask, unimpressed.

"As many things on Earth, both everything and nothing. But I assume your question pertains to monetary value? The answer is no. It has no value in those terms."

"Well, I'm sorry to tell you, that those are the only terms that mean a hill of beans to me."

"I understand that this has become your life's tragic trajectory, Mr. Rust. But all things change."

"Fine, that sulfur is brimstone. Get to the rest of it. You said 'not just any salt.'"

"Indeed."

"How so?"

"Not in composition, but where it was composed. In all chemical regards, the salt in those boxes is garden variety sea salt, sodium chloride."

"Just sprinkle it on a steak."

"And eat away," Tishbe finishes.

"So why are there fifteen boxes of it standing in the middle of the room?"

"Because it isn't what it seems. Its value hides in plain sight: a property for which you have great affinity, yes?"

"I'm beginning to lose my faith in that. And I'm beginning to get a little tired of the games, old man. So where does it come from?"

"An incredibly consequential body of water between current-day Israel and the country of Jordan."

"And which one is that?"

"Come now, Mr. Rust. Shame. I thought you were more worldly a man than that."

"Okay, I'll take a stab. The Dead Sea."

"You've redeemed yourself."

"I can surprise you every now and then."

"We'll see about that, Mr. Rust. We shall see."

Nothing's worse than asking questions and getting more in return. The other goon in the room leaves the house, probably to smoke with his buddy. From there, Tishbe changes the direction of the conversation before I can ask about the crosses. If he weren't standing here, I'd question the man's sanity. But he found out where I live, and that's not something to take lightly. Tishbe wasn't crazy as far as I could tell. He also doesn't want to take back the boxes, even though a part of me wishes he would. It's all junk as far as I'm concerned. We chat for a while about the rest of the team since he inquired. I didn't tell too much other than I'd seen most of them lately and that they were doing well. The whole thing's bizarre, but then so is my life in general. Truth be told, it was good to talk to someone, and try as my training might to detect it, I didn't feel any duplicity or malevolence in the old man. Even so, nobody likes being jerked around. The only thing that kept me from taking him out was the growing suspicion that he didn't think he was jerking me around at all. He had some kind of point, however obnoxiously cryptic it came across. Add all of these things together, and there seems little to lose in talking. Finally, he gets to speaking plainly.

"I am here to hire you again, Mr. Rust," he says leaning back against the far wall of the room, his hands buried deep in the pockets of his pressed trousers.

"That's rich," I say, tapping one of the boxes with my boot.

"If you accept, you certainly will be," he says. "The only stipulation is the following: I need you alone. No one else. No team. Only you."

"That's a dangerous proposition. There's a reason most of us with any sense don't work alone," I say intently. "And usually the mere inquiry of it raises a major flag. You don't seem like a newbie to any of this, Tishbe. So you'll understand if I've got a major flags raised in my head."

"I am aware of the usual break of protocol, but for this action I must insist."

"Something goes down, nobody's got my back. I don't like it."

"I only need you to observe, Mr. Rust. In fact, any interference in the operation for which I wish to send you will result in forfeiture of payment."

"What kind of payment we talking?" I ask, grinning from the side of my mouth. I love to deal.

"One quarter of a million dollars," Tishbe says, looking away coyly.

"That's a lot of salt."

The old man chuckles. "Dollars this time. American. I give you my word," he says clasping his hands in that church-pose again.

"What's the shot, if I *do* decide to accept that is?"

"No matter how you view me, Mr. Rust, I am a reasonable man. I understand the seemingly ridiculous nature of our dealings to this point. The boxes, the helicopter of which you correctly identified held no occupancy or weaponry, I understand your frustration and confusion."

"Real load-off," I say, scoffing.

"And your sarcasm," Tishbe says, his light demeanor giving way to a serious one. He pushes away from the wall and walks toward me slowly as he speaks. "What I ask of you will bring it all clear. Everything is for a reason. Nothing in this world occurs by mere chance. There are no dice to roll. Life is a careful series of masterful orchestrations. This very moment is the crux of your existence. There is a war, Amarillo Rust. A war of such a scope and painstaking breadth of import your mind has yet to comprehend and may never in its totality. It is a war of principalities in which you have had only a shuttering, fleeting glimpse. I am here for reasons far greater than myself. You are here for reasons far greater than your own, my young man, and you have such a part to play. Such a marvelous part, if only you choose to accept."

Something in my gut tells me to run, not to shoot. Fear fills my lungs and drops my chest into a pit of uncertainty. Elijah Tishbe has confronted something inside me, something I cannot explain, but feel a culling toward. My reason fights to reject this as lunacy, ravings of nonsense, but down in the very depths of myself, I know he's telling the truth, and though I am completely bewildered and disoriented, my curiosity and the force propelling me toward this request takes me by complete surprise. Then, of course, there's the money. Before my reason can intervene, I answer.

"Alright. I'm not one to shy from a good wager. What do you want me to do?"

Tishbe stands close now. He puts a hand on my shoulder, much like my granddaddy used to when I was young and discouraged. He looks squarely into my eyes. A quiet confidence that makes him seem several floors strong and just as solid emanates from him.

"Good. That's good. This decision has altered the course of your life, and you will be enriched because of it. What you have soon to witness will most certainly shake the foundation of your present consciousness of this world, and when it does, I ask of you only this: have faith. Hold on to that faith dearly. For you, Amarillo Rust, are now in the watchful hands of a vengefully protective employer."

Chapter 21

I'M STANDING KNEE-DEEP in snow next to an ER-Vac heli-copter pad in Lubbock, Texas. It is three weeks since Tishbe told me the action would require me to remain on-call. When the phone rang an hour ago, the gruff voice on the other end told me to get to the nearest metro hospital and to wait by the helipad. The snow didn't help much in my making it on time. I realized that asking questions was futile in this instance and since all $250,000 came through the day after Tishbe and I spoke at the farmhouse, I decided to go with the flow; that is, with one little hitch.

I don't go anywhere alone. Doesn't matter who pays the bills. I've seen too many mercs get greedy and go after the big score all by them-selves only to wind up with concrete boots at the bottom of the Potomac with a .22 bullet rattling around in his skull. I've got a transponder taped to my inner-thigh. Park has the receiver with him up on the roof of the hospital somewhere. If this team Tishbe has me hooked up with is taking me wherever the hell we're going by chopper, it can't be far, especially in this weather. Park will be able to track us on the ground. When we arrive, the plan is for him to set up on the elevated periphery and pretty much play watchdog covering me with a Leupold Mark 4 tactical scope on top of an American issue XM25. Park's good at keeping his position invisible. We're about to put that to the test.

I didn't call Bock, even if he is my obvious go-to. Bock and invisible are oil and water. Besides, he wouldn't come a hundred yards of anything Tishbe was selling. In fact, I'd have to worry more about him than I do any of this supposed *team* I've never laid specs on. I don't like keeping things from him, but in this case, there wasn't any other option.

Park and I remain incommunicado since I don't have the slightest idea whether this mysterious team of Tishbe's is already watching me or not. When I get picked up, he'll switch on the transponder and follow by car. I like Park. He's dependable and smart. Knows how to improvise and not call attention to himself. When I contacted him about this, he didn't bat an eye. Just said okay. We didn't even discuss payment. Loyalty in this business is hard to come by, but I knew early on that if I could foster that kind of trust in a team, we'd be all the better for it. That's why it irked me so when Bock brought in that 'B' team back in Albania. Don't know whether I was so mad that he did it, or that he felt like he couldn't talk to me about it first. Either way, I didn't know his boys like I knew mine. The Yak turned out to be a keeper, so did Henry Knapp. That whole Lithuania mess we went through makes me consider those two fairly integral now. But I've made mistakes before, that Dresden for one, and so a mustard seed of doubt will always remain. People can pull some awful strange things when left to their own devices. Can't win them all, but you can try not to lose them.

I hear a chopper coming in, civilian by the pitch of it, and small. Smaller even than a medical if I had to guess. I spot it approaching from the northeast, cutting diagonal in the cold air. The snow is long over, and the sky is opening up to blue. The helicopter is white with a purple pinstripe down the side: a small civilian four-seater as I predicted. I pull up the collar of my coat to cover my mouth and nose as it approaches the pad. There's the pilot and one other sitting up front. They're dressed in black fatigues, and coming down in a hurry. The skids don't even touch the concrete before the passenger hastily waves me over. I hustle to them in a hail of wind and kicked-up snow before sliding the door open and hopping inside, furiously rubbing my hands together for warmth.

I barely have time to notice the cockpit's warm before we lift off again. I slip on a set of headphones the passenger tosses me, and adjust the microphone in front of my mouth. Its foam cover scratches lightly against my mustache. The passenger turns around to face me in the back seat.

"Welcome to the party, pal," he says, and I can't decide whether or not he means it in a patronizing way.

"What're we celebrating?" I ask back over the radio crackle.

"Depends. How much you know?"

"Fair amount, I guess."

"You don't know nuthin'," the deep voice of the pilot says, not turning to look at me. The chopper heads north from the hospital.

The passenger reminds me of Everly except with less hair and a bit more muscle. Their black fatigues make me uneasy. Too official maybe.

"Sit back. Relax. We're headed to Oklahoma," the passenger says.

"We got enough fuel for that?" I ask.

"Don't worry, pal. Have a little faith."

Chapter 22

WE SET DOWN in a wooded area east of Norman, just close enough to the Oklahoma University campus to make me nervous. There's movement on the ground, more men in black fatigues, and equipment. Lots of equipment. As the helicopter digs in, I locate what must be the command center: a black tarplin on posts that waves with the helicopter's rotary displacement. A uniformed man leans in to another standing tall, chomping on a cigar, and staring in our direction. Nightfall isn't far away. Cloud cover still hovers above, blanketing the landscape in that familiar dull grey of winter that washes the color from everything.

The passenger swings the door open as the pilot runs through power down procedures. The engine churns down, and the blades start their long slowing hum. I hop out and scuttle in a crouch toward the men next to the tarplin. The man in charge, standing forceful and arrogant, glaring at me, and not in a friendly way, continues listening to intel spilling into his ear by a subordinate. Before I reach him, he takes the cigar from his mouth and spits tobacco juice too close to my boot.

"You're here," he says. Boston accent. Close cropped white hair, and harsh skin weathered with experience.

"I am," I say, realizing that I might just have to call him on his attitude.

"Rust."

"That's right. You?" I ask.

"In charge."

"Could see that at forty paces."

"Good," he says popping the cigar back in his mouth.

"Must've taken a pretty good deal of practice," I say straight into his eyes.

"Or maybe I'm just good at it."

The man in charge waves off his underling who never stops barking intel, and motions for me to walk with him. I oblige, seeing several men all in the same black fatigues bustling around. I see weapons, lots of standard issue stuff. M16s, M9 side-arms, but then there are other things I don't recognize. Two men pass me lugging an open crate of what looks to me like medium-sized cannon balls, each couple attached to one another by wide gauge cable. Opening my field of vision, I notice several of these crates. The men are taking them all over the area to drop-off points consisting of two men each. They're creating a perimeter.

"Bolos," the man in charge says. "That's what we call them any-way. Narikesh over there came up with them."

He points to a uniformed middle-eastern man with a clipboard who checks off crates as they're dropped.

"What they for?" I ask.

"Brings them out into the open, so we can see them."

"See who? Listen, why are we so close to the college? I don't like where this is going."

"Has nothing to do with that. We go where the birds drop. That's it," he says, stopping to stare down one of his men casually leaning against a crate.

The man snaps to attention and starts unpacking some kind of launcher I've never seen before, much larger than the stinger we used in Albania, but not quite the size of a 120mm mortar launcher.

"That's Narikesh's too. Good delivery device. Sure, he wouldn't mind you keeping that one operational when we're gone."

The man in charge walks off again without looking at me, instead surveying the setup for goodness knows what. I stand there for a minute watching him and wonder when Park will get here, and where he'll set up. The only open area was where the helicopter set down. We're boxed-in by residential. I can see two houses through the trees. All this movement—not to mention the chopper—will arouse mountains of attention. Wherever Park is, I hope he's got specs on all this and has a car ready. Don't see this going well for anyone. What did I get myself into?

"Alright, dammit!," I say, halting the man in charge. "I'm through with the secrecy. What the hell are we here to do?"

The man pauses and turns slowly, gnashing that cigar. He removes it slowly and starts pacing back toward me. Soon we're nose to nose. No fear on either part.

"We're here to work. You're here to observe. So observe and keep your mouth shut so we can work."

"Fine," I say through my teeth. "Tell me what I'm observing."

Then he backs up a little. Confused maybe. "The old man didn't tell you anything," he says. Not a question, but a realization.

I shake my head, feeling more than a little foolish, like someone who just figured out the joke was on him all along.

"Well, I'm not going to get into it too far because it's not my place. Elijah has a way of doing things that works. Got me into it, at least. You a military man?"

"Was," I say. "Sergeant Major, U.S. Army."

"Chiclas Taber, Chief Warrant Officer 3, United States Marine Corps retired."

"But *Blackwater* after that, I suspect. All of you," I say looking around.

"Color me impressed. How'd you figure that one out?"

"Been able to spot you boys a mile away for years. You all move the same," I say.

"Yeah, and how's that?"

"Like you own the place. Lost a lot of jobs to you boys. Lots of jobs and lots of money. Except come to find that most of you just do a good job at looking like you own the place. Employers don't know the difference till it's too late."

Taber stares at me for a minute, quiet and seething, but not without a touch of amusement. I cock my head at him and grin.

"Okay, Amarillo Rust. You may change your mind on that after today," he says and walks away again. This time I follow. "You are here to observe how we do business. Out here somewhere in this little patch of green is a friendly that we need to protect and extract to a point of safety. This is rarely accomplished without enemy resistance, and depending on the importance of the injured friendly, the resistance can get messy quickly. In fact, bogies are probably watching us right now. If they aren't, they're well on their way, which is why a swift setup is key. You never know what you're up against until you're up against it."

Just then a walkie I didn't notice on his hip squelches on. One of his men reports that post A6 is ready to fire. My head swims because for the life of me, I can't figure who we're firing at. Then it leaps out at me.

"Those houses?"

Taber halts me with a finger and then calls back an acknowledge-ment to hold through the walkie. As he does it, I scan the tree line for Park. He's got to be out there somewhere, watching and just as befuddled as I feel. Maybe he sees something I can't put together. Either way, I'm in a rough spot.

"What about cops?" I ask. "The chopper. Law's got to be on their way."

"The civilians in those houses have been dealt with, and the police? That's just a hazard of the pay grade."

"What do you mean dealt with, Taber?"

"Easy, everybody out there is fine—everybody alive that is. We just have to make sure they don't drop a dime in the limited—and I stress limited—time we're out here. Excuse me."

Taber barks into the walkie for all posts to report in, that the go to fire will be issued in thirty seconds. All posts acknowledge, one through five, with post six already having done so.

"Aim for mid-tree level. Snag the biggest branches you can find," Taber says before releasing the comm button.

"How many of you are there?" I ask, grasping at any one of the thousand questions swirling in my head like a school of herring.

He gives me a puzzled look, as if I'd asked if the earth was really round. "Twelve, of course. You should know that."

I throw up my hands in exasperation.

"Listen, just stay back and watch," Taber says. "I had to. We all had to. You'll get what you need to get if you just watch. Me explaining it to you won't help in believing it. Stick close to that armored truck over there. The bank truck. That's where we'll be heading when we have the friendly secured. Just keep your eyes open, your mouth shut, and your head down."

"How about a side-arm at least."

"I'm not stupid, Rust. I'm sure you didn't come unprepared. But I've gotta tell you, whatever you've got hiding in your boot won't mean a pile of bat crap out here. It's time. Go to the truck."

"But where's the friendly?" I ask.

"We don't know yet," Taber says dismissively, then sends his command to fire over the walkie.

I look across the posts where different configurations of men stand at the ready with M16s and launchers drawn at the emptiness of trees. The men with the launchers, one for each post, fire. Deep thuds and whistles like mortar reports send the double cannon balls end over end by their tethers. They smash into the trees, most wrapping tightly around broad branches, sending hails of dried wood shards and patches of crisp brown leaves to the ground. Then, quiet but for the cannon balls clacking to stillness against branches and each other, that or the errant sparrow escaping the disruption.

"Okay men, get ready," Taber says into the walkie. "Spotters?"

I notice one uniformed man prone on top of the truck with binoculars surveying the trees, and another at one of the points opposite him doing the same.

"Nothing yet," comes back.

Taber watches the trees intently. "Okay, spotter-post three, anything?"

Park's out there somewhere. I hope he's set up away from all this. Then a call from one of the posts closer to the trees. A spotter then mimics it through the walkie.

"Got him. East on our three. Bird's sitting propped with his back to a stump. Massive wounds to the left abdomen."

"Okay. Posts one and six, move in with caution. Three through five, covering positions. Let's have no loss on this one. Bird sustains heavy lacerations, so they're already here. Sound off on first visual," Taber says. Then he notices I'm still next to him. "Go to the truck, Amarillo. Please."

I resist the urge to defy him, and stumble off to the truck, head craned at the trees. Without specs, I'm not libel to see much from this distance, but my head is pounding. I can just make out a body slumped against a tree, just like the spotter said, and I can see Taber's men approaching, but from what I can tell, we all should have seen the man long before now. It was like he just popped into existence. None of it makes any sense. And what do they mean by calling him a bird? Wonder if Park is seeing the same thing.

I knock on the side of the truck when I reach it to let the spotter on the roof know I'm there, but my attention's still locked on the trees.

"You the replacement?" I hear from the roof of the bank truck.

"No idea," I say, barely hearing him.

Then an arm reaches down the side. I go to shake it half-heartedly.

"Want a boost or what?" the spotter says, pulling my hand up.

I step up on one of the tires as he pulls me to the roof. The spotter motions for me to lie beside him.

"Miles Halperin," He says amiably, without smiling.

"Amarillo Rust," I say.

He passes me the binoculars. "First time's a doozy, huh?"

"Yeah," I say.

"Just you wait," he says, chuckling.

A curdling scream rings out from one of the covering posts. Halperin grabs the binoculars from me before I can get a good look at whoever it is we're here to extract. I swing my head to the post and see a uniformed body fly several yards into the air and crash to the ground.

"Bogies on B3!" Halperin yells into the walkie.

"Open fire on three," Taber says, his voice booming from his position.

Automatic gunfire flares from remaining covering positions. Halperin shoves the binoculars into me and reaches to his side, trading them for a scoped Howa 1500 .308. Pushing me to one side, he works the bolt action and trains down on the scope. The rifle cracks off a round, nearly deafening me.

"Got him," I hear Halperin say through the cloud of my ringing, muted ears.

I try to shake it off and decide to slide down the side of the truck. I point the binoculars toward the gunfire and see them, or think I do. Truth is, I don't exactly know what I see through those specs.

Taber's team is perforating what seem to be three or four bogies. They look like men, but something's off. They move faster, their forearms are huge, much bigger than their triceps. Longer necks. Faces with pointed features. Narrow eyes, almost slits. They're unarmed, but I think I see claws, like a dog, black and thick, a dull sharpness to them like blunted axe blades. Clothes are tatters now because of the bullets slamming into them, but the legs are abnormally thick with muscular thighs and visible tendons from the knees down. Long feet, boney and gnarled, charred black and grey like fire-pit ashes. This is not happening. I lower the binoculars and rub my eyes until they're red before bringing them up again. Nothing changes, except there are more of them now, rushing from the trees toward Taber's men who furiously strain to hold their positions, emptying clip upon clip into the impending…things.

Taber takes turns firing and screaming into the walkie, all the while taking measured intervals toward the truck. Before I know it, I've met him on the field.

"Extraction team, get that bird to the truck. Get it to the truck now!" Taber says, noticing me without acknowledgement. "Bassong, can you back that truck up any closer to extraction team? They need your street howitzer for covery fire."

"Do what I can, sir," comes over the walkie.

I hear the bank truck growl to life behind me. The engine revs. I hear the man inside yell for Halperin, still on top and blasting back those animals coming out of the trees with the .308. His shots seem to inflict the most damage, but whichever one he hits doesn't stay down long. None of the mercs' bullets are killing them, just slowing their forward movement, relentlessly pushing back the tide. Taber doesn't seem surprised at this. I'm standing dumb like a kid at the circus. Taber grabs me by the arm of my coat and tears me away toward the truck, which careens through the brush toward the extraction team. Three mercs have the "bird" by his limbs, and I notice how tall he is, at least three feet taller than anyone else, but seemingly human at least. They struggle to wrench and pull the man toward the approaching truck. Halperin, still on the roof has stopped firing and covers his head to shield himself from branches as the truck continues back, finally stopping only yards from the extraction team. Halperin jumps down and flings open the cargo doors on the back of the truck as the three mercs load the man inside.

Taber, still pulling me with a death grip, sounds off through the walkie. "Bird is loaded. Repeat. Bird is loaded. All positions fall back and get yourselves to transport."

In some broken formation, the men, still firing, fall back and splinter off. The two chopper pilots get the downed merc to his feet and send him toward the others before making for the helicopter. The rest take off together toward the truck. I hear sirens in the distance. All bogies decide to rush the truck as well, a final push, gunfire repelling them, slowing them to an insatiable crawl, snarling and screaming to get at the body inside. One of the things stops, hunches over, desperately wheezing to catch its breath. All are covered in what looks like blood... but darker. It's pouring from the hunched one's mouth. It ferociously blows a clearing huff of breath through his nose and mouth sending a mist of it into the air before erecting itself and pressing forward again. Another creature shakes and falls to its knees, letting out an agonizing high-pitched squeal, but shortly, as all the others, it wobbles back to its feet and marches slowly forth again as if under remote control.

Halperin and the extraction team fire their parting shots and file into the back of the bank truck with the body. The driver throws the truck into drive, but waits for Taber and I to get into the cab with him. The rest of the men create a wall between the truck and those things, unleashing hell into them still. I wonder how, or even if, they're going to get away. The truck is full with four men and a body in the back and three of us in the cab up front.

"What about them?" I ask Taber about the remaining mercs, yelling over the screaming and automatic fire.

"When we move, they run," he says, nodding to the driver who releases the brake and slams the gas pedal to the floor.

"Run where?" I ask, head hanging out the window to watch as we lurch away, tires grinding into the earth beneath us.

My question gets answered when I see the chopper strafe nearer to the battling men, hovering uneasily only feet above their heads. The first man stops firing, slings his M16 over his shoulder and hops up, grabbing hold of the skids. When he pulls himself in, the chopper turns so that the merc can resume fire from the safety of the chopper. A second man now jumps to the skids and pulls himself in, switching out clips, racking the rifle and pressing fire down as well. The final merc jumps to grab the skids, but one of those things heaves forward just enough to grab hold of his ankle. The pilot pulls the yoke back to try and lift the merc to safety, but that thing just tightens its grip. Blood and meat spray from the creature until the mercs in the helicopter stop firing for fear of hitting their cohort.

"Don't stop," Taber says to the driver.

Then I hear a shot from somewhere far away. I look to the west and see a glint of something high in a tree adjacent to our position. It's got to be Park. I look back and see that all too familiar plume of an unstruck bullet hitting the ground. It's Lithuania all over again. I'm sure Park knows he didn't miss either. But, just as in Lithuania, that thing grabbing on to the merc heard the shot, and it startled just enough to let go and turn its attention to easier pray in the trees, to Park. For whatever reason, the bullets these mercs are firing do some kind of damage, something Park's and mine do not.

As the chopper rises away, the mercs pulling their rattled brother inside, I can't help but pray Park gets out. We all know I was supposed to come alone. I look at Taber, who's looking right back at me with either pity or consternation. I can't tell which—but either way—I know from his face that Park is on his own tonight, there's nothing I can do about it, and that fact scares the hell out of me.

Chapter 23

I'M HUNCHED IN the passenger seat of this bank truck as the Oklahoma cityscape floats by in a gravid fog. I see little. Thoughts flicker through my head. I'm unable to capture one for long. Everything is unsure. Will Earth suddenly stall on its axis and send all on its surface spiraling into outer space? Will all the plants simply decide to stop releasing oxygen into the air? Has my reality come apart? Nothing sits outside the realm of possibility now, but it's an eighteen-story wave rushing toward me so hard it will break my neck if I face it. I used to wonder what a nervous breakdown felt like. I don't any longer. I stand weak at the precipice of madness, and I shudder as its cold wind slices through my bones.

I hear the hum of the road, the movement and chatter behind me in the back. Just what is lying on that gurney, and what are they planning on doing with it?

"Take the exit to forty-fourth," Taber says to the driver. "There's a drop near Draper Park."

I can feel Taber looking at me and turning away in consecutive measures. If he wants to talk, I wish he'd just do it. Not sure I could even if I wanted to.

"I want to say that I know how you feel, Sergeant Major," Taber says as I stare vacantly out the window. "But we've been at this so long, I've forgotten what it must have been like. All I can say is that you get used to it eventually. Don't know when that was either, but you do. Best advice I can give you is to treat it like any other job you have. Plan it like you would any other. Execute it the same way. The fundamentals don't change. But ,I know it's a lot. Want you to know that I know."

"Thanks," I say noticing how dry my mouth is, how thirsty.

"Where now, sir?" the driver asks.

"Right, left, right," Taber says back.

I feel my mouth try to connect with my brain. I've got to ask. I have to know. "What's in the back? Is it one of those things?"

"No," Taber says almost curtly. "It's something else."

The truck pulls to a stop in front of a small church tucked inside a middle-class residential neighborhood, not much more than a shack. Leaves of brown and orange stick to a dark and icy snow near the curb. Whiter snow clings to lawns in patches. It's the time of night and cold where people don't even come outside to drive.

"I'll show you," Taber says, knocking his gloved fist three times on the metal partition behind us.

I hear the men scuttle in the back. The latches on the cargo doors release. Taber snaps his fingers in the direction of the door next to me. Blankly, I grab the handle and push open the door, stepping into the slush and bitter cold. Four men in the back routinely unload the gurney as the tall man lying on it bleeds and grimaces when they pop out the gurney's castered legs. They push the gurney up the sidewalk toward the church. Taber and the driver follow as I stand on the curb and peer into the windows of the house across the street.

There must be a family inside. Beautifully oblivious. A mom might wash dinner dishes while a child clings to her leg. I imagine the husband in front of the television, passively watching the banality of the local news, pleasantly nodding off, or thinking about whatever project he's got in store for him tomorrow at the office. I never thought I'd be envious of a life like that. The quiet predictability of it. There's safety to be found tucked in the center of the herd.

"Let's go, Sergeant Major. We're almost done," Taber says.

I take one last, longing glimpse into the window and turn back to a life exploded. I make my way to the men at the chapel door.

"This is what we were after," Taber says to me, looking down at the long body laying on the gurney.

The wounded one looks up at Taber, then to me like a nervous, cornered animal. His eyes are wild between the recognitions of darting pain from his side. His discomfort is evident. The skin is nearly transparent, his eyes fair and almost as clear. He wears what looks to be a robe or a cloak, the side of which is soaked in blood. His chest heaves with the controlled rise and fall of his lungs. He doesn't try to talk, nor does he offer anything expressing gratitude for his rescue. There appears an uneasy but knowing disconnect between he and his rescuers, almost an avoidance of direct interaction.

When the man looks at me, a feeling of iniquity rises up, building steadily until I am compelled to break his gaze so that the feeling lessens. Yet, with this a desire to look on him returns, much like that of a sunset just before the it's safe to stare, just before the brightness of the sun sinks below the horizon and the piercing rays disappear to the grandeur of its lingering absence. Inside his eyes I am both myself and someone different entirely, a part but not a whole. My thoughts are direct and singular, if not a bit foreign. I think in wide insightful swaths, unfettered by doubt, reticence or the conflict of duality. It is beautiful. Though, as again I look away, I return to the integration of my own fractured self. The familiarity of ambiguity and moral indecision creeps back. Again I feel myself, but a remaining remorse for that fact accompanies my rejoinder.

"What are you?" I ask the tall form on the gurney with blanket astonishment.

The man opens his mouth to speak, but Taber cuts him off. "He's all yours, Bassong. Get him gone," he says.

With that, the other men step aside, most of them looking at the gurney and not the man, that or to the ground. Bassong, the driver of the bank truck, lays his hand on the wounded man's and pushes the gurney through the church door, closing it softly behind him.

"Bassong's the only one who can go in. He takes them. You'll have one who can do it, but it probably won't be you," Taber says to me.

"Where does he go?"

"Up I guess. Out. I don't know. Bassong doesn't either, that or he doesn't feel like telling us."

"Why Bassong? Why is he the only one?"

"You'll have to ask Elijah that one. I wasn't in on the decision-making. Once we get the bird out of the heat and into the safe house, we're out of the picture until the next one."

He motions the rest of his men to follow him to the truck and load up like before. It's still running and warm when I get inside. The welcome heat limbers up my mind. For the time being, I've stopped asking the big questions. As we wait for Bassong to return, Taber and I stare into the streetlamps. The stillness of the neighborhood calms me.

"I suppose I should be ticked about you bringing someone else in on this," Taber says, still surveying the surroundings. "I can't though. I did the same thing. Didn't turn out so well for my guy."

"We don't know how it turned out for mine," I say.

"As long as he booked it out of there about ninety or so yards, I'm sure he's fine."

"How are you so sure? Those things didn't seem too eager to stop with us."

"Well, you didn't see them chasing for long did you?"

I shake my head. "Guess not."

"Your friend's bullet didn't hit them because it wasn't treated. The bullets have to be treated first or they hit air. Nothing but air."

"Treated with what? Pixie dust?"

Taber looks off, weary of explaining. "Salt. Treated with salt," he says, sighing.

I give an obstinate nod. "Of course."

"Look, pal. I don't really give a shake about you. You can learn or not. I'm following orders by babysitting your wise ass, so just take it in and try to learn or take off into who-give- a-ripville where we drop you."

"Take it easy—"

"No, you take it easy. This whole thing out here sucks, you get it? And we're almost out. You're almost in. You said yes to the man, and so you're in. You're the replacement, and I didn't get a say in that. Most of us have seen enough that we're lucky if we don't all end up in straight jackets when it's said and done. So don't get glib about it."

"Don't take this on the heel, Taber, but I don't know anything about replacing anybody. Elijah didn't tell me a thing but to meet you boys out here and have a look. I can't even make sense about what just happened. Every son of a mug is talking me in riddles and circles, and I've just about had it."

Taber huffs next to me. I notice Bassong in my peripheral coming out of the church and wheeling that empty gurney toward the truck. The men in the back open up and take it.

"I was a military man before and I'm a private contractor now," I say, "so I can appreciate rank, but you best back off me before you and I wake this neighborhood up and good." I glare at Taber who gives me an embittered shrug as Bassong takes his place back in the driver's seat.

"We good?" Taber asks him.

"Done," Bassong says.

"Head downtown so we can get rid of this redneck."

Then a cell phone rings. Taber digs in his pocket, produces the phone and answers. He ends the short conversation with a curt thanks to whoever's on the other end. "Cleanup crew's finished. We're gold," he says.

"Any word on my guy?" I ask.

"Nope. Must've gotten away. Good for him," Taber says.

A few quiet minutes later, Taber and his men let me out in front of a fairly well-populated, yellow building with a sign reading Abuelo's on Sheridan Avenue in the middle of Bricktown, the arts and entertainment district of the city.

"You like Mexican food?" Taber says to me.

"I'm from Texas."

"Get yourself something to eat here. It's not bad."

We share an uncomfortable moment between us.

"Listen, we're just a little jumpy to be off this tour," he says. "It's been a long time coming, that's all. Take care of yourself, Sergeant Major. Elijah's got a room for you at the Renaissance a couple blocks over. He's arranged transportation for you in the morning."

He offers me his hand. I shake it and get out of the truck. Taber shuffles into the passenger seat and rolls down the window.

"I'm sure we'll run into each other again," he says. "The world's not as big as it used to be, is it?"

"Suppose not," I say.

He offers a quick salute and motions for Bassong to pull away. I watch the truck make its way down the street, blend in to traffic, and disappear around the corner. I realize I hadn't eaten all day as hunger pangs finally surface. I enter the restaurant and hope to dream of the family I conjured up inside that home across from the tiny chapel. I hope to dream of modest and mundane things, of local news programs, and the predictability of their weather reports. Will it rain tomorrow, or will it snow? Will the sun peek out, or will the grey skies tighten their grip above our weary heads?

Chapter 24

FOREARMS, VEINED AND sinewed, writhe, swinging fractured, splintered, chaotic claws like medieval maces. Exposed tendons contract and burst forth as slugs tear in, snapping them like over-taught cables. Ruptured flesh splits away, exposing matte ivory bone above their tapered fissures for eyes, wet and black as the rivers of night. All the time they wail in their fixation, unable to sate their dogged carnalities. Gnashing and tearing for their own precious cessation that they know will never come.

I wake as in a time before, beaded and dripping with salinated sweat. It was my first private action outside the Army escorting drug mules through the Bolivian jungle. One week assignment. Alone. Only one who spoke English. Four young women in my charge. They needed me to get them to Huacaraje airport. A rival faction and my own incompetence made sure I did not succeed. All four girls died. I left them so that I would live. They were chopped down with machetes like vine covered paths, their bodies butchered for the balloons and full of white powder in their stomachs. I alone survived. I simply ran away. I left my preconceptions in the jungle, the unearned bravado, the mythic heroism and romance of working outside the official system, drained, and replaced with something else. Greif, shame, and regret. Took months to reboot, to pull myself up and accept another job. So many nights I woke up just like this. It was the old team, most importantly Bock who helped me out of it. I watched the way he worked. I studied his ability to set people aside for objectives. I learned from him to abandon ego and to release that shared humanity, that empathy, if only for the action's duration. During the operation, one must think only about the job, the objectives, and the ultimate goal. He told me, "Do the job, think of the money." Until yesterday I have been able to stand by that wisdom.

The hotel room telephone rings next to my ear. I slide up the headboard to a seated position, then rub my eyes before picking up the receiver. I don't remember coming to the hotel, or the walk over. Not even the check-in. Last thing I remember was tequila shots at the restaurant bar, and a girl. What was her name?

"Hello?" I say in a gravelly voice into the phone.

"Ah, good afternoon, Mr. Rust. I trust last night ended with some amount of frivolity, judging by your... extended slumber."

It was Tishbe. I drop the receiver and go to the window, pulling back the blackout shades. Sunlight bathes the room sending nails of it through my aching temples. From the shadows, I can tell it's late afternoon. Haven't slept this late in years, but the dull, heavy pains in my head coupled with an upset stomach and a putrid, smoky odor from deep in the back of my throat tell me what happened. It isn't like me at all. It's something Everly and Horrace would do. Drown themselves. Always thought of it as weak, but then, few have ever seen the things I did yesterday, and that fact kept whatever guilt I harbored in check.

I pick up the receiver again. "You there?"

"I am."

"What do you need? I'm going back to sleep."

"I see. 'As for thee, O king, thy thoughts came into thy mind upon thy bed, what should come to pass hereafter: and he that revealeth secrets maketh known to thee what shall come to pass.' That about right?" Tishbe says.

"Hell are you talking about, man? My head is like a jackhammer right now. Need to sleep it off."

"You won't be safe there either, Mr. Rust. In fact, sleep will only make them come back, at least in your mind. Sleep does not always

equal rest. Why not come down? I will take you for a meal. We can discuss our situation."

"My situation is: you dropped me into something I wish I never
saw, and for sure don't want to see again."

"Except you have, Mr. Rust. You *have* seen it and while today you
feel understandably overwhelmed by this knowledge, wishing only to
escape it by any and all means, most certainly the objective of your current condition in fact, your mind will return to it. Over and again you will
think on it, ponder it, wonder at its possibilities. This is the type of man
you are, Mr. Rust. This is why you were chosen. Any attempt to simply
discount and distance yourself from what must now be done will prove
feudal, and not because it will be forced upon you, no. You will come
back because you will want to come back. Even free will can be... predictable."

"Mighty sure of yourself, old man."

"Therefore, if you wish to leave, I will not stop you. You are a free
man, and so you may go. I do not wish to control you, Amarillo. What I
do wish, is that you agree to work with me. Your leaving will only delay
the inevitable. Search your conscience, truly search it, and I know you'll
find what I say to be accurate. You will come back, but when you do, I
pray you come back soon. Time is always of the essence, my boy, especially here. Especially now. Until then I bid you Godspeed."

"Wait."

Silence on the other end.

"Give me an hour to get ready," I say.

"Thank you, Mr. Rust. I knew you'd see the light. Please, don't
hurry on my account. We'll be right here when you're ready."

"Brought your euro-trash with you?"

"Now, that's not very nice. Nor is it accurate. I'll see you in the
lobby. We've errands to run."

Chapter 25

ONE OF TISHBE'S men opens the door to a black Buick, freshly washed and glimmering in the Oklahoma afternoon. I sit next to the old man as his two goons get into the front. As we pull away, my head still pounding something awful, I remember Park.

"Look, I told you I'd go alone on this deal, but—"

"Oh, Mr. Park is quite safe, thanks to… in fact, he was in a nearby hotel, only a few miles away."

"Is he still here? I'd like to see him," I ask.

"I don't know. He is out of our… jurisdiction, I'm afraid."

He's hiding something. Tishbe is a whole different breed, working on a level I've yet to understand. Plenty of people in this business put on like they know it all and have access to any information, however classified, but that's mostly a bluff. They think it seats them in a position of power. You can usually root out what they really know and don't, but I've yet to stump the old man. He might just be the real deal. If he says Park's not around then I suppose I believe him. Park's a resolute fella, but there's always a point where things can get too strange to bear. He must've found his limit. I don't know that I'll ever see him again. It doesn't get weirder than yesterday. Part of me feels responsible if he did have a break, but you take on an awful lot pulling wet work. We've all been exposed to things just as horrible as what happened in those trees, but nothing nearly as strange and logically disconnected.

"I cannot fault you for being cautious," Tishbe says as we make a turn heading south toward highway 240. "But you must understand that these things are being revealed to you slowly for a reason. I hope you are beginning to put the pieces together."

Not long after we merge with the flow of 240, I start noticing signs for the airport. The men up front are silent, and Tishbe sits stoic next to me in one of his finely tailored suits. I try again to place him. His skin tone suggests an aristocratic middle-easterner, but his suit screams Italy. I know that from working with Bock. His long grey hair, which he always wears down, possibly used to obscure that scar over his eye, makes him harder to pinpoint. The speech suggests a highly educated man, that much anyone could figure, but something about his demeanor just doesn't fit any of it. To my knowledge he has never lied, there's a knowing honesty about him that you rarely encounter in my line of work. He's never lost his cool around me. That should settle my nerves, but it only makes me nervous. But ,somehow, there is something though. Something old. Something that gives him the air of authority, of mastery, almost omnipotence. Part of me wonders why I haven't fed him to Bock yet. I should feel completely enraged. I should feel like a puppet, a fool who has been strung along and still doesn't see the end of things. But, as he said before, he chose me for a reason. On some level I'm not yet fully aware of, I must enjoy it. I know why I got into the business. It wasn't just the money. Mine has always been a rebellious, adventure-seeking soul. Tight situations usually don't rattle me. Like my grand-daddy used to say: "There's always going to be a rough patch, but that's why it's just a patch. There's always a path to cut across it if you look hard enough."

"Are you with us, Mr. Rust?" Tishbe says.

"Sorry—I just—my mind went somewhere else I guess," I say, straightening up in my seat.

"I say that Mr. Park was not ready to see what he did. You were chosen first because of your constitution. Mr. Park and the others must be told what you've seen later on, and by you."

"Why me?"

"Because they trust you. They've followed you into battle countless times, solely on the back of your word. You've neither cheated nor lied to them. Your men hold you in high regard. That's why they will listen to you, and that is why they will believe you."

"Not sure I even believe myself at this point."

"Of course you do. What you possess within you is far greater than you understand. If you did, perhaps you would have chosen a different path in your life's work. But good can often come out of the evils men trespass. Mr. Taber and his men, while effective, do not have your heart, or the sense of moral imperative you have worked so diligently to discard from your being. But we have found you now, Mr. Rust, you and your men, and at the most appropriate moment. Good may come out of this as well. Have faith."

"And what about the quarter of a million? Maybe that's the reason I'm sticking around. Maybe I smell more where that came from," I say.

"Money has motivated men since its introduction. That is true. For unto whomsoever much is given, of him shall much be required," Tishbe says, pulling back the grey strands of hair from his face, calling attention to the scar and cloudy green eye.

He grins at me, and I look away out the window. We drive into the airport's side entrance where the private aircraft are housed. The Buick continues across the tarmac, passing several planes of varying size and opulence until we come to a stop only yards from an immaculate Cessna Citation XLS+ jet. I can barely make out a pilot running through pre-flight procedures in the cockpit while a crew-member ticks his ground checks off on a clipboard. The Cessna's stair ramp is already down and waiting for us.

Before I get out, I just have to ask. "Who are you, Elijah?"

He stops with one foot on the pavement. "A humble servant, Mr. Rust, and that alone."

The crewmember and pilot greet Tishbe with enthusiastic hugs, but that's not the part that throws me. They both bow reverentially to the two euro-goons the old man always has in tow, even as one lights a cigarette and moves up the stairs past them as if not to notice. No one pays me anything more than a polite nod. Inside the fuselage, the euro-goons sit together on the first row. I make my way to the middle, taking the seat across the narrow aisle from Tishbe.

"So where are we going now?" I ask. "I'll wager it isn't Tahoka."

"That would be a correct assertion," he says, buckling his safety belt with a wide smile.

"I'm sure I've been fired from the cotton gin by now," I say back sarcastically.

"Good thing you're not really a cotton gin worker."

"So where then?" I ask, more serious now in a polite attempt to convey not only my hangover, but also rising impatience.

"To see a friend," he says, reclining his chair and closing his eyes.

"A friend," I say.

The old man sits up suddenly. "Which reminds me, you should call your partner, Mr. Bock, when we reach cruising altitude. He's been worried about you." Tishbe then reclines again, settles into his seat, and again lets his eyelids fall.

"You've spoken to Bock?" I ask, skeptically.

"No."

"Then how do you know?"

"Well," Tishbe says exhaling, "wouldn't he?" He clears his throat and then yawns deeply.

"What do you suggest I tell him?"

"Whatever you like. Lest you forget, dear boy, you've a free will. Now I beg you to allow me sleep. I am an old man and require more and more of it. I suggest you do the same, burn that infernal poison you ingested last night out of your bones. That hideous swill. Sleep, boy. Sleep."

The takeoff is one of the smoothest I've ever experienced. Let's hope the landing is the same. My father was an airplane buff, just as my boyhood friend Toby Dennis was before he got on with the air force. Guess an appreciation for keeping up with aviation just carried over. Maybe it's just a way to keep connected with people I cared about. Either way, I know a little about civilian aviation, and I know that this jet isn't supposed to be available until next year. It's brand new. I'll wager this is its maiden flight. Whoever Elijah Tishbe really is has a whole mess of money, not to mention clout. Sure, the people I work for like their toys, heck, that's usually the reason they get into the dodgy things they get into in the first place. I've seen lots of private Cessna's. I've ridden on Dassault Falcons, all sorts of Challengers, 850's all the way up to 20208's. But I've never ridden in, or much less seen a man own, a jet that hasn't been released yet. Like I said, Tishbe's on a whole other level.

When we reach cruising altitude, I string the cord of the mounted air-phone to the back row of the plane and dial in the call, making sure there's no powder on the keys or stroke capturing devices attached to the handset. While we in the team take great pains to be anonymous and untraceable, situations *do* arise. Bock and I call it the *doomsday* number. We each have a phone number that is only to be used in cases of extreme, nearly cataclysmic importance. Call it the red phone at the bottom of the president's nuclear bunker. When that phone rings, the other guy answers. That simple. Even if it means walking off a job or leaving a dinner that might end your marriage. If the number comes up, you take the call. Neither Bock nor I have ever dialed the other's, even when he showed up at the bar back in Tahoka.

With the doomsday number dialed, I hear the line transfer, a low click, then a ring. It doesn't take long to hear that familiar Scottish voice.

"Rust. Where are you, mate?"

"Bock," I say, letting out the pent up air from my lungs. "Man is it good to hear you."

"Horrace and I were set to go looking for you. Are you alright?"

"I'm fine."

"Where the bloody hell are you, mate? You haven't been checking that shambolic website of yours. Been trying to get a hold of you."

"Why? What's happened?"

"Park's gone missing too. Horrace is a whinging wreck. Acting a right fud. "

"I know," I say, but Bock just runs over me.

"Horrace got a call last night. Late. Said Park was talking all kinds of nonsense. Something about devils chasing him about. Crazy talk."

"I know," I say again.

"Well, did you know he means to kill himself?"

"Kill himself? No, Bock, he's fine. I'm sure he's—" I say, my mind racing to catch up.

"Was he with you? Did you go it alone?" Bock says, accusingly.

"I took Park along on something, yes, but I didn't know—"

"Now you're no better than me then, are you mate? Now *you're* the one stepping out. What was it for? What have you gotten into?"

"Listen, we're going to meet up soon. All of us. I'm working it out, trust me. It's all just—it's all just a little nuts, but I'm working on something for all of us. If you boys think you can find Park, then have at it."

"Where were you both?"

"Oklahoma, shadowing a team pulling some off-the-wall work, let me tell you," I say amused at my own understatement.

"Competition recon? Are you still there? Let us meet you," Bock says.

"I'm not. I'm on a Cessna."

"You're what?"

"I'm in the air."

"Going where?"

"I... don't exactly know," I say, bracing myself.

"Don't exactly know? What's gotten into you, mate? Park takes off like a mad hatter, and you don't even know where you're going? Have you both lost the plot?"

"That's a, uh—that's a good question, actually, but no. I'm still thinking fairly straight. But I don't want y'all to worry. I'm coming back soon. We'll meet up, and I'll tell you everything I know. Like I said, it's for all of us. But go ahead and find Park if you can. He's our man and we owe it to him."

"Aye, some more than others, yes? Tell me, dear friend, does any of this have to do with that Tishbe charlatan? I smell something nasty, and I'll bet me left stone it's got to do with him."

"You're a perceptive man, Bock," I say, sighing.

"Listen to me carefully, you stupid bastard," Bock says. I can tell he's bearing down on the receiver like a vice grip. "Stay away from him. Use your head. The man is a lunatic, and now Park is gone. He's no one to trust. You might be gone next, auld boy."

"I hear you," I say.

Bock planted a seed of doubt in my head, one I should have planted long ago. Had I not witnessed Oklahoma with my own two eyes, I'd slap myself in the face for entertaining any of it in the first place. I don't expect Bock to understand, but something tells me that in time, he most certainly will. In time, we all will. The most important thing now is to find Park. Tishbe didn't involve him. In fact, he discouraged, even mandated that no one else from the team come along. I involved Park, and so his psychotic meltdown and disappearance is on my hands alone.

"Give me twenty-four hours," I say. "I'll get home and the three of us can meet."

"Make it forty-eight. Park could be anywhere. It won't be easy," Bock says back.

"You two can do it. Heck, bring everyone else in on this if you have to. There aren't any secrets on this end, not for much longer at least. Trust me, the story I've got's a doozy and you wouldn't believe it if I told you anyway. Just find Park. You find him before I get home, use the number. Don't hesitate. If you can't get a hold of him, I'll make a post on the site about where to meet up. Tell everyone: Horrace, Everly, Henry Knapp, The Yak, everybody. Gonna take us all. Talk to you in forty-eight."

"Aye. Forty-eight hours. You remember what I told you about him, mate."

"I hear you."

Bock severs the connection. I move slowly down the aisle to hang up the air phone, all the while watching Tishbe. He's still asleep, that or pretending to be. Maybe Bock's right. Maybe he's just some insane businessman with too much time and cash, but that doesn't explain Oklahoma. I could smother him now and no one would know the difference. Least they wouldn't long enough for me to find a way into that cockpit. Landing the plane is another story. Maybe Bock's right, or maybe now I'm just dug in too deep.

Chapter 26

I WAKE STARING at the backs of Tishbe's goons. The Cessna's already on the ground, with the crew member lowering the stair ramp. I didn't even feel the landing. Mighty fine airplane.

Tishbe nudges me. "Ready to go?"

I rise to my feet with a groan. One of the old man's goons looks back at me with disinterested eyes. They step off the jet first, followed by Tishbe and me. He hugs the pilot again. They trade words and I search around to get a bearing on where we've landed. It's a private airstrip, few trees, and stark red mountains in the distance. The sun, bright and full above us nestled into that welcome blue I haven't seen in a while. The landing strip seems deserted, not that it isn't a functional private airfield, but no one else mills around fumbling with any of the other planes which seem to be mostly small props and trainers. Only desert breeze and wisps of orange dust occasionally come up to welcome us.

The goons look uneasy. One goes to the pilot standing next to the stair ramp and whispers something to him. The other stands watch.

"Problem?" I ask the old man.

"Probably nothing. We assumed the car would be here to meet us," he says, shielding his eyes from the Sun.

"Where are we now?" I ask scanning for movement in the small tower off to our left.

"New Mexico."

I don't see anyone in the tower. I think we're all alone out here, but the goons are making me nervous. The pilot steps back into the Cessna. I see him in the cockpit window making a call over the aviation comm. Tishbe's still looking toward one of the hangers. One of the euro-goons speaks to him in that foreign language. The old man nods and motions to me. Then the goon approaches me.

"Need your help in the plane," he says in broken English.

This is how hits happen. No one around, secluded area. If they were going to kill me, this would be textbook. Of course, they could have just as easily done it in the air, but why messy up that pretty plane?

"What do you need help with?" I ask accusingly.

"Just boxes, Mr. Rust. Please," Tishbe says.

"Don't like the look of this, Elijah. Starting to think I need to watch out for myself."

"I don't like the look of this either. We can never be too cautious in our work. The enemy is everywhere and nowhere at the same time, and the tools with which we use to dispatch them can just as easily work against us. There are boxes onboard that must be unloaded and removed from our proximity. I feel we are being watched."

"By whom?" I ask, looking around.

"We've not the time for explanation. Please. Jaoel, *Найдите, что кое-что для него отодвигает коробки от нас.*"

"You tell your goons I'm armed, Tishbe, and this ain't my first rodeo."

"I'm sure they know, Mr. Rust, but Mr. Taber was quite right, the bullets in your pistol are meaningless here. Now please. Help them unload the boxes. Jaoel is going to find something for you on which to wheel the boxes away."

"If something's on the plane you need to get rid of, why don't you just tell him to take off?"

"Because it might be our only means of escape. Take this as well, please. Tell the pilot to power up the jet and have it ready."

The old man reaches around his neck and unhooks a necklace with a small cross hanging from it. Looks like limestone, but more yellow. Ugly little thing. He places it in my hand and folds my fingers over it.

"Please take good care of this, Mr. Rust. It was a present from a good friend. You'll find the boxes—five of them—in the storage compartment next to the lavatory. Hurry, please."

I look him in the eye and decide to do as he says, following this Jaoel up the stairs while the other jogs off toward the nearest hangar. Once inside I tell the pilot to start the plane back up. I hear the jets scream to life. At the end of the aisle, Tishbe's goon swings open the storage compartment and takes out the first box. They are eerily similar to the ones from Albania I have back at Teasel's place. I take the box and haul it outside, dropping it next to the stair ramp.

"Careful please, Mr. Rust. Careful," Tishbe says. I pause at the top of the stair ramp and squint to try and see the one he calls Jaoel, but he must have disappeared into the hangar.

I take the second box from the goon and place it outside as I did the first, then the third and fourth. I'm starting to break a sweat. When I go inside for the last box, the goon meets me with it and pushes past.

"Go!" he says.

I follow him out, and see nothing toward the hangar. I stand next to Tishbe who hasn't moved an inch from the spot where I left him. The other goon stands beside us.

"Что - нибудь?" he asks.

"Nothing yet, but I feel it's close," Tishbe says.

Then I see Jaoel in the distance running toward us with a cart in tow, though it defies logic. One second there was nothing, just dust and tarmac, but as if he all the sudden popped into existence sixty yards away, there he is. He didn't exit the building, just came into visibility out of nowhere, out of the heat waves.

"The boxes, Mr. Rust. Ready the boxes," Tishbe says.

I turn to pick one up and hear a carnal, animalistic squeal. I lift a box and swing around to see something chasing Jaoel. It also pops into view as out of thin air. A hideous black, raging bull, muscles bulging in a sheen of dark sweat. I can hear the furious clopping as it bears down, the hooves ripping through the pavement like a sun-baked creek bed. I squint my eyes and notice its horns are knotted, thorned, and twisting in all directions. Its face is flat like a man's with a wide heaving nose, and the narrow eyes of a goat. Without thinking, I brandish the Colt in my ankle-holster.

"Morax," Tishbe says to his other goon, sounding panicked for the first time since I've known him. "Go, Sorush!"

The goon takes off in the direction of his friend in a sprint I would have never thought possible for a man his size. He rushes past Jaoel and launches himself toward the creature. The bull responds, bearing down on his haunches and propelling himself up. They meet feet above the ground, smashing into one another with a cracking force I can hear over the jets behind us. Jaoel presses on with the cart, not looking back. He hurls it in my direction before planting his feet and pivoting back toward the raging creature.

The cart barrels toward me. I bring up my boot to stop it and drop the box I hold on top. I can see the men struggling with the bull. Just when Jaoel seems to have a grip around the huge torso of the beast, its desperate muscled legs kick free to right itself. Sorush then cocks back a fist and buries it square into the beast's blunted jaw, sending the bull reeling on its back, and wailing once again until it scrambles its massive frame back sloppily to its feet.

"Put that infernal gun away and wheel the boxes as far from here as you can!" Tishbe screams at me.

I reluctantly holster the pistol and load the boxes in record time. Then I heft myself against the cart away from the plane. An errant wheel works against me, but I continue pushing the cart away from the com-motion behind. I hear Tishbe yelling at me from a distance to keep going. I push harder, struggling to keep control. I must be further than the length of a football field now. I've almost reached the end of the airstrip before I stop and turn and wait.

I can see the plane, but no longer hear the engines. I can see Tishbe and the pilot waving their arms for me to come back. I take Elijah's stone cross and lay it on one of the boxes before leaving the cart and jogging closer, all the while failing to spot either the bull or Elijah's men.

"Very good, my boy. Very good indeed," Elijah says when I finally reach the plane.

"Where the hell are they? Where did that thing go?" I ask trying to catch my breath.

I wipe the sweat from my forehead and grab hold of the rail on the Cessna's stair ramp, crouching down with exhaustion.

"We're safe for the time being," Tishbe says, walking over to me and patting my shoulder.

"But, your guys—"

"Oh I'm sure they're still locked in battle, unfortunately. But don't you worry about them. The two of them will make quick work of the likes of Morax."

"A what? What's a Morax?"

"A name. A demon. The real question is what he was after?"

"Well, the boxes I'd guess," I say, standing but still breathing rapidly.

"Perhaps. Or me... or you."

"Me?"

"It seems you're making quite a stir in certain circles, Mr. Rust. Perhaps we've chosen well after all."

I notice another black car, just like the one we rode to the Oklahoma airport rolling toward us. I take the Colt from my ankle holster and drop one into the chamber, raising it at the driver's side windshield.

"It's alright, Mr. Rust. This one is ours," Tishbe says.

Before we get into the car, the old man writes a phone number on the back of a card and hands it to the pilot, telling he and the crew member to wait at the Cessna for a team to reload the boxes.

"You show remarkable instinct, Mr. Rust," Tishbe says, both of us now inside the car as the driver taxis us away from the airstrip. "I trust you left my necklace with the boxes."

"Sorry."

"No, no. Had you brought it back with you, we might again have had to endure the sight of that disgusting beast."

"I'm done asking questions, Tishbe. I've given just about as much as I'm able," I say back.

"You didn't happen to notice the cross did you?"

"Didn't have much time."

"Funny. I thought you'd find it quite familiar," he says with a playful grin.

"Well it's ugly if that's what you mean. Listen, this friend of yours we're going to see gonna have anything to eat? I'm starving."

"Probably not," Tishbe says. I note the weariness in his voice. "But I'm certain he'll have plenty to drink."

Chapter 27

WE PULL UP to a small, dilapidated church circa 1970-something in a disaster movie town somewhere in the forgotten bowels of the New Mexican mountains. I always felt it a depressing state, and this place didn't do anything to change my mind. It's dry and barren, brown and cracked. The only trees in front of cheap, unkempt housing are devoid of moisture or life. Rusty trucks dot the narrow, dirt encroached streets while mostly Hispanic or Native American children ride oxidized hand-me-down bicycles up and down like zombies, wandering in hopeless packs.

Before the driver can open Tishbe's door, a pasty, rotund little biscuit of a man bursts out of the church's front door waving his hands and yelling in our direction. A tight, brown turtleneck nearly strangles his second chin, tucked haphazardly into black, wrinkled slacks which have been tailored too short, exposing sockless feet crammed into brown penny-loafers. The light weight of his black blazer ripples in the wind behind him as he shuffles toward the car with either bad hips or knees or both.

"Elijah, you miserable bastard, you promised me a letter two months ago. You better have the thing or so help me I'll..."

"Oh my," Elijah says sighing deeply, and rubbing his forehead.

The driver opens the door and Tishbe feigns a smile as he steps out to greet the little man. "Edward J. Ellison, how are you my old friend?"

"That's *Pastor* Ellison, Elijah. *Pastor*. *Ellison*. Don't start in with all this how-do-you-do crap. That's the last time I do a damn thing for free, you understand me?"

Only thing I can tell is the man isn't from anywhere around New Mexico. The curtness of his manner suggests perhaps Illinois, Michigan maybe. All the sudden, I can't blame the guy for being so upset. Tishbe's flare for ambiguity and the general hysteria that surrounds him, coupled with having to live in such an infected wart of a town could most certainly warrant a harsh greeting.

"I hardly believe you'd do anything for free, Pastor," Tishbe says. "I want you to meet someone."

Ellison looks at me like a tall pile of something moldy on the sidewalk and then turns his attention back to Tishbe. "Don't do anything for free, huh? How about that compendium in '87?"

"Really, must everything be constantly traced back to that?"

"Yes, Elijah. Everything must be constantly traced back to that, you arrogant mug. I did my part, just like I always do, and you know what? I shouldn't be mad at you. I shouldn't. I should be punching *myself* in the nuts," Ellison says with wild gesticulations.

"Then by all means, proceed," Tishbe says, waving off the driver and walking past the fat little man toward the church.

"Ha!" Ellison says. He shoots a rapacious look to me. "You hear that? The great and holy Elijah wants me to punch myself in the balls."

I open my mouth to speak, but immediately get shouted down.

"Don't hurt yourself, sweetheart," he says. "I bet this old fart has been dragging you all over creation, hasn't he? And without a second's concern for you."

"I—"

"Don't worry. You're just the next in a long line of poor sots he's going to milk every last drop of life out of."

Ellison loses interest in me and chases after Tishbe who is already halfway through the door.

"You just going to walk right in without asking?" he says.

"This is not your home, Edward."

"*Pastor*. But I live here, Elijah," he calls after him, disappearing inside, leaving me on the curb with the driver.

I shake my head at the driver as if begging for an explanation.

"Don't look at me. I'm just the driver," he says.

"Sure you are," I say, walking away toward the church.

Chapter 28

I CAN HEAR Ellison continue to goad Elijah from across the small out-dated sanctuary. The pews are heavily shellacked light colored oak with mauve fabric seat cushions. Carpet, threadbare, and dingy with use, matches the deep color of the seats. Up a short-stair level toward the front, a large wooden cross, suspended by narrow gauge wire at the points, hangs over a meager lectern. The only light in the sanctuary punches through mock-stained glass in dull patches of yellow, red, purple, and green. The place smells empty and unused, and the sparse carcasses of trapped moths, flies, and the occasional spider contrast against the pomegranate-colored carpet. As I walk toward the voices that trail through a doorway to the left of the sanctuary stage, I notice all the dust. Particles hang like glitter in the multi-colored rays that penetrate the interior, and a neglectful coat of it blankets the long untouched piano's once lustrous black body.

I more or less get what I expect when I come through the doorway behind the sanctuary where Ellison clears books, papers, and other garbage off the cushions of an old couch for Elijah to sit. He looks like a wind-up toy with one broken foot holding that stack of stuff, searching with agitation for a place to set it. The entire office is junked up beyond recognition. If it isn't all the books, mostly discolored paperbacks, stacked against the walls all the way to the ceiling where bookshelves should be, or the formless piles of paper on top of what once was once desk and seating surface, it's garbage that litters the room, most notably fast food bags, cartons, and cups with striped straws stabbing through plastic lids.

Unable to turn the anger at himself for the room's condition, and failing to find an adequate place to drop off his armful of jetsam, Ellison once again turns his frustration to Tishbe. He starts left, then right, then left again, twitching to spot an area of precious unblemished space in which to create a new pile, but sadly, the necessary real estate cannot be found. Soon, the fat little man bursts.

"Why don't you ever call before you come, Elijah?" he says unintentionally spitting. "Thought you all were the ones who invented manners for cripe's sake."

"Perhaps if you just set it down on the flo—" Tishbe starts.

"No, Elijah. That is out of the question. You know it may not seem that way to you, but I've got a system working here."

Then it occurs to him that the sanctuary, only feet away, sits vacant and ready for use. Ellison disappears out the door and returns with his hands free.

"Okay, well, you're here," Ellison says with a grand, insultingly sarcastic gesture. "Where's my letter?"

"I'm afraid I don't have your letter, Edward, I—"

"*Pastor*. Of course you don't have my letter. I shouldn't have even asked. You never have anything I ask for," Ellison says, smiling acrimoniously.

"Well, that's just not true," Tishbe says, pursing his lips in disgust, looking away.

"Do you know how much time I spent deciphering the last thing that Herald said? How much research?" Ellison says, growling.

"And you delivered—" Tishbe starts again.

"I always deliver!" Ellison says wagging his finger at Elijah, gritting his teeth. "I have always delivered for you, and I'm treated like trash. Repeatedly."

Tishbe shifts in his seat. "What you ask for in return is outlandishly unorthodox, Edward. You must understand. I'm not even certain its possible. I've offered you payment—"

"Money? You've offered me money?" Ellison screams. He shoots a look to me. "What good is money? What importance is it? Especially in a god-forsaken dung heap like this. I want more, Elijah. I deserve more than money."

"But I don't understand why? What will it prove?" Elijah says almost standing, pleading. I have never seen him so subservient.

"That I'm not crazy!" Ellison says, turning away. "That this is all real. That I'm not cracking up. Don't you get it?"

"Edward," Elijah says. He can feel the anguish in the man's voice. "You know this is real. A letter would prove nothing, my friend. Nothing. You are not crazy."

Ellison faces a wall of books, shaking his head, his palm rubbing his forehead. "We're not supposed to be involved in this. You shouldn't involve us in this. Don't you know your history?" he says so softly I almost have to lean in to hear it.

Then Tishbe stops. All compassion leaves his face. He erects himself and speaks. "You dare question me of history, boy?"

Tishbe's voice hardens, his constitution stiffens, and for the first time, he almost seems menacing. Ellison can feel it too. He shudders and turns around slowly, almost bracing for something.

"I mean only to say, remember Solomon," Ellison says, all the sudden cordial and submissive. "Did he not lose his mind amidst all his great wisdom? First Kings, chapter four, verse twenty-nine: And God gave Solomon wisdom and understanding exceeding much, and largeness of heart, even as the sand that is on the sea shore."

"Yes, and verse twelve in chapter three, I have given thee a wise and an understanding heart; so that there was none like thee before thee, neither after thee shall any arise like unto thee," Elijah quotes without a pause for recollection. "But you are muddling texts. The Bible never speaks about his madness."

"And yet it may have happened, the King's madness," Ellison interjects.

"Anything under the sun could have happened, but as humans we are privy to the canonical text, Edward, we are to look only to the Holy Bible for answers."

"Only it can be relied on," Ellison says, not so much agreeing but leading.

"Definitively, yes," Elijah says.

"And yet, as you say, anything else could have occurred in actuality," Ellison continues.

"As adding to the text, fleshing it out, et cetera. Yes, but you're not to be concerned with it."

"And why not?" Ellison asks, a grin rising on his face, each of his words punctuated by a tap of his knuckles on a desk.

"Because as humans we find it easy to lose sight of the main point, the central idea, which is God's divinity in the Old Testament, and Christ's sacrifice in the New. Any focal shift from these things to the mind could be—"

"Dangerous?" Ellison says budding open his fist near his chin.

"Yes," Tishbe says, with a defeated look on his face.

"So now you see. Dangerous. You brought us into this. You alone gave many of us knowledge that you yourself say is dangerous. Solomon had this knowledge of the way things truly are, how close we are to good and evil and the forms those take. His Gnostic text even says he was given a ring by Michael himself so that he may enslave the Jinn demons that they may work for him. The Quran substantiates this to a large degree."

"But you can never be sure of the authenticity of these outside works," Tishbe says.

"Agreed, but with the knowledge of good and evil that you have given me, this rube," he says in my direction, "Taber and the others, I'd say there's some truth to the Gnostic Solomon story."

"As you know, lies most often present themselves as the truth," Tishbe says.

"Ah, but the eyes do not, Elijah. My eyes don't lie and neither do theirs." Ellison walks over and searches my eyes. "Oh and don't think we don't try to convince ourselves that what we've seen isn't true. That we force ourselves into discounting it. That we pound it down into our guts just trying to forget these horrible things we've witnessed." He swings back to Elijah, pointing a forcefully accusatory finger. "And knowing what I've seen to be true, and letting the Gnostic text seep into my mind, letting it ferment so that my synapses form links between bits of infor- mation from here, from there, from elsewhere and otherwise, it follows that man is not supposed to be involved in this war you wage, and that man's involvement will eventually end in either death or madness. Just as Solomon. We aren't supposed to know, Elijah, and you've violated that. I do not forgive you. I do not release you from that. You know what you've done." Ellison says, finally breathing again, and pacing away, weary.

The room falls silent. Elijah sits back down on the couch as papers ruffle next to him. He too seems exhausted. Perhaps he is more burdened than anything. It was clear on our arrival that Ellison isn't an easy visit, but had I not witnessed the little fat man's disrespect and vitriol, I wouldn't have thought anyone would behave this way toward a man so seemingly regal, genuine, and outright faultless at least in appearance as Elijah Tishbe. Ellison swings around for one last salvo, though the vol- ume and energy of this one seems paltry in comparison.

"I mean, Elijah, wasn't that the true purpose of the great flood? To separate us forever?"

"That is not what the book says," Tishbe says back.

"But it could have been. Logic dictates it. I'll tell you what the book *does* say. Genesis six: 'And it came to pass, when men began to multiply on the face of the earth, and daughters were born unto them—'"

"Yes, yes," Tishbe says impatiently, "'That the sons of God saw the daughters of men that they were fair, and they took them wives of all which they chose.' We all know the story, but nothing more of it is said."

"But we might be able to piece together the rest from alternate sources," Ellison says.

"And therein lies the danger, but trust, you will never fully 'piece together the rest.' I assure you that, *Pastor* Ellison."

"Then tell me," Ellison says pleading. "Tell me the truth. Tell me what it is all for. The why of it. Tell me. I've done all you ask. Why leave it to me to pour over all this dreck," he says surveying the room, "when you could just open your mouth and let it out?"

"I cannot do that, Edward," Tishbe says, looking away.

"But why? Why leave us in the dark like this?"

"Because I don't know everything!" Elijah explodes. "I am not God. I am not supernatural. I am a man, and I do not have all of the answers. Even now."

"I understand," Ellison says, pacing the length of the room slowly, methodically, like a lion waiting just for the proper moment in which to burst from the tall grasses. "I think I've understood that for a while, Elijah, and so what have I done? I've worked. I've continued to decipher this language the Heralds vomit out. I've continued like the pious little fart I am, and you know what? I've only asked for a couple of things in return. Knowledge and proof. And when they didn't start coming my way, because for whatever reason you couldn't provide them, I realized something. The knowledge *is* out there. It's just hacked to pieces and shoved into a thousand separate works, but it's there. I can handle knowledge if the big guy wants to keep dangling it away from me like some kind of carrot, but the proof. The proof. Well, that's a much harder bargain."

Tishbe sits as on a witness stand with everything inside him fighting to remain calm. "You should be careful of your words, Edward."

"And so I ask you for a letter. One little letter written in Jaoel's hand. Written in his real language."

"The hell would you want a letter from that stinky lummox for?" I say, unable to keep quiet any longer.

I've been trying to keep up with the entire conversation, but fell back somewhere around Solomon. My granddaddy's Bible talk was awfully rusty, but I pieced together a little. Seems to me the fat man is shook up just like I am over seeing things just like I did that came out of the trees at Taber's boys in Oklahoma, that and killer bulls with human faces, and disappearing and reappearing euro-trash. Seems to me he expects to be paid for it, except he doesn't want money like I do. What throws me was why anyone would care about a handwritten letter from one of Tishbe's goons? Of course, seeing as how I can't even make out exactly what these two are talking about, suffice to say, I'm missing plenty.

Ellison looks back at me like I've got fifteen heads. He fails to remove the look when he transfers it to Tishbe on the couch. "You mean, you haven't even taught this rube the fundamentals? Did you just pick him up at the truck stop like some lot lizard? Who is this idiot?"

"Listen here, Pillsbury," I say taking a few hard steps toward him.

"It's quite alright, Mr. Rust," Tishbe says raising a hand to halt me. "It is always welcome to find yet another who finds Mr. Ellison... exasperating. However, what he says is true. Explanations are in order."

"It's *Pastor Ellison*," the little man says. "Have you ever cracked open a Bible, son?"

"My granddaddy was a preacher," I say. "Didn't take."

"Okay, well that lummox as you're calling him is an angel."

"Sure he is," I say, scoffing.

"And not just any angel," Ellison continues. "His name is Jaoel, a very powerful one. An archangel. His friend is called Sorush, a guardian of the gates."

I look to Tishbe who only nods.

"So you mean to tell me those men, the ones fighting that bull demon were angels. Wings, halos, the whole deal?" I ask skeptically.

"Bull? What bull?" Ellison asks Tishbe. "Morax? Here?"

Elijah nods, "But don't worry. They took him away. We are safe here."

"Does he know where I live?" Ellison asks nervously.

"No. Proceed, Pastor Ellison."

Ellison pauses, scratching his head. "And you saw the demon?"

"I did," I say.

"And you've seen others?"

"I sent him along on one of Mr. Taber's extractions," Tishbe says.

"Oh my, so you're—he is?" Ellison says to Tishbe who nods back.

"Did you understand what you saw? Of course you didn't," Ellison corrects himself. He smiles mischievously at Tishbe. "So you brought him here for me to explain it all to him."

"That's correct," Tishbe says. "As I've said before. Everything is for a reason."

"I see," Ellison says, exhaling. "Well then let's start at the beginning. You had better take a seat."

I look around the cluttered room and chuckle. The heavy mood in the room lightens in an instant as both Tishbe and Ellison chuckle as well.

"Perhaps the sanctuary would be more appropriate?" Tishbe asks.

We return to the darkened sanctuary. Tishbe sits next to me in the second pew. Ellison shuffles in carrying a small wooden box inscribed with Hebrew characters. He flips a switch on the wall and the fluorescent lights buzz to life above , painting the room with greenish light. He sits sideways with the box in the first pew, his arm across its back to face us.

"Now I don't like that Taber man or his methods, but here's the quick and dirty version," Ellison says, opening the latch to the small box.

"That's what I'm after," I say in agreement.

Ellison opens the box to reveal more of that yellow sulfur powder I've got in spades back at Teasel's. "You've seen this?" he asks.

I laugh openly. Ellison looks at Tishbe who shakes his head at me.

"Yeah, I've seen it. Sulfur," I say.

"Yes and no," Ellison says, taking a pinch of it from the box and letting it fall through his fingers. "This is brimstone."

"I still don't know the difference though."

"Nothing. Just the name really. That and the location it comes from which is Israel. Now I'm assuming you saw Taber's men fire those canon ball things at the trees, bolos he calls them."

I nod.

"Well those canon balls were filled with this. Any time this stuff is around, you're likely to see fireworks."

"Those creatures," I say.

"Demons. See, this brimstone brings them into this world. It forces them to inhabit the same space, the same plane of existence as humans. It only works up to a certain distance, so this is to be applied liberally around the area to ensure that nothing sneaks up to bite you in your unsuspecting butts," Ellison says, closing and re-latching the box.

"Yeah. It looked like Taber's boys were creating a perimeter with it, but they didn't see the other one until they launched those bolos either."

"The other one. You mean the one they rescued and took away?"

"Yes. The tall pale guy we took to the church," I say.

"That was an angel, and brimstone works on them too. Taber's outfit is a rescue team. They rescue angels."

"Why would angels need rescuing?" I ask. "Thought they were supposed to be all powerful. God's army."

"That they are, Mr. Rust," Tishbe says. "But as in any war, there are casualties. Demons are but fallen angels, and so both share considerable power. They surround us all the time, constantly locked in battle until the end of days, when all will be revealed to those who are and those who have been. Until that day they reside in a plane independent of our eyes."

"Just fighting," I say. "Thought the story was we all have a guardian angel that keeps us out of trouble, so we don't walk into a bus or something."

"And who do you think sent the bus?" Ellison says.

"Greyhound?" I say sarcastically.

"What Pastor Ellison is saying is that in their own plane of existence, what you may call an alternate dimension, angels and demons wage their war in a physical sense while here, only their *influence* is felt. Here we fight them in the spiritual sense. The devil is the great liar. He works by sending demons to fool us, tempt us, and coerce us to stray from the righteous path God has set forth. When we call on the almighty name of God, he dispatches angels to repel those evil hordes, allowing us time to correct our coarse and live as he intended."

"So, as far as we know, the war's in our heads, but over there it's for real," I struggle for the words.

"Oh, it's quite real in both respects, Mr. Rust," Tishbe says. "And rather than in our heads, might I add, our hearts. The devil feeds upon the desecration of our souls. It is an energy, a fuel that propels the momentum of his certain defeat: a drug if you prefer."

"So, if God wants us on this side, and them on the other side, why involve us?" I ask.

"Now, that's the real question isn't it?" Ellison says with a provocative grin. "Tell us, great and mighty Elijah, why send we miserable and weak flock of sheep to the slaughter?"

"Because the end is nearing, Mr. Rust, Mr. Ellison. The battle has crested. God needs his angels as never before. He can spare no more casualties. The hordes of Satan grow strong with this world's mounting iniquity, and I have been sent to quell it, with the help of the strong. With the help of you."

"So when one falls, we save it," I say.

"And send it back so that it may mend and march proudly into battle once again," Tishbe says.

"And you think God told you to do this?" I ask. "Just came down in a dream and ordered you? That right?"

"No, no," Ellison says cheekily. "Don't you know who this man is?"

"Elijah Tishbe," I say questioning my own certainty.

"Tishbe's not his name. Elijah *of* Tishbe, or rather, Elijah the Tishbite. It's where he's from. A town in Galilee. In that town a prophet was born, a great outdoorsman and speed runner if you take the author of Kings at his word. Fed by ravens? Predicted a great drought? Proved to King Ahab of God's dominion over Baal?" Ellison asks excitedly. "Nothing? Okay, maybe this will do it. You familiar with chapter two of second Kings? 'Behold, there appeared a chariot of fire, and horses of fire, and parted them both asunder; and Elijah went up by a whirlwind into heaven.' And from that whirlwind he descends again."

A long throbbing pause hangs between us. I remember this story from my youth, from my grandfather. He had a great respect for this prophet and his story. He told it often with a reverence I never understood, but now catch a shadowed glimpse of. His connection to the story seemed to transcend the pages of his worn leather Bible, and the fervency of his retelling resonated in my mind for years after his tragic death.

"No way. Not possible," I say in stupefaction.

"Oh, it's more than possible," Ellison says smiling wide at the look on my face. "You're sitting next to one of the only men who never died."

Chapter 29

THE CONVERSATION WITH Elijah and the pastor went well into the night, opening up more questions than providing substantial answers. Even now I am unsure if I can do it. Against my better judgment, I've done what Elijah asked. I posted on the flight sim forum that a job was available. I invited all of them: Bock, Horrace, Everly, The Yak, Henry Knapp, even Dresden though he with great apprehension.

We're to meet up in Vegas at the end of the week. High time tourist season. Elijah convinced Pastor Ellison to be something he called "The Text," our man on the inside of the church who can perform all the research and provide whatever intel we'd need to carry out our extractions. Taber's crew numbered twelve, and between Bock and I, we've got twelve of those crosses along with all the boxes of salt and brimstone, so I might have to recruit a few more men to round out the team. Now the only thing that gives me trepidation is how the boys are going to receive the proposition. If they're anything like me, and I know they are, I'm libel to be strung up and left for dead by the time I finish talking. That is, if they even stick around long enough to hear it.

I step out of McCarran International Airport to stark Las Vegas sun, the kind that bakes the color out of everything. The temperature is unseasonably hot, and it showed on those crowding around ticket counters, snack bars, and boarding gates I walked past after de-boarding. The cab line winds down the sidewalk forever, so I look for the nearest car service booth. In all my neuroticism about tonight's talk with the boys, I forgot to schedule transport to take me over to Aria, the massive new hotel and casino sandwiched between The Bellagio and Monte Carlo like an M4 Sherman Tank between a couple of Toyota hybrids. I intend on presenting it to the boys as easy as possible. Why not put them up in the biggest, newest, and nicest thing going? I even booked a meeting room in the hotel under the name Marvin Tender, CFO Base-10 Capital. Long as I keep the food, booze, and chickadees coming, the rest should take care of itself. But the real truth is I don't know what else to bribe them with.

I find a row of transportation company kiosks on the airport sidewalk and get in line to speak with the first available rep about a car. A-Line Transportation. An old, haggard lady with decades of heavy smoke in her voice waves me forward after having dismissed a small group of college kids toward one of those hotel shuttle scams. I step up, wheeling my luggage behind me. She doesn't bother with a greeting.

"Need a driver," I say routinely pulling out my wallet from the back pocket of my Wranglers.

"That's usually why they come to see me," she says in a disinterested monotone. "Shuttle's seven bucks."

"Ain't my first rodeo," I say back.

"Limo?"

"Like I said."

"Okay, tough guy. Luxury sedan and driver costs you fifty. Where you heading?"

"Aria. Give you thirty plus gratis."

"Hard bargain. Cash or credit?"

"Want me to say it again?" I say handing over two twenties.

"I'm keeping the change," she says without looking up.

"That'll work."

"Lane seven. Funny though," she says taking a business card from a stack to her right and scrawling something on the back with a pen.

"What's that?"

"Thought you might show better judgment picking a place to gather the flock, this being the city of sin and all, Amarillo," she says, looking up and sliding the card to me.

"I know you?" I say, taking the card.

"Gonna have to get used to this kind of thing now, young man. You run into trouble from the other side while you're here, you just call the number on that card. Vegas isn't the place for you anymore. Not unless it has to be."

I glance at the card and nod inquisitively. She flashes me a smile that lasts all of a sixteenth of a second before coughing for the next customer in line to approach. I walk off absently, the card still in my hand. When I come to, I'm standing on a piece of sidewalk with a weathered number seven painted in street-sign yellow. I tuck the card into my wallet.

Pretty soon a black sedan pulls up. The driver gets out, a young man who looks completely uncomfortable in his black-tie uniform and chauffeur hat. He opens the back door for me as I get inside and then heaves my luggage into the trunk. The kid immediately puts the car in drive and pulls away from the airport before I can speak. At the first stoplight, I notice him checking me out in the rearview once too often.

"Want me to tell you where I'm staying?" I ask.

"I know where you're going, sir. I've already double-checked your room and meeting reservations."

"That so."

"Yes, sir."

"You know, I chose your service at random," I say, a little rattled.

"No you didn't, sir. You just think you did."

The rest of the trip is silent. I watch throngs of tourists pulse down the sidewalks between the hulking casinos. The whole town smells of garbage covered in the sweetness of umbrella drinks. Then I see the Aria with its massive towers like reflective crescent moons. We pull into a valet lane beneath the shade of a grandly lit awning, lights dancing and moving like people. The young driver hops out and removes my bags. I open the door and slide out on my own, instantly reaching for my wallet again, a practice synonymous with nearly every possible Vegas activity. Removing a ten, I go to hand it to the driver who waits patiently with my luggage. He doesn't take it.

"Keep it," he says, "Tonight's going to be a doozy. A little advice, sir. Remember why you came. This is where they come to play."

"Why am I getting the feeling that I made a mistake choosing Vegas?"

"Because maybe you did."

"Then why the heck didn't somebody warn me?"

"What can I say, man," the driver says, walking back to the car. "Free will's a bitch."

Chapter 30

COMFORTABLY FAMILIAR SMOKE hangs in the air of
the stately meeting room, the Vegas skyline wide open beyond our table
through a prodigious windowed wall. A perfectly clear night. The boys,
stomach's filled from the meal I had catered, lounge in various states of
drunkenness around the table in overstuffed dark leather conference
chairs. There's The Yak on my left, hands folded on the table, making
the room seems small, and Horrace on my right, ash tray within arm's
reach. Several butts and mounds of ash already occupy it. Everly is next
to him, slumping down with a longneck in his hand. Henry Knapp and
Dresden sit at the far end of the table across from each other, bickering
over something I don't care to figure out. The only one not sitting down
is Bock, shaking the ice cubes in a nearly empty highball of Aberlour
Scotch. He stands facing the window to the Vegas lights stretching out
below.

I'm sure every one of them feels the tension. I hadn't yet said a
word about the job or about Park who's still missing. His absence hangs
as a great weight, especially for Horrace who hasn't uttered fifteen words
all night. My palms sweat, but I keep on fiddling with my glass of chilled
whiskey so they think it's just condensation. It isn't lost on me that I've
only got six men in the room, half of what I need, or at least think I do.
Why Tishbe would replace a team of twelve, well-oiled paramilitary men
with seven rag-taggers like us remains beyond me. Maybe the old man

thinks I've got connections to a pool of recruits I don't. I try to put it out of my mind, as I know I've got to start sooner or later before the men get restless.

"Well, boys," I say, feeling an odd lump of stage fright creeping up my throat all the sudden. "Reckon we ought to get to it."

"Money, money, money, money," Everly sings, lazily chuckling to himself and I realize how drunk he's gotten.

I can feel Bock behind me intentionally refusing to join us at the table. He knows this has to do with Tishbe, and I reckon that if we weren't so close, and he weren't so curious, he wouldn't be here at all.

"Bock?" I say.

"I can hear you just fine from here," he says behind me.

"Why, gentlemen," that sick son of a call girl Dresden says from the other end of the table. "Mommy and daddy fighting again?"

I stand up and rub my forehead. "Dresden, you're only here for the numbers. There's nobody in the world I'd rather exclude from this deal than you, trust me."

"Glad I could be of service," he says, smiling wide and raising his glass.

"This better be about Park," Horrace says, staring down at the table, a thin vine of smoke winding into his red, irritated eyes. I can't tell if it's for lack of sleep or the smoke.

"Oh, but I'll bet it's anything but, mate," Bock says patronizingly. "Your boy's gone, probably for good, you know that. We both searched for him high and low. But the fact remains. Dear old leader here was the last to see him." He turns around with that drink in his hand, the other hand in the front pocket of his grey dress pants. He walks back to his chair slowly, making a show to savor that last bit of scotch. "And we've yet to hear a fecking word of him."

"Maybe that's cause there ain't no word to say," I offer. "I don't know where he is."

"Ah, yes," Bock says throwing back the tail of his coat to sit in his chair. "But how did he get that way? That's what I want to know. And how about letting on to who you've been trotting around with as of late, yes? Go ahead and tell them. I'm sure they'd be well pleased."

Horrace looks up at me.

"Okay, Bock, so much for pleasantries. Have it your way," I say. I take a long breath. "You all remember Albania."

"Oh, you mean the cluster—" Dresden says, that self-indulgent smile still beaming at me.

"The old man who hired us, the one with the long grey hair and the scar? His name is Elijah Tishbe," I say.

"Never did get paid for that one," Everly says, accusingly.

"Well, I certainly got paid for it, dearest Everly," Bock says and somehow the room gets even quieter. "I was well paid indeed. And you know what with? Tell them, Rust. Tell them how we were paid for losing two young men in Germany for a stinger missile and shooting down a bloody helicopter in the middle of Eastern Europe. And now, of course, Park is probably dead somewhere because of it. You tell them."

I pause and shake my head endlessly, wondering how and why I've agreed to do any of this. The greater part of me wants to throw my hands up and walk right out the double-doors, that or take a leap through the windows behind me. Something inside tells me to stand, to continue. Damn the torpedoes.

"None of you other than Bock came to me for payment on that job. None of you. We all smelled something fishy, not the least of which was me. I got that palette home alone. I was the only one to do it, and I did."

"Well then, what did you find?" Bock asks sarcastically.

"Bock. Stop," Horrace says. "We know what was in the boxes, Rust. Bock told us about it. You ask me, the old man was nuts. It happens. What doesn't happen is you running off with Park and getting him killed. Kindly speak to that."

"I don't know if he's dead, Horrace. I don't," I say. "The old man says he isn't, but the last time I saw him, he was up in a tree with a sniper rifle. He was covering me. Now, he *was* chased—that I know—but it doesn't mean he's dead. We don't know that. I don't know that."

"If we get separated on a job, we always make contact on the forum when we get safe," Horrace says, pounding the table. "It's fundamental protocol."

I stand again before the boys, shaking my head, not knowing what to say. The mood of the room has taken a nose-dive. None of the men, save Yakubu, can look at me. Dresden spins around in his chair making a big show of his disinterest. He was always an outsider, even when he wasn't. Pretty soon my wits return and an anger wells up. Park is not my fault. This business is dangerous. Anyone can take a dirt nap at any time. That's just the job.

"What is this, huh?" I ask authoritatively. "Family Ties? None of you ever lost a man before? Cowboy up!"

"He is right," Yakubu says, looking at me. "We have chosen this life for ourselves. There are risks. Every man understands this. To punish him for another man's decision is wrong. Mr. Park must take responsibility for himself. I believed I was asked to come here for a job. Now I want to hear what it is."

The Yak did me a helluva favor. Bock's just ticked he wasn't in the loop, that much is obvious. Horrace is grieving. Everly's just drunk. Henry Knapp's mind is where it always is, someplace else, and Dresden, well, who gives a rip about Dresden?

"Thanks, big Yak," I say. "We all need to remember what comes with this line of work. I don't like that Park's not here any less than the rest of you, but maybe he'll surface and maybe he won't. Maybe he's dead, and maybe he just thought better about what he decided to do with life. I don't know. What I *do* know is there's a deal been offered that will send every stinkin' one of you down to the high-roller tables when you hear it. Now do you want to hear it? I'm about to sweeten your pots."

It's just then that I realize I can't tell them. Just then I realize that Tishbe modeled the whole thing out for me. If he'd have come in, guns blazing with the truth full frontal, I'd have been out of there like a hooker in church. I've got to ease 'em in like he did me. With the money. Money greases gun-toting palms like nothing else can. To some people, seeing the light is through the eye of that pyramid on a dollar bill.

"What's the job, Rust?" Horrace says, and because he does, I know I've got the rest of them on the hook.

"Contract labor on this one," I say finding my groove again.

"Duration?" Henry Knapp asks like he's taking notes.

"Not this time. It's a set number of jobs."

"How many?" Everly says, sitting up in his chair.

"Ten with the option to renew at the end of the eighth," I say.

"Fee?" Dresden asks, that perverted twinkle in his eye.

"One quarter of a million dollars per job, per man."

That one sets the world on fire. I can see each man, one after the other, actually let it sink in. I can almost hear it. Even Bock shifts in his seat.

"Wait, per man?" Everly says.

I nod.

"Per man, per job?" he says again for confirmation.

"That's correct," I say, grinning.

"Two and a half million dollars for each of us." Horrace lets it roll around in his mouth like a hundred year old Bordeaux.

"Awful cute, ain't it?" I say. "And with the option to renew. Each one of you could walk away from this stint and never feel the slightest inclination to lift a pinkie again."

I want to tell them they'll be able to disappear to some foreign beach and have exotic women pour libations into their mouths until they drift quietly into the sunset, but I can't. I know the job. I know what's in store, and I know the risks. None of them have ever imagined in their worst nightmares the things they'll see, the things they'll try and fight. Some of them may well lose their minds in the process, as Ellison told me. It happens more often than Tishbe would like to admit. I hate to visit this on any of them, but no one's forcing their hands any more than mine. They don't like the shot, then they don't have to take it. Like the kid driver said yesterday, free will's a bitch. But then, so is missing out on $2.5 million.

"But how do we know the old man's on the level this time?" Bock asks. "How do we know he won't leave us with two million in aluminum cans when it's all done and dusted?"

"Because he gave me $250,000 in cash before the Oklahoma job. It's real too. If anybody can spot a counterfeit bill, it's Vegas. Spent some of it tonight on all this. Barely made a dent," I say confidently.

"No more helicopters, I trust," Bock says.

"Not unless we're riding in them."

"Okay, I'm comfortable in speaking for the table that we're interested. But, I've got to know what we're doing, mate. What's the job?"

I mull over what to say next. Don't want to scare them off. Want to keep them focused on the cash for now.

"When I was in Oklahoma with Park, the old man had me meet up with a team. Called it an extraction team, but it was really a rescue team. Fella heading it up was named Taber. Had twelve men. Every one of them ex-Blackwater." I can hear the huffs and sighs coming from all directions. "I know what you're thinking, and I thought the same thing, believe me, but these boys had it down. They knew exactly what they were doing, like they done it a thousand times before."

"Who is there to rescue in Oklahoma? Somebody kidnapped?" Horrace asks.

"In a manner of speaking, I guess. More like beaten to a pulp and needed evac in a real bad way. Point is, these guys were good. Opposition showed up and these Blackwater types circled the wagons, laid down fire, loaded the package up, and got him out. Clockwork deal."

"How did Park work into all of this?" Horrace asks.

"I hired him independently of the old man. Needed him to watch over me in case something went wrong. Neither of us knew what was happening till it did. The rescue team loaded me up and hauled me away before we could do anything for Park. My hope is that he got away before the hostiles caught up to him. Haven't heard a thing since."

The room is silent. I half believe most of them stopped listening after they got the dollar amount in their skulls. Bock is busy thinking in his chair though. I don't like it.

"You're leaving something out, mate," he says. "I don't know what, but you are. You were in a plane when I talked to you. Obviously Horrace and I couldn't find Park, but you seemed pretty cozy with the old bugger."

I think hard on what I'm going to say next.

"Listen, you boys are going to have to trust me. I don't want to send you in with a bunch of questions, but I'm gonna have to because that's the way it was done to me. It worked, so I reckon that's the best way to do it. What I will say is that if you agree to do this thing, it couldn't be more different than any other action you've ever been a part of, and more dangerous to boot. If you've got doubt, any doubt, then don't go along on this."

My voice soaks in their minds. Maybe I've never seemed so serious. That's probably because I never have been. I still have trouble reconciling what I already know, and shudder at the thought of discovering more. I can imagine how they feel because I've been there.

"Our job is to replace Taber's rescue team and continue their work. Our employer, strange a pickled egg as he may be, is extremely powerful, and very resourceful. For some reason he chose us, and trust me, when you get to know the man, you'll learn that he has good reasons for everything he does. Nothing is left to chance. Our rescue team, while incredibly important, is only part of a *much* bigger picture. We'll have support when we need it, and a gigantic expense account as well. Believe me when I say, this is no joke." I look into each man's eyes, right down the line. "Now, I know we all got into this work for different reasons, but we all share a few things. We each have a thick skull and enormous pair, and that's how I know it's going to work. Money's great, sure, but sometimes glory's even better. This chance won't ever come around again. Not ever. So I've got to ask you, each one. Who's with me?"

Chapter 31

IT DOESN'T SURPRISE me a bit that Dresden decides to take off for Carson City after the meet at The Aria. Henry Knapp just said he would go back to his room and catch some sleep while Everly, Horrace, and The Yak opted for a late night at some dance club called Pure over at Caesar's. That left Bock and I to get reacquainted downstairs at the Gold Lounge.

The place isn't as low key as I was hoping, but Aria is fairly new, so the bar is slammed with tourists and locals alike checking out the new digs. There really wasn't any other place to cool off as long as I was with Bock since he's such an Elvis fan. The bar is modeled after Graceland, so they say, but I doubt the king would approve of the mood lighting or European-style tables and seating in deep browns and gold. Bock seems at home. He spotted a couple of females straggling from the herd at the expansive island bar, so he makes a shot for them under the guise of getting us drinks. I doubt I'll see him for a while.

Bock always had a way with the ladies. His rough Scottish speech lends an air of mystery to his refined appearance. We even lost him once to a Welsh girl. She ended up leaving him, but we thought he'd found the real deal there for a while when he started to shrug off work. Guess you can't take the merc out of the man after all. I have a feeling he hit her. The break-up was fast and hard. When he came back into the fold, he carried out things a bit differently than before. More brutal. Everybody's got a heart, and nobody likes it busted, not even Bock.

I sit across from an empty seat at an intentionally low-lit table for two. I survey the clientele, but all the faces seem to blend together. I wish Bock would come back with a drink, but I'm not holding out too much hope. I'd get it myself, but I don't want to lose the table. I promised myself that tonight would be for drinking and forgetting. Ellison told me that a job on one of Elijah's teams has a tendency to consume a man until there isn't much left but an endless loop of nightmares, questions, and in the end, madness. Might be better if I try to not pay much thought and live like the masses for at least one night.

I watch a well-put-together waitress with red hair and a short black skirt float from table to table effortlessly taking orders while at the same time ingratiating herself in the conversations of customers. How does she live? What is her life? There's got to be a simpleness to it that makes that pillow feel awful soft at night. Either way, she's got the job down pat. She spends no more than a minute-thirty per table. I watch her quickly evaluate each one just before the approach. *What kind of people are these? Where do they come from? Will a flip of my hair or a shake of my tush bring me a larger tip?* All that in a couple of seconds. It's a raw talent to size a person up so quickly, much less several people at once, but she does it in grand fashion. A real pleasure to watch.

I'm on deck. She's finishing up handing off drinks to the table of young, snot-nosed businessmen next to me. Their ice cubes sparkle in the light through their gins or vodkas. Those punks act like they're in a two-bit strip joint, pawing at her and acting boisterous as a pack of sloppy hyenas. A thought comes over me to get up and drag them out by their skinny black ties like little doggies on a group walk. Before I can figure out why the thought came to me, that pretty waitress with the short black skirt stands over me like the most beautiful portrait sprung from canvas and come to life. Before I can take her in, she sets down her tray and sits in the chair across from me.

I crack a smile before she's all the way down. Probably thinks I'm three sheets to the wind already. We smile at each other for a beat. She knows how she looks, and it seems like she's done sized me up.

"Howdy, partner," she says in a cute, costume twang that alerts me that she's not from anywhere near the South.

"Howdy yourself," I say, wondering how she figured me for a Southern fella, then remember my Wranglers and boots.

"Come around these parts often?" she continues her playful ruse.

"First time, darlin. First time. Nice place though."

"You don't say," she says giggling in a way so it isn't annoying or condescending. "I'll bet you're an Elvis man." She leans in when she says it, like she's actually interested. It takes most of what I've got not to fall for it.

I shake my head. "My buddy over at the bar is though," I say pointing.

The waitress looks over, noticing like I do that one of the two women already has her hand on Bock's shoulder.

"Something tells me his mind isn't on The King right now," she says.

"I'll bet you're right," I say. "Said he would bring me back a whiskey, but I guess by the look of things that's gonna be your job."

"And here I appear," she says, raising her hand.

"There you appear. Ambassador of bourbon with the pretty red hair."

"You like?" she asks lively, gently taking hold of a wisp and turning it up so she can see.

I nod, grinning, lulling myself into her voice.

"It's not real," she says. "Had it colored last week. Don't know how I feel about it yet, but if you like it, I guess I made the right decision," smiling even wider.

"Man," I say, sitting up and shaking my head, "you really know what you're doing don't you. You are *good*."

"What do you mean?" she asks acting incredulous.

"I've had my eye on you, sugar, and boy can you move around this room. I bet you make a mess of tips that would make an old country boy like myself tear up."

"I do okay," she says laughing, possibly genuinely.

"'Do okay,' shoot. They made a helluva decision when they hired you on."

"I like your mustache," she says, changing the subject with the ease of the slide on a well-oiled .45 Lugar carbine.

"Alright little lady," I say jovially. "You've already got me on the hook for a drink. You can stop pouring it on."

"I'm not pouring it on. I really do," she says, raising those perfectly arched eyebrows, the light coming off the table lending a tantalizing glint to her irises.

"Well in that case, I thank you."

"Let me ask you a question before I bring you that whiskey."

"Shoot."

"If your friend happened to come back to the table with both of those girls, and one of them were for you, would you take it?" she says, serious, but still with that sultry grin of hers.

"One of them?" I turn to look again. "I don't know. Probably not if I'm being honest."

"Good," she says, standing, pulling her skirt down into place.

"Why's that?" I ask.

"Well that means you're alone tonight. I'll be alone too. I'm out of here at a quarter to one," she says, picking her tray back up and moving closer to pass by. "My roommate went home to visit family in Indiana. She and I like to get breakfast after our shifts. Maybe you can fill in, Texas."

"I reckon I can do that. How'd you put me from Texas?"

"Everybody comes to Vegas. Doesn't take long to size a man up. Especially when he's a Texan," she says sauntering away. "See you back here at a quarter to one."

I figure she will.

Chapter 32

AFTER SPENDING AN hour or so at a mid-stakes blackjack table at the Monte Carlo, the smell of cigarette smoke mixed with the restaurant's greasy morning breakfast service seeping into my pores like an infection, I decide to return to my room for a shower before meeting the waitress back at The Gold Lounge. I think about the boys as I slip on a fresh pair of socks. I wonder if the Vegas nightlife will change their minds about joining up with Elijah's team. I had the one shot to convince them, and depending upon how much they lost at the tables, on drinks, and other entertainment, the promise of a quarter of a million per job must be burning in their heads just as much as mine. I pull up my boots, grab the room key-card and head out to meet the girl.

I hadn't even entered The Gold Lounge when I feel her hand on my shoulder. She put that lustrous auburn hair up in a ponytail and changed her clothes. A group of long red strands curve down her forehead and mingle with her left eyelashes. I can't say it didn't perk me up a bit, but my antenna was already up. It had not yet struck one thirty. I remember the old woman in the car service booth back at the airport, and the card burning a hole in my jeans pocket, not to mention the kid driver who dropped me off. I knew the good guys were monitoring me, but that just made it all the more obvious that the bad were most likely doing the same. Caution is as effortless to me as breathing, but if the other side thinks sending a pretty face in a short skirt was all it would take to put my guard down, well, they don't quite know me yet. Of course, that whole "keep your enemies closer" thing can end up biting you in the hinds too, but there's nothing wrong with trying to get inside your opponents' head. Whether the waitress standing in front of me with those sultry green eyes and a body that could send an old heart to a fresh grave was here to love me or kill me, that's yet to be determined. But I will find out.

Before I can greet her, she wraps her arms around me like we've known each other since summer camp. I return the hug at fifty percent.

"Glad you showed, Texas," she says.

"My how you've changed," I say, stepping back and giving her a playful once over.

"Oh, this? No, they cut me pretty soon after you left. The crowd thinned out too much, I guess. Just had time to run home and freshen up. You like?" she says, presenting herself like a *Price is Right* model.

"I have a feeling you'd turn heads wearing a trash bag, Red."

"That's cute. Already giving me pet names. Listen, I thought we'd skip breakfast and go for a drink instead. Still have some time, and I know a great little place off the Strip if you're up for it?"

"Always in for some local flare."

The walk to the bar was filled with all the regular get to know you stuff. I have my cover-story down pretty well, but tried to keep it light and focused on her.

Soon we step down into the bar through a narrow stairway just off the sidewalk. It's the kind of place that tries too hard to look like a speakeasy. Even had a slit in the metal door for the burly security guard to evaluate the prospective clientele. It's all for show. Vegas isn't much for turning down spending money.

Of course, the guard knows her, so does the bartender. We take a couple of seats belly up to the bar. She orders a scotch. I note that. Scotch drinking women are always to be watched closely. I order a Maker's neat. I can feel her watching me too as the bartender pours my whiskey and sets the glass on a fresh napkin. I take a look around the bar and notice the signs on the wall, all old political campaign propaganda without discernable party affiliation. You've got Mitchell vs. Haskins '72, Rodriguez vs. Duval '88, among others. I finally recognize a familiar one: Nixon vs. Humphrey in '68.

I point at the sign and lift my drink off the bar. "So, which one are you?"

She looks over at the sign. "How old do you think I am, Texas?"

"Come on, you gotta know who Nixon is," I say taking a sip of whiskey.

"Okay, well, the other guy, I guess, right? I mean, who would be for Nixon?"

"Well, I reckon he did win, so I guess plenty."

"That was before they figured him out, though."

"Imagine so, but nobody can see the future, Red."

"Maybe, but we can certainly see our past."

The bar is far from full, but I'm a little surprised to see so many people at this hour. It isn't like the other places around Vegas at this time, full of chip-losers and addicts. Sure, there are those, but suits and dresses too, wide-awake and filling the place with conversation.

"Been waiting for you to ask my name, you know," she says.

"Well I already know your name, Red," I say feigning offense.

She laughs. "Okay, Texas, so tell me yours."

"John," I say, comically offering a handshake. "John Cash. How do you do, Red?"

"Uh huh," she says with a snide grin. "I'm Evangeline Terrace."

"Pretty. Sounds like a song."

"I actually haven't heard that one before. That's nice. So we've already established where you're from? What do you do?"

"I work at a cotton gin—well—did work at a cotton gin."

"Did work?"

"Suppose I got laid off, and if I didn't, I think I'd question the competency of management and go ahead and quit anyway."

"What'd you do to get fired?" she asks sportily.

"Played hooky."

"Bad boy," she says, slugging back her scotch like a pro.

She rests her glass back on the bar and taps the rim with a finger, all without looking at the bartender. He fills it.

"Where are you from, Miss Terrace?"

"Me? Oh, Indiana."

"Like your friend."

"Roomate, yes. She had a death in the family, so I'm holding down the fort," she says lightly knocking on the bar with her knuckles.

That's when I notice her hands for the first time. They're not like the rest of her. Hard. There are calluses, and a few old scratches that have scarred to a flat redness.

"I'm gonna guess you weren't always a waitress."

"What makes you say that, John?"

I point at her hand. "Those hands know work."

"Family business. My dad ran a slaughterhouse. I know, not exactly date conversation, but."

"Meat packing. I love a juicy steak," I say nodding at the bartender to pour again.

"Smaller actually. Goats and sheep."

"Interesting. Don't hear about that every day."

"Full of surprises," she says right into my eyes, and all the sudden I think I know where this is going. Question is whether I'll let it go that way. All the signs point to this being a set up, but Troy fell for the same reason, and there were a lot more Trojans to stand up to the assault.

"So you worked the slaughterhouse for a while. Didn't much like it I'm sure. Dirty work. So Vegas came calling and you were all too ready to enlist. That right?"

"Not quite a shocker that a twenty-one-year-old girl doesn't like coming home smelling like blood every night to her parents' house."

"Hey, don't get me wrong, Red. I don't blame you," I say, smiling. "I'd have done the same thing. I certainly would."

A moment passes between us. She's moved closer without me noticing. Doesn't bode well. Even though all the signs match up, I'm not getting a dangerous vibe off of the girl, at least not physically so. She's trouble all right, but maybe just the kind I'm looking for.

"You gonna stare at that drink all night or are you going to take me on a tour of that room of yours, John?" she says those eyelids of hers just falling past the crest of her pupils.

I chuckle. "Awful forward of you, darlin. Making me think you do this a little too often."

"Can't a girl like the way a man carries himself? Guys like you don't exactly grow on trees around here. Besides, my roommate is usually here to keep me in line."

"When the cat's away, huh?" I say, unconsciously leaning in.

"The mice will play," she says, her bottom lip pressing softly into mine. "At least for one night."

The kiss is brief, but it tells me all I need to know. I was all-in to go down without a fight.

Chapter 33

EVANGELINE PULLS ME by the hand all the way back to the Aria like a kid after a carousel. I can feel the tension when we get into the elevator. We both wish we were the only ones on it, but the four others speaking Japanese to one another, smelling like chimney soot only heightened what I knew would follow. Luckily they got out on floor six, one below ours. Didn't give us much time, but we steal a long kiss before the doors open again. This time I lead. We hang a left and make our way to my room. I let go of her hand and fumble for my key card in front of the door, but she keeps on going. I watch her continue down the hallway noting the numbers on each door.

"We're right here, Red," I call down to her.

She doesn't pay attention. Then she stops in front of one of them. It's Bock's room.

"Come here," she says in a serious tone I had not yet heard from her to this point.

It takes me a second to rouse myself off the high I'm on, whether it be from the girl, the drink, or both. All the sudden I realize I'm unarmed. But if she wanted me dead, she had plenty of opportunities before now. If it was Bock she was after, it would have been much easier to take him out at the bar after I had left. I glance both ways down the hall, and seeing nothing, decide to cautiously walk over to her. I want to give her the benefit of the doubt, but I do so at my own peril.

"My room is back the other way," I say when I reach her, trying hard to figure out the angle.

She looks at me, then the door, then back at me again. I can sense the agitation, the nerves. A vein in her forehead bulges slightly. Her heart rate has elevated.

"Kick down the door," she says.

I wonder if I heard her right.

"Do it," she says.

"The hell are you talking about, Red?"

"Listen, your friend is in there, and he's in trouble, so do as I say."

"Look, sweetheart, I don't know what you're into, but he's probably already got two girls in there—"

Just then she takes me by the back of the head and plants a kiss on me that I'll probably never forget. All the sudden I feel a calmness come over me as she backs away. I am completely disarmed.

"Please, Rust. Trust me. They're going to kill him."

I cock my head, but then remember that most of the other craziness that's occurred in recent memory, while defying all discernable logic, has ended up having teeth. I step and rear back driving the heel of my boot into the wood beside the handle. I hear shuffling inside, but the door doesn't give until the second kick. The lock snaps and the door slams against the wall inside the room.

Red storms in. She's already drawn a small revolver from god knows where. I can smell sulfur. I look down at her free hand and see a clear baggie bulging with the yellow powder. One of the women from the bar lies on top of Bock on the bed, while the other woman watches on at the edge. She has a knife waiting at her side. All are naked. The women are heavily tattooed. Bock, more surprised than I've ever seen him reacts, throwing the woman on top of him to the side like a ragdoll. He goes for the nightstand drawer, for that .45 of his that I'm sure he's got inside.

I scream his name, still bursting in, both of us thunderstruck. He doesn't know what to make of seeing me. He pauses for a split second before seeing Red next to me, rearing back with the baggie and launching it at the wall. He moves again for the drawer, throwing it open.

The naked woman at the edge of the bed leaps toward Evangeline with the knife. Red raises the revolver as the baggie bursts against the wall, sending a shower of brimstone pluming across the room. That's when they come into view. Two demons appear, one behind each woman, both naked and beautifully grotesque at the same time. They dance around the women, singing some screeching chant that causes me to cover my ears. The demons are identical, slender and white with beautiful faces but for wide mouths filled with row upon row of gnashing needled teeth and the thickest lips I've ever seen. They also have four arms each with one set bound tightly behind their backs with wire cutting into their wrists. The free arms wave wildly above them, like charming snakes.

The woman with the knife charges Evangeline, wailing with her demon close behind. I hear a shot from the revolver strike the woman in the forehead, spraying the demon with blood that seems to make it all the more excited. Evangeline fires twice more, this time at the demon. It falls to the floor, still trying to screech out that piercing song through blood-choked gurgles.

Seeing this, Bock lets out a string of curses while scrambling off the bed with that .45 of his. He leaps over the bed to see the woman he threw away getting to her feet with her demon right behind. He draws down on the scarier of the two and unloads a full clip into the remaining demon. All shots pass right through like a mirage. The woman it stands behind smiles wide and utters out some hateful string of her own before Evangeline pumps her last three slugs into her demon, sending it crashing through the seventh floor window behind, screeching and wailing all the way down. Evangeline then runs over snatching the naked woman by her thick black hair and drags her out of the room. I look to the floor and notice that the first demon she shot is slowly waking, and so my attentions turn to Bock who huddles in the corner of the hotel room, frantically trying to reload that .45 of his without success.

"We need to go," Evangeline says, disappearing into the hallway with the squealing woman in tow.

I scuttle over to Bock and lay my hand on his shoulder. He continues fumbling with a fresh clip as if he doesn't recognize me, unable to insert it with all of his shuttering. I say his name. His eyes are wide toward the window with that sulfur smell still polluting the room. I say his name again and once more before he looks up at me. He is unable to speak.

"We have to go now. It will come back. We have to leave," I say as calmly as I can muster.

"I'm bloody counting on it coming back," he says, near tears, trying to well his fleeting bravado back up.

"You don't want that, Bock. Let's go," I say, pulling him to his feet. "Get your clothes and fast."

Soon we're in the hallway again, Bock covering his privates with balled up slacks. Evangeline stands in front of my hotel room door. She wraps the butt of her revolver against the naked woman's jaw, who struggles to break free from Red's grip.

"Open the door, Rust. We don't have time," Evangeline says.

The whole thing was so fast, only now do we see a few brave people poking their heads from random rooms. I quickly swipe the key-card and hustle everyone into the room, forcefully closing the door behind.

"Give him a shirt and some shoes," Evangeline says toward Bock, throwing the woman against the far wall by her hair.

She crashes into the table and crumbles to the floor, still uttering a string of nonsense.

"The hell do we do now?" I say, my hands deep in my suitcase for something to give Bock to wear. "You woke up the whole stinkin' Casino."

I throw Bock a shirt and an extra pair of old running shoes I always bring along. He catches them and drops that .45 of his on the bed, his senses returning, but still clearly shaken.

"We walk out of here like nothing's wrong. Act drunk if we have to. Get a car." Evangeline says, standing watchfully over the naked woman.

"You filthy—" Bock says, now sloppily dressed and stamping toward the woman on the floor.

I grab him before he can kick her.

"What were you going to bloody do to me?" Bock yells, working to wriggle away from me, spitting. "What were those things? Who is she?"

"I will tell you," Evangeline says over him, "but we have to get out of here first, Thomas."

"How does she know my name?" Bock asks me, backing down enough for me to release him.

"I have a feeling she was here to make sure we didn't get into trouble," I say. "Looks like we failed."

"He failed," Evangeline says to me, then looks at Bock. "Don't you know enough not to take strange girls home from the bar, Thomas?"

"Yeah? And what does that make you?" he says back, glaring.

Neither of us have a good answer for that. Instead, Evangeline digs through my suitcase with one hand, the other with the gun trained at the woman on the floor who slowly cranes her head up. She's grimacing with a thin spill of blood coming from the corner of her mouth.

"*Puta, tu Dios, te dejará a la putrefacción conmigo. Vamos a bañarnos en sus entrañas,*" the woman says.

"Shut up," Evangeline says, scowling at the woman.

"What now? Doubt she's just gonna follow us out like a good little doggie," I say. "And the demons will be back any second won't they?"

"They can't do anything now," Evangeline says, tossing a couple of articles onto the bed behind her. "We're far enough away from the brimstone for them to show up again."

"That shite in the boxes makes this happen?" Bock blurts out. "Thank the saints I got rid of it."

"You threw it all away?" Evangeline asks. "All of it? And the salt too?"

"Right into the feckin' lake, sweetheart and with bloody good reason, I see now," Bock says.

"Stupid," she says.

"Hey, relax, Red. He must've just gotten rid of his half. I've still got mine back at my place."

"Just half. Well, that makes it all well and good then," she says. "That stuff doesn't come easy. I can't believe Elijah trusted this moron."

"Oh eat it, you whinging—"

"Okay, okay. Just hold off," I say. "Let's figure how to get out of here before the cops throw us into the meat locker."

"I've already got that worked out," Evangeline says at the woman beneath her with red-stained teeth. "I'm going to knock her out. Then we're going to dress her and carry her out likes she's a friend with a drinking problem."

"That's sure to work," Bock says sarcastically.

"It will work. Good night, princess," Evangeline says before slamming the revolver into the side of the woman's face.

Chapter 34

THIS EVANGELINE TERRACE is the real deal. I like her even more than I did when she was just a haughty waitress at a casino bar. Not two minutes after she made a call to the same number I suspect was on the card the old woman at the car service booth wrote down for me, the young driver from before showed up and hurried us into a limousine. She knew just how to deal with the cops and casino security. When they approached us in the hallway, and even in the lobby, she turned on the waterworks and asked all the right frantic questions. She asked them if it was a terrorist attack over and over, stopping them before they had a chance to stop us. She told them we had heard the shots and ran to get her friend from another room who got too drunk at the club. She asked them if we were all going to die. They not only let us pass, but also pawned off a casino security guard to escort us out to the entrance who apologized the entire way.

Now we're headed out of Vegas, the four of us sitting apart from each other in the limousine cruising down highway 15 in the middle of the Mojave Desert toward Barstow with nothing but time to think. It's silent for a long while with Evangeline staring out the window, and Bock staring down at the floor of the car.

"You reckon she'll ever wake up?" I say breaking up the rhythmic pulse of the road.

Evangeline comes to and looks at the unconscious woman next to her. Strangely, Evangeline doesn't seem to mind the woman's head resting on her lap.

"She'll wake up," Evangeline says, turning her attention back to the side window.

"If I didn't know better, I'd say you made friends the way she's laying on you."

"She just got mixed up with the wrong side. It happens."

"That so?" I say back.

"Yes. It does."

"What sides?" Bock finally speaks up, the frustration in his voice hanging heavy around us. "Is this the job you were talking us into, mate? This what all that talk about the quarter million quid was about? Monsters, mate? Bloody crazy tattoo hookers and four-armed monsters?"

"Didn't want you to find out about it this way, Bock. I promise," I say.

"Exactly what way were you going to show us that we wouldn't soil our drawers over, mate? Which way was that pray tell?"

"I don't know. It isn't like it's all sitting clear and pretty with me yet either. It's... a big shock."

"Right grand shock it is, mate. What's it all about? Are we to carry wooden stakes and crucifixes about with us? Wee vials of holy water, then?" he says flushed with acrimony.

I search for the words. "They're not vampires."

"Some of them are... Kind of," Evangeline says.

"Well," Bock says, throwing up his hands. "There we are then. Vampires then. Tell me, miss, will there be any werewolves? I mean, there must be werewolves because I witnessed you shoot silver bullets at that bird I was about to make love to. And the two other things: am I to gather those were haunted specters, or the Loch Ness monster's hatchlings? Do they have breakfast cereals named after them? What were *they* now?"

"Demons, Thomas," Evangeline says, sighing. "They're all demons. Come in all shapes and sizes. Just like us."

Bock points at the woman lying in Evangeline's lap. "That there is a demon you say?"

"No, Thomas. This is a woman. A familiar, a satanic loyalist, but a regular woman."

"Aye, I was about to get very familiar with her friend indeed. That is before you shot her between the eyes."

"Listen, you're not going to understand this all at once," she says, exasperated. "Some of us don't understand it the entire time we're on the job."

"But this," Bock says acerbically pointing again at the unconscious woman. "This one here. You can enlighten me about that, yes?"

"Whatever. Sure," Evangeline says dismissively. "This woman is what we call a familiar. Sometimes demons can attach themselves to specific people and in a certain way, control them."

"You're talking about possession," I say.

"Yes and no. I mean, a demon can't really control a person fully. Humans still have free will, but their demon can... suggest things. Strongly suggest. Like a drug addiction. They can promise things. If the person allows them in, the demon can stay, and there's only one thing someone can do to make it leave."

"And what's that?" I ask.

"Tell it to. Call on God. Switch teams, as it were."

"Ah, but there's another way isn't there. I've seen it with my own two eyes, miss," Bock says antagonistically.

"Meaning?" she ask with attitude.

"Why you can blow her face off and send her to Hell yourself."

"She was coming at me with a knife, Thomas. Don't start talking to me about morality. I wasn't there to protect *you*. I made a choice, and had I made a different one, you'd be the one in Hell right now, so show a little respect," Evangeline says forcefully.

Bock shakes his head sits back. Another long silence fills the car. I'm not quite sure what to say. I always knew Bock would be the toughest one to get through to. Horrace won't be easy either, but Everly will follow me blindly into the bowels of the Earth if I ask him. Henry

Knapp's dead on his feet and probably looking for a quick way to get back with his deceased wife and kids anyway. I have a sneaking suspicion that Yakubu already believes in all of this, and Dresden, well, he seems the type that would jump at the chance to scrap with something even more evil than he is. But I always knew Bock would be the toughest, and it looks like that's been taken care of for me.

Twenty or so miles further down the highway Evangeline has passed out, and Bock's on his way too. I'm sure I'll be next. Going through something so traumatic begs the soul for sleep. I figure this is as good an opportunity to gauge where Bock's head is at, independent of Evangeline's interference. I quietly cross the aisle and slide in next to Bock. I poke his shoulder and he slowly rouses.

"How you holding up?" I ask.

"How do you think? Are you mad?"

"I know," I say. "Believe me, I know."

Bock notices that Evangeline and the woman are still asleep. He checks to make sure the driver's partition is still up before speaking.

"What I can't fit together, Rust, is how her bullets landed and mine didn't. I emptied an entire clip for mum's sake. I know I'm a better shot than that," he whispers.

"You remember back in Lithuania, on that old road across the border?" I ask. "You were in the cage of the truck and something happened. You heard a gunshot."

"Aye, nobody would talk about it. Figured you shot a boar or something."

"Well I was shooting at a man and the same thing happened to me. And you know I don't miss with that pistol. I had the elevation. I had the roof to steady my shot. All of it. Still I missed. But I didn't. Just like you."

"Who were you shooting at?"

"There was a group of guys on the side of the road beating the ever loving life out of two others. Brutal scene, I'll tell you that."

"Out there? That road's in the middle of the bloody countryside. There's no one out there."

"I know," I say, "that's what made it so surreal. One minute they were just there. I don't know. I couldn't believe the two they were beating were still alive, but I remember the eyes on one of them. I don't know how, but I just felt like he didn't deserve what he was getting, and so I tried to put down the one holding him up while another one just kept punching him over and over. It worked on me pretty good, so I tried to take a shot. I did it. Passed right through him like he wasn't even there. Just like a ghost."

"Just like mine."

"Just like yours... That fella Elijah put me with in Oklahoma? That guy Taber? He told me you had to treat the bullets to get them to strike."

"Treat them. Treat them with what?" Bock asks.

"Salt. Salt from the Dead Sea itself. I don't know, it... does something to them. Not sure what, but they hate it. Burns them something fierce, but it's the only way."

"That's what was in the boxes. That's what I threw away," Bock says, staring off.

"Reckon so. But now I have a question for you. Did you bring some of that other stuff, the sulfur, on the Lithuania job? The Russian gun-running thing" I ask.

"Aye."

"Thought so. Well, turns out that's pretty important as well."

"I didn't see those creatures until she threw a bag of the shite at the wall. Knew what it was the second it came open. But why?"

"Well, as it was explained to me, at one time God let angels mix with people, before the flood and Noah with the arc and all that. Well they started taking a shine to human women because all they did all day was watch, they were called the Watchers. So the Watchers come down and sleep with the human women because they 'found them fair,' or some such business. That created a whole race of half-human, half-angels."

"Rust, come on mate, where'd you pick up this silly garbage? Next you'll tell me there's a wee hobbit with a ring to throw into a fire-pit."

I chuckle. "I'm telling you, Bock, look it up. It's in Genesis. Well, not all of it. The little fat guy says he's pieced the whole story together from several sources, but—"

"*Who* showed you?"

"Pastor Ellison, but don't worry about that now," I say.

"*Pastor?*"

"It's who I imagine we're on our way to see. You'll meet him. Miserable little cuss, you'll like him. Digs scotch more than you do. Anyway, his theory is that God decides after a while that these giants that angels and man produced aren't working out so well. They're throwing their weight around normal people and consuming too many resources or whatever. So, God sends the flood to wipe them and most everyone else out."

"Noah's ark, yes? Do you really believe this, Rust? And what's that got to do with the sulfur anyway?" Bock asks.

"I don't know what to believe. I mean, I remember some of what my grandfather told me when I was a kid, but this part, no. Ellison could be crazy for all I know. But he says it's after that flood that God basically resets everything. Starts over. Clean slate. And when He does, He forever separates the world of angels and the world of men so nothing like that would ever happen again. The separation also keeps demons from tearing us to pieces and eating all the little babies, setting the world on fire, et cetera. Now the angels and the demons can have their war that's gone on for however many millions of years, and over on this side we can live our lives. The angels and demons can influence us, protect us, tempt us and everything else, but physically at least, we're separated."

"With good reason," Bock says.

"Yep, but every so often the two worlds or dimensions or realities or whatever you want to call them can... bleed over. Sometimes angels come to send us a message, or to hold the hand of a dying man so he isn't alone. Maybe a demon wants to grab hold of someone's ear, or the devil wants to come and tempt someone in person. That kind of thing, so I'm told, happens, just not often. It takes lots of energy and even more effort to cross over. There is, however, one way man can do it, and from what I gather, *only* one way."

"Sulfur."

"Bingo. The sulfur binds the two worlds together for a short time and in a short distance. Anybody, human, or angel, or demon, for that moment, as long as that sulfur is active, instantly exists on the same plane."

"So we can kill them. Or they can kill us," Bock says.

"Hate to say, but it seems to be a one way street. They can kill us alright, I've nearly seen it, but we can't kill them."

"Why not?"

"Because in the scheme of things, we're like dung beetles throwing poop at timber wolves. We're real low on the totem pole. The only things that level us are the separation and the salt. As long as we use the sulfur to bring them into this world, we can see them, and as long as we treat our bullets with salt from the Dead Sea, we can hurt them, repel them. Keep them at bay just long enough."

"Just long enough for what? If angels and demons are so powerful, what's the point of us getting involved? Why would God need us?"

"I asked the same question. Apparently that war on the other side between angels and demons is coming to a head. Angels are dropping like flies and God can't spare any more casualties. Since that fight takes place here on earth, albeit on a different plane of existence, we're a lot closer to the action than anyone else. Rather than Heaven send down its own extraction team, Tishbe needs us to rescue an angel from time to time when one gets himself into a pickle."

"We can do that?" Bock asks.

"I've seen it done, and when done right it's mighty nice work, but just about the most dangerous thing you can get yourself into."

"Certain death more it seems."

"But that paycheck's awful pretty."

"Aye."

We sit quietly for a moment as the desolate desert turns to Barstow townscape.

"So, you in Bock?"

"Quarter million quid per broken halo?"

I nod, already knowing the answer.

"Suppose you'll have to put me in coach. I'm ready to play."

Chapter 35

AS WE DRIVE through town, Red having woken up and shoved the tattooed devil-girl to a seated position, Bock and I can see the distant flare of Fort Irwin's massive solar project in the distance. Seemingly hundreds of rows of reflective panels soaking up the sun's rays point skyward.

"Fort Irwin military base," Red says, noticing us.

"I know," I say. "I was stationed here for a stint. Instructor."

We pull off the highway at a truck stop alive with drivers gassing up, kicking their eighteen tires, and grabbing a bite before pushing through the rest of the Mojave. Red tells us that there's a contact at the base that supplies teams from time to time. There's some good stuff going on over there. Lots of training. I've even seen a prototype or two in use.

I ask her what we can expect to be outfitted with. She tells us that we take whatever the contact gives. It's usually just a crate or two. Mostly ammunition, but there's sure to be a few weapons mixed in. Then I tell her that my team is capable of getting procuring our own munitions, and that we know what we like to use and would rather do it that way. Red tells us that the supplies aren't only for us. Several teams, many without our connections need what's in those crates, and whatever isn't used gets sold off, the revenue from which is added to team expense accounts. She doesn't let on how many teams are out there working or much of anything else. Maybe she doesn't know. Elijah would be smart to have everyone on a need to know anyway. Makes the troops more manageable and focused on their own projects.

"I doubt we're to get many military crates in this limousine," Bock says.

"Don't worry. It should already be loaded up in one of those eighteen-wheelers over there. We're transferring to it once I find out which one," Red says.

I look over to a couple rows of semi-trucks parked tightly at the edge of the lot. Must be thirty of them, maybe more.

"Well, which one is it?" I ask.

"You two must be hungry," she says. "Go get yourselves something to eat. I'll find the truck."

"What about this one?" Bock asks, pointing to the exhausted woman next to Red sneering at him.

Without a beat, Red grabs hold of the woman's neck and instantly brings a pistol to her head. "She and I are going to have a discussion."

"Oh, I gotta see this," I say.

"Suit yourself," Red says back. "Bock, open the wet bar next to you please."

Bock opens the door to reveal a small wooden box much like the one Pastor Ellison had full of brimstone back at his church with the same Hebrew markings etched all over.

"Open it up," she says to Bock.

Bock opens it, and realizing what's inside, shoots a wild look back to her. "Are you bloody crazy, lass? You want more of those things to show up here?"

"Relax. Nobody's looking for her," she says, then looks to the woman she grasps by the neck. "Are they? Have you figured out yet that they were just using you?"

"Then why do you need this?" Bock asks, closing the box and tossing it over to me.

"Just making sure. Besides, don't worry, as long as the brimstone is in a box like that, it's inactive."

Red tells me to take a pinch of brimstone and flick it in her direction. I do so cautiously. I realize I'm holding my breath, even after I flick it. The car is silent. I can feel my blood coursing, Bock's too, but Red seems calm as a cucumber. The other woman's hopeful eyes dart around the limo's interior, waiting for a demon to save her from us. It doesn't happen.

"See?" Red says to her. "They don't care about you. I could kill you right now and they wouldn't raise an eyebrow. You are nothing to them."

The woman's eyes have turned downward, and she begins hard, panicked breathing.

Red peers deep into the woman's pupils, lowering the pistol. "I cast you out, any unclean spirit, along with every satanic power of the enemy, every scepter from Hell, and all your fallen companions; in the name of our Lord Jesus Christ. Be gone and stay far from this creature of God. For it is He who commands you."

The air inside the limousine expands and contracts with Red's words. The woman trembles and cowers as I notice goose pimples erupt from her exposed skin. She makes no sound, but only crumbles further with each piercing word from Evangeline's mouth. Bock and I sit paralyzed. When Red completes her recitation, the air clears, our heads return, and the woman lies crumpled on the floor of the limousine heaving as showers of tears. Tears not of fright, but of an impossible longing to be that which she once was, back before she had taken a side she now realizes had done nothing more than rip away, layer by layer, her inmost humanity, and replaced it with a frothing hatred for goodness and hope, and of love itself. Her acceptance of evil had robbed her of her being, and not only that, but also of the recognition of it. All of the sudden it became impossible not to care, and if not care to at least pity the woman crying on the floor. Even Bock's visible consternation lessened to some degree.

Evangeline gently brought her hand to the woman's chin and raised it softly so their eyes could meet. "Now you know what you have done, but now you also know you have a choice from now on. You've been given a second chance that most in your position will never see. Leave this place now, and live. Call on Christ when you need help, because it is not me, but He who has saved you today."

The bewildered woman nods. She reaches behind her for the door handle, unable at first to break Evangeline's gaze, sniffling all the while. She opens the door and stumbles out of the limousine toward the truck stop in a fog.

"What are you?" I ask.

"You'll be able to do it too, given time," she says.

"What kind of time?"

"As long as it takes for you to believe it," she says.

Then Bock speaks up. "You're going to tell me that God sees nothing wrong with leaving a crying woman at some truck stop in the desert hundreds of miles from her home, yes? We'd do better to put her out of her misery right now."

"I didn't say *you'd* ever be able to do it, Bock," she says with irritation. "Just like I'm sure you won't ever understand what I'm about to say. As I told you before, I didn't come along for you. I came for your partner. He wants to include you? That's his decision. But that woman's journey has just started, and finding her own way home is what it's all about."

"Okay, you two, how about we just find this truck and get out of here," I say. "Bock and I will go get us something to eat while you find the right one. After that, what's our next move?"

"We take the truck back to Elijah. He's assembling the rest of your team as we speak. We'll meet them, and you'll be debriefed on your first assignment."

"Already going on our first rescue?" I ask, trying to think more about the money than anything else.

"You're close, but there's still one member of the new team we need to find."

"We?" Bock asks.

"I'm guessing she says that because she's part of the team now, Bock," I say.

"Shite."

Evangeline gives me a nasty look. Guess she expects it from Bock.

"Don't get me wrong, Red. I was there when you dealt with things back at the Casino. You're welcome on my team anytime. I just don't see who else we need here."

"Well, you've got your muscle, and you've got me. You've got Pastor Ellison who I'm guessing is our Text—"

"Our Text. What does that mean?" Bock interjects.

"He's the guy that tells us how to fight whatever we have to fight," I say.

"But you don't have your Herald yet." Red says.

"Herald? As in: Hark the Herald angels sing?"

"That's right. If the Text tells you how to fight, the Herald tells you who, where, and when."

"Whatever," Bock says. "The only person I care about is the one that hands me the money. You just get us that truck, lady. My mate and I need a good stiff drink."

Chapter 36

"WHAT KIND OF bloody truck stop doesn't serve scotch?" Bock says too loud.

"You want a beer? You can have a beer," says the fat, bearded bartender sweating from the other end of the bar. "You want a whiskey and you can have that too. But we don't serve scotch here. Or cosmos, or margaritas, or fuzzy navels neither. You want scotch and you'll have to haul yourself over to scotchland."

"Scotland, you feral—" Bock says.

"What'd you say, punchy?" the bartender says, slapping down his washrag, and prompting onlookers to turn their heads.

"He said he'd take a beer, bud. Me too. Two beers, kindly," I say to diffuse the situation. I turn to Bock. "Take it easy, man. We don't need the attention. Think that limousine parked out here in the desert and that wailing woman stumbling out of it wasn't enough?"

Bock nods defiantly, and ceases glaring at the bartender.

"I'm gonna go take a leak," I say before stepping away. "You okay to handle yourself?"

"Aye."

It's your typical filthy truck stop restroom. Walls once white, now show a grimy cream streaked with years old splashes of faucet water, urine, and otherwise. Dirt and oil mixed with swill from the mineral deposited sink sits in pools on the floor where its slope fails to direct it to the crusty drain. The old, dust-glazed light bulb hangs exposed from the ceiling, swinging gently with just enough light to shadow some of the worst stains. There are two unoccupied stalls. I take the first one I come to and decide to drop trough and take a seat, closing the metal door behind me as best as I can. I hear measured dripping whether it be from the faucet or the drain in the floor. I think about what Evangeline had said in the limousine just before we got out, but my mind becomes tired quickly. I lull myself into the drip, clearing my mind. I yawn, but then hear a whisper. Sounds like a woman, but lower, more harsh, almost androgynous. I figure it's coming from the women's restroom on the other side of the wall, but it sounds closer. It morphs into a series of obscene groans, low like heavy morning fog before rising back up to the whispers. They are the rapid whispers heard in an audience mid-performance—brief, choppy hisses. Then the whisper sounds like a child humming light and lonely, but it fades away seconds later. Now a deep echoey groan that seems a thousand miles away. It trails off too. Only the drip returns.

"Amarillo."

"What?" I snap back mainly out of a knee-jerk surprise.

Quiet for a moment, then the whispering woman again. A few seconds later a giggling child joins her. My hands begin to tremble. I can't stop them, my hands or the voices.

"Amarillo," they say in unison, and now a deeper one, tinny, wet, and garbled. Three deep and sorrowful voices tear into my skull. "We intend to feast on you."

They trail into the recesses as air across the blades of a fan. I bend down and peer under the stall next to me. No feet. I'm alone. Voices return. They're coming from deep inside that filthy dripping floor drain.

"We intend to feast on you. Your agony delights us," and more giggling from the child's voice. The woman continues to whisper inaudible breathy swings, as the low voice wells up again from the depths of the small circular grate like a thick bubble threatening to burst its foul contents across the floor. "Your agony delights us. We will savor your flesh, as we tear the meat from your fractured bones."

Not knowing what to do, I slam my fist against the metal wall of the opposing stall only to hear the drip again, but the drain gurgles and the voices return.

"We intend to feast on you. To feast on you. We will feast on you and drag your worthless soul to the fires of Styxx and come inside."

I gather the nerve and frantically hoist my pants, breaking from the restroom in the process of zipping up. I hurriedly rush over to Bock who's about to take a sip of beer from a mug and take his arm, forcefully pulling him away. He looks down at my pants, noticing my unbuckled belt flailing wildly, and my grappling to keep the Wranglers up around my waist.

"The shite's gotten into you, brother?" Bock says trailing awkwardly behind me as I march him toward the exit by the arm.

"Hey!" the bartender calls after us with patrons seated both at the bar and in the booths surrounding it staring at us. "Hey, you didn't pay for those beers."

I stop and turn, glaring at him and pointing. "There is something majorly wrong with your bathroom, fella," I say and pull Bock out of the truck stop.

Evangeline waits in the driver seat of a red semi-truck just beyond the doors, revved up, engine grumbling and ready to go. I move around to the passenger side, hop up, open the door, and get inside. Bock follows and shuts the door behind him. Evangeline notes my discomfort. Bock says nothing.

"What happ—" Evangeline starts.

"Just drive, Red," I say. "Just drive."

Chapter 37

I SWEAR I'VE never traveled so much in my life. I thought I knew what jet lag was, but that's all been replaced by an entirely different animal. My hands tremble from dehydration that I can't seem to quell, and I'm liable to crack the clavicle of the next person that breathes in the wrong direction. Red says you get used to it, and if you don't, you won't live long enough to regret it anyway. We're back in Lithuania. Everyone showed, and it doesn't much seem like any of them had the slightest problem with my not calling the shots anymore. Don't quite know what I was expecting. A merc's a merc, and a merc loves money. The guy pointing at it is the guy who calls the shots, and that's Tishbe now.

We're in a poorly lit, sparsely furnished roach motel in the bad part of Alytus, tucked between closely packed concrete buildings no more than four or five stories each. This town's different than most. In fact, this tiny area of about three or four streets would be the only thing resembling the drab, crumbling post-communist Eastern Europe. Alytus is a manufacturing town of a hundred thousand people mostly living way above the national standard. As we drove in, I told Everly if I kidnapped and blindfolded an American and dropped him in the middle of Alytus' residential neighborhood, I bet when he pulled off the blindfold he'd think he was in a suburb outside of Cleveland. Only thing that looked Lithuanian about it at all was the surrounding flora and this district.

There's Yakubu bouncing a rubber ball off the floor in the corner like a teen on lunch break, making the ball look like a speck of dirt in the hand of Colossus. Evangeline's dressed like a schoolmarm sitting next to the dingy fireplace and talking to Elijah. Horrace and Everly enjoy a smoke over a half-hearted game of chess, the hotel's pieces so old and used they might just crumble in their hands. Bock and Henry Knapp stare out of the hazy front window of the small lobby that's more like a medium-sized living room, watching people on foot, bicycle, and car on their way to work. Dresden still hasn't come down from his room. I'm sure he's still drunk. I'd dismiss him, but it looks like that's not my call anymore. Tishbe's in charge now. I'm just his field general.

We had three weeks in between Red dropping Bock and I at the airport in San Bernardino. I made good use of my time. I like to be proactive. Sets me apart from a lot of mercs, even some in my own team. What's that they say about chess? You win if you think five moves ahead? Personally, I don't know how anyone can think five moves ahead on anything, so two moves is good enough for me.

There's a private construction outfit run out of Spain by a guy named Xavi, who for the right price, will build anything you want quietly. I hired him to come out to Tahoka. Told him I needed something underground for a team. A clandestine HQ of sorts. A subterranean base. None of it was new to Xavi, and so he brought up a band of seventy non-English-speaking illegals from Mexico and a couple of foremen from Spain to break ground out at Teasel's. I had some plans mapped out and ready to go when they showed, not to mention a whole mess of cash that Tishbe and I will be paying off for some time to come.

The headquarters would be underground. We'd enter it from a door in the floor beneath Teasel's living room. I wanted it automated and secure, so Xavi rigged up a fingerprint reader on the doorknob. The user had only to press his thumb on bottom of the knob for a quick scan. Only an authorized individual would even know the thumb scanner was there. For all visual intents and purposes the doorknob was just a doorknob. Xavi is brilliant at hiding tech, and the scanner was no exception. Upon successful entry, a rectangular hatch of wood-slat living room floor

would automatically slide away, and another hatch, this time heavy rein-
forced steel would open by way of hydraulics. The authorized individual
would then encounter a staircase leading downward to the HQ. A motion
detector would signal the individual's entry and close the hatches, thus
returning the living room to, well, just a regular old dilapidated farmhouse living room.

With Xavi's input, I figured we'd need a bunkroom, a small mess
hall, a conference room complete with a long round table that would
make King Arthur jealous, and all the tech we'd need to plan and debrief
in Pentagon style. Of course, all that's just the gravy. What the HQ really
needed was an arsenal. A metal room about the size of your average convenience store would house everything from six-shooters to Javelin missiles, all in four hydraulic, floor to ceiling, optic-scan-secured hideaway
vaults. Two room-length steel islands would rise from the floor and
compliment the vaults in the center of the room. You can never have too
many guns. Go big, or don't go at all.

Xavi then suggested a four-bay shooting range with top notch sound
dampening and a bulletproof viewing area to hang off the side of the
arsenal. Music to my ears. I almost had him throw in a monster living
area for myself, but I remembered some advice from the old team: It's
almost impossible for guys like us not to mix business with pleasure, but
you do so at your own peril. Besides, the HQ should only be used when
necessary. This way the off chance of being discovered would be mini-
mized, as would unnecessary wear on the hatch hydraulics. Xavi's group
broke ground the day after the plans were finalized.

But there was still one problem. The HQ would be the natural place
to house our supply of salt and brimstone. It would require its own room,
but the enemy would find the place eventually, resourceful as they are.
Our best defense is our dimensional separation, but with cases upon
cases of brimstone just sitting in the open, any old demon could cross
over and take us out unsuspecting. That's when I had an idea. Both
Evangeline and Pastor Ellison had those small wooden boxes with the
Hebrew writing on them and brimstone inside. I remember both of them
saying that as long as the brimstone was housed in the wooden box it was

inactive. If I could get my hands on enough of that wood, I could line the walls, floor, and ceiling of the supply vault with it, in effect creating a giant box that would render the brimstone inert until we brought it out.

I made a call to Ellison. I could hear the whiskey in his voice. It evoked even more of that chafed attitude that I was still getting used to. After trading a few barbs, I learned that the wood was extremely hard to come by. Should have guessed that. He said the wood had to come from trees in the garden of Gethsemane, believed to be along the lower slopes of the Mount of Olives in Jerusalem. It's the place where Jesus and his disciples prayed the night before his capture by the Romans. This particular site is automatically imbued with powers to subdue paranormal activity because it's the only place man successfully took down the divine.

Needless to say, the location is locked down by the Israeli government, and it is almost never vacant long enough for anyone to sneak in and start chopping trees. But it can and has been done, usually through a series of payoffs to government officials and both the care-taking Church of the Agony as well as the Russian Orthodox Church of St. Mary Magdalene that overlook the area. Because negotiation of such waters is both expensive and politically treacherous, oftentimes items and structures built from said wood in the past can more easily be procured, dismantled, blessed and marked by Kabbalah rabbis to be used for our purposes.

Ellison added that further use of Kabbalah by teams is greatly discouraged, and its effectiveness incredibly sketchy at best. He told me a couple of stories about teams in the past putting so much emphasis on weaponizing Kabbalah mysticism, even going so far as to employ rabbis as sorts of spell wielding wizards. It never worked, resulting in team compromise, even death. I assured Ellison that if he could get me enough wood to line the vault, we'd stay away from anything else concerning it. He agreed, and a few days later a Chinook dropped a payload right at the construction site. I offered to pay, but Ellison laughed me off and asked in that condescending rasp who I thought I was working for.

And so back at that rat hole hotel in Lithuania, I look pointlessly down at my watch and conclude that Xavi and his boys must be putting the finishing touches on the HQ as we speak. Best to keep it on a need-to-know until we finish this job. We've come to get Brigita, the little girl we liberated from the Kostonov brothers, who is our Herald. When we finished gun-running for the Lithunaians, I sent Horrace with the girl to find her a safe place to live. She had no family, and so later Horrace told me he dropped her at an orphanage here in Alytus. That orphanage sits only a couple buildings over.

The plan is simple enough. We send in Everly and Evangeline posing as prospective adoptive parents. They've been in contact with the orphanage by phone and snail mail for a couple weeks already. The meeting with the orphanage staff has been set for 9 A.M., an hour from now. With any luck, Everly and Evangeline will just happen to choose Brigita as the one they want to take home. In that event, the unsuspecting adoption process of a little Latvian girl to your average Midwestern American married couple will begin and take about a month or so to complete. That's the way we hope it goes down. The best jobs are pulled off when the other side never even knows a job was pulled. We've got all the paperwork drawn up to make it look legit. But if the enemy has figured out the little girl's role in things to come, that orphanage is probably already compromised and teeming with demons and their familiars, or both. In that case, the gang's all here and strapped to the nines. If our little plan doesn't work, we go in without brimstone to keep the worlds apart and take the girl by force, hopefully dealing only with familiars and loyalists. Loyalists and familiars we *can* kill.

We haven't had a chance to doctor our own ammunition, so if the orphanage is compromised and they're guarding the girl with hopes of turning her to their side, a sad and cruel possibility that I'm told has happened before, Elijah has handed down some of Taber's unused ammo. I figure the best thing to do so as not to waste salt rounds on human loyalists is to tape a salt round clip to the bottom of one loaded with regular cartridges. Each clip will point in opposite directions. If it's just loyalists, we pump them full of regular rounds, but if they've covered the area with brimstone and demons show, our boys simply eject the regular clip, flip it around and lock in the salt. Should take about a second. Regular clips remain unmarked while we wrap the salt round clips with a band of white electrical tape so there's no confusion.

"Mr. Rust, a word if you please," Elijah says from the fireplace.

I walk over.

"I trust your men are ready?"

"Ready as they can be. A few of them still don't know the full story, but they're good with a gun and won't hesitate to unleash Hell on anything that comes after them."

"Heaven, Mr. Rust. We unleash the power of Heaven upon them."

"Whatever you say. You're looking very... ordinary," I say to Evangeline who sits next to Elijah in a conservative grey pantsuit with that red hair in a ponytail.

"Look the part though, don't I?" she says.

"You look like a banker to me," I say with a grin breaking my lips.

"And you look like all you need is a John Deer trucker cap and a lip full of Copenhagen to finish yours."

"Hey Red, the snuff's in my back pocket, and I prefer Caterpillar."

She chuckles. Elijah doesn't.

"And what of your man, Mr. Everly?" Elijah asks. "I detect a great deal of nervousness. Are you confident he can perform?"

"He'll get the job done. Everly's more than he looks. I have complete confidence."

"Excellent. I must say that time is of the essence, as trite as it may sound. The enemy proves emboldened by the day. Their victories are on the rise. With every angel they successfully fell, word returns to Hades, and their resolve increases exponentially. Nothing delights them more than the defeat and tarnishing of something pure. I fear greatly for the little girl's safety."

"You *do* expect she's still alive in there."

"I do. The girl Brigita is far too valuable for both sides to simply do away with," Tishbe says. "A Herald can see things the average man cannot. As life simply passes before us, unfolding with the banality, disorganization, and chance most take at face value, the Herald views events, people, and the interlocking determination of it through connective, some would say, wide open eyes."

"You saying the girl sees the future?"

"I'm afraid it isn't as simple as that. A Herald instantly takes into account the whole of an individual. They see the trajectory of a soul. You see, a soul can be mapped. Moves can be surmised and predicted, often with great accuracy. The uninitiated might say that a Herald knows when a person will die and where their soul will go when it does, but this is an oversimplification. The Herald is not a soothsayer. The Herald merely concludes the inevitable outcome of the intersection of individuals.

"Is an event anything more than an intersection of individual souls after all? Doesn't the aggregate polarity of those souls generally determine the outcome of the intersection? The event? With the blessing of and consultation with the Holy Spirit, the Herald will either confirm or deny the validity and probability of the outcome he or she has reached. History has proven that God must use a system such as this, of course, his omnipotence greatly supersedes that of a human Herald's, and so we cannot be sure how God arrives at his operation, but we do know that the fight between good and evil takes place at the *event*, at that intersection of polarized souls, good or evil. Wherever one finds good and evil attempting to occupy the same space, one will find angels and demons warring over the human soul or souls involved. To follow the logical chain, angels and demons occupying the same space must battle. Evil cannot exist in the presence of Holy goodness. Christ's light will always attempt to consume all evil surrounding it. It's as simple as that.

"Where battle occurs, will good win or will evil? When the Herald analyzes and predicts that good will win, the Herald need do nothing more than send a prayer of thanks. But when evil wins the battle, Mr. Rust, the Herald calls on us, for where evil has won, there will be injured angels left in their destructive wake. Those angels must be rescued and sent back home. The enemy can use the girl in much the same capacity, for the Devil has teams of his own, and they are far more brutal in their executions than you can imagine."

"Well, it's all so clear to me now," I say sarcastically.

"You joke, Mr. Rust, but the facts remain. The enemy has grown strong. Their momentum builds at an alarmingly exponential rate, and it is up to you and your men to help turn the tide."

"Now *that* I understand," I say. "Everly's gonna do fine, and I've got all the confidence in the world in Red here, but if things run off the rails, we'll get that little girl out one way or another."

"That's the spirit, Mr. Rust. Might I say that my confidence in you all runs deep. The girl will be recovered. Of this I have little doubt. If it comes to it, be alert and be ruinous in your rendering of whatever evil you come across. The Devil fights mercilessly, but we must show him that the armies of Christ offer even less mercy to those that would dethrone his divine sovereignty. Awe them, Mr. Rust. Awe them and strike a crippling fear in those who fear nothing but the Almighty Himself. You are the trigger at His finger, so fire away."

Chapter 38

IT'S PINS AND needles from the second Everly and Evangeline leave the hotel. Conversation gives way to the clicking sounds of metal as magazines are checked and rechecked. Slides are pulled back, chambers are loaded, and grips firmly meet determined palms.

I look to the corner where Yakubu sits hunched over, his massive hands wrapped around the broad stock and barrel of a 5.56mm Ultimax 100 light machine gun that would look like a skinny German MP40 sub in anyone else's. His eyes are closed to the floor. I think he's praying. I walk over and wait until he's finished.

"Praying?" I ask.

The Yak nods.

"Who to?"

"I pray to Christ Jesus."

"You don't say. Wouldn't have pegged you, big man."

He peers up to me. "If you had come from where I do, you would pray to him too."

"Well, you might not know it yet, but looks like you found the right team to hook up with," I say, patting him on the shoulder and heading over to Bock who stands at the window again, wiping down that shiny .45 of his.

"Gonna make it?" I ask from behind.

"I keep running through my mind whether we should have told them, mate."

"The boys? They'll be okay. Wouldn't believe us if we did."

"Perhaps so," he says to the window.

"Doing a good job covering up that tremble in your hands though," I say.

"Toss off."

"Hey, I've got it too, man. Imagine we will for a while. Just keep thinking about the money."

"Trying," he says.

But it's eating at me also. Just because Bock and I didn't get the scoop before we confronted Hell on earth, doesn't necessarily mean we're the better for it. The orphanage will be confined quarters. Would only take a swipe of a demon claw across the back of the neck to take out one of our men permanently. We told the team that the white clip was only to be used if something gets out of hand. Didn't tell them what. Luckily, the money Tishbe's offering has blinded most of the men to the logic of our little exercise. They might just choose not to question why a backup mercenary team is needed on a mission to adopt a little girl. Stranger requests have come our way, though, and it's the default merc attitude not to ask questions when a price has been agreed upon. Just follow instructions and get the job done. I question our secretive approach, but like I said, the rest of them wouldn't believe the truth until they saw it with their own eyes anyway. Letting on too early might just blow the whole deal. Those of us in the know would be discounted as either nuts or liars, and we can't risk losing a single man before the job's done. I've seen each of them in action plenty of times, and none take threats lightly. They all come prepared and ready to play. Still, I'm nervous. To know Bock is also comforts me.

Just about that time, Dresden stumbles down the stairs. He's dressed like a cartoon character in a bright orange prison jumpsuit, twirling a three-fingered bowie knife in one hand and a Glock compact 25 with a tactical light attachment flashing like a disco strobe with each twirl. I waste no time.

"Get back upstairs and change," I bark at him. "This isn't a damn game."

Elijah stands, anticipating a violent altercation, which I must admit sits only a breath away.

"It's how I work, Rust. I love it when they see me coming," he says smiling petulantly.

I get nose to nose, spraying spit through my teeth. "Not on my team. That stupid costume will get us killed. What are you thinking?"

"Oh, I'm sorry. This is your team?" he says, stepping back theatrically, still twirling the knife. "Funny. See, I thought it was *his* team," he says pointing to Elijah who stands cautiously but calmly to the side.

I look over to Tishbe for some support. My right fist is clenched and ready to pop. Tishbe says nothing. Just stares. It's a test, isn't it? Has to be.

"Twirling that knife like you want to use it," I say square in his eyes.

"You know how well I can use it," he says, a devilish smile narrowing at me.

"You're right. I have. But then, I'm not a defenseless pregnant woman, so who knows how it'd work against somebody who can handle himself, you sick son of a—"

"Ah," he says scoffing, chuckling. "Chicago. I see. You won't ever let that one go will you, Rust?"

"She had nothing to do with the job. Nothing!"

"She was in the room. She was with them. Ask Bock, he knows its true."

"I don't need Bock to tell me what happened in Chicago. We were both there, and you murdered her."

"That was the job," Dresden says.

"That was not the job, mate," I hear Bock say behind me. "The job was to take out the sheik, not his wife, and not the unborn kid."

"It was a hit for god's sake. They wanted him dead. End the bloodline. What do you think would have happened if we left her alive to have that kid? It would've grown up to take the sheik's place and the contract would've been null and void. I made a call. I did us a favor carving her up!"

"It was my call, you arrogant punk. My call!" I snap.

Dresden takes another step back, shaking his head violently, fighting back all kinds of urges swirling around that perverted skull of his. He points the knife at me. "They would have found us. They would have killed every last one of us. You know they would. You do not mess with a cartel like that."

"I don't know that and neither do you. We're not monsters. We're not like you. We don't kill women and children."

"You keep telling yourselves that. Hypocrites. All of you. I did the right thing, and you know what?"

I wait for his answer; my teeth clenched so hard I think they might shatter.

"I enjoyed it."

I glance over to Elijah. He gives me a nod so small I can barely see it. Not that he needed to. My mind was already made up. It had been four years ago after Chicago when I told Dresden if I ever saw his face again I'd paint the walls with it.

I leap toward him and knock the gun out of his hand, but it leaves me open to a knife strike. I feel his other arm raise for a stab. As he sends it rushing down, I manage to roll away from it and grab his free hand at the wrist and elbow. I use the momentum to fling him at the stairs. He stumbles and crashes into the stairwell, throwing him off guard and unintentionally burying the bowie knife into a carpeted stair. I ready myself for retaliation. He works to free the knife, but in a second's time realizes the action's futility. Instead Dresden uses his weight to come around with a spinning back fist. I dodge it narrowly, feeling the air displacement it creates and unleash a cracking blow of my own to Dresden's jaw that throws him off balance again. He's no match to my standup as long as he doesn't have time to go psycho. I throw another hook with my left, but he's come to and leaned away from it. It's all the time he needs to grip one of his hands deep into my shirt, his red, wild eyes careen toward me. The head butt slams into my face like a mack truck, and all the sudden I'm seeing double. I fumble backwards, trying to get my feet back under me. I can just make out Dresden going for the Glock I knocked out of his hand.

I hear the distinct sound of Bock brandishing that .45 of his and racking the slide. He'll put one between Dresden's eyes before he can take me out, but before it happens, my double vision returns the disjointed images to one. I see a giant black arm shoot out and take Dresden by the collar of his jumpsuit, lifting him off the ground. I hear Dresden choke and Yakubu speak.

"The gun or your arm. Which do you wish to meet the floor?"

Dresden continues to lose air. My wits are back, and I see Dresden still considering drawing down on me even though his feet are nearly two feet off the ground.

"I will tear your arm from your socket, Mr. Dresden. Please believe me," Yakubu says, glaring up at him. "I can do this."

"And I'll make sure you feel it before I bury a round in your forehead, Dresden," I hear Bock say behind me, the barrel of his .45 trained down.

Realizing his inescapable predicament, Dresden exhales and drops the Glock. Bock immediately holsters his pistol, but Yakubu continues holding the man wearing the orange jumpsuit in the air. I can tell he wants to make good on his promise. Elijah finally speaks up from near the fireplace.

"I believe you can do it, Mr. Yakubu, but I also believe your point has been taken," he says. "Please lower him to the ground."

The Yak heeds Elijah's instruction. Not only does he set Dresden down, but he does so with care, all but readjusting the bright orange collar of his jumpsuit for him.

"You are an exciting little man, Mr. Dresden, I'll give you that," Elijah says. "But it seems redemption has again eluded you. Your services are no longer needed. Perhaps greener pastures await you elsewhere. I'm sure you wouldn't be so brazen as to ask for compensation as your involvement in this team has no doubt come to an abrupt but justified end."

Dresden stares at Elijah as if there's anything he can do about it. A heavy moment is shared between them. In regular fashion, Elijah Tishbe expresses not only the absence of fear, but of interest as well. Dresden picks up on this.

"I'm going upstairs to get my stuff and them I'm out of here," he says turning toward the stairs before uttering under his breath, "Hypocrites."

"I think you have all you need, Mr. Dresden. All you deserve. You have your life. Now leave and inject your foolishness on this group no longer."

Dresden stops and turns to look each of us in the eye. All stare back in varying levels of consternation. He glances down at the bowie knife still buried into the stair, and to the Glock lying impotent on the floor. His shoulders slump as he wipes a spot of blood from the corner of his mouth that I'm proud to say I am responsible for. He walks slowly to the hotel door, but stops before leaving. He swings around to Tishbe, pointing at him.

"I better not ever see you again," he says with what little authority he has left.

"It will be a dark day, indeed, Mr. Dresden. Now run along. I am sorry I misjudged you so. I would advise you to get used to your little uniform. It should make your inevitable incarceration much less difficult."

Having nothing left in his reserves, Dresden spits a red clump of blood and mucus on the lobby floor before disappearing into the Alytus streets.

"Very good," Elijah says without skipping a beat. "That was exciting wasn't it? I urge you all to get back to readying. Our two brave scouts should return soon. But if they have met with retaliation, the resistance you're likely to encounter will make Mr. Dresden appear paltry by comparison."

Chapter 39

FOUR HOURS AND counting since Red and Everly left for the orphanage. The boys are growing weary. So am I. The only one not showing any sign of wear is Elijah, who seems lost in the smoldering fireplace.

"Take it easy on the coffee, boys. Give you the trebles," I say. "And get away from the window, Horrace."

"Think they might have a spotter?" Bock asks from across the room.

I don't know the answer to that, but I know our people should have been back by now. I start second guessing the plan about now. We didn't wire Everly or Red for sound. Didn't want any tattle tails. Was I too confident they could get it done with words? Maybe. Can't put anything past anybody now.

I'm five seconds from asking Tishbe for a go to breach when Horrace comes over for conversation. "How's time, boss?"

"I don't know, Horrace. Part of me thinks we need to move, but..."

"Who knows."

"Yeah."

He leans in close and lowers his voice. "This isn't a regular recovery is it?"

I lean back. My eyes tell him all he needs to know.

"I've been thinking. Had a lot of time," he says. "You don't send in unarmed people to adopt a kidnapped kid. Think it's lost on me that this just so happens to be the same orphanage I dropped off a little Latvian girl several months ago? I'm no rocket scientist—"

"Far as I know," I chuckle.

"Well I'm not, but something's going on. Bock seems like he's in on it, you and Elijah clearly are."

"How you figure?" I ask looking off. Way back in my mind, I knew this one was too big for some of the boys to swallow. "Maybe they want to get rid of the kid. Tell the parents they still have her. Collect the dough and disappear. They'd never find her."

"C'mon, Rust. I'm smarter than that."

"Maybe it's a grudge thing. They want the money and lose the girl too."

Horrace shakes his head, almost thinking of it all as a game. I can see those wheels turning, but he doesn't have to go far. "I don't know what you're up to, but we've been a team for a long time, Amarillo. I don't appreciate being kept in the dark because that means one of two things."

"Being?"

"One: Most of us, the ones not in the know, we're expendable."

"Trust me, Horrace, that ain't it."

"Or two," he continues, "you don't think we can handle what's really going on."

"Like you said, you're a smart man."

"Okay. Well just a word of caution, pretty soon the rest of them will catch on to the little show you're putting on, and they're going to think about that whole thing with Park. They won't be any more pleased than I am."

"Well, I appreciate your candor, Horrace, but you know—" I start.

"Money motivates men, but so does the feeling they're getting jerked around. I'm saying that as a friend."

I've never seen Horrace more adamant. I think Elijah hears us somehow, but he's not letting on. He's still settled in that chair with his hands crested on the top of his cane, his long grey hair hiding, but a glint of those eyes searing into the fire. I turn back to Horrace who's been stone the whole time.

"Alright," I say, lowering my voice further. "Alright, Horrace, I'll tell you, but before I do you have to understand there's a reason I tried to do it this way."

Just then noises come from the hotel door. They're soft at first, scratching sounds. Takes a while for most of us to react, but pretty soon all movement in the room stops.

"You hear that?" I ask Horrace.

He looks to the door and nods, slowly bringing up the sidearm from the holster at his waist. Henry Knapp's closest to the door. He's already got his pistol drawn. You could hear a bug sneeze in the room. Elijah hasn't moved. It's like he knows. I want to throw him into that fire because of it. The scratching grows louder and we hear a muttering out-side. Female, but low, like a distressed wheezing. I motion to Henry Knapp. He slides down the wall toward the door. The rest of the boys move to defensive positions. Yakubu quietly sets a table on its side and rests the light machine gun's tripod gently on top. He crouches with his hand ready to rack the drum. Henry Knapp checks the rest of the men, making sure they have position before he opens the door. Horrace has gone prone on the floor next to me finding time to re-holster the sidearm and trade it for the UMP40 sub strapped loosely over his shoulder.

The scratching gives way to a voice, ticking outside like an old clock. Bock refuses cover and simply brushes one half of his trench coat to the side revealing the grip of that shiny .45 like an old western movie. I move to the cover of the stairwell on the other side of the door from Henry Knapp, picking up the Glock I knocked out of Dresden's hand earlier. I check the clip and slowly work the slide. Then I nod to Henry Knapp again. His hand moves gradually toward the door handle. That hoarse voice on the other side keeps ticking. Elijah hasn't moved. I whisper his name, trying to get his attention, but he offers no response.

I give Henry Knapp the okay. He quickly squeezes the latch, and throws the door open. Yakubu uses the noise of the door to rack the light machine gun and train down the sight. He sees what we all do.

Evangeline is belly down on the ground, slithering like a snake. She raises her head. Her eyes seem cloudy, and her nose, obviously broken at the bridge, streams blood. We don't know what to make of it. She lowers her head to the floor and stabs one of her arms into the air, her fingers like claws. Her hand reaches out and slams into the hollow wood floor, pulling her wriggling body inside. She repeats the motion until she's all the way in. Henry Knapp instinctively darts his head out of the doorway a couple of times to check for tangos, but finding nothing, he swings the door shut and locks the deadbolt swiftly.

For a short moment, we all stare at Red on the floor. Normally we would swarm and cover a downed team member, but her movements are inhuman. Her torso undulates like a serpent. Her joints pop and crack. No one makes a move for her, and so I know my eyes aren't playing tricks.

"Lix—lix—lix," the body on the floor utters, face still hanging to the wooden slats, a pool of blood forming beneath it from her injured nose.

"And who are you?" Elijah finally speaks. He still hasn't turned away from the fire.

"Lix—lix—lix, who are you?" the slow, gravelly voice says.

"You know who I am," Elijah says back.

"What the—" Horrace says, shimmying back a bit and searching my face for answers. He's panicking.

I try to show him some confidence, but there isn't much to give. Then Evangeline's head swings up like a marionette, her spine arching back so far I think it might snap. Her bleary eyes point toward Elijah.

"Leader of the foolhardy," she says in long breathy exhalations. "How far you've fallen. Just like a human."

Elijah rises slowly and turns, the oranges and yellows of the fireplace reflecting in his eyes. "Interesting choice of words, demon."

"Lix—lix—lix," Red says, the repetition tapping like skipping vinyl.

Yakubu is strangely calm, his eye never leaving the iron sight. Bock only narrows his. He's almost grinning at the grotesquery of the woman on the floor. Henry Knapp and Horrace seem the worst. I can see sweat beading on Knapp's forehead as he realizes he's too close for his own good. Horrace has shuffled back against the wall with nowhere left to go. He'll be the first to snap if I don't speak up.

"Horrace," I call out. "Take it easy, buddy. Breathe. Henry, nobody fire. Stand down until I say otherwise. Everybody chill down."

Having heard me, the body swivels as if on an invisible axis at the waist. It faces me, unrelentingly frozen. I see no life in her eyes. "I see you," she says.

"I see you too," I say trying hard to not show my pulsating nerves.

"Lix—lix—lix. We want you," she says, head jerking sideways with a corner of her mouth jagging upwards.

"You want him for what, vile spirit?" Elijah asks.

The body contorts further, her excruciating back somehow bowing more with the head craning up as it swings to face Elijah. "A sacrifice. Just a sacrifice."

"You cannot have him or anyone else in this room," Elijah says, resolute. "They have chosen their side."

"Have they?" she says. Her body pivots behind her to face Henry Knap. "Lix—lix—lix. You've not chosen. You've—not—chosen."

Henry Knapp's eyes bulge and he stumbles away down the wall tumbling backward. He scrambles to his feet and raises his gun clumsily at Evangeline.

"Wait, Knapp, don't. Just wait," I scream with my hand out.

The body pivots again and this time her head dances on her neck at Horrace. "What side?" the head barks at him. "What side? What side?"

Horrace is on the verge of tears. Suddenly the body freezes and the head jolts to Bock, then slowly stretches forward. "And you... Lix—lix—lix."

"Enough!" Elijah says, striking the butt of his cane loudly on the floor. "What have you done with our other one? The man."

The body still faces Bock, who studies the figure with the scrutiny of a scientist. "We bind him lix."

"And so he lives? You hold him?" Elijah asks.

"We hold him. We lix him and hold him with us."

"And the little girl?"

"The girl," the body repeats, swiveling on the floor again. "Lix. She lives. Still she lives. With us she lives with us. Lix—lix—lix—lix."

"Why do they still live?" Elijah says.

One of Red's arms stretches out, pointing in my direction. "We want him."

"You cannot have him. As I've said before, I command you to speak your name," Elijah says. "Who do you serve?"

"Lix—lix—lix."

"Do they live if I go with you?" I ask.

"Do not think of it, Mr. Rust. To give an inch is to give it all," Elijah says. "You, Mr. Knapp." Tishbe produces a cellular phone from inside his jacket and scrolls through entries. Finding one he presses the send button and tosses the phone across the room to Henry Knapp. "The man on the speakerphone will be one Pastor Ellison."

"Ellison!" the woman wails, slightly coiling.

It distracts Henry Knapp. The phone bounces off a chair and hits the floor. Knapp scrambles to pick it up. "H-hello?" he says, raising it to his ear.

"You must ask him the meaning of this word she continues to spill forth," Elijah says, still fixed on the wriggling woman. "Find the meaning of this 'lix.' I have business to attend."

"Lix—lix—lix," Evangeline sputters like the rattles on a diamond-back.

"Who the hell is this?" scratches through the cell phone speaker.

"Oh, sir, hello?" Henry Knapp fuddles.

"Speak up, you jackball. Who?" It's definitely Ellison.

"Uh, sir, my name is—"

"Mr. Knapp!" Elijah says hurriedly.

"Let's just shoot this crazy bird," Bock threatens.

"Bock. No. Stand down," I call back as the intensity mounts.

"Is that you, Elijah?" the voice on the phone says. "Who's the idiot holding the phone? Put Elijah on the line, damnit."

Bock has enough and stomps over to Henry Knapp, swiping the phone from him and walking back to his original position. "The auld man is busy, codger. My name is Thomas Bock and we've got a situation."

"Go ahead," Ellison says.

Elijah steps up to Red and crouches so that their eyes meet. "You'll not hurt this one, demon. The order of Christ will command you to leave this body."

"Lix—lix—lix—lix—lix," she says, casting a spray of blood into his face.

Tishbe doesn't react, only stares deeper into the cloudy eyes before him. "I will know your name and you will leave this woman. She is protected."

"None are protected. No protection. Give him to us," the body points at me again. "Let us see him. Lix let us see."

"You are curious are you? You sense something," Elijah says. "You will not harm him?"

"Let us see him. See lix."

"You are not to be trusted."

"Let us lix him. Let us see."

Then from across the room, Bock into the phone. "Does the word 'lix' mean anything to you?"

"Styxx?" Ellison says, struggling to hear. "Of course. The river of the damned. Lake of fire."

"No. Listen. 'Lix.' L. I. X," Bock enunciates into the phone.

I can see from the stairwell that Horrace has shut down. There's no emotion on his face. He's flat on his stomach, finger now lazily on the trigger, his sub leaning over and his eyes transfixed on Evangeline's inhuman spine arching into the air like some kind of tortured root.

"Your time is nearing an end," Elijah toys with the possessed woman as the room nervously anticipates Ellison's answer.

I think to myself. If this thing on the floor is just Red possessed, and Everly and the girl are still alive in the orphanage, we can't waste time with all this talking. I've seen enough to know that everything can flip on a dime and everyone could end up dead real quick. I've got to go. Next to Elijah, I'm the only one on the team that knows enough about what we're up against. The captain goes down with the ship. Before anyone can notice, I'm already out the door. As I leave, I hear Ellison growl the demon's name over the speakerphone, "Lix Tetrax."

Elijah calls after me, but I'm already down the street, talking myself up like a linebacker emerging from the locker room. I see the orphanage in seconds, only two buildings away. The streets are vacant, silent. Wind curls trails of dust and refuse where concrete meets their darkened alleyways. Dresden's around here somewhere, and all the sudden I realize that the Glock I hold isn't loaded with salt rounds. I'm pretty much unarmed and marching toward the Devil. What form will it take this time? What does this thing want with me and how can I fight it? I'm just your average stiff working for a check. I don't see the future and I'm not some Bible character that God cared so much about he sent fiery chariots to take up to the pearly gates. Why ask for me?

The weatherworn sign above the door to the orphanage reads something in Lithuanian. I breathe deeply and check the window for movement inside. A woman, a nun I think, sits at a shoddy reception desk. It all looks on the level. Maybe this Lix Tetrax was lying. Elijah said that was their *real* power anyway, the lie. What if they just wanted me out in the open for Dresden? Let fate take its course. Dresden I can kill with regular rounds. Besides, I don't think even he's so stupid after the whooping he just took. More likely he's on his way back home, that or in some pub looking for something to dominate. Either way, I'm passed the point of no return. I'll take my licks and hope there's no brimstone inside. The girl is the mission. From what I can tell, she might be the only one on the team who isn't replaceable. Bock can take the lead if I end up meeting the maker. I stop the shakes, crack my neck, and turn the handle to the orphanage door.

Chapter 40

A SLIGHT YOUNG woman with dirty blonde hair haphazardly hidden beneath a nun's habit pours tea into a cup atop a simple desk. The room looks like a rotten Easter egg with its pastel paint in blues and pinks cracking and peeling from the walls. The black and white checkered floors remind me of a hospital except filthier. There is the smell of mildew, but something else. Sulfur. I'd know it anywhere by now. A lump rises in my throat as the young nun views me, evaluates me. She tries to suppress a giggle.

"You know why I'm here," I say in a matter of fact tone. "Where's my guy? Where's the girl?"

The young nun raises her eyebrows as I speak and feigns compassion, tilting her head ever so slightly and nodding it dramatically with my words. When I finish she goes into a giggling fit and I feel myself tense up. I'm not even sure she speaks English, but I've had just about all I'm willing to take.

"Well," I say, widening my stance and pulling the Glock from my belt. "I'm here, lady, so tell me where the hell I'm supposed to go."

She lowers her head and giggles again. She brings a hand to cover her mouth. There's a stairwell to the left. Might as well check it out. As I move cautiously up the steps, I glance back at the young nun at the desk. She's eyeing me like a cat watching an injured bird flailing helplessly on the sidewalk. I head up sideways so that I can keep her in my sight as well.

The heat must be turned up on the second floor. My face is going flush. I'm met with a darkened hallway of closed doors ahead of me. Don't know where to begin. Heck, I don't know what I'm even doing here alone. The smell of dirt, mildew, and sulfur reach intolerable levels. Should I just start kicking doors down? Should I pull out my cell and call Elijah for backup? Was that thing possessing Red telling the truth that Everly and the girl were still alive and that all this demon, Lix Tetrax, wanted was to meet me? What kind of name is that anyway?

I take a few steps down the hall, my boots on the wood sounding my arrival. As I creep down the hallway, inch by scurrilous inch, the suffocating heat presses in. I start to fight collapse. The heat to my back blisters and when I turn, I see the stairwell I had just ascended ablaze. I leap away from it, further down the hall lined with aged whitewashed doors. I heard nothing, not a spark. Saw nothing, not a flicker. The stairwell just went up silently and all on its own.

I feel the first droplet of sweat break on the back of my neck. It's only going to get worse from here. Need to work fast now, with purpose. Suddenly the kicking down doors option seems just as good as any. I rear back and kick the first door to my left. It comes apart like the rotten wood it is revealing a small dormitory filled with leaky bags of brimstone clumsily suspended in the air by lengths of twine. I turn and kick down the door to my right, and find the same thing. I feel a rush of wind in my face and hope there's not a back draft brewing. I call Everly's name and hear nothing but fire raging behind me, consuming wood and paint from the walls, spewing toxic smoke in a vertical spill across the ceiling like a black river. I call the girl's name now listening hard for a response. Nothing. Door after door I smash, the noxious smoke licking my lungs. I cough as the consistent emptiness of the rooms taunt me into a frenzy. I call the names out again, this time receiving another rush of air and the giggle of the young nun at an impossible volume loud enough to hear clearly over the fire that continues consuming the hallway behind me. The voice takes turns giggling and letting out endless strings of that horrible sound Red kept making: Lix. Lix. Lix.

Only three doors remain. The sounds of the nun threaten to drive me mad as I wonder whether they are actually in the hallway or just inside my head. Either way, the distraction hinders my progress. I call the names again, and the door on my right juts out as if someone pushed it. I hear faint, muzzled struggling from inside. I kick the door and though it looks just like the others, it fails to give. I kick again, but my boot bounces off as if the door is made of poured concrete. I can hear Everly's muffled pleas inside, and so I kick once and again over and over until I feel the bruising of my heel overtake my persistence.

The door next to me shudders, and a little girl's scream comes from behind it. I switch feet and kick at that door, but it too proves impenetrable. I beat on the doors with my fists, with my open hands, I rush them with all the weight of my body, but they will not give way, and all the while the torrential flames behind me threaten to set my clothes ablaze. My face drenched with sweat, my muscles spent, and my hope fleeing into the relentless conflagration, I scream out. "What do you want from me?"

The only door left clicks open. A cool swath of air breaks from the blackness, and I hear both Everly and the little girl Brigita say, "We are here. We are safe. Come and see."

I didn't fall off a turnip truck. Those voices sound like Everly and the girl, but I know they aren't. I pound on both of the doors for a few seconds longer until my knees start to buckle from the heat with the fire only feet from where I stand. The voices again invite me inside with the nun's fading giggling and goading repetitions still trailing up and down the hallway. I scream and relent, taking hold of the knob on the cracked door. It is freezing cold. I swing the door open in a desperate attempt to cast light from the fire inside so that I'm not entering blindly, but it is no use. The frigid blackness of the room repels any light whatsoever, and so at the last moment, I duck inside, into that insatiably refreshing cold. As the door closes behind me, I am awash in the pitchest black I have ever experienced.

Were there any light at all, I would see my breath the room is so cold. I hear no trace of the fire beyond the door or the struggling of who I believe to be Everly and Brigita. The nun's maniacal giggling has disappeared, but it's the smell that bothers me. The ever-present sulfur remains strong, but it's the dirt now that takes precedence. More like mud. In fact, with the smell, the temperature, and the dampness hanging thick in the cold air, I feel I'm standing in an earthen pit rather than a constructed room at all. The only thing I hear is a low squishing, a slurping, like the bubbling and frothing of tar pits.

"Lix. Lix. Lix. Now you are with us," comes from somewhere in front of me. The voice is lazy and several octaves below the norm, sounding stuffed, like a man speaking with a mouthful of sewage.

I glare into the darkness and instinctively begin feeling for walls. "Where are my people?" I ask in defiance.

"At the hotel with me, excrement," The tired voice says.

"You know who I'm talking about."

"Lix—lix. Burning. They are burning."

"Let them go. I'm here now. You have me."

"Will not. Lix—lix—lix. Will not let anyone go."

Guided by outstretched hands, I search the void in a desperate attempt for orientation. I walk a few blind steps to my right, and finding only more emptiness, I turn to my left, determined to find something, anything to help me negotiate this god-forsaken blackness. Finally, my outstretched fingers stab into a damp and slick surface. A wall. The room is as I feared. We are in a wet hole in the earth, me and this... thing. The room has disappeared. The hole is cylindrical from what I can tell as I slide my hands along its mud-slicked surface. The darkness accentuates the chill of inexplicable wind that whips unceasingly along the rounded surface of the walls, cutting straight through me before continuing to complete the circle and double back again with renewed strength. The cold wind's force increases with each pass, barreling by again and again faster and faster, until I must force my fingers into the wall just to stay on my feet.

"I am the Lix Tetrax. Languish in wretched exaltations," the voice says, directionless, locationless in my mind.

My fingers tear into the mud walls with slimy bits and pieces carried away by the unrelenting wind. Dirt and mud invade my teeth and eyes that strain in the black to see anything at all. Soon the wind picks up such a speed that my fingers have no choice. I am flailing completely horizontal on the cylindrical wall. My right hand catches wind and pins back, soon the force of the air is too much for my left.

I tumble along the walls, sometimes rolling sideways, swirling at bullet-speed end over end, my feet crashing into the walls of muck, boots inadvertently flinging more of it into the cyclonic thrush that howls without boundary. A few more slams into the wall and I'll be knocked out cold. Only thing I can do is go as limp as possible. They say it's the only reason the drunk nearly always survives the crash when no one else does. He's relaxed. Muscles are loose. I'm doing my best, but I'm libel to crack an arm, maybe even my neck with this flailing. Instead, I decide to make myself into a ball. I fight the inertia to bring my clenched fists and chin to my chest, and my knees as high up as I can. While the action saves me from breaking an appendage, it also speeds me up. Directions and orientations are meaningless. The mud wall is seemingly at my back, my nose, and my sides all at the same time.

My body pulls away from the wall. Though the wind remains rushing through my ears, my body stops spinning. I feel suspended in space, though in the matte blackness, I cannot tell whether I'm moving at all anymore. I release my appendages cautiously lowering my arms and extending my legs. No ground meets my boots, yet my body remains completely motionless as the thrush of wind races past my face. As I stare into the void, I note a blue hue in the distance. The wind slowly brings me to it.

A simple mound of blue luminescence comes into view, like a rounded loaf of soft white flesh. I study it and my surroundings in hope to make out anything resembling an escape. No luck, the glow only illuminates itself. I stare into it as the sound of wind decreases.

"Welcome, descendant, to the Lix Tetrax," that full, bass driven voice says, and all the sudden a slit appears in the loaf, horizontal, the full width of it. As the slit widens, a giant eyeball appears behind it, and I know now that I'm staring at the demon's head. The eyeball is like a goat's, a bulbous eye with a jagged horizontal black slit in the middle serving as the pupil. Always hated goats.

"What do you want from me?" I ask.

"It is as my minion attested."

"To see me? You just wanted to see me? Well, here I am. You see me."

"I see you. Lix—lix—lix. You fail to evoke fear in us."

"Ditto," I say, and too brazenly as the blue head rises up high above mine.

The blue luminescence liquefies, flooding down, spilling and pulsating like a syringe filled with some neon vaccine, down the body of the beast, lighting the entirety of it. Now I see the glow is bright enough to illuminate our surroundings. I am indeed suspended in the air by the tight cone of a vortex, and we are indeed inside a deep hole, the sides of the cylindrical walls ripped and torn by my boots and hands, mud and yellowed roots sliding down its dampened walls. I look up to blackness above, while below more mud with dark puddles of moisture reflect the horrific blue vision before me.

This Lix Tetrax is a slug. A giant, blue slug that can light himself up like a neon ad in Time's Square. The absurdity of it should bring fits of laughter if it weren't so... real. He's got to be the size and weight of a semi-truck, fuller at the bottom and narrowing all the way up to the head that seems several stories above me. That's when I notice the vortex has ceased, and I'm dropping toward the thick pit of puddles. I splash into one of the brown pools, soon realizing that these are filled with anything but water. As I struggle to stand, I do my best to clear my face of the thick viscous fluid that covers me. Then I remember that this demon before me looks like a slug, and I know what I'm covered with. I turn to one side, hunch over and vomit twice. The giant slug actually laughs.

"We sense a worldly strength in you, descendant," the demon says.

"You do, do ya?" I say sarcastically, still trying to clear myself of the sludge that covers me like coagulated chicken fat.

"But the soul. Grievously weak. Lix—lix—lix. Nothing to fear in you. Not like him."

I finally find my footing in the ankle-high muck, my face mostly free of the goop. I have to tilt my head nearly all the way back to see the demon's eye so far in the air.

"Not like who? Who do you think I am? Let my man and the girl go." I say, still awed at the sight of the glowing behemoth in front of me.

The eye lowers slowly. Lowering and lowering until it floats at my level. Pupil darting. Studying me. "You are unaware," it says, not so much as a question, but more of its own realization. "The fool from Tishbe has not told you."

"Told me what?" I ask, trying hard not to cower at the eye as big as my entire body.

A crash and splinter of wood comes from behind me. Before I can swing around to see, I hear Elijah's voice. "Now!"

A barrage of gunfire above lights the edges of the hole. I hear the demon groan in pain. I turn to see four barrels blazing next to Elijah who casts his cane down to me. It stabs into the soft mud at my side.

"Stab it, Mr. Rust. The eye," Tishbe calls down.

I quickly drop to one knee and snatch the cane with my right hand, swinging it instinctively behind my back as a Bo staff before taking it with both hands and rearing back. I throw every ounce of remaining force into the cane and plunge the tip deep into the demon's eye. Fluid gushes out, covering me once again as the blue head reels back. The strongest wall of wind takes my feet from under me and sends my body slamming into the mud wall behind. I slide down nearly unconscious, just in time to watch a thousand bullets, like piercing rain thud into the surface of the great demon eliciting more of the thick substance with each puncture. The demon cries and shrinks, as do the sides of the hole. I can't tell whether it's the sides of the hole lowering or the floor that rises slowly to bring me level with my men who continue to hail gunfire down on the beast. The mud starts to evaporate. The demon continues to wither and coil and shrink upon itself, its booming groans of pain deadening as well until my eyes flutter, and a buzz overtakes my mind. I feel myself passing back into blackness. My focus decreases. The last thing I see is Bock strobing toward me by light of his blazing guns.

Chapter 41

I AM SITTING in the pews of my grandfather's church in Wylie, Texas again. I am seven years old. My parents sit next to me, eyes on the pulpit where my grandfather preaches yet another Sunday sermon, Bible raised above his head. Smatterings of the congregation sound their agreement, covering the sanctuary in "amens" and "yes, preachers." I look to my mother. She notices me and smiles down. I see my father's heel tapping the floor in time with the organ that accompanies my grand-daddy's vivacious scriptural recitations when the doors of the sanctuary creak open behind us. Someone enters mid-service. I strain to see, but the tall pew obstructs my view. The congregation turns. I look to the only thing I can see, my grandfather up front. He freezes. He lowers his Bible. He glances to me, prays silently, and closes his eyes for the last time.

Chapter 42

"HE'S COMING AROUND."

"Let him sleep. It's just a twitch."

"No, I saw his eyes open."

"Leave him, I said."

"Go get Bock."

My eyelids crane open like I'm lifting a couple hundred pounds. That buzz in my head slowly trails off. My focus returns and I realize I'm on my back, covered up. Florescent lights above me. I work to turn my head, the soreness in my neck sends a shooting pain all the way down my thighs. I see Bock again, this time grinning over me.

"Aye, boyo. Welcome back."

"Bock," I say, throat hoarse as ever. "Where?"

"I tell you, brother. You know how to make them, don't you?"

I slowly reach out my hand for Bock to pull me up. He takes it and pulls slowly. I hear the vertebrae in my back crack back to life as I sit up on the bunk. We're in the HQ I had Xavi construct under Teasel's farmhouse. Wasn't the way I imagined the ribbon cutting. Didn't think they'd be the ones to show *me* around.

"How long was I out?" I ask, rubbing the sleep from my eyes.

"Days," Bock says. "Touch and go. Good thing old Horrace here's a doctor after all."

I look over to Horrace who stands behind Bock with his arms crossed, a lit cigarette hanging from his mouth. I hear movement in the adjacent room. "We had you pegged for a professor, Horrace," I say gently lowering my legs from the bunk and resting my feet on the cold and slick concrete floor.

"Like what you've done with the place," Everly says from a bunk across the room.

"Everly?" I ask with as much excitement as I can. "You made it."

"Barely," Horrace finally speaks up. "He's got some healing to do."

"What about the girl?" I ask, struggling to my feet as Bock works to steady me.

"She's in the kitchen with Evangeline."

"So everybody made it out?"

"Aye."

"How did you get into the orphanage? The fire," I ask.

"Fire? What fire?" Bock says.

"There wasn't any fire, you idiot."

I turn to see none other than fat little Pastor Ellison, a highball of whiskey in each hand. He pawns one off to Bock and takes a sip from the other.

"Okay, the mud hole? The wind? The big blue slug? Any of that there?" I ask.

"I think he's still off the plot," Bock says, grinning again and swirling the whiskey in his glass.

"Lix Tetrax is a very powerful demon, boy. Doesn't work the way you'd think. Not like most of the others anyway. I'm told you found the brimstone," Ellison continues, leaning slovenly up against one wall of the bunkroom.

"Tons of it. Rooms of it," I say.

"Well, I don't have time to go through the whole thing. Long story short, he used it to take you to him. He didn't come to you. Not in any way you'd understand."

"What were you all shooting at then?"

"Elijah got rid of whatever was controlling Evangeline," Horrace says. "He took us over to the orphanage, and when we busted in, some crazy nun rushed us spewing some language I've never heard. The Yak put her down before she could get to us."

"Where is he? And Knapp?" I ask.

"Found your little gun range, mate," Bock says. "Haven't been able to tear them away since we got here."

"When we got to the orphanage, we went upstairs and saw that you'd smashed up all the doors," Horrace continues. "All except two. Everly and the girl were in them, bound up like mummies. You didn't see them?"

"Couldn't get the doors to open," I say, looking apologetically over to Everly's bunk. "No matter what I did."

I finally notice that Everly's beat up pretty good. His jaw is wrapped up and there are bandages all over his face with red swells everywhere else. He looks away as soon as he sees me.

"Well what about the other door? You go in there? The pit?" I ask.

"You were crumpled up in a heap on the floor, Rust. That's where we found the priest sitting on a chair in front of you," Bock says.

"Say again."

"Lix Tetrax sets fires and controls wind, but those aren't his best powers, you see," Ellison blurts out. "What he does really well is 'render houses dysfunctional.'"

"Meaning?"

"Well you saw what he did to Evangeline, didn't you son?"

"Possession?"

"In a sense, but he can't do it unless there's a fissure in the soul," Ellison says. "We've all got them, and usually somebody like Evangeline would be able to rebuke it. But like I said, everybody's got a crack in the armor."

"I figure priests and nuns who run orphanages would be immune, wouldn't you?" I ask obstinately.

"Maybe, sure. But not if your orphanage was just a front the international child slave trade, huh?" Ellison scoffs. "You sure know how to pick 'em Horrace."

"How was I supposed to kno—" Horrace starts.

"Evil comes in all shapes and sizes, my good man." It's Elijah, just rounding the corner into the room. "Do all men share the same color of skin? Of course not. Nor do they share the language in which they speak, or the country and climate in which they live. Why should the armies of Heaven and Hell deviate from this truth? Imagine the myriad provinces and the beautiful differentiations to behold in the vast expanses of heaven. Imagine the harsh regions of the underworld, their terrible variety limited only by the forms and methods to which suffering can be ascribed. Divergent surroundings beget divergence among their inhabitants."

"And so that slug possessed everybody in the orphanage—" I say.

"He possessed the wicked therein, Mr. Rust. Long before we arrived. The evil one knew of Horrace's act in leaving the girl there, believing in his limited, and therefore blameless knowledge that she would be safe. The wicked one dispatched the Lix Tetrax who promptly took hold, compelling the nun and her priest—perhaps without their own understanding—to acquire brimstone and to place it about the orphanage. They were certainly fed reasons by the demon to bind Mr. Everly and the girl, and to offer it poor Evangeline so that she too may be possessed in order that you were lured. Even now I wonder if Mr. Dresden were compromised, and that his outburst served only to throw us off our better judgment. One can never be sure of these things. The Devil also works in mysterious ways."

"But why leave us alive? Any of us?" I ask. "He could have had the priest or the nun kill Everly and the girl. Heck, they could have killed me if they wanted to."

"They almost did," Horrace says. "That priest was holding a knife over you just before we broke in."

"So the gunfire was you putting down the priest," I say. "But the cane. You threw your cane down to me and I stabbed the son of a slug right in the eye."

"Ah, the cane," Elijah says. "There is still much you don't understand. The staff has long been an instrument of God to show man the power he may wield along with His blessed approval. Even in the holy book of Exodus, long before my own time, God told the shepherd Moses to cast down his staff, his greatest protection, only to have it turn to a serpent on the ground before him: a snake, the nemesis of any shepherd and his flock. Moses was afraid, but God instructed him to take the serpent up by his own bare hand. Moses was reluctant of course, but did as he was asked through faith, pushing through his fear, and the serpent once again returned to a staff."

"What're you getting at, Tishbe?" I ask.

"Do you not see? Perhaps I was instructed to cast down the staff to you, Mr. Rust. You could have done anything with it, even nothing at all. But you took up the staff, didn't you? You took it up, and through great courage and fear of your own struck out at the serpent until only you and the staff remained."

"But you're telling me that giant slug wasn't even there."

"Oh the demon was there, Mr. Rust. He was there for you, and you smited him. You passed the test and thus sealed your destiny. You've officially chosen your side, and much to His approval. And as you have chosen the right side, we in turn have chosen the right man. It is finished, and you may now consider yourself and your team, activated. Everything is in place. All members are assembled—"

"We've got ourselves a bat cave—" Everly says.

"Ha, indeed you do, Mr. Everly. And now that you've saved the life of your Herald, the girl Brigita," Elijah says. "I should expect your first rescue to occur shortly."

I can't believe it, but I'm buying most of this. Seems like the rest of the boys are too. They've seen enough by now to know it's not all smoke and mirrors. Suddenly we hear Evangeline calling out from the next room.

"Elijah! Something's wrong with Brigita!"

"Ah," Tishbe says too calmly. "Shortly has become presently it seems."

Bock holds out his hand. I take it and give a good solid shake.

"Alright then, brother," Bock says. "Let's go and make ourselves rich."

Chapter 43

SO MUCH HAS occurred, even after so many years in the business. I must admit, I've got butterflies again. Maybe it's because I know that this time we're up against a completely new kind of enemy. Everywhere and nowhere. Unarmed but as deadly as could ever exist. Worse than the simplistic old saying, "things that go bump in the night." More like, "things that tear the face off your skull before you even hear the bump."

Tishbe and Ellison tried their best to prepare me for what the little girl, Brigita, would go through in her "spell." None of us were ready for it. It comes on as a convulsion, a seizure. Guess that's why only a few people can even spot a Herald. They act just like someone with epilepsy, and display characteristics found in some autistics. Of course, it seems everyone is autistic these days. Back when these things weren't so understood, I imagine Brigita would've been thought as possessed herself and possibly burned at the stake, Salem style. Talk about irony.

Later, I asked Red how Brigita's spell came on. She said it started as trembling, almost vibrating. The girl seemed to get tight, eyes trained in on an invisible point in space. The trembling stopped and she froze. Her mouth began to froth and Red said she could hear her little teeth begin grinding so hard she thought they might shave down to powder. The trembling returned and Brigita began fluttering her lips with indiscernible Sounds. Ellison called it "the receiving," Likening it to a fax machine making a connection. Though he said he couldn't be sure, he suspected the strange sounds were a language, possibly the very one angels communicate with. He was fascinated, and said that he had spent many years trying to decipher this language. Ellison is driven in that way. His thirst for what some would call forbidden knowledge overrides pretty much everything else except fast food and whiskey. Apparently coding this angel language continues to elude him as he says the sounds don't translate well using our alphabet. Somehow they just don't fit. That's why he was so keen on getting a letter written by one of Tishbe's angels in his own language. He said it would be his codex, his springboard into successful translation, his Rosetta Stone. Something tells me he won't stop trying, even without the letter, and part of me fears for the little girl's safety. Ellison can be overbearing to say the least. No tact. No polish. I'll have to keep an eye on him around the girl. She's got enough problems.

Red told me that Brigita snapped out of it just about a minute or so in. She asked for juice in Latvian. Luckily, Horrace was there to translate. Only after downing a couple of glasses did she reveal the location of the downed angel. That couldn't have been coincidence. I'll assume that Heralds need to replenish something whether it sugar or vitamin C quickly after a "spell." We'll need to keep it on tap at all times. Ellison made a call and one of those black Chinook choppers showed up in short order to take us to the site.

We're headed to Del Rio, Texas, a border town down south. Ellison and Elijah stayed behind with Brigita and Everly who still need recovery time. Before we left, Ellison mentioned in passing that we should expect several more extractions from the Texas-Mexico border due to the fierce drug wars raging across the region as of late. This border is a hotbed of violent activity both physical and spiritual since most of Mexico's populace is devoutly Catholic, even the criminals.

I had hopes of tweaking some strategy and tactical weaponry before our first rescue. Taber and his team had a system, but I noticed a few things that could have been revised. We inherited all of his equipment and methods. Even though I believe there is a much better brimstone delivery device than the bolos, it seems we'd be bound by them for at least one job. When the chopper touches down at Teasel's we have to scramble. I always take an interest in what my team chooses to mount up with. I insist everyone take as much Kevlar as they can manage and still maintain a minimum of 85% dexterity. The weaponry's up to them. Bock and Henry Knapp are almost exclusively partial to semi-automatic selections, pistols and shotguns. Of course Horrace is known to opt for a single burst FN FAL or "light automatic rifle" as it's translated from Belgian. Yakubu seems to be enamored with that hulking Ultimax 100 light machine gun he picked up on the Brigita orphanage job. Guess it's the only one he's found that really fits his size. I'm going to stick with the trusty P90 sub and my Colt revolver as a sidearm. It's agile, compact, and rapid fire. It should be mentioned that we're low on salt-treated ammo from Taber's old stash. Apparently treating ammunition is a difficult process to master, and the time to experiment just hasn't been available.

Can't say I'm not surprised to see Red on the chopper with us. Figured the whole possession thing would steer anyone clear from action for a while. I'm always impressed by this woman's constitution, and look forward to learning more about her as time permits. At first I thought she only brought a sidearm to the party: a Smith & Wesson compact 9mm. I can't imagine that would be enough to repel this kind of tango, but then, that wasn't the only equipment she brought along. She had the chopper crew load up a crate too, a good sized one about 4ft. X 2ft. Nobody knows what's inside, and she's not offering any explanation. I'd ask, and I'm sure Bock's curious, but we've got more important things on our mind. The mortars and brimstone bolos seem to be standard issue among extraction teams, and so I was informed by the crew that these were already in the chopper payload.

"Five clicks from drop point, gentlemen... and ladies," the pilot says over the PA.

We all take the cue to check our weapons and body armor. Red produces a screwdriver and gets to work popping open the crate. Sitting next to her is Henry Knapp. I notice him taking a peek, but can't seem to make sense of what's inside.

We are to be dropped a half-mile from the location of a downed angel in an open desert area surrounded by low, sandy hills dotted with cacti and brush. I'm comfortable with this terrain. Only difference from home is the hills. The armored bank trucks have been placed at insertion for us. We'll take them to the site and go to work. This is usually where my blood pressure spikes.

I feel the Chinook descend and peer out the open cargo doors. Sunset already underway, I see the trucks parked neatly below. I motion for Bock to take the first truck. I'll drive the second.

We hop out at touchdown. My men unload the mortar and bolo crates. Red hangs behind and says something to the co-pilot. He assists her in taking a complicated looking apparatus from the crate at her feet. The copilot lifts a large tank with thick shoulder straps, much like those seen on the backs of deep-sea divers or WWII flamethrower infantrymen. He slips it over Red's shoulders. He snakes two tubes running from the tank down her arms where one palm-width cylindrical device for each hand sits atop heavy, chain mail gloves at the knuckles. Red slips on the gloves as the copilot tightens the straps: two over the shoulders, one across the chest, and one on the back end of each glove by the wrist.

I watch astonished, like I'm seeing the Grand Canyon for the first time and notice that the rest of the team has done the same. We've all got the same inquisitive look on our faces as Red approaches us at the trucks.

"Let's go, gentlemen. Burning daylight here," she says cheekily delighted and faking annoyance at the attention. She passes me muttering, "I'll tell you inside."

"Okay," I address the men. "Everybody pile into Bock's truck. Looks like Red's gonna need a wide berth with that tank strapped on her back. I'll take her with me. See you at the site. Start setting the mortars in a 360 formation at the center. We won't get the friendly's exact position until we pop the bolos."

With that, we're all tucked in. Bock's GPS guided truck pulls away in a cloud of dust. I'm in the driver's seat of the other one with Red in the cargo hold. I reach behind me and slide the viewing window open so

I can talk to her. Before I can start, she delivers it like she's had to a thousand times.

"Two small gauge air lines wrap from the air tank down the arms of the user to chainmail armored gloves upon which the steel cylinders sit. The cylinders are basically retractable pneumatic cattle puncher bolts about four inches long, shaved down to the shapes of crosses and treated with Dead Sea salt. Pressure sensors around the outer rims of the punchers, usually through a striking motion of the user, detect contact and activate the pneumatic bolts, thrusting them out at a thousand feet per second, drilling an instant cross-shaped puncture wound into the target before retracting back into the cylinders just as fast as they were expunged. Fire rate depends upon the user's punching speed, as well as a small trigger on each palm that can toggle a 'rapid-automatic-fire' mode which can virtually perforate anything coming into contact with the user's fists at a rate of six punctures a second. Obviously this mode disables the sensors around the rim of the contact device. Questions?"

"Uh... well. Guess that pretty much sums it up," I say, grinning wide, and fighting a strange sort of adolescent arousal. "Don't mind getting that close and personal?"

"Love getting up close and personal, Amarillo," she says, and for the first time I see a glimpse of that bubbly girl I thought was a waitress back in Vegas. "Would have thought you'd know that by now. Want me to make you one?"

"Think I'll stick with bullets, sweetheart."

"Your loss," she says smiling.

Chapter 44

BY THE TIME Red and I pull into the clearing off the dirt road, the men have already started work setting up the mortars in admirable fashion. For good measure, I opt to park my truck on the other side of the prospective battlefield. Better to spread out the odds since we don't know the exact position the fight or extraction will take place. This way we've got two exit options. The wooden Hebrew boxes that render the bolo brimstone inactive until such time we load them into the mortars are stacked as they should be. I get out of the truck and pop the cargo hold. The men watch Red take a short hop out with what I've decided to call "The Thumper" on her back. She stands next to the mortars, and helps the boys position the show.

"Everybody listen to Red until we get the hang of it," I say walking up. "She's done this thing several times. Take her word as mine."

Bock joins me. "Could use a couple of flood lights, mate. We'll be in the dark soon."

"Take it from somebody who's seen it, my man," I say. "This thing goes down the way it should and we'll be out of here with the package before the Sun drops."

"Nothing like being dumped into the frying pan," he says.

"I hear you. Do me a favor and help Knapp fire off the bolos on my mark. Horrace, you'll hang back by one of the trucks with that FAL since you've got the ACOG sight. Pick 'em off as they show. Yak, stack up a few crates about thirty yards from the mortars and repel tangos from that position with the machine gun. Where do you want to be, Evangeline?"

"We'll stick close to Yakubu's LMG position until we spot the downed angel," she says. "Then you and I will rush and extract under his covery fire. I think Henry and Bock should do what they can, but primarily move to the trucks ASAP. The enemy is painfully predictable. They see us with an angel and they will turn all of their attention that way."

"Sounds good," I say. "Positions everybody?" I move over to Red with my arm raised. "Fire bolos on my mark."

Only the sounds of desert now. Only the smell of dust. Wind rustles brush. Distant jetliners push through 30,000 feet of sky. Crickets welcome the impending night. I check each man and remember that whole thing with Park in Oklahoma. I drop my hand. Henry Knapp pumps a set of bolos into the first mortar. Bock releases the hammer, sending that first bolo out into the open in a thunk of white smoke. I watch it careen through the air, crest, and begin its arc to the ground about two hundred yards away. Another thunk, and the second set of bolos is sent away, then a third, then a fourth. I watch each pair smash into the dirt, and wait for a few seconds.

Nothing. I start to doubt our little Herald. I wonder if she's too young or just misidentified. I wonder if it's a talent that must be groomed and refined, and if Elijah had sent us into the proverbial lion's den without a staff. Another test perhaps, the cruelty of it stirring inside me as doubt takes hold. What were we doing out here? Onlookers would think us hopelessly insane, playing some kind of comic book game. But just as the skepticism threatens to envelope me, I make something out in the distance.

As the smoke threatens to clear, I hear confirmation from Horrace back at the truck on our right. "I think I see it. Eleven o'clock."

Still quiet as concentric plumes rise into the air. The distant body on the ground groans and rolls to its side.

"Do we wait or go now?" I whisper to Red who crouches on the other side of Yakubu. The Yak glances at me, and I motion with my eyes for him to keep watching the smoke.

"Toure'," Red says to the big man with the Ultimax resting on a tri-pod atop the crates. "Lay down a few rounds just over the man's head. Like a semi-circle. But do not hit him, Toure'. Can you do that?"

"I can," he says, and wastes no time. He looks down the oversized iron-sight and cracks off six or so deafening rounds, just like Evangeline told him to.

That's when a blood-curdling scream I haven't heard since Oklahoma pierces the area like a pig with a slit gut comes from some-where behind the angel.

"Now," Red screams as she scrambles around the crates and makes a run for the body.

I hop over the crates and follow. "Don't you hit us, Yakubu," I call back.

"Yes, boss," I hear him say before opening that Ultimax back up again.

I hear the bullets whiz past our ears and two reports from Horrace's FAL far behind. They're here. Red and I are in full sprint across the desert terrain.

"Over there," I hear Bock yell, but don't have time to take my eyes off the angel who I now see is desperately coughing up blood and cra-dling his insides close to his body cavity.

There's still residual brimstone in the air mixed with South Texas dirt. Just enough to obscure a clear line of sight. The demons are in there somewhere. If they've got brains in their heads, they know to hide and stalk us in the smoke. Just as I think of it, we're five short yards from the angel as a shape leaps at me from the haze. Same angular dog legs. Thick thighs. Tendons. Covered in matted brown hair. A thick, segmented tail like a rat flails behind it, helping to propel its body toward me. But it's the face this time. Eyes bulbous and sharp like a goat behind a flat metal mask. Is it wearing armor? Slim, forked arms more blunt than pincers, with three sharpened nails at the ends. Thick, bark-like skin protrudes from patches of that wiry hair.

I fail to raise my P90 in time, instead going into a halting slide. The heels of my boots tear long gashes into the dry ground. The thing tackles me and I am instantly vulnerable on my back staring up at death poised over me, ready to strike, its sinewy canine legs straddling my torso. I glance over to see Evangeline pivot on one heel and unleash a powerful haymaker at the beast's face. The cylinder on top of her glove activates and the thumper shoots out faster than my eye can register. As her fist recoils, a perfect indenture three inches or so in length punches through the demon's metal mask like a .45 slug through crate paper. It all happens so fast, it takes a second before its dark blood wells up in the wound and begins to spill onto my Kevlar vest. The demon doesn't even have time to scream before a second punch punctures its rib cage, then a third to the kidney, a fourth and final blow again to the rib cage.

I scramble back to avoid all the blood. The demon shudders, in so much pain and surprise it can't even scream. It furiously wipes at the wounds with its forked arms, exhaling deeply.

"Come on!" Red says, pulling me to my feet.

Another demon runs toward us from the smoke, but is quickly put down by Horrace's FAL far behind. Two more make for us from the side. Yakubu cuts them into pieces with the Ultimax. I can hear him screaming over the barrage from either excitement or fear. We reach the angel. I crouch down to check its wounds while Red stands guard waving for the trucks. The demon Horrace hit with the FAL rises and skips toward us almost like a kangaroo trading sprints from feet to tail, feet to tail. Yakubu is busy with three more demons approaching from further away, still screaming and making that LMG barrel burn orange. Red scrambles to block the demon bearing down on us, its forehead trailing blood each time it hops forward. She flips a switch on one of the cylinders. The pneumatics thump in automatic mode sounding deep and constant like a turbo-charged sewing machine.

"We're just about to load you up. Stay with me," I say to the angel who looks up at me with a cautious hopefulness.

I press down on his hands that hold his wet entrails and I'm struck by how pale and human the angel seems. He's tall again, just like the last one, and there is a separate dimension to his eyes that widens the gap between our beings. This one wears a tattered brown cloak. The sash has been torn away. There are no genitals. I try not to notice and cover the angel up as best I can, remembering Taber who told me not to speak much to them, that though they look like us, and though they're on the same side as we are, that they're still very different beings, and that we don't mesh on levels we may not see. That our sinful nature offends them. I don't know if I buy all that. If I was ever torn open like this one, I'm not sure I'd care how sinful the guy trying to get me safe is.

A horn sounds from one of the trucks. I look up and see Bock bearing down on us from the driver's seat. Henry Knapp's with him. The truck's tires kick up thick trails of dust into the air as the engine growls. The last glimmer of sun casts sharp beams onto the battleground. Horrace stops firing and now follows Bock close behind in the other truck. The Yak has run out of ammo, and furiously clamors to expel the empty drum and replace it with a fresh one. This takes his focus off the two felled demons that take the opportunity to rush him. I scramble to one knee and try to use the red dot sight on my P90 to take them down before they reach Yakubu. It will be a feat. A P90 sub isn't ranged for that distance, but I've got to try. Yakubu, as big and powerful as he is, sits in the open like a honey-baked ham on Thanksgiving.

I hear Red's thumper to my left on automatic relentlessly tearing into demon meat. She's got that one under control. The one Red fights finds its voice and lets out one of those piercing wails. I raise the red dot a little higher than normal to gauge distance and let off three and four round bursts at the two demons skidding toward the Yak as Bock's truck slides to a stop only feet from the angel now laboring to breathe next to me.

My shots ring out. I can't take them both, but I hit one with a full four-round burst in the exposed thigh. The next time it tries to bare weight on it, the leg gives way, sending the demon tumbling to the ground end over end in a rush of dirt. I scream out Yakubu's name. He sees the demon as it leaps for him in the air. The Yak brings up the light machine gun in both hands like a staff in order to deflect the beast. It takes hold of the gun in the forks of its hands. I see the big man's leg muscles nearly burst through his pants as he throws all his weight against the creature. I'll be darned if he doesn't push it back like a defensive lineman. The creature seems surprised at the human's strength and so digs its claws into the ground for leverage. The Yak yells and continues pushing. The demon slides backward, wrenching away the LMG from Yakubu. Now it's hand-to-hand and from everything I've been told, you never tangle hand-to-hand with one of these things. The big man grabs the creature around the neck anyway with one of those massive hands. The thing on the other end seems just about as shocked as I am, as it hangs limp just long enough for Yakubu to crash a fist into the side of its head. The force sends the metal mask flying off to the side. It hangs from the demon's head revealing a rotten mess of wet flesh and teeth beneath it. Just one problem, his fist isn't treated with salt, yet it still made contact. Remarkable contact. But how? The Yak goes for another punch, but I know better and leave Red with Bock and Knapp who have charged out of the truck and unlocked the cargo doors.

Red tells them to load the angel up while she repels any opposition, though the remaining demons all seem downed for the moment. But a moment can change, and Yakubu's is about to. I rush toward him with my P90. No way it will allow one of us to clock him twice. I call to him, ordering him to let it go and get to the trucks. He doesn't listen and instead cocks back that monster fist again. The demon comes to and brings the forks of one arm together, ready to go for a stab. I stop about forty yards from them and bring the red dot to my eye. I squeeze the trigger knowing the risks. Yakubu's far too close to be safe from the P90's erratic spread pattern, but there isn't much choice. Thankfully most of the clip slams into the demon's side-mass, but one of the slugs tears through Yakubu's forearm. He let's go of the creature's neck and unleashes a devastating thrust kick which sends it stumbling back several feet, just enough for me to drop my spent P90 and take up my Colt revolver. I plant all six rounds into the staggering beast, even hitting it once in the uncovered face. Teeth, bone, and flesh splinter off as Yakubu makes a run for the grumbling trucks with one hand over his wounded forearm. I crouch to pick up the P90 and run that way myself, seeing a litter of bleeding demons struggling to their feet and staggering toward the trucks that wait for the Yak and me. Everyone's loaded, the team and the angel. I can smell victory. I wave my hand for Bock to head out since he's running the truck with the angel. Yakubu and I pile into Horrace's. When we're safely inside, he puts the truck into gear and grinds the tires into Del Rio dirt, covering the trailing demons in earth and exhaust. *Via con dios, el diablos.*

"What now?" Horrace asks as we pull both of the trucks onto Cinegas road.

"There's a church on Lupita in Del Rio. Red knows what to do. Just follow," I say, turning around to the cargo area. "You okay big Yak? I sure am sorry about that. Should be a first aid kit back there somewhere."

"The wound is close to the surface, boss. I thank you for saving me."

"Yeah, we need to talk about that. Those things are too strong to be throwing down with unarmed, even for a big boy like you. To be honest, I'm surprised you can even do it."

"I learn that the hard way."

"Looks like. Not again, okay?"

"I will do as you say," he says searching for a med-kit, droplets of blood dotting the cargo floor.

A few quiet moments pass, as Horrace finally remembers to flip on the headlights. We remain quiet for a while listening to the radio scan for stations across the expansive desert static.

Chapter 45

MAKE NO MISTAKE. I'm well aware it's my first time running a rescue team, and truth be told, I feel like I'm second in charge to Evangeline anyway. But I've got to tell you, I honestly thought more would have gone wrong. Guess that's the genius of old Elijah Tishbe. Said he searched far and wide for Taber's replacement. He must've meant the entire replacement team. We worked like a well-oiled machine if I do say so myself. Of course, Yakubu could've been a little more with the program. I feel like he was firing mainly off adrenaline and disbelief. Scratch that. It wasn't disbelief. I think it may have been confirmation. There was something in his eyes that said, "Aha. I knew it. Now I can see you. I always knew you were there, but now I can kill you."

Horrace did pretty well, his aim notwithstanding. He's usually far more accurate with a FAL, but under the circumstances, I'm not gonna bust him on that one unless it becomes a habit. My boys know how to calm their nerves, and I think Horrace will find his sea legs soon. We've got to find a way to get Bock and Henry Knapp more involved too. Spent too much time running for the trucks and shuttling them around. Whether they like it or not, I can see myself having to pull rank on their weapon selection. Be better if they could find that out on their own, but I've got the feeling we don't have the time. Not with this kind of enemy.

These demons are senseless the way they're put together. Always heard demons were nothing more than fallen angels. Haven't seen an angel yet that hops around on a giant rat tail or sprints around on dog legs, and what's the deal with that armor? Makes me wonder if fallen angels get changed somehow when they switch sides. God punishing them maybe. Disfiguring them. Don't know. Either way, just makes our job harder when you can't predict what you'll be up against on a given day. The intel sure would be useful so we could outfit ourselves accordingly. Course the only one who could have any idea what the demons look like ahead of time would be the angel, and if the other ones we rescue are as torn up as the one we just extracted, there's not likely to be any head's up from their end.

The mortars are cumbersome, clumsy, and inaccurate. Guess that's why nobody outside those Arab cave-lobbers use them anymore. Two hollow cannon balls with welded chain holding them to each other. Archaic. Feudal. Unimaginative. They've got no intrinsic propellant outside a completely clunky, bulky, and not to mention extremely heavy independent delivery device. The mortars have to be carried to the site, each in their own crate, then leveled, set up, then primed, and you can bet your first shot will be a waste for judging distance. Talk about inefficient. Not sure what Taber was thinking, but the whole mortar bolo system will be the first to go. Thinking I'll put Horrace and Everly on weapon R&D. Horrace can apply the physics and Everly has an extensive knowledge of modern weaponry since the civil war era. The job is tailor-made for Park though. He and Horrace would've had a blast at it. But that's life I guess.

We're almost to our turn. I pick up the CB to call the other truck. "We're gonna take this next left on St. Peter, Bock."

"Aye, St. Peter," he confirms.

"So what happens now? I mean, where exactly do you take an angel to get stitched up?" Horrace asks, the visible signs of exhaustion creeping over.

"We don't stitch him up," I say. "We just take him to— Daddammit."

"What?" Horrace says with a jolt. "What? What?"

"Sorry," I say sighing. "Forgot about something. That's all."

"Forgot what?"

I pick up the CB again and call the other truck asking for Red.

"What's the matter, Amarillo?" I hear her say as the truck in front of us makes the turn down another dust swept Del Rio street.

"Who takes him in?" I ask, a little embarrassed.

"What do you mean, 'who takes him in?'" she asks.

"The angel. Who takes him into the church?"

"You don't know?" She's not happy. "You didn't set this up ahead of time? You're kidding, right?"

"No. I'm not kidding. I forgot about—"

"*Forgot.* This is the most important part, Amarillo. Elijah said you had the whole team down."

I hear the CB jostle on the other end. Now Bock's voice comes through. "What's this bird going on about, Rust?"

"Taber said only one team member was able to actually take the angel into the safe house. The church. I don't know who that is."

"Who gives a shite? We'll all take it inside. You can take it inside if you want. What's it matter?" he says.

"I don't think it works that way. Get the feeling that the wrong person takes the angel in and something bad happens."

The CB scratches again. They must be yanking it from each other's hands. Now it's Red again. "Bet your butt something 'bad' happens. You better figure this out or we're royally screwed, Amarillo," she says. "It's just a matter of time before they send more demons to intercept this angel. This is the part that has to be fast."

"It's okay, isn't it? We don't have any brimstone around. Should be fine, right?" I ask hesitantly.

"Rust. I'm looking down at an empty gurney right now. The angel has crossed over again, but the rule is, once we get to the elevator—"

"Wait. Elevator?" I cut her off.

"Yes. Elevator. That's what most teams call the church, the extraction point. I don't know, the place where the angel gets sent back up. The elevator. Anyway, when we get there we're supposed to make the sign of the cross in brimstone on the angel's forehead just before we bring him out. He crosses back over so we can see and protect him. We wheel him up to the door, and the designated member takes him inside."

"Look, I know all that, sweetheart," I say. "But Taber said he didn't know why his man, that Bassong character, was the only man who could take the angel inside. He said he wasn't in on the decision-making. Elijah must have told him."

There's silence on the line for a minute.

"Well, what are we supposed to do now?"

I muster some confidence. "We'll do what my team does best. We improvise. Tell Bock to pull over. Ready the bird, Red. We're here."

The trucks pull to a stop on the southeastern corner of Westlawn Cemetery. More howling dirt cuts through clumps of manicured green hedge amid all the close-cropped yellow brush. Rows of ground level markers with the occasional granite tombstone surround us. The small cinder-block chapel sits to our right, moonlight glowing off its flakey white paint. There are no lights inside. No traffic on the surrounding roads. No resistance so far.

I take another quick scope of the area. Seems quiet enough, so I hop out. Yakubu stays put in the back. Hope he isn't loopy yet from blood loss. Horrace follows me to the other truck. Bock and Henry Knapp get out and open the cargo doors just in time for me to see Red dip her finger into one of those wooden boxes of powdered brimstone. She makes a cross seemingly in mid-air as the horribly injured angel is painted back into our existence. He's trembling, and bleeding something awful. It spills over the sides of the gurney like a knocked over syrup bottle at the edge of a breakfast table.

I motion to Horrace and Henry Knapp to wheel out the gurney. Red has unstrapped herself from the Thumper. Sweat rings under her arms and across her shoulders where the straps dug in show the fatigue running a weapon of that size can take on a person. "Alright, captain," she says sarcastically. "We need to do this fast. What's your conclusion? Who goes in?"

"It's my mess. My fault. I'll take the bird inside," I say.

"It's almost never the team leader," she says back.

"That's what Taber said, but what choice do we have?"

Horrace barks my name. I turn to see two sets of unwelcome swirling red and blue lights approaching up the road at a clip.

"Great," I say. "Police."

Two squad cars. Local. No sirens, which is a good sign. But for them to get here so quickly, I have to wonder if they heard the gunfire back in the desert. The Texas-Mexico border is a dangerous place to do business. The local law is already on high alert for anything out of the ordinary, and they've learned to have twitchy trigger-fingers. We might just be flat against the wall on this one. I'm not into killing cops, but my boys and the mission always come first. I can feel the men tense up and become aware of their side arms. Think. Think.

Just as the squad cars pull to a stop behind our trucks, I feel Henry Knapp's calm hand on my shoulder as he passes me and heads for the officers. There are two of them, only one in each car. They haven't drawn on us yet. Another good sign in a sea of bad ones. The angel's still got brimstone on his person, and so we're vulnerable for another attack at any time.

"Where the hell have you been?" I hear Henry Knapp bark as he stomps up to the policemen.

"Calm down, sir," the nearest cop says, holding out his hand. "This is private property."

"No kidding, patrolman. What's your name? I put a call in twenty minutes ago," Knapp continues undaunted. "Is this how Del Rio PD responds to assistance calls? No wonder you're having such a cartel problem around here."

"Sir, back up now. We—" the cop behind the other one starts.

"What, you need ID? You need ID? Who's your superior? I'm going have his hind-quarters in a sling when I get back to Langley."

Knapp holds out one steady hand and reaches his other into a back pocket. The patrolmen's hands instantly move to the hilts of their belt-holstered 9mms. He produces a wallet and flips it open, presenting it arrogantly to them. I can see the shimmer of some kind of badge in the squad car lights. Sly son of a gun. He somehow kept his credentials when he left the agency. That or he had some mighty authentic looking ones made up.

"That going to work for you, officer?" Knapp says. "Can we move on now?" he says, methodically flipping the wallet closed again and returning it to his pocket.

"You're FBI?" the first officer says. "What about them?" he says pointing to us.

"And the bank trucks," the other one says.

"Do you need an explanation of our entire mission, patrolmen? That how it works? I don't think so." Knapp steps up to the first officer and plants a finger in his chest, driving it in, accentuating his displeasure. "I radioed twenty minutes ago for support assistance on our operation that was, up until you jackwagons decided to blaze your lights, clandestine. We could have been slaughtered out here! You know how many cartel members with automatic rifles could be moving on our position? This is a federal drug operation in progress and so help me your bumpkin PD will not blow it for us. Now who is your superior, officer?"

The first cop looks dumbly back to the other one who offers him nothing but a shake of his head.

"Who is he?" Henry Knapp raises his voice.

"Diaz," the cop Knapp hunches over, chest heaving, says.

"Your superior? Diaz?" Knapp says.

"No him. He's Diaz" the buffooning cop says pointing at the one behind him.

"You his superior?" Knapp barks to the other one.

"No. I'm officer Diaz, sir," the one in the back says.

"And who are you, jackass?"

"Cokely, sir."

"My god, are we really doing this?" Knapp says turning his back to the officers and walking back to us. "You two get your tails back to the road and make sure no one enters this cemetery until we sweep it for our fugitive," he says over his shoulder. "You understand me? I've got half a mind to accompany you back to your HQ and hand your knuckle-headed asses to your sergeant myself. Now, go!"

The officer in the back, Diaz, wastes no time in sinking back into his police cruiser. The other nervous one can't help himself. "Uh, but, sir? Wh—what about these bank trucks, sir?"

Henry Knapp turns on his heels and breathes deep. "They're bait cars, Cokely, you idiot. Now get out of here before I take down your info and have you fired all the way from Virginia."

"Sir," the remaining officer says before skulking back into his cruiser. They both pull away as Knapp stands before us with his eyes closed, quietly willing the policemen to buy it all without checking.

"They gone?" he whispers to me.

"Yep," I say, a smile creeping up my face. "Now that's impressive."

Everyone seems to be in agreement.

"We need to get him inside, Rust," Evangeline says at the gurney. More blood pours over the side. I can see the angel's breath now. It isn't even cold outside.

A small glimmer of light dances through the dingy windows coming from inside the chapel. The light intensifies, moving again from window to window. Bock looks at me. We all draw our side arms and train them at the door to the chapel that shudders and rattles, then stops. The light blinks off. The door opens.

"Impressive indeed, Mr. Knapp." It's Elijah, emerging like a medieval innkeeper. All that's missing is a lantern in his hand. "Wonders never cease."

We all lower our guns and collect ourselves.

"Where'd you come from, Tishbe? Was that supposed to be another test?" I ask, shaking the nerves from my hands.

"A test? No," Elijah says moving softly to the gurney and laying his hand on the mangled angel's upturned palm. "The time for tests is behind us. But I think we've found Mr. Knapp's calling."

"What do you mean?" Henry Knapp asks sheepishly.

"You have emerged as 'The Anointing,'" Elijah says, grinning.

"The hell is that about?" Bock says.

"There are positions in the team, Mr. Bock. Each man has a distinct purpose in this team, as in life. You, Mr. Rust, are 'The Shepherd,' the team leader," he says to me. "Mr. Knapp is 'The Anointing,' the one who administers the brimstone cross to the angel's forehead and delivers him inside the church. Pastor Ellison is 'The Text,' your spiritual and informational advisor. The little girl Brigita is your 'Herald,' hearing the very words of God. As the worldly gentleman he is, and with his vast knowledge of so many languages of Earth, our scholarly Horrace should perhaps be known as 'The Interpreter.' If so named, angelic words will become clear to him. Mr. Yakubu, showing marvelous physical strength in the face of certain death against the minions of Satan, I suggest he become 'The Judge.' His blessed will allows physical contact with the enemy possible without need for intermediaries. And Mr. Everly back at your headquarters, having sustained remarkable injuries that would fell any man of his meager size, only to offer himself to be placed in certain peril once again, might I suggest the ever important designation of, 'The Meek.'"

"Does every team have these positions? These labels?" I ask.

"Well, the exceptional ones, but none in a long while, I'm sorry to say. Did I not tell you there were parts to play?" Elijah says turning his attention back to the angel. He gazes down upon him like the epitome of beauty. "Be strong, Hofniel. Your heavenly creator anxiously awaits your triumphant return." He says it so softly and with great reverence. "He prepares a sumptuous celebration for you."

The men stand in silence as the door behind Elijah opens on its own. The angel tenderly lets his eyelids fall. His laborious trembling ceases. The face of deliverance washes over.

"Mr. Knapp," Elijah says quietly. "The agony you have felt for your departed family has led you to this moment. Your protective valiance and quick action at the site of ascension has marked you. Free from violence. Free from bloodshed. Come with me now and I will show you how it is done, and in it you will feel close to your wife and daughters once again. In your new purpose, you will know they are safely with Him. In His rapturous arms, their pain is at an unreachable distance. Come and see."

We watch Henry Knapp as he drops his eyes and arms. His flushed cheeks shimmer with tears. A great weight of many painful years lowers slowly from his shoulders. He wipes his eyes and looks at each of us as the longing he burdened to carry for so long seems to slowly wear away. Suddenly he can breathe again. I nod to him. He looks to Elijah, then the angel, then back to me. I nod again and grin. He exhales his anguished past deeply, and follows Elijah as the gurney floats inside unassisted. Just before they disappear, we note the angel's hand reach out and take Henry's, leading him forward, unafraid.

Chapter 46

WE HAVEN'T SEEN Elijah since that night in Del Rio almost five months ago, but that didn't stop business. Most of the team has quietly relocated to Tahoka. I figure some of them waited to do so until their payment from the first rescue cleared. When that last bit of doubt was replaced with dollar signs, it was back to work. My team waits on call twenty-four seven, day and night. Extraction to the rescue site, usually by helicopter, arrives minutes after Brigita finishes a spell and Horrace translates. It was just as Elijah said, too. Once we named Horrace 'The Interpreter,' Brigita started speaking in a language I've never heard anywhere, and I've been everywhere. But Horrace seems to understand it anyway. Language of Heaven, I guess.

Our enemy is smart enough to know who we were, and where, and so the team all ended up trickling into the small farming town of Tahoka, Texas on their own time, quietly shopping the paltry real estate market. There's no use in hiding anymore, not from the enemy or each other. It's a set team now, and it would work far better centralized. Each one had their reservations. Tahoka sleeps heavy at night, and works hard in the fields during the day. Nothing much happens here, and some of the boys resent it. I don't blame them. Talk of relocating the HQ rumbled about for a while, but when I confronted the team one day, telling them that we could relocate, sure, but that I wasn't interested in footing the bill alone, most of them backed off after I told them the price of a new headquarters.

Horrace loves the new underground HQ more than any of us. He picked up a small one-bedroom apartment on the edge of town by the grocery, but he's rarely there. He spends nearly all of his time in the armory, that or the testing range beneath Teasel's with Everly, wrapped in the excitement of weapon development and application. Everly found a small parcel of land several miles northeast off FM 400, near the lake. When he isn't in the testing range with Horrace, he's at home remodeling and pouring patio slab in pursuit of the perfect bachelor pad. Henry Knapp found a residential in town not two blocks from First United Methodist on 4th Street. He's begun to attend services. The congregation has taken to him from what I hear. I *do* wonder what he must have seen in that Del Rio chapel with the angel and Elijah. Whatever it was, it changed him. His trademark brooding has given way to a committed diligence toward his new position as The Anointing.

One thing the team *did* like was how far their money went in a sleepy place like this. Bock went most extreme. A few years ago, a writer of western novels with a healthy readership passed on. He had built a secluded monument to his own agoraphobia west of town on forty or so acres of well-manicured land. It sat vacant ever since, that is, until Bock found out about it. The fee for our first job wouldn't even make the down payment, but he bought it anyway. Guess he'd been saving up more than I thought over the years. I haven't made it out yet, but he's allowing Red and Brigita to live out there in the mansion with him. At first, I wasn't sure how to feel about it, but after talking to some of the others, we decided it would be okay. Besides, what was Bock going to do with all that space?

I don't delude myself, the little girl is the most important of us all. She goes away and the team is rendered completely directionless. Red has taken to her as close a mother figure as someone could without adoption, and so the two of them stick together at almost all hours of the day and night. We bandied about the idea of enrolling her in public school, but Ellison said that would be a terrible idea. He said the girl had a gift that most people would consider a severe mental disability. He said that if Brigita went into one of those spells at school, teachers would notice and likely call in all kinds of specialists that would start asking lots of unwanted questions. Might even be taken away and locked up in some nut house. I agreed with him, but couldn't help but feel bad for the little girl. She'd been marked for something that seemed to rob her of a life on her own forever. Wonder how God would answer that one.

Even though Red had willingly taken primary responsibility of Brigita, it was always Yakubu who seemed to have the tightest bond with her, even from the beginning. We included him in the conversation about she and Red moving out to the mansion with Bock. He felt the same way I did, inexplicably leery, and so The Yak moved into a foreclosed farm as close by as he could get, about a quarter-mile south. It wasn't that we didn't trust Bock, heck, I trust him with my life, and have good reason to several times over, but Bock was never someone you'd call warm to the opposite sex, much less children with what some would call disability.

Toure' Yakubu took to living in Tahoka better than anyone, maybe even me. His hulking musculature warded off whatever residual racism remained in this part of the Texas plains, and he was always eager to help a neighboring farmer or rancher when called upon to corral animals, move equipment, or stalk the usual predators that threaten the local herds. Yeah, the people took to old Yakubu just fine. The summer heat suited him, as did the harsh, dirt-laden winds that blew relentlessly across this flat geography most months of the year. But most importantly he was close to Brigita, always at the ready if ever she found herself in need of protection or comfort. I can't think of anyone better for the task.

In the unlikely event Evangeline, Bock, Yakubu or the rest of us somehow fail to keep the little girl out of harm's way—if the enemy is out for anyone it's her—we had her "tagged." It's a harsh term, I know, but the idea came from Horrace and it was a good one. We had Henry Knapp work his magic on procuring us an ankle bracelet just like the ones felons under house arrest wear. The latest in anklet technology is small, wristwatch small, so that's how we disguised the transponder. Horrace and Everly designed a working digital faceplate to set over the anklet face. Red painted it up pretty with butterflies and colorful yellow and green flowers all around the strap. Looked just like something you'd find hanging at one of those kiosks in the middle of the mall. When we had Yakubu present Brigita with her new "watch" she let out a precious little yip while trying hard to lock her skinny arms around The Yak's neck. We never told her that the wristwatch was basically a lo-jack, constantly pinging her position back to our HQ computers, just in case she was taken or wandered off. Not that we could have told her anyway, as only Horrace speaks Latvian, but with Red's help, her English was slowly coming along.

So with the team pretty much settled in, Horrace and Everly constantly developing and testing, Knapp becoming more and more involved in the church, Bock enjoying the fruits of his labor, Yakubu laboring for his fruits out at the farm, and Evangeline doing her best to educate Brigita on her own, it wasn't long before we were put back into play. If Brigita was out with Evangeline, either at Bock's or in town somewhere, all Red had to do was record whatever Brigita said during one of those torturous spells on a voice recorder and hustle back to the HQ for Horrace to decipher. Luckily Teasel's was far enough away from Tahoka for most anyone to notice all the chopper activity, and it didn't take but ten to fifteen minutes to have the team assembled via SMS alerts sent to their smart phones.

We've pulled two rescues since Del Rio, each with their own... inconveniences. The first job took place near Odessa, Texas, just under half an hour south by helicopter amid fields of oil derricks and tumbleweeds. One of the mortars Bock tried to fire off failed, and the ones Henry Knapp managed to get into the air didn't explode on the ground like they were supposed to. I can't wait until we get rid of this technique. We improvised like always though, but I knew a better system could be implemented if only I'd had the time to develop it. Elijah hinted as much when he gave us our direct titles. Brigita as our Herald and Ellison as our Text made perfect sense, even I as the Shepherd was self-explanatory. The Yak was the Judge because he can hurt these things with sheer blunt force trauma, but why is Everly the Meek? I mean, I know what Elijah said, but how do we use him? What's his intended purpose? I'd need to have a powwow with Pastor Ellison as soon as I find the time to get away.

The second job took place off a highway near Phoenix. It was a battle for souls recently deceased. We showed just moments after a major automobile crash took place. A bus full of high school baseball players from goodness knows where. Couldn't make out the school's name because the bus was a twisted mess of metal, blood, and yellow paint. Looked like a blowout might have set it off. I started understanding where and why the angels showed up. Demon's will try to drag your soul away to the hot place any way they can. Those poor dead teenagers would be trophies down there. I'm sure some of them wound up down below anyway, but not all of them. Some of them must have been saved. That's why the angels showed up to claim them. There was a skirmish, probably a whopper judging from all the death inside that bus. Hope the good guys got away with everybody and dropped them at the pearly gates. One angel wasn't so lucky, but we picked him up and took him to the nearest "elevator" as Red calls them. His injuries weren't nearly as bad as the one in Odessa, but he still couldn't make it back to Heaven without help.

The most disturbing thing about both of these rescues wasn't the amount of bloodshed, or even the conditions of the angels. I suspect the rest of the team has noticed it as well, but they aren't saying. I'm not either. Sometimes to give something a name is to make it real, and whether we're all just in denial or not, I don't want this to be real. With each rescue we make, with each innovative use of tech or weaponry we employ, the odds are quickly and increasingly slipping out of our favor. There are more demons now, greater numbers of them to contend with as the jobs funnel in. It's like they know we're coming, and they're calling reinforcements before we even get there. I fear they will overrun us soon if we don't do something about it.

On a more upbeat note, Henry Knapp has taken to his new moniker of The Anointing quite well. He pushes the gurneys in confidently now, always holding the willing hands of the angels. Taber's man, Bassong, didn't even do that. Wonder if it was just technique, or if Knapp has some deeper connection to them. With each extraction we're moving better, taking to our roles and carrying them out with greater precision and efficiency. With each extraction we receive payment with a swift assurance that we'll be needed again soon; and therefore, paid again soon. It buoys the men's spirits, but I'm starting to see cracks in some of them, like it isn't all about the money anymore. The fissures are small, but I see them. Makes me nervous. It's a fine line to walk for a merc. The money keeps them honest, keeps them aware, grounded. Once the driving force becomes an ideal, well, that's what always gets people into trouble. See, you can reason with a man when you're talking money, but too often reason goes right out the window when you're talking about his faith.

Chapter 47

I AM EIGHT years old again, back in the pews at church. My grandfather has stopped preaching. He stares wide-eyed at the church doors like everyone else. I struggle to push myself up to see who's entered. I stretch and lean, but my mother holds me down into the seat. I see a flash of something, then darkness.

I wake up suddenly. A noise. The hairs on my forearm stand at attention. Someone is in the house. I've moved the bulk of my personal arsenal to the HQ beneath Teasel's, so I decided to deactivate most of the security measures. Maybe that wasn't such a good idea, but I've still got my wits and my Colt revolver. I have another pistol filled with salt rounds, but I'm not too worried about needing them. I've taken great pains to rid my house of brimstone. That cuts the threat level down to a four out of ten. I can deal with most thugs before they even realize I'm home.

I roll out of bed and hit the floor, snatching my stockless Remington 12-banger pump action. I had a modified red dot mounted on it several years ago with the laser unfocused to spread pattern size. I did this for three reasons. Number one: damage accuracy. I could maim rather than kill easier by painting my target with only an outside edge of the red. Number two: It helped blind the perp without giving my position away as much as a small LED would. Number three: It looks really cool.

While prone on the floor, I pump the 12-gauge. I hear scuttle from the blackness of the living room. I crawl forward and turn down the hall, away from an exit, a counterintuitive move that would throw off most common home invaders. Two sharp blasts into the bedroom I just vacated tell me whoever's inside has good ears and means business. Most likely isn't theft. This is a hit job. My ears ring, and from the sound, the perp's got a small caliber pistol. My Remington can turn that into Swiss cheese. He doesn't know it yet, but now I'm stalking *him*. The living room has two entrances. I hop to a barefoot crouch and move slowly through the darkness toward the second entrance, counting my steps, hoping to flank. Through the heavy ringing I hear a muffled clatter followed by a string of curses. Whoever's in my house is male, human, and as blind as I am in the dark. Only difference is that I know the layout. That gives me all the upper hand I need. I go back to my stomach and silently push myself into the living room and work my way between the legs of a heavy oak side-table, using it as a prospective blast shield. I wait for just the right second before I spot him with the red dot sight. No need to give up my position until the perfect moment. I prop my elbows on the floor and get ready, breathing slowly to lower my heart rate as much as possible.

Just then a pickup truck revs outside. The tires crush through the dirt and for a brief moment the truck spins around, painting the living room windows with headlights that burn beams of hot white through the slats of the wooden blinds. I take it as a gift from above, and just before the headlights swing in the opposite direction to ready a quick getaway, I spot the intruder. Droopy blue jeans. Biker t-shirt. Tats all over. Bald. The light glints off a thick loop earring. I train the shotgun, forgetting the red dot sight altogether and let off a booming cluster of pellets at him. Most of them miss and rip into the wall behind him, but just enough cut into his left shoulder. The man winces and lets out a pathetic yelp.

The room goes dark again and I pump the Remington to chamber another shell. The spent plastic casing plocks off the living room floor, as my front door bursts open. Another man charges in by moonlight. Looks just about like the one I shot give or take a few hairs. He's got something bigger than a .38, and he's already firing full bore around the room in automatic. I reach over my head and topple the side-table in front of me. He's unloading that clip blindly, so I cling close to the overturned slab of oak and wait for him to spend that sub to empty. Pieces of my life in showers of glass, tufts of padding, splinters of wood and plastic fly into the black air, illuminated by the rapid, methodic clap of a barrel snarling fire. I clinch my teeth and judge whether to pop up and let loose a few of my own. Before I can think, the man stops firing. I spring into action, flipping on the red dot sight and pointing it in the aggressors' direction just long enough to see the second man's hand shoot out and grab the back of the other one's t-shirt to pull him out of the house. I let loose a shot anyway, but it's too late. They've made it out, but I'm not gonna let it end that easily.

I hear the truck race away down the dirt road making a break for the highway. I pull on my Wranglers and boots, deciding not to waste time on a shirt. My Colt is in my left boot, and I'm gripping the Remington hard while scrambling outside for my truck. I start it up, throw it into drive and give chase down the dirt road. They've kicked up so much dust, Mr. Magoo could tail these idiots. Pretty soon their truck's within eyeshot, a blue late-model Ford. Their tires squeal onto the highway. Lucky there's no traffic. For the first time I glance at the dash clock to find it's nearly half past three in the morning.

The Ford heads toward town. Need to be careful. I think to put a call into Tahoka law enforcement to let them deal with these jokers, but realize I didn't bring my cell. That means the team's out of contact too. Guess it's just me. I'm not complaining.

They take a hard left on 2nd street, then another on "M" putting them south again. The route seems deliberate. Maybe I'm still groggy from sleep, but now I'm thinking I could be heading into an ambush. But why in town? Why risk it? They could set up an ambush anywhere they liked. Back on the dirt road would have been much more opportune. No cops. No witnesses. Of course I'm assuming these punks are pros. I shouldn't do that, but the introduction of an automatic weapon tends to guide thoughts in the professional merc direction.

I watch their truck skid wildly down the main drag of Lockwood Street, heading straight for *Sharkey's* Bar—and I don't mean in the general direction. They've hit a slick patch or suffered a blowout because their truck inexplicably careens across the solid yellow lines, then over the curb, actually picking up speed through the bar's parking lot until smashing into the side of the darkened establishment with the force of all hell. The front end explodes into the brick and siding before bursting into a fireball. The concussive force nearly shatters the windows of my truck. I screech to a halt in the middle of the road to assess the damage. Nobody could have survived that crash. The tangos are barbeque. I'm more worried about *Sharkey's*. The local watering hole has caught fire, and with all those bottles of booze inside, I hope the volunteer firefighters get here quickly before much of Tahoka's commercial real estate chars itself to a quick end.

That's when something strange happens. That building, the one with the flaming truck hanging out of it, its neon sign flickers on like its open for business at almost 4 A.M.. Lights inside the frosted windows come alive too, and it isn't from the flames. I sit perplexed as the door of their truck opens up like it's not engulfed in fire. The passenger steps out seemingly unharmed, but completely enveloped by fire, his head like a struck match. He calmly walks to the driver's side intermittently dropping sparks and cinders of himself to the pavement like liquid droplets. The burning man opens the door to check the condition of his friend. A crispy, inanimate body falls out of the driver's side. The burning man shrugs, deciding instead to walk to *Sharkey's* entrance. He's not hopping around or convulsing in pain from the intense flames clinging to him like orange waves. He's not rolling on the ground in agony like anyone else would, no, the burning man walks at a leisurely pace to the entrance, and strangely finds the door unlocked, as if bars were always open at 3:30 A.M..

I hear the purr of my truck engine and the crackling bar burning in front of me. I realize I'm in the middle of a wide and empty road with two firearms and no shirt on. I pull into the parking lot and roll down the window, hoping to hear sirens soon. Nothing. No sign of movement anywhere whatsoever, just the fire and that *Sharkey's* neon sign buzzing above me. I feel a pull to step out of the truck, to turn off the ignition and just step out, regardless of the police or anyone else that must certainly be on their way. My hand seems to move on its own, turning the key backward and shutting off the engine. I leave the truck behind and make my way to *Sharkey's* door absently evaluating the flames running up the side of the building with growing intensity.

Suddenly I'm inside, and not alone. The bar is bustles full of customers though I could hear nothing of the sort from outside only seconds ago. Patrons—none I recognize—shoot pool from the tables or hunch over rounded four-tops with their drinks of choice, laughing and conversing. Every stool at the bar is taken. Most are smoking cigarettes and taking turns swigging on thick, glass mugs of domestic lager, swatting intermittently at errant flies that attach themselves to faces only to dart away and bother another. No one seems bothered by the burning man from outside, now poised over the bar wrangling for the tender's attention. I stand in the middle of the scene wondering whether or not I'm dreaming, or even alive. The thought crosses my mind that perhaps I was the one who crashed.

Every so often a patron either walking by or glancing at me from a table will raise their head and greet me by name with a disturbing joviality reserved for old friends. I continue to search the room for any face at all can I recognize, but everyone seems foreign to me. *Sharkey's* has plenty of shadowed corners where the harsh, smoky light only threatens to encroach. I extend my search to them, first the far right. The tables are populated with shady patrons in conversation. I look behind me to another corner where smoke begins to seep into the bar from the emblazed truck that no one seems to care about. A group of older men sit only feet from the fire that begins to snake up the wall. One stands and intentionally plunges his arm into the flame. It catches fire and the rest of his cohorts chortle in congratulation as the fire creeps up his shoulder and down his jacket. He begins to cry and wail while the others cheer him on. He falls to his knees as the fire overtakes him completely. The others take their seats again and intently watch him burn between grinning sips.

"Amarillo," someone says behind me.

I swing around.

"Amarillo," comes from another at my back.

I turn again.

"Amarillo," from across the room this time.

They do not stop speaking my name, but repeat it over and over until the bar is filled with a cacophony of sound that reaches a deafening crescendo that all the sudden stops as quickly as it started.

"Hello, Amarillo," comes from behind me, a singular voice. I recognize it.

I turn to see old Teasel standing before me. It's impossible. The crowded bar has become a silent audience. The only thing I hear are the men burning, the old one on the floor, his hair snapping intermittently, and the driver at the bar standing there like he's supposed to, on fire, his blackened face melting before us all.

"Teasel?"

"I am here."

It takes a while for my mind to focus. Teasel's not dead anymore. He seems just as tired and fed up as when I laid him to rest at the farmhouse, back when the game warden sent me to stop him from shooting that shotgun at his chickens.

"You shot me," he says so matter of fact that I'm not sure how to respond. Part of his head is missing, and whatever blood hasn't coagulated to a black at the edges of the blast radius drips onto his shoulders in messy, stringy clumps.

The crowded bar just watches along like it's all some kind of show. I do my best to remain composed.

"Look, Teasel," I say, dropping my head. "I—I just did what I thought would be best for you."

"Tried to help me? That right, son?"

I nod my head, unable to meet his cold eyes. That's when a Mexican fella sitting at one of the tables next to me speaks up.

"You feel that you delivered him?"

"What?" I say.

Then another voice from across the room. "From what? From death? From unhappiness?"

Another voice coming from the bar. A woman this time. "His life was over after all. You saved him from living anguish. It was your call to make."

"And you made it," Teasel says. "You certainly made it."

I'm confused. I'm locked up. An old woman sitting alone close to the bar stands. "Are you too foolish to answer for yourself, boy?"

I shake my head instinctively.

"So what are you waiting for?" comes from a middle-aged fella with close-cropped hair. Looks like a soldier on leave. His face is torn up like he walked into an IED. I don't think any of these people are alive. The closer I look, the more dead they seem. Some of them are just pale, but others wear the more violent moments of their demise quite openly. I can't believe I didn't notice before.

"What the hell is this?" I finally work up the courage to say.

"Exactly," Teasel says. "You feel like you did me a favor by killing me, Rust? Look at me. Do I look different to you? Do I look...happy? I'll never say goodbye to my daughter. I'll never see my wife again."

"Teasel, please," I say.

"They are all here for my delight," comes in a heavy accent from a darkened corner of the bar. "It matters not by what hand."

The bar remains silent but for the flames that have proceeded to engulf the entire front wall, running up and down it like a rippling yellow river. No patron moves away from the fire, but only sits allowing it consume them as well. They sit in silence when they catch fire, making no attempt to escape the conflagration's punishment. It is as if they feel they deserve to burn. The rest of them, the others at tables and at the bar itself pay no attention to their pain, they only sit and listen in some twisted reverence to the one in the corner.

"In a way, I have you to thank. You've sent me many of your own volition. I am always pleased when one of you decides when another of you should die. It spares me the effort. You fail to realize the consideration that goes into it all. For you, it is a mere flick of your trigger. Boom. Another soul is sent away like so much paper in a burning barrel of garbage." A hand emerges from the shadow and gently waves back and forth through the light. "Fly away paper. Fly, fly away."

"Who am I speaking with?" I ask, patience waning, but well aware that I've little firepower or means of escape should the group rush me for whatever reason. Then I hear a chair scoot across the floor, and two shoes clomp toward me. A figure emerges from the shadow, and finally I *do* recognize someone in the bar. The old Russian man from Latvia, the one from the Lithuanian gun running action. The old man playing dominos who spoke to me in English as we nervously waited by the airport for Horrace, Yakubu, and Henry Knapp. I remember him telling me to calm myself, that my men were close and that we should learn the language if we wanted to work in foreign countries. I took him as a spotter for the Russian gunrunners, but it seems I was wrong about that. His appearance hasn't changed a bit. He hunches over with those same searing black eyes and that mop of unkempt grey hair that seemed to melt right into his bushy mustache and beard.

He slowly raises his right arm and points his finger and thumb at me like a gun as he walks toward the bar. I see him mouth the word "boom" and snap his thumb down to his index finger, just like he did in Latvia behind that fuel depot as we drove away. He stops in front of the burning man standing at the bar.

"What is your name?" he asks the man on fire.

"David, master," the burning man tries to say through gooey, melting lips.

"I *hate* that name. Before you cease your suspension, know this: All of your pursuits, all of your allegiance to me has been worthless. You are the same mound of refuse you always were. I *hate* you. I owe you nothing. I promise you everything, and you get nothing in return. You will languish beneath my heel as all the rest and I will crush your skull forever as easily as you once breathed."

"But, master, please. I have sworn m—"

The old man snaps out his hand and plunges it through the man's flaming mouth, closing his grip around the man's tongue and tears it from him. The burning man groans and coughs up a black tar that runs down his chest. The old man tosses the tongue over his shoulder. One of the eager patrons catches it. Those at his table fight over it, knocking over glasses of whiskey and beer, toppling the table. They act as if the severed tongue were manna. The fat, bald man who wins it, growling and yanking it from the hand of a weaker woman stares at the tongue, finding it as disgusting and horrific as I do. He brings it reluctantly over his head, squeezes more black tar from its open wound and lowers it into his gaping mouth, crying all the while as if fighting against his terrible urge to consume it.

"You have," the old man continues at the burning one. "You *have* sworn your life to me. You have. In hopes of reward. I've promised you so much, haven't I? And now you're ready to collect, aren't you?"

The man nods sorrowfully and reaches out to the old man for comfort. The old man stolidly denies it, laughing at the frailty of the burning man's intentions. "Ha ha. So weak. Of so little value. Of no value at all. Meat. You are only meat, you are burning meat and your languor is my mirth. But come close, David. Come close," he goads the burning man who withers toward him. "I do have a single promise to fulfill to you." He grabs the burning man's head and sinks his fingers deep into his charred scalp, pulling it toward him and snarling violently. "May you forever struggle to fill your lungs with ash from my fires so that your entire being be flooded with the searing ache of hopelessness. Die now and be received by my minions that they may torture you with a fervency of the unfed masses of hell. Let them feast upon you until time itself grows weary of your anguished cries."

With unquantifiable anger, he heaves against the burning man's head and hurls him into the air with a jarring force and sends him crashing into the opposite wall. The man's body crumbles to the floor and lies there limp, continuing to smolder and burn. Then the old man, fingernails filled with blood and ash, turns his attention back to me.

"You don't remember me, boy?"

"Sure I do," I say, my voice trembling as the fire works to overtake more and more of the bar. Yet the air grows icy cold with each and every step the old man takes toward me. "Latvia. You were with the Russian gunrunners—their spotter. Told me to calm down, that they'd wait for us. Good advice. Owe you a drink."

"You have been under false assumptions."

"I remember you pointed your finger at me like a gun as we were driving away too. Can't believe I remember it."

"You have no idea how difficult it is to walk among you for even the shortest time. If your life is a blink it is too long. I do admire the way you dispatched the old farmer to me though. Such compassion. Little did you know that he suffers now with the rest of them."

"Watch your mouth." I can't believe I just let it slip.

"You tell me to watch my mouth. I should be offended, but I fail to be. Would you be offended if a cockroach told you to 'watch your mouth?' Certainly not. Your kind is so blind and vain I will never understand how you were chosen. You deserve nothing. You deserve less than nothing. You are shit on my heel, and yet I bother with this endless campaign as if the ends aren't already determined. Why? The greatest question, 'why.' Your God won't answer it either. He refuses. None of his creations will ever know why we do anything or why we are here and your kind there. It is all a fool's errand, and we are his miserable pawns to be shoved across the board and handled like toys. Discarded. Banished."

Finally, I figure out who I'm talking to. The great deceiver. The Morning Star himself, now fallen and disgraced, his name a poison on angelic tongues, and the bane of all mankind who are led by his lurid promises and untruths. Here before me stands Lucifer himself.

"See," he says slurring, slugging a full shot of Jim Beam he snatched from a table of silent watchers while motioning for another from the bartender. "You thought I was talking about the Russians in Latvia. I wasn't talking about the Russians. I was talking about us. Us, here in this room among others. We would wait for you to join the prophet before we destroyed you; and in certain manners, we did just that didn't we?"

"How so? I'm still standing here."

He hovers inches from me. He's shorter, but those dead black eyes scorch right through mine. I have never felt so intimidated. I have never felt so scared, or with such an awareness that I am truly alone.

"You stand as long as I allow you to stand. You will cower at the brush of a hair should I require it. I have dominion here. Not God. I am the ruler of the Earth, and by your surprise it seems the great Amarillo Rust does not know his own history."

"I know that we're on opposite teams."

"Teams. How quaint. Explanations must be so rudimentary. Your pig brain has no understanding of greater things. You haven't the slightest inkling at how difficult it is to converse with such a lowly animal as yourself. Your language is so nebulous. The imprecision of it is nothing short of staggering. Humans seem only able to talk around something, never arriving at a definitive point. The very construction of your feeble mind's processes are offensive to creation. Did you know we had met before? Do you even remember?"

"I told you, Latvia. Old man at the card table."

"Oh no. Long before that. You were only a child."

I look around at the faces populating the bar as the fire intensifies. A beam in the roof gives way and crashes down in a hail of sparks on two tables of patrons. The mangled faces are expressionless. Vacant.

"Care to remind me?"

"I'd be surprised if I could. You've dreamt of it countless times, Amarillo. It keeps you up at night. We haunted you as a child though you never knew that all the while, as you sweat and clung to the covers in the darkness, that I encircled you with demons so closely that you could have felt the breath of their rotted insides on your cheek."

"What are you talking about?"

"The nightmares of your grandfather's death. Frank Rust. The pathetic pig preacher," he says theatrically popping the alliterative words. "Elijah hasn't told you. He's kept it from you, but I won't. I'll tell you everything. All you have to do is ask." All the sudden he sounds just like you think he would. He accentuates every 's.' I don't know whether it's real or if he's just toying with me.

"My grandfather was murdered."

"Yes. Go on. Go on," he says, almost giddy.

"Some nut killed him one Sunday."

"Yes! On the holy Sabbath—yes."

"While he was preaching," I say, hanging my head, the emotion returning.

"And you were such a young boy to see such a thing. Such a terrible thing. Yes. You were eight. I was watching with the most excitement. You were in church that day. I sent that man to kill him. Of course, he didn't know that. Of course not. To that man, your grandfather represented all the broken promises of a painfully unfair god. If I remember correctly, the 'nut' as you call him recently lost both his job and his wife in the same day. You see, he worked at a local paint store. The owner would fornicate with the man's wife while the silly man enjoyed after hours drinks at the local bar. When the wife told him the truth, that she had fornicated delightfully and repeatedly with his employer, and that she would do it over and over given the chance, he came to your grandfather for heavenly advice. What a crock of shit. But your grandfather was nowhere to be found that day. Not when the man from the paint store needed him. Well, the owner, his secret having come to light, fired the man in short order. He did it by phone so as to avoid conflict. Humans love to avoid conflict don't you know, especially when they know they're in the wrong. This is all so funny because only days before the man had received a similar call from his doctor explaining that it was actually a degenerative neural disease responsible for the pain in his hands and forearms. His wife didn't even know because she didn't care. She was too busy exploring all of the glorious carnalities with his employer. And because your grandfather wasn't around to tend to his flock, the man from the paint store, now jobless and hopelessly ill found his wife at the beauty shop that Sunday and murdered her with a hunting knife. Very brutal. Very admirable. Blood painted every corner of the shop. Mirrors, walls, windows matted with clumps of sticky crimson hair. Of course, then he found his employer at the paint store taking weekend inventory. He murdered him too, but not before violating him with brushes and mixing sticks—whatever he could find. He even created a new shade of red. Yes he did. So messy, but so very lovely. The police found a fresh gallon canister of his entrails shaking back and forth in the mixing machine. And because your grandfather abandoned him—"

"My grandfather did not abandon anyone," I say, feeling my muscles tighten and my fist clench.

"Because your grandfather and his god abandoned this poor, foolish little rodent, he decided to go to church on one last occasion. Your grandfather's sermons did droll on and on, if you remember. My little paint-mixer entered the church, this time with the pistol he once kept beneath his bed to protect his cheating whore wife. Came in just about mid-sermon, didn't he?"

"Yes. I remember now," I say, trembling with adrenaline, remembering.

"And, boom," the old man said, again pantomiming it as he did in Latvia.

The bar is silent for a moment, except for the encroaching flames along the walls and ceiling, that and those flies that seem to populate by the second.

"The man who killed your dear grandfather is here, Amarillo. In this room," he says, looking around. "Reveal yourself, pig."

An expressionless man shoots to his feet like a marionette, staring blankly in our direction. I look at the man as hatred washes over me.

"Want to kill him back? Want to kill him back? Want to kill him— want to kill him?" the old man asks titillated.

Then the expressionless congregation says it in unison. "Want to kill him?"

"Already looks dead to me," I say, trying with every bit of fortitude to hold back.

"Ah, but that's the majesty of Hell, boy. You can kill and kill and kill again. Kill kill. Thrill kill. No limits. Death and suffering are but hourly errands, and all are punished with great enthusiasm. Even your grandfather."

"Where is he?"

"I have him defecating into the mouths of children. Oh, he is well. Very, very well indeed. I save the worst for those self-important human vermin who delude themselves into thinking they have the slightest influence over my affairs. You are inconsequential. You are nothing. Less than nothing. Your existence sickens the universe. Bacteria. Molecules of disjointed carbon scum. I hate you all so much. I hate you. I hate you. I *hate* you. I hate you and you will all suffer with me until I cease to draw breath. I will exploit your free will at each and every turn of your useless trifling moments. I will make you trust me only to crush your spirits. I will delight in your doubt and disappointments, and I will leave nothingness for you to take hold of at night as you sleep. You will be separated from Him, that hypocrite who denies me a place beside him, much less above him. My greatness will be measured by your decay and in your souls' collective banishment from that infernal light he fools you into reaching for. His lovely little creations. His lovely little lemmings. His trash imbued with the divine spark that stupidly rabble about having no appreciation for what they are. For what they possess. I will exploit it and lead you away from him, and he will watch and cry for what I do to your souls. I will tear them apart, and nothing you and that pathetic prophet of yours could ever do will change anything! We will put down two angels for every one you fools send back to him. All of your work is for nothing! I will place you down beside your beloved grandfather and watch as you both choke on my vomit!"

I don't know if it's just my being ticked off or if some change has come over me, something speaking to me, through me maybe, but whatever it is, it doesn't want to be quiet anymore. "Tell me then, Devil. If all of our work is for nothing; if we puny little humans don't matter and can't do a thing to screw up your operation, tell me something: Why are you so worked up about it?"

The old man stops and stares at me through those black eyes looking like the whole flooding current of Hell would burst right out. He shakes and trembles. I see his knuckles get white and tight. He takes a deep breath and fills his lungs with fire. I knew something bad was coming, maybe the end. Then something occurs to me. It is a rhythm in my mind, a melody from years past, so far away it's almost out of reach but by the moment its clarity comes forth in layers. It is the voice of my grandfather. The echo of the sanctuary pulses through stanchions of my memory until, inexplicably, I know what to do.

"You know?" I say. "I just remembered something my granddaddy used to say to me. Back before you killed him. Know what it was?"

Satan doesn't respond.

I grin. "Better get ready for it."

Again he only blears at me through the deepest of eyes, black as empty space.

"The Lord is my shepherd," I say with a spontaneous confidence. "The Lord is my shepherd and I shall *not* want."

"Stop," the old man says.

"He makes me lie down in green pastures. He leads me beside still waters. He restores my soul." I close my eyes.

"Make him stop," comes from one of the patrons. Expression returns to their faces. Anguish. Anger. Pain. Regret. Flies dart about the room, swirling around my head until the buzzing threatens to deafen me.

"He leads me in paths of righteousness for His name's sake," I continue.

"Do not go forward," the old man says, heaving as everyone in the bar starts to cry out for him to stop me.

I take a step toward him, my grandfather's words—no—the Lord's words spilling as from a golden cup I thought had left me long ago. "Even though I walk through the valley of the shadow of death."

I hear and feel a pool of snakes twisting through my boots, curling around my legs beneath me. I lift my eyelids to see two of them rear up and strike, sinking their fangs through my jeans and into my flesh. I grimace and try to push through the pain, continuing to recite, but not just recite, to feel the words with a conviction I don't know that I've ever possessed. Another beam weakens from the fire raging all around and breaks loose from the ceiling, crashing down on more people. A thick black smoke envelops the room, starting only as a haze but darkening with increasing rapidity.

"I shall fear *no* evil," I say, gritting my teeth and willing myself forward.

Wails emit from all around, the gnashing of teeth and screaming comes forth from the agonized faces in the bar. Fire begins consuming the writhing bodies who call to the old man for respite, but find none. The Devil holds my gaze as I slowly creep forward. More snakes leap up and strike, pumping dangerous amounts of paralyzing venom into my flesh. I feel the injections course into my bloodstream, thick like oil searing through my veins.

"My rod and my staff... they comfort me," I say feeling woozy. I fight to keep my knees from buckling.

And then a magnificent thrush at the front of the bar. Wood and glass explode inside. Both my and the old man's attention shoot to the direction of the crash. It can't be. It can't be, but it's Park and four others, all outfitted like SWAT with crosses painted on their Kevlar vests, unleashing tremendous waves of automatic gunfire into the bar, chopping down wailing patrons with salty hot metal. The old man looks back to me and snarls.

"The next time we meet I will tear the soul from your beating chest," he says, and as if by a disastrous sweeping wind, his legs fly out from under him until he's hanging upside down in mid-air. He extends both arms in the sign of an inverted crucifix. The sound of a thousand thrashing wings rises over the fire. His body cavity unfolds upon itself into a bubbling mass of rotted flesh and bone, like a beating, swirling cylinder, abruptly disappearing from existence with only the smell of molded death and a plume of darting flies left in its wake. I look down. The snakes are gone though the fire continues to rage all about me. Bullets from Park and his men tear into the patrons who scream and wail with renewed agony.

"Park," I manage to say before my focus comes undone, and reaching out my knees give way. The last thing I see is my blurred vision falling to meet the smoking barroom floor. A hand shoots out for me, but everything goes black.

Chapter 48

BLINDING WHITE LIGHT above me. Woozy. Motor functions lethargic. Feel drugged. My eyes creep down my arm. IV tube. A figure stands over me like a heat wave. Speaking. Blurry. I shake it off. Pat my eyelids. The form sharpens. It's Henry Knapp leaning over my bed. Cheap white blanket pulled up to my chest. I hear the beeping of the heart monitor. Smell the antiseptic bleach on the floors. Must be a hospital.

"Rust," Henry Knapp says in a rapid hush. "Go along with whatever I tell them."

"What happened to me? Where am I?"

"University Medical. Lubbock. You were laying out in the parking lot of *Sharkey's* while the place burned," he says, checking behind him for onlookers.

"I saw Park," I say in a heavy, graveled voice as if I haven't spoken in months.

"Wha—?" Knapp says before cutting himself off. Three men enter the room. One's a doctor complete with lab coat, stethoscope, and clipboard. The other two I'm guessing are law.

"Awake I see," the doctor says, approaching me. He puts the ear buds in and places the cold metal pad on my chest to listen to my breathing.

"How long's he been under?" one of the suits asks.

"That's two days and just about five hours," the doctor says, still listening and moving that cold metal disc around my chest. "Vitals look good. Chest is clear. You're strong as a horse, Mr. Rust."

"Thank you, doctor," the other suit says. "Mind if we have a minute with him?" the other suit asks.

The doctor nods, marks something on the clipboard, and leaves the room, placing it into a slot on the door.

"Mr. Knapp," the shorter, pudgier suit says. They've got to be detectives. Easy to spot. They never can seem to keep their ties straight or their shirts tucked cleanly. "Surprised you made the trip. Witnesses usually don't take such an interest. What is it, an hour or so drive up? Sure you don't know Mr. Rust?"

"Give or take an hour, sure. Tahoka's a small town, detective," Knapp says. "I'm sure we've run into each other a few times."

"At church maybe?" the taller one says. "Don't want you to get nervous but we asked around about you. Just procedure in homicide cases. The locals say you're quite the pillar in the community. Very active in the church."

"Makes for a good witness," the pudgy detective says.

"Homicide case?" Knapp asks.

"Possibly, but we don't think there's much to it. Seems pretty straightforward really. Hope you don't mind going over it again with us. Tahoka sheriff's department isn't equipped to handle these types of cases, so they turned it over to us. Again, hope it isn't too much of an inconvenience."

"Not at all."

The tall one hasn't taken his eyes off me since he showed up. The pudgy one scribbles disjointed notes into a flipbook. Henry Knapp is calm and cool. I act more out of it than I am until Knapp lets me know what the shot is.

"Says here that you were driving up to church at about four in the morning when you saw a blue Ford truck veer into oncoming traffic. A '93 Dodge—that would be Mr. Rust here—reacts, spins. The Ford makes a hard left, overcorrects and smashes into the side of the bar, bursting into flames and catching this, uh, *Sharkey's* on fire. So Mr. Rust was the oncoming traffic. That right?"

"Yes, sir," Knapp says.

"Why were you going to the church at four in the AM, Mr. Knapp?" the tall one asks, still staring at me.

"I run a Bible study at six o'clock every Thursday morning. Farmers mostly. I hate to say that I hadn't read the lesson yet so I thought I'd go up and do that, start the coffee, arrange the chairs. All of that."

"I see," says the pudgy one, not a note of suspicion in his voice. "So you witness the accident—I'll go ahead and call it that—but what worries me is that you then see Mr. Rust here exit his vehicle and enter the bar?"

"That's right."

"Now why do you think he would do that?" the tall one says, then to me. "Why would you do a silly thing like that, Mr. Rust?"

I offer a groaning noise and make a show of hacking up a bunch of nothing.

"I assume he went in to try and help," Knapp says. "He looked panicked. I knew there wasn't much chance of anyone in that truck surviving, what with the explosion and everything. When he didn't come out for a while, I decided to run in and get him. I've heard that smoke inhalation kills more people than the actual fires. Do you officers find that to be true?"

"Smart man," the pudgy one says, continuing to scribble notes.

"I pulled him out into the parking lot to a safe distance from the fire and called 911. That's pretty much it."

"Didn't happen to see the dead body next to the truck or the one inside?" asks the tall one.

"No, it was very smoky and dark in there. Mr. Rust here didn't make it far, so when I saw him I just grabbed him and got out."

"Why'd you go in there, Mr. Rust? Is it like Mr. Knapp here said?"

"Tried to help them," I say in a pathetic broken up slur.

"I see. Okay," the short one says, flipping his book closed and clicking the head of his pen back inside its housing.

"Just one problem," the tall one says. "How did all those bullet casings get on the floor of the bar, Mr. Rust?"

I can feel Henry Knapp tense up. The air is sucked out of the room. Have to think fast. I can tell my boy's got nothing for this one.

"I—I shoot pool there. Arlin. Bartender. Keeps a gun behind the bar. For security," I say in a lazy garble. "Fire must've set them off. Heard the shots when I got inside. Hit the floor. Must've passed out. All the smoke."

The detectives look at each other. The short pudgy one shrugs. "Checks out," he says to his partner. "Explains the shoulder wound on the deceased we found inside the bar."

The short one turns to leave, shaking Henry Knapp's hand and motioning for his partner to follow. He stops just before they turn the corner. "You're both very lucky. We found some pretty nasty weapons in those crispy perps' truck. You'll hear from us if we have any other questions. Thanks so much for your help, Mr. Knapp, and Mr. Rust? You should thank him too. Looks like you had a guardian angel watching over you that night."

I can't help but grin when I hear their shoes clop away down the hospital hall. I look at Henry Knapp and shake my head.

"How do you do that?"

Knapp smiles. "Just have to know the questions before they ask, right? I was FBI after all. Surprised they didn't ask about all those bite marks on your legs though. What on earth happened in there, Rust? I heard the explosion from home and wouldn't you know it? I just couldn't help but think it had something to do with you. Lucky I'm still a light sleeper. Most of the farmers in that town would need something nuclear to wake them up."

"Afraid there's no luck about it. I told you, it was Park. He saved me. I saw him."

"It's just the drugs. The smoke. They've got you on a nice drip."

"I'm telling you, Henry. It's not the drugs. It was Park. He was there. He had a team. He busted in and filled a whole barroom of demons with salt rounds. Least I think they were demons. You didn't see any-thing?"

"No. Just you shirtless and unconscious in the parking lot. One dead guy burnt to ash next to the truck. How could that be, Rust? Park's dead for all we know, and if he isn't, he's been out of the loop for ages. How could he have known where you were, what's more that you were in trouble?"

"I don't know, Henry," I say, throwing back the covers and grab-bing hold of the IV in my arm. "But I mean to find out."

Chapter 49

I'M SITTING IN my pickup on the street in front of Ellison's church in that New Mexican dump of a town he calls home. Drove through the night and didn't bother to call ahead. I need answers, and I don't have time to ask nicely. Up to now I thought we were on the periphery of this war, but one thing I'm sure of now, the Devil doesn't show up to chat with bit players. I'm in way deeper than I ever wanted to be, and I've got a feeling it has something to do with my grandfather. But that's just the tip of what I need to know. I walk up the sidewalk and wrap on the church door like I've got a warrant. Takes a while for Ellison to shake his muffin-hips to answer. When he opens up I get a deep waft of whiskey and mildew. Neither of us say hello. His bloodshot eyes tell me he's been up for a while, certainly drinking and pawing through those dusty books of his. No rest for the weary I guess. He leaves the door open and walks off into the sanctuary toward his office. I close the door behind me and follow him back. The only light that makes it through the stained glass is from the moon, and as I step into his perpetually cluttered office with books, papers, and whiskey bottles scattered about, he's already plopped behind his desk. A small lamp with a year's coating of dust on its shade illuminates the workspace.

"Well? What is it?" he asks unimpressed.

"Got questions."

"You don't say. Well, I seem to be your baby sitter while Elijah is away so hurry up so I can get back to drinking."

"Have a glass for me?"

"No. What's your question?"

"Come on, Ellison. I'm gonna be here 'til I get what I need to know, so we might as well have a little fun doing it," I say.

Ellison labors behind him, finds an empty glass, and tosses it to me on the sofa along with a half-full bottle of cheap scotch.

"It's dirty," he says. "The glass"

"Not for long," I say back, pouring some. "So where is Tishbe? Need to talk to him."

"How should I know where the welching old fart runs off to? You got *me*, so go ahead."

I knock the shot back, then pour another before corking the bottle and tossing it back to the pastor. He catches it and does the same like we're 30-love deep in a tennis game.

"Okay," I say. "Couple of things. First, one of my men, the one I took with me on Taber's rescue mission? Thought he was dead, but he's not. Least I think he's not."

"Park. The Asian one. Yeah, he's alive."

"You knew?" I say, instantly angered. "Ever gonna let me in on that?"

"He's got nothing to do with your operation. Why would I?"

"Because he's my man, Ellison," I say, feeling my grip vice down on the glass.

"Not anymore. The Catholics snatched him up. Saved his butt too when you all left him in Oklahoma."

"What're you talking about?"

"The Catholics have their own force. We don't play nice together. Don't agree on some of the finer points. They've got their own system. It's full of pomp and that divine providence nonsense. We sometimes catch each other shadowing missions and what not. Anyway, he's taken up with them. Why do you ask?"

"Because he saved my life the other night."

"He did?" Ellison perks up. "Well, you're not an angel, so…"

"I know. I was surprised too, but he was there all right. He and two others with big crosses painted on their vests. Guns blazing."

"Guns blazing at what?" Ellison asks with scrutiny. "We didn't send you on any rescues the last few weeks."

"Funny you should say, but before I tell you, I want to know about my grandfather," I say returning every bit of his scrutiny.

"You do," he says, taking a drink and shaking his head slowly at the desk. "You do—you do. Only a matter of time, I suppose. Elijah wanted to keep it a secret. Didn't want you running around with all these expectations in your head."

"Tell me."

"Alright. I'm only going to tell you this because I didn't agree with Elijah's decision to keep it from you. I can't say it won't give me a little pleasure to defy the arrogant son of a skunk too—but alright—your grandfather, Frank Rust; bit of a legend."

"How so?"

"He was the first. He was like you, but better. Much better from what I understand."

"You knew him?"

"How old do you think I am? Whisky adds the years but—hell no, I didn't know him. Elijah found him. Your grandfather fought in World War II."

"U.S. Army. Stormed the beach."

"Uh huh. Know he was captured and shoved into a Nazi pill box? Beaten within an inch? Almost gave up the ghost? All that?"

"Sure do. Didn't like to talk about it much. Learned most of it from my father."

"Your dear old daddy tell you how he made it out of there? Why he became a preacher after the war?"

"Not really. Assumed they freed him when the Allies took the beach."

"Funny word. Allies," Ellison says, stroking his chin with his old desk chair squeaking as he rocks back and forth. "Soldiers didn't get to him. Allies of a different kind did, I suppose, though their purposes weren't as altruistic as you might think."

"Well if you say he was the first, then I'm gonna take a wild stab and say some angels broke him out of that pill box."

"You'd be right. Elijah was there too. You can imagine how quickly it all went down. Probably didn't have time to mull over the terms."

"Terms for recruitment, I take it."

"That's right. Of course, the polish of Elijah's lofty speeches weren't as finely tuned. He was new to this thing too back then, remember. Imagine you lived some four thousand years ago, never died, got taken up to heaven in a fiery chariot to live among the angels—wherever that is exactly—I'm not even positive it's a place as the human mind can comprehend. And then one day—poof—you're sent back down to Earth with a mission. *Very* different time. *Very* different place. The confusion of it all must have been... incapacitating," the pastor says, almost lost in the gravity of it. I can tell he's pondered it for years, envy gleaming through his eyes like napalm.

"Reckon that would be a tough one to weather," I say back, motioning for the bottle.

The request jars Ellison out of his trance. He corks the bottle again and tosses it over. Before I pour, a question. "But why him? Why my grandfather of all people?"

"If you haven't already learned this: the little we as humans are allowed to know about all of this amounts to Octopus dung in the Pacific. I don't know why he was chosen. All I know is that he was good at it, rescuing angels. Preaching too, but that—as you now get—was just a side-job. He developed a system that has fallen by the wayside now. Good system though. All about who's got the biggest gun now."

"And here I was thinking that the war put the fear of God into my granddaddy."

"Nope. That was Elijah. Brilliant move really. We don't know if God set up our little corp of angel rescuers or if one of the archangels did, but it was successful. Very successful. Caught the leadership of Hell completely off guard. Our men above gained a sizable advantage at first.

Angel forces far outweighed their demon counterparts. Humans know this as the post war nineteen-fifties. Family values. Clean streets. Cohesive families. Prosperity. All that. Good won the war after all, even when the odds were against the world.

"Many in our circle—myself included—think Hitler was in the know, maybe that he was even the Devil's human prodigy, and why wouldn't they what with the holocaust? Best way to twist the knife into the almighty is to wipe out his chosen people. Some think our angel recovery teams were started as a direct result of Nazi successes before America got involved in the war. Remember, every corporeal act for or against His moral code has a spiritual battle behind it. When the Nazi's won a battle, killed an innocent, marched into a sovereign country covering it ankle-deep in blood—that meant angels lost a battle too. That meant angels fell. That meant His numbers were down, and it strengthened the kingdom of Hell. My guess is that pretty soon more angels were being dispatched to recover their injured than were actually engaged in battle, giving further advantage to the bad guys. God used America as an instrument of righteousness against the Nazi Reich. His will was done. God won. The United States won. Maybe that's why nineteen-fifties America was such a happy, orderly, God-fearing place for a while, or seemed to be at least. Elijah and I choose to believe that your grandfather was an integral part of that success. The Devil must have as well, because he sent a man to kill Frank Rust, and that man *did* kill him. You know that. You saw it."

"I did, I mean, I blocked it out for a long time. Must have. But recently—mostly in dreams—I know that I did see it." I'm staring straight through the coffee table, replaying what I can remember. Then I look at Ellison across the room. "Know what else I saw, Ellison? The other night? When Park busted in and pulled me out of that burning bar?" I ask.

Ellison waits impatiently, for a moment forgetting the glass of scotch resting thick and warm like molasses in front of him.

"I saw *him*."

"Him who? Your grandfather? Ha—that's imposs—"

"The Devil. I saw the Devil. He came to me."

"Came to you? At some bar in bumstick Texas? Don't think so, chump," he says, laughing me off, but still hanging on my words as if dangling over a cliff.

"He was there and he told me about how he had my grandfather killed. Every last detail. He had a horde of people with him, all sitting around the bar like any Saturday night. But they weren't like any demons I've seen yet. Seemed human."

"Once human more likely," Ellison says. "But if I believe you, and that's a big *if*, I'm quite sure who came to you was not Satan."

"Said he was. Looked like he was."

"The great liar ring a bell? Come on, kid. Let me tell you something: the Devil is going to take form in front of some piddly human just as soon as God himself will. It's not going to happen. If I *do* believe you, trust me, you saw something else."

"Who then? What then? He was scarier and more powerful than anything from the other side I've ever come across, or likely will ever," I say.

"I don't doubt that. That you have right. There's only one other aside from Lucifer that can manifest himself and a cadre of damned souls at the same time into our world without brimstone. Just one," Ellison says, grinning.

"That's what those other people were?"

"Yes. They were souls that have already gone to Hell. Dead souls. Lost souls. Only the devil and his second in command have the power to cross over at will and bring along his captives. No other demon has the authority. Let me ask you, were there flies?"

"Flies? As in buzz-buzz?"

"Yes, idiot. Flies. House flies. Horse flies. Insects with little translucent wings. Flies. Were there flies around the bar?"

"Didn't notice at first, but when he disappeared, he broke up into a plume of them," I say recalling an image that will forever be seared into my brain tissue.

"Yes. Yes, oh my. You, sir, were visited by Beelzebub."

"And what the hell is a basilbob?" I ask halfheartedly, still clinging to my original assertion while the scotch sends waves through my thoughts.

Pastor Ellison doesn't even look behind him to grab hold of a compendium from the bookcase. He drops it on the desk with a hefty clump. Dust curls out from its pages as he opens it up and flips through. He stops about halfway in and clops his finger on a page, waving me over to come and look. My knees pop as I push to my feet, still feeling the effects of that night at the burning bar, and the IV drip at the hospital, and the scotch. I make it to the desk and lean over to get a look at the book in the musty light.

"Beelzebub," I read. "Prince of demons. Originally an idol of the Canaanites, means 'Lord of the Flies.' Beelzebub identifies himself as the ruler of all demons because he was the highest-ranking angel in heaven and is the only one left of the heavenly angels who fell." I stop reading and look to Ellison. "Oh no."

"Uh huh."

"That's bad," I say.

"The commander in chief doesn't go into the field. But his general does, and they're almost always just as scary," Ellison says, closing the book and turning his focus to the last bit of scotch in the bottle.

I turn around and run my hand back and forth over the stubble on my chin. I pace the room slowly, trying to ascertain the implications, the options. My head is a mess of worry and questioning.

"The Devil knows who you are, where you are, and he's so ticked off that he sent his last remaining five-star-general out to rattle your chains. You just became a wanted man. Even more than you were before. A hundred fold. A thousand fold. It's time to be cautious and it is time to be prepared."

"But why me?" I ask. "There's teams all over the place. Just because my grandfather was the first? Why would that have any significance now? I mean, we don't do anything that other teams don't do, and he doesn't send out this Beetlejuice fella out to harass them. Not the big guns. Besides, he said that he already had my grandfather in Hell with him, so why me? What are you not telling me, Ellison?" I ask, just about as close to being scared as I've ever been. My cheeks are flushed; my heart beats rapidly as the cloud in my head sends flurries in all directions.

"First, he doesn't have your grandfather, and he never will. Your grandfather is in Heaven as he rightly should be. Elijah has spoken with him several times. That was a lie, and as we know, that's the thing the bad guys are best at," Ellison says with a tacit concern I've yet to register in him until now. "It's what your grandfather managed to *do* that Beelzebub wants to prevent from ever happening again, that he must prevent from ever happening again. I suppose he thinks you, being Frank Rust's blood relation has the knowledge to do what he did as well." He says it to himself more than to me.

"But I don't have the knowledge of whatever the heck it is everybody thinks I can do," I say, throwing up my hands. "What did he do?"

"Okay, well if you read on in the book I just had, it says that Beelzebub is the last remaining angel to have fallen to Hell with Satan, right? The original ones. The ancient ones. Every other demon in Hell, any other demon you've fought is something else, came later, spawned, less powerful, something, I don't know how it works, but he's the last."

"Okay," I say urging him to continue.

"So where did the other ones go?" Ellison asks.

"How on earth should I know?"

"It's rhetorical. I don't know either, no human does. But I know what happened to *one* of them."

"Hurry up, Ellison, what?"

"The demon Abezethibou. One of the original fallen," Ellison says. "Your grandfather killed him."

I feel as if I've taken a shotgun blast full-bore to the chest. "But I sat here with both you and Elijah and you both told me that humans can't kill demons. You said that. 'Humans can't kill demons,' you said. Much less one of the originals."

"And ninety-nine million times out of one hundred million, that's true. Humans are not supposed to be able to kill a demon. It completely upsets the order of things. Only goodness can kill a demon, massive goodness. Tremendous righteousness. Sinlessness. Blamelessness. No human has the capacity for it. Only one human, Christ himself, both God and man at once could ever have the power to actually kill a demon," Ellison says, his voice raising.

"So how did my grandfather manage to do it?" I ask.

Pastor Ellison stares at me, his mouth agape, struggling for some kind of answer I know isn't coming. Like so many other things, most other things concerning our charge, I know he hasn't the slightest. But, because he's Ellison, he finds something to say anyway.

"For a long time I thought that it was Frank Rust's system that gave him the power. I thought that he found the perfect, perhaps intended way to carry out his ops, and that's what resulted in him killing Abezethibou. Instead of rescuing angels by repelling demons through the greatest technology or through superior team numbers, he looked to scripture and used a small team, designating each of them with a biblical label to exemplify their strongest traits. See, he recognized that it wasn't just him who was important. Taber and all the others never figured that out. God didn't just choose Frank Rust. God had a hand in everything, in everyone that joined the team, even when it looked like coincidence or his own decision. He knew God was in complete control.

"Frank Rust knew the bible, and that is what made him so damn dangerous. He saw through the surface level. He saw beyond it, made the connections, and drew parallels to the deeper meanings. It's just like how Christ taught everything in parable. He rarely conveyed anything without one. Frank knew that it wasn't the parable that was important, it's what the parable signified. He converted that common understanding as it pertained to spiritual battle and used it to his advantage in physical battle. It was brilliant. When I read the history, I was in awe of the simplicity and sheer effectiveness of it. No one ever since could pull it off. He called one The Herald, one The Interpreter—"

"I know," I say. "Elijah told me about the names. Didn't say they came from my granddad, but we've got all the stations filled."

"But, you don't know what to do with them," Ellison finishes.

"Well, not all of them. Most are self-explanatory but—"

"Which ones are you having trouble with? Maybe we can figure it out together," Ellison says, brushing debris off an old legal pad and picking up a pen.

"The Judge and The Meek. I don't know what to do with them. I know Yakubu's our Judge and Everly's the Meek, but I don't know how they fit in exactly," I say.

"And we don't have much time to figure it out. If Beelzlebub has come to find you, which it appears he has, then his attack will happen soon, and trust me, nothing is written of this demon to suggest he takes anything lightly. I think it's safe to say that your primary objective has gone from angel recovery to basic team survival."

Chapter 50

ALL OF A sudden, $250,000 doesn't seem like much money, at least not enough to be chased around personally by the prince of darkness. The team doesn't know about the price on my head because I've kept it close to the chest. Won't help anyone to know. Wouldn't do anything but scare the blood out of them anyway. Status quo. Business as usual. That's the only way to do this one. I even asked Ellison to try and send a rescue or two our way, just so we can prepare and implement the strategy he and I worked out: my grandfather's strategy. Something tells me we're going to need it soon, and this time in a defensive nature. I wish Elijah were here He has a way of quelling fears, of inspiring confidence when the chips seem scattered across a dirty floor. But he's not here, and seems like nobody will be able to find him.

Of course, Ellison can't send us work. Only the man upstairs can, through our Herald, that little Brigita that I can't ever help but always feel sorry for. The agonizingly sheltered and suffocatingly controlled life she's been all but relegated to. Evangeline's done a bang-up job with her. She's slowly learning English, almost enough to have a full conversation without Horrace having to hover over and translate. Red tells me the little girl's got a shine for teddy bears. She's just a regular little girl in that way, a regular little girl that wears a GPS locator on her wrist that she can't take off. A regular little girl who God or somebody speaks through while she foams at the mouth and convulses on the floor, seizing like a bug sprayed with insecticide. Yeah, regular little girl all right. No friends. No real family. I know she's much better off than before we rescued her from the Kostonov brothers; I shudder to think what they did to her in that cabin, but I can't honestly say that she's got it good now because she doesn't. She's a prisoner. In some ways we all are, I guess.

I'm standing in the muted silence of the HQ armory, the only sound the low howl of the ventilation system. You'd be surprised what eight feet of West Texas earth packed above you can mask, sound or otherwise. It's nearly 7 A.M.. Can't sleep. Drove over from my house down the road that's starting to look like a pincushion with the last break-in by the Satanic loyalists. Sounds ridiculous even as I say it, *Satanists*, but that's what they were. Funny, they're willing to lay down their lives for promises of grandeur delivered to them by the greatest, most adept and dedicated deceiver in existence; then, they're surprised when he welches on it all just like I saw him do to that burning man at *Sharkey's*.

I stare up at the twelve jeweled crosses Tishbe gave us in the beginning with my arms folded. We still don't know what to do with them, or what they're for. Maybe they aren't for anything at all other than symbols. Maybe they were payment, just pop the jewels out and sell them. Who knows? When I asked Tishbe about them months ago, I just got a blank stare. Ellison has no idea what they are either. He says they came from Jerusalem. He guesses they were given to me because they were given to my grandfather's team. Just tradition. I asked if other teams had their own set of crosses, and he said no, that there was only one set, only twelve, and that we were the only team that had them. Ellison called them Sepulchers. I told him that to my understanding a sepulcher is a tomb. He responded by telling me they were found in a tomb, and that he didn't know what the official name of these ornamental crosses was, but that as long as he's been in the know, they've been called Sepulchers. I dropped the subject, and viewing them now, each one sitting atop its own chromed weapon cabinet like owls perched on leafless winter branches, my mind grows tired of questioning everything. At this point I decide— for my own sake maybe—a cross is just a cross.

"You know I wonder about them too," comes from behind me.

Caught off guard, I turn to see Everly staring up at the crosses positioned neatly in a line all around the armory. I give him a look like I don't know what he's talking about.

"The crosses," he says. "They're beautiful. I wonder where they came from. Who made them. What they're worth."

"Sure," I say. "All that's occurred to me too. Went and met with Ellison."

"That's what Bock said. You know, you really shouldn't leave him in charge when you're gone."

"Why's that?" I ask.

"I think living out at that mansion's starting to get to him. He rarely comes in anymore. We're all left to our own devices, not that we can't handle it. I just think if you put a guy in charge, well, he should be *here*."

"I'll take that under advisement," I say, finally realizing how out of the loop I've been.

"Another thing, Rust," Everly says, and I can feel the apprehension in his voice. "We've been together for a long time, all of us, yeah?"

"Sure," I say, turning toward him to offer my full attention.

"Well, you remember when Bock had that girlfriend way back when?"

"That one he almost married? How could I forget? Almost tore the team apart."

"You remember how it got toward the end when that relationship started to turn? How he got? Toward women, even on jobs? How he got even after it was over?"

"Sorry to say I do," I tell him, stroking my mustache between my fingers. "He got meaner than usual. Got brutal."

"Well, I don't know what's going on with him. Maybe it's just being cut off from people around here, or if the weirdness of the job's getting to him, but something's off. And it's not just me. A few of us see it. We all know Bock's not the nicest guy in the world as it is, but he's got Evangeline and Brigita living out there with him. She doesn't talk about it, but I think she and Brigita have moved out of the main residence and into a guesthouse near the edge of the property. It's not good."

"I see. Okay," I say concerned that I haven't seen or noticed any of this before. "Why didn't anyone bring this to my attention sooner?"

"You're gone a lot, boss, even when you're not, you know?" Everly looks away, but do I know exactly what he means.

Everyday I'm confronted with more questions. A piece of the puzzle gets set and it only leads to other questions. I'm beginning to agree with Pastor Ellison: Humans are not meant to be involved in this war, not like this. It's just too much to wrap your head around, and clearly more immediate issues are neglected long enough to become California fault lines.

"I'll go out," I say to Everly. "Get a handle on this. Sorry I didn't before now."

"Sure, Rust," Everly says, walking over to one of the weapon cabinets. He opens it and takes an M203 assault rifle with an M16A1 attached launcher down from the pegs, then a Springfield .45 ACP handgun as well. "I know you will. You've never let us down."

Those words are like fire in my chest. I can't leave without telling him. After all, his job in the new strategy might just be the most dangerous, and the poor son of a gun doesn't even know it. I meant to spring it on him right before the next rescue, so he wouldn't have time to think on it too much, but these men trust me, and I have an obligation to show some respect. "Listen, Everly, I need to talk to you about something. I intended to wait a while, but I think it's the right thing to do."

Everly stops, noticing my seriousness. He sets down the weapons on the glass case in the middle of the armory. "Okay, Rust," he says with a little apprehension.

"Ellison and I figured out what we think your role as The Meek will be in the following ops," I say. "But you're not going to like it. Hell, I don't like it, but we've got to give it a shot. You and I both know that the enemy is starting to understand our methodology and we've got to change up our tactics before somebody gets themselves dead. Frankly I'm surprised it hasn't happened yet. Apparently most teams lose members early on, and you know that Bock almost bit the dust in that Phoenix rescue a few weeks back."

"They're getting smarter," Everly says, nodding. "More numerous each time. They're overwhelming us."

"Yeah, maybe not smarter though. I think they're just learning. Turns out my grandfather was the first Shepherd. He put together the first team toward the end of the war. We think that's why Elijah recruited me. Us."

"Wow, no kidding? You're serious? And you didn't know? Your dad didn't?"

"Nobody knew. Ellison says that he was good. *Really* good. Same thing happened to him. Demons got wise to his strategy. He lost a few men. It was grizzly. So he came up with a system, one in which he had unprecedented success," I say. "Those names we all go by? The Meek, Judge, Shepherd, all of them? My granddad came up with them. They're based on principles—I'm talking biblical—and we're going to try them out. Give it a run."

"So why am I The Meek?" Everly asks. I register a slight tremble in his voice. He can sense something less than great coming.

"You're slight. You're fast. Lean."

"I don't get you," he says.

I pause for a moment, but there's no good way to say it, so I just do. "You appear… weak. Now I know you aren't, but that's how the demons see you, and we've got to use that to our advantage."

"I don't like where this is going, Rust."

"I don't either, trust me. Everly, you've got the hardest job in this whole deal, and for that I'm sorry, but we've got to do it." I take a deep breath. "You have to go in first, and you have to go in alone. There's something about you they like. They look at you like candy. I'm sure you've noticed that they tend to go after you first."

"I've noticed, but I didn't want to say anything. Hoping no one else would. I mean, would you?" he says, looking away.

"No. I wouldn't say anything. I wouldn't. But we can't change it either. I'm protective of you, Everly, and if I didn't think you could pull this off, I wouldn't put you in the position."

"Just get to it, Rust. I'm stroking out over here," he says, and I've never seen Everly so small. He's terrified like he knows what I'm about to suggest. "I'm going to be bait aren't I."

Only somebody who's gone up against the things we have would appreciate the overarching weight of that thought. To go against an enemy so ravenous and powerful alone would send any regular Joe charging for the exits, but Everly's not some average Joe. He's a tried and true merc like the rest of us. His mettle is not and has *never* been in doubt. Not by me anyway. Bock's another story, but that's Bock.

"I hate to call you bait, but yes. That's just about the size of it if I'm being honest."

"I see," he says, eyes to the floor. He's got to be seconds away from falling apart. I don't think any less of him.

"This means you can't have any weapons," I say unsuccessfully masking a hint of pity. "You go in. We hang back. We pop off the sulfur from distance. The demons see you, and we're betting it'll send them into a frenzy. They'll be blinded by the sight of you. They'll charge, Everly. They'll charge at you like Great Whites to bloody water, and you've got to stand your ground. But, I promise you with everything inside me that when they charge, we'll be right behind you and just as intent to push them back before they reach you."

"Why can't I have any weapons?" Everly asks, hopeless as a jackrabbit in a field of coyotes. "I mean, come on, you've got to give me something."

"We have to make you as vulnerable and attractive to them as we can. If they see a weapon on you, they'll know it and be cautious. Suspicious. You've got to appear... completely helpless."

"Rust—"

"Everly, I know. I know," I plead with him. "But there are reasons for all of this. You *have* to trust me. We will have your back. We will not let them get to you."

"I don't see why we can't succeed through superior firepower. Like we always have. This is crazy. We've been successful so far. I just—"

"The game is changing, Everly. You know it is, and this is historically the most effective way to go about it. No other team besides my grandfather's has been able to pull it off as well as he did, but that's why I've been activated as Taber's replacement. I can make this work. I will make this work. We can do this. We have to."

"But how can you know that?"

"Ellison and I were talking. He says that he's noticed a pattern, one that I think Frank Rust did too, and that's why he developed this streamlined system. It seems like the more resistance you throw up to the demons, the more demons show up to combat it. More guns, more demons. Larger team, more demons," I explain. "More demons, Everly, and you've got the greater likelihood of becoming overwhelmed. They don't have restrictions on their numbers. We do. Taber went the way of adding more guns and bigger team numbers, but he also had the worst success rate and the highest casualty count. Pairing things down increases our odds, not theirs. I know it sounds counterintuitive, but the numbers don't lie."

"It increases *your* odds, Rust, not mine. My odds just went into the toilet."

"Not if we do our job. Not if we follow the plan," I say, realizing that our voices have raised enough to bring Horrace in from the firing range. "Now Ellison is prepared to offer you significantly more money for subsequent jobs. You'll be the highest paid one of us... by a lot."

"By how much exactly? How much is me dangling out like chum to monsters with really sharp teeth worth to the cause?" he asks, glaring at me.

"Half a mil," I say hurriedly. "Double danger, double pay."

Horrace looks on as we're both silent while it sinks in. Horrace is the first of what I'm certain to be many registrations of discontent.

"I'll do it. I'll do anything for $500,000," Horrace says, and by his lighthearted attitude I can tell he hasn't heard anything else we've been saying.

"No you wouldn't, Horrace," Everly says back without breaking his stare. "No you would not."

"Why? What do you have to do?" he asks.

"Let's call a spade a spade, Rust. I'm not The Meek. I'm The Meat."

Chapter 51

I DIDN'T QUITE know how to end the conversation with Everly, so I switched the subject over to Red and Brigita. Horrace said she'd checked-in minutes before I arrived at the HQ, said she was taking Brigita to McDonald's for some breakfast. Everly said she and the girl had been going there a lot recently. The fast food joints are on the other side of town close to the highway in order to catch the trucker traffic. Luckily, the new Wal-Mart is over there too. I've been thinking of picking something up for Brigita for a while now that it's dawned on me that I haven't really spent any time getting to know her. I keep looking at her as a sad little girl with a terrible affliction, not as a team member like I should. As the team's Shepherd, I need to know my whole team, not just the ones I find it easy to get along with. Brigita is possibly the most important team member we've got. I need to treat her accordingly.

As I scroll past that all-too-familiar Tahoka scenery, the Quick Sack on the corner with that yellow plastic bag slipped over one of the broken pumps for as long as I can remember, the new post office where those two old farmhands from Escuela's place hang out on the bench, and that broken down, paint-chipped colonial I think about buying and rehabbing every now and then, my thoughts turn to *Sharkey's*, and to Park, who saved me. After talking to Ellison, all conjecture that he had been a figment of my imagination melted away. One thing didn't make sense: why not contact us, one of us, anybody, and let us know he was still breathing? Why the secrecy? Was it just part of the Catholic operation's code? Cut yourself off from anyone or anything? Doesn't make sense. Any way you slice it, even if the Catholic teams and ours don't get along, we're still fighting the same enemy. Why not make a move to get on the same page? The whole thing sounds like pre-9/11 interagency squabbling; the jurisdictional pissing contest the CIA and FBI found themselves tangled up in too much to notice two giant passenger jets careening into glass towers, and one into their own Pentagon. Foolish if you ask me. What could possibly put our two factions so far apart? Maybe that was Park's overture by saving me. They clearly know about our ops, both when and where they go down. They know our enemy just as well as we do. Seems to me we should be fighting this war together. Wouldn't mind some of their resources either. I caught a glimpse of the gear Park and his cross-chested boys had. It was better than ours for sure. The Vatican's never had a problem with style.

Not that our gear isn't great. Wherever our cash comes from, we've never had a problem getting it. Horrace and Everly have been feverishly working on our new tech pretty much since our team was activated, and I must say, some of their prototypes are downright exciting. For example: the horrendously clunky bolos and their equally antiquated mortars? Gone. In place of them we've got a grenade launching system.

Grenades seemed to be the obvious brimstone delivery system. The problem was, the boys couldn't figure out a way to press the brimstone powder tight enough for it not to come apart while flying through the air. They tried adding water and baking it down to a cake-like composite, but that didn't work. It made the brimstone break up in clods and chunks when it hit the ground. It lost all of its powdered quality. The brimstone needs to remain a powder, so the tiniest particles can circulate in the air. That way you get the best coverage. It would cost three or four times the brimstone quantity to bake it into grenades than if we could keep it in powdered form. I'm sure that's why Taber's men used the bolo technique.

But then, Taber didn't have Horrace or Everly or their own underground mad scientist laboratory to play around in. Horrace figured up a glaze. They press the brimstone into grenade shape and then paint it with a hot resin. As the resin cools the shell hardens like a clay, almost a thin terra-cotta type shell. Doesn't take much to break apart, and we still get the benefit of a wide powder plume. And that's not where it ends. In a stroke of brilliance, Everly came up with our own flash-bang concept.

Flash-bangs are non-lethal grenades designed to incapacitate tangos without killing them. Typical flash-bangs explode with a blinding flash of light accompanied by a respectable concussive wave from the explosion that should disorient a target just long enough for the user to rush in and take the upper hand. Everly's flash bang is designed for the user to get a quick and safe glimpse at any demons that may be in the area without putting that user in immediate danger. I didn't buy the concept at first, but once he explained it to me, I couldn't believe nobody thought about it before. The idea is simple. Everly inserted an extremely quick and hot burning phosphorus charge in the middle of one of the new brimstone grenades. Throw the flash bang, it pops, you get to see if any of the hell-spawn are around, and just before they can tear you to ribbons, a delayed second charge ignites and almost instantly incinerates all surrounding brimstone from the area. They're over there. You're over here. Safe. We haven't put it through paces in the wild, but we've got proof of concept in the gun range.

Not to be outdone, Horrace applied the failed brimstone-cake grenade idea to something that would work for us in fine fashion. Salt grenades, and unlike Everly's flash-bangs, they *do* hurt. You don't want the brimstone to clod and fragment, but that's not necessarily the case with the salt. The bigger the chunks of salt to send flying at demons the better. They developed a filler that prevented the sodium from breaking down at a high baking temperature. It binds to the salt and nearly turns it into rock. Throw in a charge powerful enough to crack that puppy into a thousand shards of Dead Sea hurt and you've got yourself a salt grenade. They're pretty too, look like fist-sized pineapples made out of packed snow. They've been tested. We're still digging bits of it from the range's concrete walls.

If demons weren't so ugly, I'd almost feel sorry for the first one that takes the brunt of a salt grenade. They used the same technique for our bullets. We used to treat our standard lead bullet rounds with the salt, just soak them in a salt water mixture then re-attach them to dry casings, but not only did the treated bullets only yield minimal target damage, they also resulted in the increased incidence of rapid corrosion and weapon jamming. Not anymore. The boys use the same cake-like salt mix for the grenades and bake it into trays of bullet molds. They run the baked bullets through the brimstone grenade glaze, then get set aside to cool and harden. Once that's done, we slap regular casings on the back of them and—boom—you've got yourself a full on salt bullet, 110% stronger and more painful than our original solution. Just put these four new weapons together and you've got a serious game changer on your hands.

They've come up with a little something for Yakubu too. It's in a case on the floorboard of my truck, a big one. I'm gonna run over and see him at his farm after I finish with Red and Brigita at McDonald's. I've been out of pocket too long, and if Bock has gone to his dark place again, it's gonna take some sorting.

Chapter 52

I SEE EVANGELINE and Brigita sitting at a booth through the window as I ease my truck into the McDonald's parking lot. I picked up an orange and purple teddy bear at Wal-Mart that sings high-pitched parodies of pop songs when you squeeze the pads of his paws. Don't know if Brigita will like it, but I tried. While I rambled aimlessly down the toy aisles, I got a call from Pastor Ellison. He asked for a progress report, so I gave him one; told him about the new munitions and the willingness for the team to adopt the new system. I could almost hear him licking his teeth with excitement about the salt bullets. I didn't tell him about some of the discord within the team. Didn't think it would serve any good purpose. Besides, I can handle it. I've had to manage Bock's mood-swings for years now. I think I can do it again. Then Ellison properly brought up the fact that we should practice our new system and equipment, put it through its paces out in the field. I concurred but told him that only Brigita could inform us of assignments. He told me that wasn't entirely true. He said that, of course, use of Brigita's "gift" was indeed the only sure fire way to see action, but we *could* always play the odds.

"Go where bad things happen, Amarillo," he said in that unhealthy rasp of his. "Go somewhere good once had a foothold, but seems all but lost now. Lost to the darkness so that evil flourishes and becomes the norm. You find that place, and you're likely to see fireworks, my boy."

"Seems a little... out of our jurisdiction," I told him. "Doubt Elijah would approve."

Well that sent a shockwave through him that erupted into the angriest mushroom cloud you could ask for. A myriad of spit and expletive-laced rhetoric barked through the handset. He didn't like being second guessed, and by all this, it was obvious that Elijah had personally reprimanded him at some point for suggesting a team go out on their own looking for trouble. If there was one thing that Ellison hated, it was orders, and if there was one person he hated getting them from, it was Elijah Tishbe.

I told him that I understood that Elijah wasn't here, and placated him by agreeing that, yes, maybe his attending to other business without telling us could be taken as a sign of wavering commitment to the team. But I never once believed it. I can trust Tishbe completely now, but Ellison is another matter entirely. Ellison wants to *be* Tishbe. He wants to call the shots. He truly feels that he should be taken up as a prophet just the same as Elijah was all those years ago, in a hail of heavenly fire engulfing that holy chariot rising and rising still after being brought inside its light. But that wasn't the place for him, even I can see that.

Ellison is selfish and worldly and filled with a hubris I usually reserve for drug lords. But he is good at what he does, very good. His skill in accurate translation of the ancient texts is unmatched. His intellectual abilities of intuition and deduction are of an extremely high level. Elijah knows this, and that's why Ellison is still around. See, the way I figure it, a man can't really tell what's in another man's heart. You can catch glimpses of it, of a man's true nature, but you can't really ever see inside. Sometimes what's inside is protected so much, held so tightly that things get crossed, hardened—and for a hundred different reasons—until all the goodness in him is a light surrounded by four feet of granite packed each way. You'd never know it by the way he walks around, by the way he talks and acts, and maybe even some of the things he's does, but behind that granite there's still a little light flickering in there, a little sphere of some kind of wanting to do the right thing, to be righteous, hopeful, to love. It's small, and it's been covered up by years of hurt and wear and disappointment, but it's in there all the same. You just can't see it anymore. Sometimes a man can't see that light, not even in himself, but I think Elijah can see it. God can see it too, and that's another reason Ellison's still around. "God's got a hammer, a chisel, and an arm that doesn't tire," my granddad used to say. "Anything can be redeemed." Maybe I'm starting to see things that way too.

Funny, if you would have told me three years ago that one day I'd be tapping on the big window of a McDonald's with an orange and purple teddy bear in my hand, I'd have called you crazy. Of course, if you would have told me three years ago that I'd be ambulancing injured angels to elevators—next stop the pearly gates—working out MP5 jams because we've got to mow down monsters from Hell and salt from our bullets got stuck in the slides, I guess I would have called you crazy then too.

So, I'm in front of the window, tapping away over the clamor of kids climbing and sliding on the plastic playground behind me. Evangeline's back is to me, I see that perfect curve of her neck as she takes her French fries one at a time between two fingers, working them like airplanes before popping them into her mouth. Brigita faces me, and I can see she takes great joy in the show she puts on for her. I watch for a moment, thinking about the girl, and about Evangeline, still speculating silently about how someone like her gets into this business. Then Brigita sees me, she smiles wide and waves her hand excitedly, rapturously even, that GPS tracker watch forever around her little wrist shifting with her arm in a blur of color and sparkle. Evangeline turns to see me, smiles a meager moment, and turns back around.

I walk around the side of the white brick building, the smell of greasy remnant clotted bags shoved into a nearby garbage can with a red-domed top remind me why I don't eat the stuff. I enter the establishment with the teddy bear.

I stand next to their table for a brief moment, peering down to Brigita with the toy behind my back. My look beckons her to locate its obvious whereabouts. Brigita giggles, Evangeline forces a smile, and I open my mouth wide. It causes Brigita to mimic me, her eyes like dinner plates. At that moment, I pull my hand around, revealing the bear to her great delight. She claps and giggles as I offer it to her. She eagerly accepts the bear and hugs it tight, causing it to elicit one of its squealing songs. This new development may have been more than she can take. She holds the bear away from her as far as her arms will extend. Her mouth goes wide again, no sound. She flashes a look at Evangeline who feigns surprise along with me. The three of us hold the look for just a moment before Brigita wails and giggles in excitement once again bringing the bear close to her chest.

"Looks like you're a hit," Evangeline says.

"How're you doing, Red?" I ask amiably.

"What do we say, Brigita, when someone gives us a gift?" she asks the girl instead of answering me.

"Thank you," Brigita says, and I can barely detect an accent at all.

"Whoa, girl. You speak very nicely," I say. "You're very welcome. Does your hamburger taste good? Do you like coming here?"

"Cheeseburger," Brigita says, nodding with her mouth full.

"We don't talk with our mouths full, honey," Evangeline says, passing the child a napkin.

I turn my attention to Evangeline who doesn't seem well. Her color is off, her hair a bit ragged, not the striking, vivacious woman I met in Las Vegas.

"Been hearing some things," I say stealing a fry.

"Yeah, well I'm not surprised. Might hear more if you were around."

"I deserve that."

"You do," she says looking away and sucking cola through her white and yellow striped straw.

"To be fair, you have no idea what's been going on with me, you'd be happy not—"

"Don't hand me all that, Rust. I'm—we're all going through some stuff too," she says referring to the two of them.

"I've heard. Bock?"

"How could you work with—" she says, her eyes narrowing at me as if to set me in the same category.

"Heard you two moved out of the main house. To the guest one around back? That right?" I ask with honest concern.

"He drinks," she says staring deep into me. "When he's bored, and he's always bored, he drinks. But you knew that."

"It's been a problem in the past, but—"

"When he drinks he gets... violent."

"With you? With—"

"Yeah, Rust, he gets violent and he gets royally angry that Brigita's dolls are on the floor of a room he never goes in. And then he even— Forget it."

"He didn't try to—"

"Not to her, no. He hasn't hit her yet, but he's sure hit me, and that's not all."

"You can't be serious, Red."

"You think you know this guy, but you don't. You don't."

"Red I've been with Bock for—"

"You do *not* know him," she says, her eyes welling. Brigita's smile has gone, all emotional expression has vanished and now she absently sits humming and staring at her food.

With one elbow on the table, my hand kneads my forehead. I've heard another woman say this about Bock. *Now you know he is an animal*, I hear a voice from the past say. Only one, and she ended up... missing. How can this be? "Come live with me. I can take you. Come live with me," I say before I can even think.

"What, and wait for another group of Satanists to grate us into cheese?"

"You heard."

"We've got money, Rust. We don't need a man to take care of us."

"Then why do you stay?"

And just then, right there, I can tell by the look she's giving me that there's far more going on in that mansion than I thought, more than she's telling me. They weren't roommates at all. They were playing house, and now it's on fire. She cares for him. Bock and Evangeline. Where have I been? How couldn't I have seen it? She hated Bock. Loathed him. I guess if you cram two good looking people like that into the same living space, nine times out of ten something's going to happen, but this? Part of me is sad for Evangeline and Brigita, but another part of me, a growing part of me is furious, not only at Bock for sinking back into that dark region of himself, but for him feeling the justification to get amorous with her at all.

And then something clicks. Clicks or shuts off, shuts down, snaps maybe. I don't know. I bolt up from the table, emotionless. "I'm going to take care of this, but meanwhile, we're all still on the clock. The boys and I will be shoving out soon on a training mission. I want you here watching over Brigita. We're testing out the new system. You two will be safe in the HQ while we're gone. Bock will be with me, you hear? Get some sleep. You don't look good."

As I move away, I hear Evangeline in a soft voice. "Don't hurt him, Amarillo. Please."

I look back and direct a shameful look at her. I remember a woman with strength beyond most men, now reduced to groveling for the well-being of a one who drinks scotch and uses her like a heavy bag. This team has been compromised, and I cannot allow that to continue.

Chapter 53

I'VE ONLY BEEN out to Yakubu's farm once, and it didn't look like much then: just a big patch of cracked earth and some paint-chipped pipe fencing next to a modest, orange-bricked, two bedroom and a wraparound porch. Under his care, this bruised and forgotten spot of the Texas plains has become resurrected. Yakubu planted cotton, row upon carefully measured row of it spanning the length of the field in front of the house. Both the fence and the small house's wraparound porch have received refreshing coats of white paint.

I walk up the creaky wooden steps to the front door, almost knock, but I hear grunting and swing around to see Yakubu in the distance kneeling down over a cotton bush. I leave the porch and walk down a dusty aisle between cotton bulbs. The closer I get, I come to find The Yak's got one of his massive hands wrapped around the hilt of a medium sized cotton bush about two feet across. He's working to pull it from the ground with his bare hands.

"Think you might need a shovel for that job, podnuh?" I ask.

Though the Yak doesn't look up, I can sense the smile in his voice. He grunts. I hear the muted pops of stubborn roots from deep within the soil beginning to give way. "I would use a shovel if I had brought one with me, boss."

"What's wrong with her?" I say referring to the cotton bush. I know the answer, but I'm just making small talk. The bush's bulbs have withered; it's branches spindly and weak.

"It has died. I must remove it before the rest of the cotton notices."

"Notices?" I ask skeptically.

"They will begin to grow weak also," he says giving one final heave. Sweat droplets break over his forehead as the muscles in his monstrous arm tighten. He pulls up, more pops and thumps register from the soil until he wrenches the bush from the ground completely. A shower of dirt cascades from its tangled roots. Yakubu faces me with the bush in his left hand like Perseus raising the head of Medusa. "You see, boss. The weakness is gone. Now the rest can be strong again."

We walk together toward the house mostly listening to the cicadas and breeze slipping through fields of grass on the next farm. Yakubu starts to break the bush down into twigs just shy of the porch steps.

"I will burn this in the winter," he says coolly.

I nod and grin. There has always been a gentleness in Yakubu that only unsettles me having seen him embroiled in battle with both the living and the dead. He fights even harder with the dead, the demons, and I think that's why he sticks around. Maybe when you're as strong and powerful as Yakubu, you're just searching for a worthy opponent in a sea of inferiors. All I know is that it's not the money. He doesn't spend it, that much I know, in fact, it seems almost a game with him, to see how much he can do with as little as possible. Take this farm for instance, it's a working farm but it doesn't have to be. With all the jobs we've pulled together? Yakubu's made more money than anyone in this town ever has, yet he works the farm himself, yields a decent crop from it, sells that and puts the remainder back into the farm by way of renovations or equipment.

I look to the far side of the house and see what seems to be a brand new John Deer tractor tucked under a corrugated steel carport. Instead of the standard green bucket for moving dirt, the implement on the hydraulic arm is a giant jackhammer; its gleaming chromed bolt sharpened to a point protruding proudly from the yellow hydraulics encasement. Must be as big around as a hundred-year-old oak stump.

"See you used some angel-money to get you a new tractor?"

"Yes. You know, I have a feeling the dry air and all the dust shortens the life of engines. It was like that in Africa too. Do you like it?"

"Sure. What's the jackhammer for? That thing's gigantic."

"One of the past owners had—what did they call it at the store—had a bomb shack? You know for bombs? To hide from them?"

"Oh a bomb shelter."

"Yes, a bomb shelter. They put it right out here in the middle of my garden, but I am not afraid of bombs. I would rather plant tomatoes. I enjoy tomatoes."

"I see. Good, good." I listen to the breeze for a moment and decide to change the subject. "So why do you do it, Yak?"

He takes a strong, deep breath and surveys the farm proudly. "One part of my life is very ugly. Very angry. Very mean. To be involved in it can torture your soul. I must balance this with something beautiful, something normal. If I do not, my soul is at risk. If I dwell on the ugliness, I too will become ugly, just like Mr. Bock. Yet if I choose to dwell on God's beauty that is all around us, right here, my soul is washed clean."

"But we work for God, Yak. We save angels. We're the good guys. How is that ugly?" I ask, realizing this is pretty much the first real conversation we've ever had. I have underestimated this man's thoughtfulness.

"The angels are the only reason I continue. I fight for them because they have fought for me. This does not mean that it is in the best interest of man to be so close to evil that you can reach out and touch it with your own hands," he says with his free palm up then snaps it closed into a white-knuckled fist.

"You said something about Bock before."

"Yes," he says, turning his attention back to breaking down the dying cotton bush. "He is your friend."

"Sure, yeah, he's my friend, Yak, but you've noticed something too, haven't you?"

"I care for the child, boss," he says, pausing, closing his eyes.

"I know you do."

"But you are my boss. Mr. Bock is your friend, and I am a good worker, yes?"

"You're excellent, Yak. Irreplaceable. Just tell me what's on your mind."

Yakubu straightens up and drops the cotton bush. He looks me dead in the eye and lays it out.

"I check on her every night, boss. I jump the fence and move through the shadows of the moon to the big house where she stays, with Evangeline... and him. I look through the windows to make sure she is well. I have seen many things in the nights I go to check on her."

"I knew that's why you bought this place, Yak. You wanted to be close to Brigita, to protect her."

He nods. "I feel... responsible for her life. I saved her from the two bad men in the cabin, but now there is a third."

"A third bad man? You mean Bock?"

He nods again. "As I say, I have seen many things. But he is your friend, and you are the boss, and so I will not speak of it anymore."

"No, Yak. I need you to. You don't understand. Bock has acted this way before. I just saw Evangeline and she told me her and Brigita have moved into the guesthouse because Bock hit her. I know they've been sleeping together. You don't have to protect him. I know what Bock is capable of, but I can stop him. I just need to know what you've seen."

"I am not protecting him. I would never protect him. I am protecting you and the girl, boss."

"I don't need protecting, Yakubu. I run this outfit, and now I need you to tell me what you know," I say, giving him my best authoritative demeanor: back straight, chin high, cold stare. I'm the old king of the pride making one last stand against a bigger, stronger, and younger version of myself. Yakubu could snap me like one of those cotton bush branches if he wanted.

"Yes, boss," he says averting his eyes out of respect.

I exhale with relief.

"I have seen Mr. Bock many nights," he says. "Always with a bottle in his hand. He stumbles around the house, singing with his glass in the air. Sometimes he throws things and screams as if he is speaking to someone, but no one is there. I have seen Evangeline try to calm him, and instead he strikes her. At these moments I think to break through the window to stop him, but then he starts to cry and kneels down to apologize. She holds his head in her hands. Many times they end up making love. At these times I move around to Brigita's window and see her fast asleep. It is all so confusing."

"I'm surprised she can sleep through all that... commotion," is all I can think to say. What I'm hearing does not sit pleasantly.

"The girl is like me, boss. She has lived too much life for her young age. We have both been surrounded by much worse, and so anything less we find a way to tolerate. She retreats from her nightmare to sleep. The girl sleeps often, boss. Very often."

"I just can't figure why Red would have stayed so long?"

"I have seen them together many nights, boss, and often the bottle is in her hand, and while I have witnessed him strike her, I have also witnessed her strike him. They wear dark smiles on their faces when they fight each other. Their love is angry too. At these times they are not themselves."

"Not themselves," I repeat under my breath. It's almost too much. How could this have happened, and what precipitated it? Bock can get mean and sadistic as they come. You've got to keep him on a tight leash. I've failed in that, but Evangeline? What's come over her? She seems so protective of Brigita, but the way Yakubu's talking, it sounds like she all but neglects her at home. Something's not right. "The boys back at HQ said that Evangeline's been acting... distant."

The air hangs heavy between us. There's just too many irons in the fire: Bock and Evangeline. Brigita. The new system. Elijah's still MIA doing whatever it is he does, leaving only Ellison on our side, guiding us in a manner I find tenuous to say the least. Yakubu looks reticent to tell me something.

"There is more," he says, a graven look flashes across his face. "A few nights, Mr. Bock leaves the big house and goes to the stables near the front of the property. There he meets with someone in the shadows. But only a few times have I seen this."

"Meeting with who?"

"I do not know. It is dark and I do not wish to give away my position in fear that I will not be able to check on the girl without being noticed. It is a man. An old man I think. By the moon I have seen only his hair. Only once. It is long and grey."

"You don't—Elijah?" I ask, dumbstruck.

"This came to my mind as well. It is a thought I wish to deny. I have seen him, but pray I am wrong."

Am I being usurped? Used? Is Elijah making back room deals with a man that's clearly gone off the reservation? Tishbe isn't stupid. He must know what's going on in that house. He must know that Evangeline's started some kind of ungodly relationship with Bock fueled by alcohol and whatever other bad things I've either unconsciously decided not to see, or worse, just failed to piece together. Why did I allow them to move into that house with him? But then, why wouldn't I? Bock is my friend, my partner. I thought that manic slip he went through all those years ago was an isolated incident that he'd changed, learned from it—I don't know—figured out how to cope and simmer down, but now? Now. Now, I just don't understand anymore.

My trust in Elijah has been hard won, but he did win it, and if Yakubu's right, and Bock has been covertly meeting with Tishbe, I've got to trust that in his own way he's got things under control, even if I'll be damned if I can see how. I was hired—no—I was recruited for a reason, to do a job. I've got to keep it together and focus on the job. Everything else will have to wait. The best I can do is go and talk to Bock directly, but I've got to keep Yakubu out of it. He just might be the only thing protecting the girl now. What I know has got to come out organically. Can't let on. They obviously want to keep whatever sick thing is going on between them a secret by the way Evangeline talked her way around the truth earlier. Best thing I can do is try and separate them somehow.

"Listen, Yak, I'll take care of what I can, but we've got a job to do. Can I count on you to keep your eye on the ball?"

"Of course, boss," he says without wasting a beat.

"The boys back at HQ have something for you. I brought it over so you can get yourself acquainted."

I open the door of my truck and lift out the heavy Samsonite brief-case. Yakubu motions for me to follow him to the porch. I set the briefcase down with a clump on the worn, wooden slats and click open the hinges.

"You know you're The Judge, right?" I ask before opening the case. "You know what that means?"

"I believe so. Samson. I have read the story many times. It is one of my favorites," he says kneeling.

"Good, then you might get the reference."

I open the case slowly to reveal an oversized steel gauntlet of sorts resting neatly on a bed of dark grey foam core. The chromed gauntlet catches a beam of sun and gleams up, causing us to shield our eyes.

"May I?" Yakubu says with a grin.

"It's yours. Go ahead. Made especially for you," I say, leaning back slightly. "It's got a salt polish you'll have to reapply before each mission, but then, I'm not sure you even need it."

Yakubu's hand takes up the steel gauntlet. I could fit both of my arms into it. The armored glove is designed to run all the way up the arm, past the bicep and to the shoulder ending in a series of gilt latches that clamp and lock under the armpit. Its impenetrable surface resembles a tortoise shell down to the elbow hinged with two wrought gears, one on top and one below. Down the forearm is ribbed with layered segments that rise to semi-sharp edges. The remaining mandible section is fash-ioned into a massive fist that only Yakubu could fill. But that's not the best part. Solidly clamped forever in the fist, all in one smooth continu-ous form factor appears the weapon end of the gauntlet, a scythe-like blade sharp as the finest katana. It arches out fluidly from the right side between pinky and palm. Extending on the left between the palm and trigger finger curves an even longer bladed edge almost a foot in length notched with bone ripping teeth like the back of a hunting knife.

Yakubu doesn't slide his new weapon on at first, but holds it up proudly in the light admiring the craftsmanship of it with a grin that tells me he's already figuring out the martial possibilities.

"Recognize it?"

"I think so. 'With the jawbone of a donkey, I have piled them in heaps,'" he recites, smiling.

"'With the jawbone of a donkey, I have killed a thousand men,'" I say back, recognizing the passage from somewhere in the annals of my memory, unable to hide a grin of my own.

"Judges fifteen, sixteen," the big man says, sliding the elephantine gauntlet over his right arm for the first time, clamping the latches and working the gears of the elbow with preternatural familiarity. It's so pretty he could have been born with it. Then he gives me a curious look, that thing on his arm gleaming like the hand of God. "I have heard you quote the scripture before, and please do not be offended by this, but you do not seem to be a man who would be familiar with the Book. How is this?"

"Might say the same thing back to you," is all I can think to say.

Yakubu chuckles. "I see. What is the expression? Looks can often deceive?"

"Something like that, yeah. My granddaddy was a preacher. Guess some of it was bound to rub off."

"And you feel it is only by accident that you now have been brought back to God?"

"Yak, I'm not even sure that God knows what we're doing and if He does that He even approves."

"He approves, boss. He approves. Of this I am certain," Yak says.

"How you figure?"

"Because we are still alive. That is one reason. There are others."

"I'm interested," I say.

"How much money do you have? From working for Mr. Elijah, how much money have you earned?"

"Don't have the slightest."

"You see?"

"Not sure I do," I say back.

"You do not know because you are like me. This is no longer about the money, and yet we were only drawn to this work by the money. That which brought us to His work has now become only about His work. We do this because we want to do this. Ask yourself if I am correct. Any other people would have quit, would have run for the mountains by now only at the sight of these demons. We do this because we must do it."

"I guess part of me still doesn't want to believe that," I say, looking off to the fields.

"He needs you to believe, boss. You already do, you just cannot admit it to yourself."

"I guess when a kid sees Superman get his head sprayed across the back of a church pulpit, it might get them questioning God. Questioning whatever the hell his 'plan' is anyway. Guess I just didn't want any part of it from then on."

"Your grandfather," Yakubu says in the softest voice. "He was killed."

I nod.

"My father was killed also. And my mother. And my four brothers, and three little sisters. The men who did this was possessed by the Devil. They tell me he was just a warlord, that it was only to strike fear, so he would gain power in the village, but I do not believe them. The Devil moves, boss. He moves like a swarm of bats looking for food in the night. He finds good things and destroys them, eats them. He is a hunter. That day he found my family, but he did not take me."

"Did you hide?"

"I did not hide. I looked him in the eyes, all of them. He could have killed me. I was only a boy, but he did not. Do you know why?"

"No," I say under my breath.

"Because he was not allowed to. I was protected by God. This was not the warlord's eyes I stared into—it was the Devil's, and he knew I saw him for what he really was. God noticed too, and so he protected me for many years. Many difficult years. Until I met you, boss. That's when I knew why I did not die that day. He would turn my pain into righteous anger against the one who killed my family. Now I have been blessed enough to do it, and no amount of money in the world can sway me."

"You really believe it," I say, not a question but a statement.

"So do you, boss. Do you think the Devil would only stop at your grandfather? Would he not have loved anything more than to kill you too, and make your grandfather scream and cry in Heaven?"

"Hadn't thought about that."

"But he did not. He *could* not. God would not allow it, and so you see he has protected you too."

"For many years," I say staring through the big man.

"For many difficult years, yes? And now he has brought you back, and he has given you a righteous anger too, and he has given you the means to unleash it, hasn't he, boss?"

"Yes, I suppose he has."

"So do it, but do it for the one that has protected you. Say his name and let it burn the evil spirits we fight. Let it burn inside of you until the blaze cannot be contained. Our work is a gift, boss, and to do it well we must do it with His name on our lips. I had a dream about you only nights ago. The Devil came to you and threatened you, but you did not move. You spoke from the scripture, just as we did today, and you know what happened?"

I do because it truly happened. Somehow Yakubu, the most faithful of us all had seen what went down at the bar with Beelzebub, but in a dream. He saw it, but none of the others did, that or they aren't saying so. Yakubu saw it. It's the faith. I think faith is the key. You have to believe it; not just believe it, but believe *in* it. In good. In righteousness. You have to believe that good can win—*will* win. Now I know this team, this mission, and this work are bound tighter than I ever thought possible. I'm starting to see that there are no coincidences, and that nothing is ever left to chance.

"You spoke the Word and he disappeared," Yakubu continues. "God protected you, and he can protect us all again if only you trust him and believe."

"I think I do," I say, a bit surprised at myself. "I think I do believe that."

"Do not think, boss. Say it. Say it and make it so. Do you believe that God has protected you?" Yakubu asks, leading me. He turns around and hurriedly lifts up an old pail of rainwater from next to the porch with his free hand.

"God *has* protected me," I say, the words pass through as a wave of memories of my grandfather. They storm past, rushing through. I feel safe. I feel young. I hear my grandfather's delicate voice as we fished so many summer days on the soft green banks of Lake Ray Roberts. I feel the gentle strength of his hands clasped over mine as he would say our nighttime prayers while kneeling next to my bed. I remember the safety and comfort when tucked in his lap on Christmas mornings with the cold white outside and the wonderful scents of the holiday all around.

"Do you believe in Him again, and that his Son died for you, and that he wants only the best for you while you are among the evils of this earth?" Yakubu asks with a fervent intensity.

"I do," I say, remembering all the actions in foreign lands, the too-close calls: the helicopter crash in Laos, the near capture in Bangkok, the field of land mines in Lebanon. Any one of them could've killed me, but none of them did. I chalked it up to luck, to training, but I was wrong. Nothing could have kept me, could've kept any of us alive for this long without some hand in it all. Something guiding it, making moves fall into place. Elijah was right all along. Yakubu knows it so deep down in his soul that it can no longer be questioned, and now, so do I.

Everything has changed. That's when I feel a rush of water over me. It's hot and it doesn't smell good, but the pail of rainwater Yakubu soaks me with might as well be the morning tide on white Caribbean beaches. It takes all the regret and uncertainty, all the built-up morally nebulous triviality and grey-shaded decisions I've made for decades along with it, right off of me and down to the ground where the soil just soaks it up like it was never there at all.

"Good," Yakubu says as I am jostled back to awareness. "Consider yourself baptized."

I stumble and wipe the water from my eyes, shaking my head like a dog drying off. "Think you could have warned me there, big Yak?"

"If I had, would you still have let me do it?"

"Probably not," I say, composing myself. I finally look back at Yakubu who is just about on the verge of breaking into a laugh as big as all Texas, but I beat him to it, and for the better part of a minute, we're yucking it up there on his porch steps. It's been too long since I've shared a good laugh with anyone. But sooner or later, we need to get back to business. We've got a job to do, and I've got more purpose than ever to do it. "Well then, now that I'm sopping wet like a three-legged mutt, I guess there's only one thing left to do."

"What's that boss?"

"Ready to try it out?" I ask excitedly, pointing at the shiny new weapon on his arm.

"Yes I am," he says, stepping off the porch like the lord of all gladiators, anxious muscles rippling beneath his tank top, all the way in his element and meaning to do considerable harm. His undeniable confidence makes me think this new system is actually going to work. I almost get chills.

"Now we just need a place to do it," I say.

"What do you mean? Brigita has not had a vision?"

"No. Nothing's come up in a while. Ellison said we'd probably have to find our own action on this one."

"How do we do that?"

"He said to go where terrible things happen. Got any ideas?" I ask.

"Yes I do. Can you find an airplane?" he says without taking his eyes off the new toy.

"I can try. Where we going?"

"Home."

Chapter 54

WE'RE EN ROUTE to Fiabuggo, a small village in the African Darfur region of Sudan about a hundred miles east of the Chad border. In his usual form, Pastor Ellison didn't, or rather wouldn't, come through with transport, but an old friend did, and on short notice. Yakubu, Everly, Horrace, Henry Knapp, and I sit patiently on the passenger benches of a C-17 Globemaster transport jumbo deep into the ninth hour of our flight. Bock is with us too. Hasn't said ten words since I collected him from the mansion yesterday after I spoke to The Yak. Something's way off with him. I needed to split Red and Bock up, so I had Ellison sit with she and Brigita back at Tahoka HQ. Ellison wasn't thrilled to make the trip down, but the way I figured, it's the least he could do.

I've spent most of the trip getting the men acquainted with the new system, running it over and over ad nauseum. We cannot afford to lose a team member on this exercise. Among all the other toys Horrace and Everly came up with, now we've got something to keep The Meek, or as Everly calls himself, The Meat, safer than an exposed slab of sirloin. Horrace had a flash of genius to modify an EOD or Explosive Ordinance Disposal Suit, the ones our boys in Afghanistan diffuse roadside bombs in; layers upon layers of sheet steel and Kevlar, bulky and clunky like an astronaut's gear or those old timey diver suits with the big bronze bulb helmets. Horrace managed to pack a few layers of salt in the leg protectors, chest plate, blast collar, and helmet too. I don't have the slightest idea how Everly's supposed to move around in it, but I'd rather him have some protection when he goes in alone. He'll need all the time he can get before Yakubu rushes in with his bladed gauntlet. He's got to get to Everly before the demons tear into him. I trust he will. After Yakubu lays into the attackers, that's when we pop out of cover and press the attack with those Dead Sea bullets and grenades. Horrace and Henry Knapp are charged with locating and initiating evac of any injured angels in the area. We're going in lean and clean.

In the moments I'm not drilling the plan into my team's heads, Bock and I trade stares. I keep hoping he'll pipe up and talk about what's been going on at the mansion with Evangeline, Brigita, and whoever it is Yak says he's been meeting with, but mum's the word on his end. My patience is tried. I consider letting loose on him, but that's when my old friend Chic Taber emerges from the cockpit to have a word. Who knew he still had connections, or that his munitions developer, Narikesh, moonlit as a pilot for the Indian military back in the early nineties.

"Drinks? Peanuts?" Chic asks playfully without showing it on his face.

I offer a small note of amusement.

"We're about half an hour from drop-point at Fiabuggo," he says. "There's a dirt strip seven or so clicks south of there. It's probably too small for the C-17, but it's nothing but dirt and the occasional bush out here so we ought to be fine."

"Thanks for the truck," I say flicking my head to the quarter-ton pickup that's tethered down in the cargo hold.

"Hang on to it tight," Taber says. "If the tangos don't get you, the Janjaweed militants will. They've been systematically moving through the region exterminating the nomadic non-Arab population. Your man Yakubu was right to suggest this place as a hotbed of spiritual activity. But that truck's the only thing that'll get you and any angels back to this plane in one piece. You've never experienced heat like a Sudanese dessert. It'll gas you before you know you're gassed. That truck means your life."

"Will do," I say, offering a handshake.

He takes it and leans in close. "Didn't Ellison tell you about going out on your own looking for trouble?"

I nod. "He said not to."

"Well so do I. Suicide mission if you ask me."

"I hear you, but we've got to get our game plan down quick. I feel like there's a fight coming for us."

"Coming for you?" Taber asks, confused. "That's not how it works, *compadre*."

"Not till now. Just have a feeling. A real bad one."

"What does Tishbe say about that?" he asks.

"I'll ask him if I see him," I say.

"He take off again? He does that."

"Tell me about it," I say. "If something does happen and the bad guys decide to take the fight to us back home, can I count on you?"

Taber releases my hand and turns, laughing. "Nope. I made my money, Rust. Already put my time into the cause. I'm just lucky to be alive."

I can't say I blame him.

"Gentlemen," comes over the PA. It's Narikesh from the cockpit. "Please return your seats and tray tables to their full upright and locked positions. We are go for landing."

Just before Taber reaches the cockpit, he turns back to me. "Good luck out there, Rust. My contact tells me there's been a raid on a band of locals in the area less than half a day ago. Make your way southeast and you should see some action. Narikesh and I will hold off any tangos that decide to follow you back to the plane from here. Other than that, your team's on your own. You're a damn fool for doing this, you know."

Trust me, Chic, I say to myself. I know.

Chapter 55

WE FEEL THE C-17's roaring jet engines grind down to a whimper as the heat of the Sudanese surface causes the plane to tremor and shimmy slightly across the thin air. The landing gear unlocks and hums beneath us, causing more heavy vibrations around the fuselage. The initial jolt of touchdown feels hollow and uncertain as I can feel Narikesh working the tail to gain more control of the colossal transport jet to keep it straight on top of the mercilessly shifting dirt of the strip. The engines bluster alive again, this time in reverse, working with earth-rattling horse-power to slow the aircraft, all the time continuing to slide in dangerous measure left and right on its unsure footing. Soon, we thankfully hear the metallic groan of the brakes lock down and cut culverts into the desert as we pull a stop.

Not a second later, Chic Taber reappears and waves me along to the cargo hold where we begin untethering the pickup truck. I tell the men to suit up. Everly's got the biggest job with that EOD suit, so I instruct Horrace and Henry Knapp to assist. Everly's noticeably and understandably the most nervous. Bock remains seated for a moment before I catch his eye. As if jarred from a trance, he collects himself and walks over to Chic and I to help with the truck straps. There is a noticeable distance in Yakubu's eyes as he opens the case and takes up his gauntlet. He isn't afraid—that's not it—he seems sullen, almost mournful to be back in

Africa. He pulls on the glimmering gauntlet and clamps the latches behind his bulging bicep, and then the forearm each with a taut quietude.

With the truck unstrapped, Narikesh hits the switch to open up the cargo hold. The staggering glare of African sun pours into the fuselage as the tremendous hydraulic moan vibrates the entire aircraft. I cover my eyes until my irises adjust. When I open them, I see the African countryside. It's greener than I expected with loose smatterings of brackish trees and their weary green leaf patches above lanky grey trunks. The area surrounding the airstrip is vast with deep orange, brown and black dirt. Dead grasses cling hopelessly to the edges. As I step down to the earth I look north and realize we are at the edge of the green where Fiabuggo village meets the Sudanese dessert. Where we're going is desolate, the orange and black dirt meets the rolling sands less than a mile south only to be broken up by craggy, clodded hills like skeletal brown icebergs in the hot sea of sand-swept ochre.

Yakubu stands beside me, taking a deep breath. He is transfixed by the sands. Bock is already in the pickup having loaded that new M-110 semi-auto sniper rifle with the Unertl 10x scope on top. The engine growls as he shifts into drive and slowly its mud treads meet the dark terra firma. Henry Knapp is next off the cargo floor. He hands me a SCAR-H assault rifle, locked and loaded, which I rest on my shoulder. Knapp's got an H&K G36 assault with a 1.5X telescope sight and spare transparent magazine of regular rounds clamped to the left side of the inserted one. We all have those since there's a chance we could run into Janjaweed militants. Horrace will work the M32 "six shooter" grenade launcher from distance first with the brimstone loads, then he'll switch the drum and fire off salt grenades when the demons rush Everly and Yakubu. Everything works as planned and there will only be a fraction of the resistance we're used to.

Horrace passes me with a small television monitor tucked under his left arm. He notes my confusion and just whispers to me that it's just one of a couple of surprises he and Everly have up their sleeves. I take that at face value with a playful curiosity.

Taber gives me one last nod as we mount up. We lift Everly, packed tightly inside his EOD suit—sans helmet for now—into the bed of the truck. Bock insists on driving, so I'll ride up front with him. The rest of the boys pile into the back. Pretty soon we're off the dirt and onto the sands heading southeast toward the waypoint that Taber's contact set for us.

We drive for a while, two clicks then three before I can't take anymore of Bock's silence.

"You know I know, don't you?" I say keeping my eyes on the dessert horizon.

"What would've been the point in telling you, mate? I know how you feel about her," he says doing the same.

"I don't feel anything except a need to get our job done."

"Sure, Rust."

We let it sit for a minute. I can't say it doesn't sting a little, but I'll be damned if I tell him that. Not that he needs to hear it. Bock knows me better than pretty much anyone.

"Whatever it is you think you know, I promise you this, Amarillo, you don't know the half of it."

He gently guides the wheel to the left toward a craggy outcropping of rock in the hazy distance, trying not to show anything to me. Inside I'm boiling. Inside I'm thinking about Vegas, about that first time I met Red and it's killing me. I'd have to be stupid not to know why. She had me from way back and Bock knew it even then. Maybe that's why he played the silent card on me. My brain's getting rusty. It feels encrusted with hard layers of dirt. Here I am pining over a woman, a team member, something I simply would never have done in the past. Never. The rules of the game don't change, only people do, and that's often what gets you killed. I've made that mistake and I didn't even know it. Part of me thinks Bock was just protecting me again, not from her, but from myself. The confusion mounts in my mind turning everything into a liquid mess until I don't know what's right anymore. All I know is the job, that's all I've known for as long as I can remember. The job will get you through.

Used to say that in the early days when the sight of blood and dead men still affected me.

I remember that rainy night so long ago in Berlin when angels and demons were tales I had left sitting in a pew at my grandfather's church. Back in Berlin when it was just another job in a long string of them. I now realize my humanity had been stripped by then. I had no real emotion left. No empathy. No pathos. Berlin was where all this craziness started. Get the stinger. Get the stinger. We need the stinger for the Albania job. It ran on an endless loop in my mind. I didn't think about the sniper who took out two of my team prospects before we even knew he was there. I didn't spend one second of time thinking about those two young men who lost their lives, everything they knew and loved evaporated at the end of a muzzle. I couldn't even tell you their names, and I even trained one of them out of Fort Sill. They were fresh out of the U.S. Army, but where were they really from? Were their parents still alive and would they ever find out what had happened to their sons? Didn't even cross my mind. I had shut down long before then, and my hubris kept telling me that I actually cared about my team. That I was one of the good ones. Now I know there's no such thing. I was part of the game, total and complete. I had no one, and I had nothing.

And then I remember that Bock was the one who took that sniper out all on his own. One shot, one kill, through the nighttime city lights and the rain that fell like molten beads. Bock was my friend. Still my friend, or so I think. Is he protecting me now too? From myself? Maybe my emotion for Red is the sniper now, and Bock just stepped in to save my neck one more time. It's all swirling. I'm dizzy and think maybe Bock isn't the problem after all. Maybe I'm just waking up from a life-time slumber of denying that which makes me human. Maybe now, knowing for certain what most people only have faith to believe is real actually is, perhaps my soul stirs again and it scares the rest of me to death.

"She's not what you think, mate," I hear Bock say from somewhere far away.

The truck yaws just a bit on the Sudanese sand. Thin streams of smoke rising from the outcropping are closer now, but still several clicks away. Bock tells me her story. Things I don't know. Things I wouldn't have believed only minutes before.

He tells me the part about Red's family, about the slaughterhouse in Indiana. About how her father ran it, and she worked with him from the time she was just a girl. That part I knew. But then Bock tells me that her father used to drink. Maybe it was the cries of the animals and all the blood that ran down those slaughterhouse gutters. Sometimes he would disappear for days on end. He left she and her mother to run the operation on their own only to find him curled on their porch steps stinking of whiskey, no one knowing how long he'd been there.

He tells me about the night that changed her. Father came into her room one summer night. She could smell the alcohol from his breath on her cheek as he put his weight on top of her. She was nearly eighteen then. At first she struggled, but the hand cupped over her mouth deafened her cries. Thoughts of college and everything she knew drifted away when he finished and wordlessly stumbled out of her room, leaving her there in a tear-filled heap on the bed.

Evangeline tried to put it out of her mind. Her father went on like nothing had happened, even beginning to believe that he actually didn't do it. Life for everyone else went on as usual while hers became locked in that moment when the earth and all its reason had turned against her. She went on for a couple of weeks, hoping against hope that it had been a dream—not a dream—a nightmare. The days in the slaughterhouse moved like pulsating mud, and she existed through them trancelike and unsure until it broke. She left, packing little.

Bock tells me that she took one of the work trucks and headed down the highway by cover of night, leaving everything behind north to Montana. She remained in her trance, not remembering the days and nights in that truck alone without even the fleeting signals of the radio for company. She simply pulled over when she needed to sleep, and resumed up that highway when she woke until the trees grew thick casting long shadows over the hood. With each mile, the pain eased, and thoughts of a future began to take form.

Evangeline finally stopped driving when the trees opened up into the brightest green she'd ever viewed. She guided her truck toward a great steel building on the horizon shimmering in the noonday sun, a familiar building at the edge of Hilger, Montana, population 4,000. Slaughterhouses were in her blood, and Evangeline could always spot one of her own. Hilger was just far enough away from life and everyone she knew. She thought she could be safe here, so she stopped driving.

It didn't take long for her to find work at the new slaughterhouse. She rented a room at the motel for the first few weeks until her accumulated paychecks could afford her a place of her own. She chose a singlewide trailer next to all the others. It reflected her on the inside at least, nondescript in every way. As the paychecks came, she populated her new home with furniture she found at the flea market the first Sunday of every month, and soon life became more bearable, the weight of her father lifted slowly as if by a slaughterhouse crane from her thoughts, and ultimately she emerged anew.

Hilger had one restaurant, one church, a school, a post office, a few basic shops in the town square that could survive that tiny economy, and a bar called Cole's Tap. This was the real town center, Hilger's living room. Evangeline soon came to the realization that if she wanted any friends at all, Cole's was where they would be found. Evangeline was always pretty, even then, and so it didn't take long for her to become something of a celebrity around town; that strange young thing with the pretty red hair that showed up one day, out of the blue; the girl who knew the slaughterhouse business like the back of her hand, but didn't seem to have any history at all.

Naturally the men gravitated to her first, single or otherwise, but there was one woman, Mindy, the slaughterhouse secretary who worked in the office with Mr. Olestop. She became her confidant. Mindy was a single mother of two though only one lived with her. The other, a boy of fifteen, lived with Mindy's mother in Great Falls. She and Evangeline would meet at Cole's at the end of most days, warding off the advances

of some of the younger men in town and gossiping about reality television, which was just about the only thing to gossip about in Hilger.
Mindy loved her vodka martinis. Tom, the bartender, had ordered the
martini glasses especially for her. Everyone else drank domestic lager,
but Evangeline and Mindy were martini girls. The hazy olive juice in
those tall-stemmed glasses made them feel cosmopolitan in a funny kind
of way. Pretty soon the whole town started referring to them as the
"Martini Girls" too. It was endearing at first.

But as most things, endearing can turn to disenchantment awfully
quick especially in a tiny little town with nothing else to do. When
thoughts of her father rose in her chest, Evangeline had Mindy buy her
another drink. Pretty soon she found herself taking home fifths of vodka
from the convenience store after she left the bar. Evangeline began
missing work, waking on the couch of her singlewide with the front door
spilling afternoon light and breeze onto her eyelids. She began to accept
the advances of more than a few locals—some married—but it was when
Mindy announced that she would be moving to Great Falls to be with her
other son that Evangeline really began to unravel.

After Mindy was gone, Evangeline's life revolved around Cole's
hours of operation. She still went to work of course, but her rise up the
company ladder had come to an abrupt halt at floor manager. She
became increasingly undependable. She flirted too heavily at the bar
through slurred phrases, her hair frequently unkempt and her weight
plummeting. The bottles accumulated in the kitchen garbage can, and not
long after, one of the men at the slaughterhouse, Tolouse, an overweight
Native American with a stray eye served her a pink slip, but he slept with
her first before dropping it on her nightstand like some kind of payment.

That was when Evangeline knew she had nothing. Hilger *was* the
slaughterhouse. There would be no other work. Her reputation in town
had sunk to an unemployable level, and so all that was left to do was
drink to make it all go away. When the money ran out she depended on
people at the square to offer up whatever they could. She returned home
one night to find herself foreclosed upon and locked out of her trailer.

Only a damp cardboard box split down one side held her clothes. Everything else was seized.

For a while she lived around the square. She tried the steps of the courthouse, but the sheriff grew tired of running her off and threatened to lock her up, so she moved on. Her truck provided shelter for a while, but the gas had run out, which didn't matter because the alternator went dead some months ago anyway. She developed all kinds of health problems. Her back was a mess from sleeping anywhere but a bed. On good days one of the old shopkeepers would forget to lock up the back door and she would slink inside.

Of course, through it all, Evangeline wasn't stupid, she knew when the liquor trucks would make their deliveries to Cole's Tap. She'd hide behind the dumpster or a tree and wait for the uniformed delivery man to wheel a dolly of bottles into the back door before sprinting out for the truck, ripping open the cardboard lip on a case and snag a bottle of vodka or whatever hard stuff she could get her hands on. She knew it was only a matter of time before they would catch her. Evangeline was now the town bum, that or the town whore depending on who you asked. Any money she made from the latter went right back into Cole's anyway, so Tom didn't bother her when she stumbled in most of the time.

But one night was different. One night, sitting at a table in the corner eyeing the rest of the residents bellied up to the bar like monkeys, most not paying her the time of day save for the odd drunken fool she once called a friend propositioning her in a daze of liquid courage. That night a stranger walked in. He was young and well dressed—at least for Hilger—pressed slacks, a long navy coat, and shiny black shoes with little silver buckles on the bridge. He seemed to spot her even before he entered the bar. But no one else seemed to notice, which was strange given his obviously foreign appearance. He smiled at her from the entryway though she was obscured by shadow. His teeth were so white, his eyes a brilliant, distant green.

The stranger walked over to the bar and held out his hand. Tom, without even acknowledging him popped the top of a longneck and gave it to him as if he were a regular with a standing tab. Then the man came over and sat right across from her at the small round table, staring into her eyes. It was the most pleasant and caring face she had ever seen.

"Evangeline," he said and it was like a breath from the ocean floating over the coolest shores. "You were made for so much more than this."

She felt something inside of her for the first time in so long. It welled up in her chest and soon she felt her heartbeat again. The man set down his longneck and gently slid his open hand across the table. She stared at it as if it held all the promises of youth and providence. The feeling pulsed through her and crept like life-giving waters up the roots of a tree until it reached the bottom of her eyelids, pooled, and threatened to crest. Evangeline felt her hand begin to reach for his. His smile never faltered, only seemed to embolden itself as her fingers came inches from his.

Suddenly two men stood over them with empty bottles in their hands. She knew them both, and knew them often. That kindness and hope that almost overtook her seized back into the depths and disappeared. She knew what was coming, but for her condition, hazy and weak with fatigue and regret, she could not warn the stranger.

The two men shouted drunkenly and one slapped his hand forcefully on the seated stranger's shoulder, clamping down hard so that the material of his coat wrinkled uncomfortably in the grip. The other man did the same, accusing the stranger of trying to take advantage of a sick woman, an audacious claim that disheartened her even more knowing that the two drunks held only those intentions themselves and several times over. Before she knew it they had dragged him away, their dirty, meaty arms locked under the stranger's own. She watched as the stranger's eyes remained locked on hers for a while, but then fell to the floor as they continued to drag him out of the bar. He did not resist. Others followed them outside like wild animals hoping to catch a glimpse of the gallows. He had done nothing to her or to them, and they would crucify him for it.

It took all of her strength to rise from that chair. She stumbled to get her bearings, using the tables and chairs for stability. She made her way outside in time to witness the crowd encircling the two brutes who only paid her coins for pleasure, coins for pieces of her soul. While one beat the stranger, the other held him upright. They took turns. She stood on the steps bracing herself on the railing, watching them pummel the kind eyed man until blood poured from his mouth like molasses onto the white of his shirt.

That feeling swelled up inside her again. She locked eyes with the poor man who she knew in her heart only wished to bring life back to her. She knew it was his purpose for entering the bar at the moment all seemed lost. In his eyes she recognized the knowledge of what was about to happen, and in his eyes she recognized that he would do it all over again, for her.

She felt her hand leave the railing, and her feet move down the steps. A power had returned to her, a rage that sent a rush through her legs and soon she was clawing through the crowd, screaming from the depths of her broken soul, teeth gnashing and fingernails wailing like claws against the two filthy brutes who stole her only fleeting chance at redemption. Soon there was blood in the air, their blood, their flesh under her nails in a chaotic flurry. Perhaps it was only in shock that the crowd as well as the attackers began to splinter and disperse. She had come undone, and her vengeance would not keep quiet any longer. When all was said and done it was only her screams that lingered along with the heaving of her chest as she stood protectively over the stranger. It was only the two of them now, and it all stopped when he raised his head. He was trying to smile through the blood, through the cuts and the bruises he didn't deserve. She had saved him, and the flood of it all sent her rushing away into the night, even as the stranger did his best to call after her.

She didn't know why, but Evangeline ran for what seemed like miles, blindingly into the night until there was no light but the stars, and still she ran until the stars were swallowed up by the trees. She had reached forest, but she would not stop even then. She ran deep into the early morning until the muscles in her legs jittered and fired their last pulses of stability. She sputtered to a halt and reached out to grab a tree, sliding down the harsh texture of the bark to its hilt, and there she believed she had died. At the bottoms of trees, the wind filtered by swathing needles above, Evangeline finally felt peace.

But no death greeted her the next morning, only the heat of the Sun that punched through holes in the forest. Evangeline woke with the deepest throbbing headache she had ever experienced. Her mouth open and dry as crisp fallen leaves. Her vision slowly focused on the waving treetops, and a smell invaded her nostrils. It was strong and pungent. She rolled over with bits of the forest floor clinging to her greasy skin and tattered clothing. A bubbling sound captured her attention from the right. She squinted, but seeing nothing tried to rise to her feet. Her legs groaned their disapproval, but she knew she was lost in the depths of the trees, so she turned round and round to try to gain her bearings, but it was for nothing. She was lost and could find no exit. How far had she run? In which direction? Only that pungent smell guided her, and so she followed it, that and the bubbling sound she now identified as a spring. It was close. She needed water. Her belly had been deprived of food for the last couple of days, and so water would be her only means of survival. She trudged through the trees, around the cover of dense vegetation and over downed logs grown over thick with moss until it all opened up to reveal a hidden pool. It was encroached with dark, wet, algae-slicked rock that appeared several feet deep. The surface of the small pond steamed with the thin broth of nature. It was a hot springs that butted up to a rock face maybe nine feet high. The warm water trickled over the rocks above, winding its way serpentine down to the pool. She now placed what she smelled as sulfur. She knew the water would taste every bit as bad as it smelled, but there was no other option, and so she knelt down as she imagined hundreds of animals had before her. She cupped her hands and began to drink mouthful after mouthful, willing her tongue not to taste the clear, odiferous, life-giving liquid.

When her belly was full, she placed her hands on the slick rocks aside the pool and breathed in deeply, letting sulfuric air mix with the freshness of the surrounding forest filling her lungs over and again.

But someone was watching her. She lifted her eyes to see a man, or at least what she thought was a man perched at the top of the rock face.

He just lurked up there silently, staring down at her with eyes as black and shiny as polished onyx. Something about his skin wasn't right. It was grey, maybe greenish, and his ears seemed to dangle and crane away from that slick hairless skull. Certainly this was a hallucination. She closed her eyes and shook her head, and when she opened them again, the man, or what she knew as no man she'd ever seen was hovering inches from her face, crouching, staring, and breathing something putrid that wasn't breath at all. Evangeline screamed and jolted back, scuttling away on her elbows and aching heels. The thing didn't react as a man, it only tilted its head curiously and widened its glassy black eyes.

It was going to kill her. She knew it, and even though death seemed like the most welcome respite only hours earlier, the death that confronted her now hollowed out her very core. She screamed. Tears poured down her cheeks. The thing grinned and hunched down ever so slowly, its sinewy muscles tightening, contracting, ready to leap and ready to devour.

Then a pop on the forest floor, like the snap of a great branch and the rustling of leaves. The smell of soil plumed into the air and standing between she and the cold, crouching thing was the stranger from the night before. His back was to her, but even then she could tell he was completely unharmed, showing no signs of the beating from that tragic night before. His clothing seemed freshly pressed and when he looked back at her and winked, his face was as pristine as the moment she first laid eyes on him. The crouching thing erected itself in a flash and bared its teeth with a growl like a wild dog. The stranger's eyes narrowed at the naked thing before him, and all the sudden, behind her was another man, an older one with shoulder length grey hair, a beard of the same, skin weathered by the sun, and a scar over his left eye. He too was dressed immaculately in a three-piece suit and the same silver buckled dress shoes. He offered his hand to her, and through some preternatural strength raised Evangeline to her feet effortlessly before looking deep into her eyes and speaking.

"He who came to save you was blameless, and only you protected him. So shall you be saved as well. My name is Elijah Tishbe, and you were meant for so much more."

Chapter 56

GUESS EVERYBODY'S GOT a story, and Red's is a doozy, but we're a hundred yards from those pillars of smoke and I can all but smell trouble. I tell Bock to stop the truck. The brakes hiss as the tires sink into the orange sand. It's as flat as West Texas out here, and so Bock won't have the luxury of an elevated position. I'm sure he'll choose to stand on the truck bed and use the roof as a setup for the M-110 tri-pod to snipe. From there he'll get a good look at what I already have: six or so domed huts built out of animal hides and whatever these poor dead nomads that pepper the surrounding sands could find. Two of the huts are smoldering either from unattended cook-fires or from the torches of genocidal marauders that seem to have moved on to kill some other poor group of frightened Sudanese. Next to the pillaged camp is a rock face, split and cragged with more of that burnt orange rock maybe seventy feet tall, a couple of stubborn saplings clutching to the side, straining for sun, looking just as weary as everything else.

Even from this distance I can smell the blood. Those people were gutted. There's bile in the air. I hate that Everly's going to be sent in alone, but we've got to try this out, uncomfortable as it may be for him to see the bodies on his own. Not that Everly hasn't seen his share of gore—even caused some of his own—but he's a sympathetic soul, and always has been. That's why he's our Meek, and a deal's a deal.

I slap the side of the door, signaling the men to dismount. I feel the weight on the shocks lift a bit with each man's departure. The truck gives a pretty good roll when Yak hops out.

"Back to business," I say to Bock who callously unwraps a cigar from its plastic. "We're not done, you and me. I'm gonna want to talk to you a little more when this is over."

"I assume you do," he says as I open the door and slip out, adjusting the waist of my jeans as I stand on the sand.

Horrace already has a cigarette lit. He casts the spent match for the rolling sands to swallow up. Everybody except Bock moves back to the bed of the truck and helps Everly down to the desert floor, looking like a forest green Michelin Man. When he's got his legs under him, I once over the suit again and notice a couple of three-fourth inch gauged pipes protruding from underneath the forearm plates on each arm of the EOD suit. They look like muzzles, but by the hurried and slightly uneven blowtorch cuts on the ends, no bullet would travel down them and breach properly. Horrace catches me looking and again tells me it's a secret. Part of me feels like I ought to know everything about this suit they've concocted strictly for tactical reasons, but I know how hard Everly's got it. He's going in first and alone, so I guess I can ease up on protocol if that makes them feel better. Might be fun to see whatever it is in action anyway.

"One thing I will tell you about though," Horrace says, lifting out the small video monitor from the back and resting it on the sand before going around to the driver's side of the truck and popping the hood. "I'll tell you all about the helmet."

"Okay, but we need to get moving. The sun's sinking fast," I say.

"Just give me one minute," Horrace says. He picks up the monitor again and sets in on a corner of the engine block. He attaches a couple of wires to the back of the monitor and flips up an antennae next to the terminals. "Gentlemen, if you please, will you crown Mr. Everly?"

Yakubu picks up one end and Bock, who now has that unlit, four-inch Arturo Fuente tucked firmly into his jaw, picks up the other. The helmet is heavy with Kevlar and steel, yes, but the blast shield that covers the face, thick like aquarium Plexiglas, is what really gives it heft. They lower the dome over Everly's head. His worry is palpable as sweat beads already take form on his upper lip.

I stand in front of Everly and we stare at each other through the glass. I don't say anything, just look at him, trying my best to convey confidence and an assuredness that he won't be harmed, and that we'll be right behind him when the demons show up. We remain there for a moment. I see him give the slightest nod to me, so small I'm sure the rest of the boys don't even notice.

"There's a latch on the back," Everly says to me in his muffled voice through the blast shield. I reach around back and clasp the latch, then I pat his helmet and turn to Horrace who finishes up attaching wires to the truck battery. He presses the power button on the small monitor and it flickers and buzzes to life. A picture takes shape. It's Henry Knapp, staring into at the encampment. I look behind me to see the real version of him doing the same thing. Everly's helmet faces Knapp.

"The helmet's got a camera rig in it," I say to Horrace, patting his back with a hearty force. "You've outdone yourselves."

"Now we can see what he is up against," Yakubu says with a smile, working that elbow gear on his gauntlet with great anticipation.

"That's right," I say, "but you won't be close enough to see the monitor, big man. You're going to hang back, sure, but off to the side, just far enough away so the tangos don't see you, but close enough that you can make it to Everly in time. It's a three-layer scenario. Everly, then you, then us, got it?" I ask checking everyone. "Let's lock, load and rack 'em up, k? Nice work on that camera, Horrace."

Then I notice that Henry Knapp isn't checking his rifle like the rest of us are. He hasn't taken his eyes of the huts yet. He just stands there like a scarecrow. I walk over to him.

"You ready to go, soldier?"

"There are two here," Knapp says, pointing. "One in that hut, and one at the foot of the rock face. Right there."

"Two of which, angels?" I ask.

He nods. "There and there."

"How do you know? We haven't popped off any brimstone yet."

"I don't know," he says, turning to me. "I just do. It's a... blue glow, kind of."

"And you see them."

He nods.

"Okay, well what about demons. You see any of them?"

Knapp shakes his head. "I only see the injured angels. We need to hurry."

"You got it," I say, making hand signals for everyone to get into position. I motion for Yakubu to move fifty yards up and to the left. Everyone else is ready to go with Horrace and myself by the monitor. Bock' staring down the sniper sight in the bed of the truck above us. Knapp is to the right ready to provide suppressive fire. Horrace hands me a single ear headset with a telescoping mic so I can talk to Everly. I slip it on as he jacks it into a port on the monitor. I check the Sun; it's lowering. The The burnt orange bottom curve threatens to sink below the horizon line. The desert is pitch quiet.

"Okay, Everly," I say into the mic. "You're a go, my boy. Start walking toward the encampment. You'll see brimstone flash-bangs coming over your head when you reach the ten-yard mark from the objective. Be alert and report any and all sightings. Break a leg, kid. We're right behind you."

Everly gives us thumbs up and begins the lonely trudge toward the smoking huts and the rock face beside them. Somehow everything gets even quieter. Clouds form in the distance further south. The Sun continues to set and we can hear Everly's boots slough through the sand for what seems like an eternity. He looks like an astronaut alone on the barren landscape of Mars. I turn to the right to see Henry Knapp's mouth moving at fifty miles a minute.

"Knapp," I give a hushed yell over to him. "What are you doing? You see something?"

"I'm praying," he says back.

I turn back to the monitor, "Good idea."

Pretty soon I hear Bock up on the truck bed say that Everly's fifteen yards from the camp. I nudge Horrace and he picks up the M-32 grenade launcher.

"Go on the flash bangs," I say to Horrace before opening the line to Everly. "Here comes the brimstone, Everly. Stay sharp."

Six deep thuds plunk out over the desert as Horrace paints the scene with flash bangs. They make the tall arc through the air like roller pigeons high over Everly's head before thumping into to the ground at different spots from left to right. The first flash-bang explodes next to a hut on the edge. I turn and look at the monitor. The screen goes white for a second, followed by a small fog of brimstone. The camera jostles along with Everly's nerves, and as the picture returns to normal, it seems there is nothing to report. Then another flash and an ear-piercing hiss like a thousand fresh slices of bacon hitting a greased pan all at the same time. It's the phosphorus charge working just as it should, burning all the brimstone out of the air. The screen goes white again, even more intensely than before. The process is repeated as the remaining brimstone flash-bangs explode around the camp. None yield any sight of demons. That is until the final one bursts off the side of the rock face. The camera hurriedly pans over.

"I heard something on that last one," Everly says through the ear-piece.

"Try and get a visual," and just as I say it, the glaring white screen returns to normal.

"Oh, no." Everly says. "They're here!"

I see two of them on the monitor clinging to the rock face like spiders on a wall, except only their eyes resemble arachnids. A row of jet-black spheres, like wrap around sunglasses gleam above the snouts of dogs—no, not dogs—hyenas. Their teeth chatter and grind as they hiss and whine like the carrion-eating beasts of the safari. They have the hands of men or large apes, but the rest of them look like hyenas as well, patchy hair dark and wiry with hunches on their back standing at attention. Everly sees them, and they see him.

But as suddenly as they are there, they are gone again as the phosphorus charge burns up the remaining brimstone in the air. I try to calm Everly.

"We saw them. Two right? Only two?"

"Yeah," he says breathing hard. "Only saw two. That's good right?"

I motion to Horrace to switch out the drum and use straight brimstone grenades this time. I whistle to get Yakubu's attention, letting him know he's on deck, and then respond to Everly. "Yes, yes that's a good thing. Shoot, remember Odessa? Must've been ten of them on that job. Just stay calm. We're almost ready on our end to send over the brimstone. Now they'll attack, but big Yak will be on them before you can say—"

"Mississippi?" he says and I can tell he's panicking and breathing even faster now.

"That's right, just stay tough, son. Stay tough and hold your ground. The Yak is on the way. Here comes the brimstone. Just hold on."

"Hurry, Rust," Everly says. "They're probably right in front of me now, hurry up and pop off the freaking brimstone."

"Now," I order Horrace, and he pops off six of the straight brimstone grenades in tall contrail arcs just like the flash bangs. This time the brimstone will hang in the air for what we hope will be the duration of the battle. With any luck, we'll be able see through the plumes well enough to engage without hindrance. Just before they explode, I slap the hood of the truck to get Bock's attention.

"Not until the Yak has gotten-in the first couple of licks," I warn him. He returns a half-hearted nod before returning his eye back to the sniper scope.

The brimstone charges explode. The monitor is awash with sulfuric haze. I strain to see. Horrace is a step ahead of me, changing out the M-32 drum once again to include the Dead Sea salt grenades.

"See anything yet, Everly?" I ask into the mic.

"Oh my god, they're right in front of me. Rust, help."

Then I see them, hunched down in an attack position right in front, just like he said, their mouths drooling onto the sand, teeth grating, and necks jittering with excitement to devour a soul. They savor an easy kill with an anticipation that is difficult to watch.

"Yakubu, hoof it!" I scream, as the big man's heavy feet fight to gain traction in the sand. His heels kick up seven to eight foot crescents of orange sand behind him as he rushes to get to the demons before they attack. The screen is vibrating with Everly's fear. He is totally helpless inside the EOD suit, or so I think.

Horrace rushes over and tears the headset off my ear, barking into the comm. "There! There! They're close enough. Release the aerosol, man. Blow the aerosols!"

Just then the screen goes flush white again and I hear both of the demons shriek as if they were right next to me.

"Bloody brilliant," I hear Bock say as I turn, straining my eyes into the distance catching a glimpse of two thick white streams of smoke erupting from those pipes I noticed underneath the forearms of the EOD suit. The smoke billows for five or so seconds before it's completely spent, curling furiously off the desert floor, and obscuring everything like a fog. I see hair and flailing grey appendages through the smoke.

"The hell was that?" I ask Horrace.

"Call it a saltblaster," he says, glowing with pride.

"Nice touch, but you think Yakubu's going to be able to navigate through all that? And what about our visual?" I ask it just in time to see Everly fly into the air about seventeen feet and fall in slow motion downward, crashing into the ground in a wash of sand.

"He's hit," Bock says looking down the scope.

"Oh no, move in!" I call out.

"No. Wait," Bock says.

The white salt aerosol slowly clears to reveal Yakubu hoisting one of the hyena demons in the air by the scruff of its neck. He holds it suspended there while he cocks back that punishing right hand, the one with the colossal gauntlet, and sends a blow its way that could shake the foundations of the earth. The strike nearly rips the snout right off of the demon, and the scythe blade at the back of the fist follows slashing a groove so sharp into its neck that it doesn't even have time to bleed. The creature careens through the air, flailing like a beetle on its back double the distance it threw Everly.

We stand in awe at what Yakubu just managed to do. I hear a thump by my foot. It's Bock's cigar. Must've fallen out of his mouth. I can see how it could.

"Okay, let's press 'em," I return. "There's still one he doesn't have a hold of. Fire away, Bock."

"Aye," he says, bringing his eye back to the scope and pulling the trigger. The recoil rocks the truck's shocks, as the salt round rips through the hamstring of the other demon that nearly sinks his teeth into Yakubu's shoulder. The shot slows it, but it's gonna take more than that to put it down for the count.

"Suppressive fire, Knapp," I call over. He lets loose in three round bursts, slowly walking toward the target, his mouth still silently moving ninety-to-nothing.

"Hit him again, Bock."

"All day long, mate."

Another shot, another shriek.

"Horrace, disengage this monitor and roll the truck up to the huts for evac. Knapp figures there are two friendlies in need of assistance."

"Will do, Rust. Man, I can work with this. Only two demons to deal with? Smooth sailing."

"Don't jinx it. See you at the camp. I think I see one of the angels now. He's laying with his back to the rocks. See him? Pull up and load him first. I'll get the other one. Knapp says he's in that hut over there. Let's move."

I hustle toward the camp popping holes into the one Yakubu sent halfway across the desert with a single punch, just so he stays down and out of our way. When I get there, I see Yakubu lifting Everly to his feet. There's a pretty mean tear in the torso section of the EOD suit. The other demon is on the ground too. Every time it tries to stand either Henry Knapp or Bock drills it with a hot salt round. These pure salt bullets are far more effective than the treated ones. They sizzle when they hit. Sounds like breakfast.

"Boss," Yakubu says next to Everly. "Help me with this helmet."

I plug a couple more rounds into the first demon before slinging the SCAR-H over my shoulder. We lift Everly's helmet off. It's a sauna in there. Looks like someone locked Everly in and forgot about him. I ask if he's okay.

"You promise me one thing, Amarillo. You promise me," he says.

"What's that, son?" I ask.

"Not Africa. Never again."

Yakubu gives a deep belly laugh.

"What—you could stand to lose a little water weight—huh, kid?" I chuckle.

"Next time we do Africa, you're in the suit." Everly says.

"That one's trying to get up again," Horrace calls over to us, pointing.

"He will not," Yakubu says, straightening up and stomping over. He stands over the demon, grabbing the wound he created with his gauntlet and pulling its crippled, black blood spurting body closer to him. "When the Philistines burned Samson's wife alive and he killed a thousand of them all by himself do you know what he said to justify it?" He asks the demon, but I don't think he expects an answer. It just coughs up more of the black stuff and stares into him with that row of onyx eyeballs. "Samson told them, 'I merely did to them what they did to me.' Now listen, you filthy monster. You killed my family. Everything I knew was gone, and you took it from me. My brothers and my sisters were children. They were children! Tell your boss I will do to him what he has done to me. I will do it again and again until God himself comes to claim me. Do you hear me, demon?!" And with that he raises an unsympathetic fist and sends it crashing into the creature's jaw, splintering bone against his metal, dislodged teeth littering the sand.

Henry Knapp pulls back a curtain at one of the hut entrances and disappears inside. Horrace and Bock are already lifting up the injured angel next to the rock face into the bed of the truck. "We'll get you out of that suit, Everly," I say before calling Horrace over to do it. I walk to the truck. Bock and I look at the angel together. The angel's eyes dart back and forth to us. He looks confused as we trade looks. His hair, dark and greased with sweat and blood falls over his left eye.

"It's okay, you're safe now," I say to the angel.

"You speak," he says, struggling, "as if you know."

"I am, and you are."

"Do not be so certain," he says, and I think he's looking at Bock.

I hear Henry Knapp calling me from the hut. I tell Bock to watch the angel and the rest of them to plug those demons when they try to get up again. Knapp comes out of the hut to meet me. I ask him what's going on, if there's another angel in there like he thought. There is.

"It wants to talk to you," Henry Knapp says.

"Talk to me? Why? They don't want to talk, and when they do it's only to you."

"I know, but this one wants to talk to you."

"Okie-dokie. Be back directly. Get them to bring the truck over here so we can load up. We should get back to the C-17 ASAP."

I crouch into the hut. Angels almost always seem androgynous to some degree, but this one is decidedly more female. Her hair is so blonde it's almost colorless, but long and beautiful, nonetheless. She has a deep gash just below her sternum. I can see some kind of organ bubbling up through the wound. It's hard for both of us to breathe for different reasons. I kneel down a little timidly. Like I said to Henry Knapp, angels generally don't want to talk to us mortals, and when they do, it's to our Anointed. That's Knapp, not me, so I'm a little nervous.

The angel tries to take a deep breath before speaking. "I am not supposed to speak so directly. May the Trinity forgive me."

"I'm sorry?"

"Your sin nature is… contagious. Not only to other humans, but to us as well."

"I'm sorry."

"The prophet Elijah of Tishbe has not left you."

"Forgive me, but, I—none of us have seen him in a long time."

"Time," the angel trails out of her mouth. She tries to offer a weak chuckle, but instead emits a terribly wheezy cough. "The prophet has not left you... but was taken from you. Find him... save him... as he saved you."

"But—where?"

"The girl...knows. The girl."

"Brigita."

"The girl knows the truth," the angel says, then smiles. "Do you not recognize me, child? Of course not... how could you? It was so long ago. You see—I was...the one who watched over you when you were young. When you were a child in the west. I delighted in you... but you disappointed Him, pulled away, denied us, and so... we were separated."

I feel my stomach sink. There is something. Something deep. Resonant. There is a familiarity to her. I felt something leave me not long after my grandfather was murdered. A weight was taken away, but not a restrictive weight, a comforting one, like a heavy winter blanket that keeps the chill at bay. After it left, I felt exposed. I hardened. I let my old beliefs and convictions weather away layer by complacent layer. I became something else. Something cynical. Now I know what that weight was. The weight that left was her, this angel. Somehow I know that she attended to me, that she watched over me. Somehow I know that she was my guardian, and I find myself markedly ashamed in her presence.

"I came to you in moments. Once as an older woman who snatched you from the street just seconds before those tires crushed your bicycle. Once as a stray dog in the lot behind your school who played with you one long and effortless summer day. Once on a Christmas snow watching your family pray, dine, and celebrate from the window. I have missed you, Amarillo... But you see? God is good. We are together again. And now you see me as I truly am." She cups her hand over my cheek.

Though vaguely, I *do* remember those times. I remember falling off my bike. I remember a woman I had never seen pick me up and yank me to the curb before a man fooling with groceries in his passenger seat mangled my bike under his truck. I remember meeting a happy, thick-haired black and tan German shepherd mix in the junk lot I used to play in behind the house. We had a wonderful time frolicking over the hills and piles together, but when I went back the next day, the dog wasn't there. I remember these things. This is real. "I am so sorry I turned away," I say to her.

"You were in so much pain after your grandfather... I wanted to comfort you, but your angry words were against us, against all that he stood for. Your soul had been saved since the time you were young, that would never change, but our blessings we had planned for you had to cease. When you turned from Him, we... could not stay with you. If only you had turned toward us... toward Him."

"I was foolish with so much of my life. But I'm better now. I know what I have to do. Things were so bad when you left." There are tears in my eyes. It's been so long I don't even recognize the feeling. It is almost as if my grandfather has returned to me.

"I'm sorry we had to leave. I loved you so, sweet boy."

"Do you... have a name?" I ask clasping my hand over hers.

"Sensenya," she says, and I let her name glide over me like wings over water. *Sensenya*, my guardian angel.

Suddenly her hand shoots out and grabs my arm. She sits up. Her eyes go wide. "Evil is coming, my child. Go. Now." She pulls me toward her as she sinks back to the floor.

"We're getting you out of here," I say running my hand over her forehead. "Knapp! Get that truck over here now. We have to go!"

Henry Knapp pokes his head into the hut. "Uh, Rust?"

"What?"

"Better come see this."

I tell Sensenya that I'll be back with the truck, but emerging from the hut, I see the last flicker of daylight on the horizon, that and an ever-mounting wall of dirt and sand just in front of it. The brass-colored sand-storm approaches with a low rumble accompanying it, a tsunami of sand. The rumble grows louder as we all stand together. Both downed demons start to chortle and hack their approval of the tremor as the earth vibrates beneath us.

"What in the shite is that?" Bock asks.

I focus on the sound as best I can, even going so far as closing my eyes. Rumbling. Not one thing. Many. Clumping. Kicking up sand. Oh no. "It's the Janjaweed marauders. On horseback. They're coming back."

Nobody needs instruction; we all furiously switch out our salt magazines for regular rounds. They're coming fast. I run for the hut and scoop up Sensenya, placing her right next to the other angel in the bed of the truck. I jump into the driver's seat and angle the headlights toward the oncoming militants. The headlights go bright, then dim, and then go bright again only to dim down almost to nothing.

"Let's go," Everly says. "We can make it back to the plane. They're just on horses. We can beat them."

"Not anymore," Horrace says pointing at three trucks much like the one we've got, punching through the wall of sand, tires spinning over the desert.

"Come on," Everly says, now free of the EOD suit, leaping into the back of the truck. "We've got to try. There's too many. We'll be slaughtered here."

"Everybody mount up," I scream. I jump into the driver's seat, Bock next to me with that .45 of his ready as the rest vault into the back, careful not to land on the angels already laying there bleeding. "Horrace, did you bring any regular grenades for that M-32?"

He shakes his head. With everybody in the truck, I turn the key. Nothing. The engine doesn't even turn over once. I see on the periphery that the two demons we put down are finally struggling to their feet. One of the boys in the back pumps a couple rounds into one of them before realizing he'd already switched to regulars. The bullets pass right through the demons leaving them unharmed, only striking sand behind them. I try the ignition again. Nothing. Again. Then it comes to me.

"Daddammit, Horrace," I say.

"What's the bloody problem?" Bock asks as we both realize that it's all academic now. The Janjaweed are pretty much all over us. We're not getting out of here alive.

"Horrace jacked with the battery terminals to hook up that monitor. Must not have tightened them back well enough. They came loose. We're dead in the water."

Bock takes charge. "Fine," he says and opens the door to get out. "It's dead, mates. Get out of the bleeding truck and get ready for hell. Take that silly gauntlet off, Yakubu. Grab a gun like a man, yes?"

Everyone dismounts again searching around for cover, but it's no use. I tell Horrace to pop off a couple of brimstone grenades before the marauders get here, just to see what we're dealing with. I suspect a whole mess of demons will be following that group of militants. They're close enough to see that they number somewhere around fifty-strong. If we don't create some kind of brimstone perimeter, we won't detect any demons until they're right up close and personal since even our remaining unexploded brimstone grenades will still bring our worlds together. Better to see the enemy coming. At least then you have a fighting chance, but truth be told, whatever chance we have is almost all the way back at the plane by now. We've never fought both demons and humans at the same time, and never against this many humans, well, maybe once in Panama, but like I said, never demons and people together. Those angels in the back aren't in any condition to help either. We're cooked. Horrace blows off a couple of brimstone grenades forty yards in front and behind of us. That ought to be enough.

The Janjaweed trucks come first, men in the back pointing AK's at us. Then come the horses. Lots of horses and lots of bad guys, some wearing camouflage, and most in crude turbans. They encircle us like Little Big Horn. Then we see the demons. Hell certainly follows with them. There are just as many of those rabid, spider-eyed, gorilla-handed, hyena demons as there are militants, but they hang back. They know that if the militants see them, their focus will be off of us, and they'd rather the militants kill us. Easier that way. I look around for the two we put down, but they must have staggered off into the darkness. The only thing I see are the headlights from the surrounding trucks blazing at us like we're already splayed out at the morgue.

One of the Janjaweed steps out from the passenger seat of a truck, the leader I assume. He rips off his sunglasses and yells something. I look at Bock because I know what he's thinking. He'd like to drive a bullet *Raiders of the Lost Ark* style right into this joker's forehead. But he does that and we're minced. There are no less than fifty guns pointing at us, all makes and models, and at least one RPG; each one itching to fire.

"Not yet, Bock," I whisper.

"When then?" he says back. "I'm getting back to that plane."

"We're all getting back to the plane, Bock, just calm down."

"Guys?" It's Everly.

"You've got ten seconds the way I mark it," Bock says with that .45 of his trained in on the face of the Janjaweed leader.

"Don't do it, Bock. We might talk ourselves out of this one. Might be the only way."

"Guys?" Everly interrupts again.

"Talk your way out of a religious genocide, yeah? I'll believe that in hell. Seven seconds."

"Bock, I'm warning you."

"Rust!" Everly yells.

I look around at the Janjaweed marauders. I didn't even notice that the leader had stopped yelling at us. Everybody's focused on the sky. The demons behind them are fluttering about, nervous. I look back at the boys in the truck; they're looking up too. Sensenya's arm reaches up from the bed of the truck. A single blood-stained finger points to the sky. How bad can it be? I look up just in time to hear a thunderclap that riles the horses, jostles the trucks, and nearly takes the rest of us off our feet; then, just as sudden, the booming of a tremendous horn as deep as the Mariana Trench.

My ears are ringing something fierce. The sustained note rattles my ribcage against my guts. A giant circular cloud teeming with lightning crackling and snapping inside hangs less than a hundred feet above our heads, electrified and alive. The flashes illuminate the desert surroundings like strobes. I can finally see there are far more demons behind the Janjaweed than I originally thought.

"What now?" Bock says.

The Janjaweed leader standing alone, his brazen legs shoulder-width, tries to mask his awe by barking something to his men, but they aren't paying any attention to him. He yells out the order again, and again no one responds much to his disapproval.

"Take it easy, boys," I whisper quietly to the team, my eye on the orb above. "Easy now."

As if provoked, something white hot flares up inside the cloud, then an arc of lightning crackles out and strikes the ground between the militants, the demons, and us. An ozone smell hangs in the air, and the ground bubbles into glass at the site of the strike. But that's not the weirdest part. A man now stands there too. Not just any man. He makes Yakubu look like a Pomeranian. He radiates incalculable confidence and strength. The African night fails to encroach upon him or the others like him that shoot down in separate bolts until their number equals seven. The armor covering their chests, forearms, and shins suggest Greek in origin. The deep blue tint seems like steel, but has a strange pearlized quality that I'm totally unfamiliar with. It's pretty for sure, and looks like it could take one hell of a wallop too.

The biggest one from the first thunderbolt has his hair up in a thick, red ponytail. His facial hair, a full mustache arching down to a beard of the same burning red intends to hide a long, puffed scar running along his jaw line. In their hands they grip swords, ones like I've seen before in old military history books. They were called Kilijs, and they were brutal; slightly curved like your run of the mill Turkish saber, but with one important feature. The blade thinned out at the curve, but then broadened out significantly toward the tip. This provided weight to the blade's top third, giving the swordsman superior balance and heft on both ends. With weight distributed as such, this puppy could quite literally slice a man in half, meat, bone, everything, and all with one well timed strike. No hacking required: an astonishing, brutally effective bladed weapon. Vlad the Impaler carried one back in the fifteenth century, and he was feared as few before him, or after, for that matter.

Through the men's unflinching seriousness and thick, hulking musculature, like the toughest Spartan at Thermopylae, I knew these men were angels, but not just any angels. These had to be the big boys. These had to be originals, at least the red-bearded one walking up to me was. The closer he gets, the more battle-scars I see. He gets taller as he lumbers forth until he is one foot, now two, now three full feet taller than I. Their swords literally smolder, red and hot as fresh out of the forge with a thin twist of smoke rising up from their razor sharp tips. None seem particularly concerned with either the heavily armed Janjaweed or the legion of demons behind them. The angels stand with us in the middle of a circle of death, and they are unafraid, almost dismissive of the danger in our midst. The red-bearded one is only interested in me, and he doesn't look happy. He looms over me like a thirty-story building. I see his chest heave beneath the armor at my eye-line. His eyes pierce down at me, and though they churn with disapproval, there is a natural, gentle concern behind them I'm not sure he could extinguish even if he wanted to.

"Blessed be the Trinity," he says in a low, gravelly voice to which the other angels behind him instantly reply, "Who wields the power of all creation, all destruction, and whom one day will judge all things."

"Indeed," he snarls down at me.

All falls silent in their midst, the demons, the Janjaweed, and us. The cloud from which the angels came flares like a solar storm, emitting the whitest radiance, converting our immediate patch of dark and dirty desert into the perfect luminescence of daylight.

"There is one thing you humans do better than any other souls in the universe," he says leaning over and casting me in total shadow. "The wrong thing. You can always be counted on to act foolishly, and without fail choose that which you have been warned against. You will test all that surrounds you until the odds become…" He looks around the rim of armed horsemen and frothing demons. "Insurmountable… So tell me, Amarillo Rust, how will you fare without intervention?"

"So—so you know who we are. What we do. That were on your si—side?" I stammer out. I have never felt so small, so powerless.

He glances behind him and shares a laugh with his cohorts. "I know that if not for the prophet Elijah of Tishbe who is faithful in all things, you vermin would still be using your little combustive machines on souls just as black and tainted as your own for your true god of green paper."

"It's not like that anymore," I say.

"Perhaps not for some of you. The African for one," he says pointing to Yakubu, "Your heart is attuned, but do not be proud for your life has not been lived without serious trespass. And you," he says, pointing forcefully at Henry Knapp. "You may be blessed to speak to us and enter holy ground with us, but your faith is new as well, and so you are sloppy and childish and brazen in it. You have far more to learn than you think, and so do not be proud also. The one you call Everly there, the small one. You offer your life for a cause but you know not what. For goodness? For goodness and for money? Wonderful. Goodness is not sufficient, little man. He requires your soul to be inscribed with His name, not just the nebulous ideal of goodness, for all of you, all of you," he says to everyone on both sides, "owe a debt to He who saved you by grace. Not by works, and you must name Him or your goodness is self-serving and meaningless.

"And you, Amarillo Rust," he continues, lording over me again, causing me to shrink inside myself, "You who was instructed in His truth by a man I call friend in Heaven disappoints me greatest of all. They call you a Shepherd, but it has taken you this long to become one. You who should have been all your grandfather was on this earth and more, but when confronted with difficulty, fell not to your knees, but on your back where you squirmed like a worm for too many years. You have lied. You have cheated. You have stolen, and you have killed. You followed an ugly path, and only when shown in a corporeal sense what is hidden from the eyes of most humans their entire lives and still they believe through faith alone are you returned to that which you should never have fled. Bah! Shame on you, Amarillo Rust. Little boy. Little dog.

"You wish to be commended for your work? Any of you? You seek our commendation? Do not forget it was money that brought you to this point, and while for some of you the focus of your toils has shifted to Him, know that I do not approve of humans doing our work, and know that I am *not* the one who sympathizes with the infirmity of you humans. I am *not* the one who would forgive your wickedness. In fact I detest—so often detest—your nature, and do so because I revere and cherish the Trinity's unblemished perfection. While I do not understand your worthiness to be granted souls or your ability to express free will, God sees it fit, and so it is not I that you have to fear, for I do what I am told. I swear to protect what he loves and holds dear. I do what is required, and I do it for righteous reasons. *That* is why we have come to do battle alongside you. Leave the two injured angels you carry. We will return our own *on* our own, as it should be. Use your crude weaponry to dispatch of these genocidal transgressors and then leave. They sent many Christians to their graves this day. We will take care of the demon rabble. You are in the presence of Michael, the archangel and his personals. None of you shall be harmed today."

With that, the light above us explodes even brighter, and a thudding clap of thunder booms out across the desert's expanse signaling a call to battle. Michael and his angels raise their swords and let out roaring battle cries as the demon horde smashes through the line of horsemen like sprigs of water through the cracked hull of a frigate. The Janjaweed are caught off guard by this—many for the first time seeing the creatures at all—and that's where I see our chance.

"Their pants are on the floor. Open fire, boys," I scream, and the team does so in methodic fashion, first taking out the men in the trucks, then starting on the horsemen who fall like cleared timber, most struggling to bring their mounts back under control for the demons pushing past them toward the indomitable angels.

Horrace and Everly go fully automatic with their assault rifles quickly spending their first clips as empty casings clink off our truck and stab into the sand like brass porcupine quills. Bock's decided to take that .45 of his into the lines, and there is wisdom in it. Most of the Janjaweed are carrying unwieldy AK's and are still fighting with their horses that continue to kick up a fog of sand. That dust is perfect cover, and Bock's .45 is maneuverable and agile in tight quarters. He streaks between horses, there then gone, punching lead through foreheads until his first clip is spent. Seeing Bock's effectiveness, Henry Knapp takes off into the fray using his compact submachine gun in much the same manner. Fish in a barrel. It's all about range. My boys know how to play it. The Janjaweed prove woeful amateurs. By the time a militant turns a rifle on one of my boys, they're already dead. I provide covery fire for them from behind the truck while Horrace and Everly pop in fresh clips and permanently perforate anything human. There's a lot of blood in the sand now, and none of its ours, so the chance of zero percent casualties turn out to be pretty good once the numbers start to whittle down and even out.

Doesn't take long for Horrace and Everly to run out of ammo the way they've been firing on full-auto, so I instruct them to take Sensenya and the other angel out of the back. I look over to the angels and demons battling next to us. These demons are simply no match. There are only about twenty or so left, but it could have been a thousand. The angels' smoldering blades hiss through demon bodies in glowing blurs of swordsmanship, a caliber and fluidity simply unmatched on this Earth. The smell of burned hair flushes across the desert as steam bursts from freshly sliced torsos as effortlessly lopped off limbs toss helplessly into the air. Soon Michael and the others run out of open earth and must step up to fight on a rising platform of dispatched demon body parts. Their footing is sure, and their strikes relentlessly true. They make no mistakes, and they show no signs of tiring. I see Michael glance over at us, and seeing that our work is nearly done with Knapp and Bock finishing off the last few Janjaweeds, he leaps from the rising pile of bodies from which they fight and walks over, letting his brothers take care of the rest. I brace myself for another round of criticism and possibly a strike, but this time Michael stops at a comfortable distance.

"Gabriel tells that my temper often gets the best of me," he says. "You must understand that even I am not without flaw. I only see what humans have been given and I... grow weary of their shortfall. I so strongly disapprove of the prophet's methods only because I fear the burden and danger of confronting evil in such a literal sense is too great for the human mind and soul to bear. It is a regrettable subject of much debate in Heaven. I have seen many of you mutilated for it, and I have seen many others turn toward the very darkness they once fought against. Even now in my jaded disappointment, I still care for your kind. I also know that Elijah has no authority to administer his work without the approval of God himself, and so perhaps some of my anger is... unjustified. Only He is omnipotent, and so the end product of Elijah's charge is yet to be determined just as the destination of your mortal souls are yet to be. Each has a path. Some will rise. Others will fall. It is not for me to proclaim your ultimate guilt or innocence. Before I take Qaspiel and Sensenya home, I will bid you farewell and give you a chance to say goodbye. I believe Sensenya has something to tell you. It is not often a human meets his guardian while his heart still harbors beating."

The angels in the distance hack the final demons to pieces, easily doing what we in our many battles have never been able to do, to kill a demon cold and dead. Michael walks off toward them as two others pick up the two injured angels. Just then Michael stops and turns as if receiving a message on some invisible earpiece.

"You, Toure' Yakubu. Your faithfulness is appreciated. Your heart walks in the light. You played a great part in returning Amarillo Rust's heart to God, and away from earthly compensation. These things shall be added unto you. Stay true to this course and one day you may serve under my command. There is a larger fight brewing. One in which all of creation is involved; one in which all of creation is at stake. Think on this, human warrior, and continue to live accordingly." Michael walks away, returning to his personals as two of them gently lift an injured angel each to take them back to Heaven.

As they pass, Sensenya's hand, fair and weak, reaches out and takes hold of my arm. The angel carrying her stops as I move closer to hear her words.

"Do you—do you remember the prayer you and your grandfather would... say every night?" she says, wincing from pain. Her wounds seem to have festered in the short time we were apart. "'When the devil comes to steal your day—'"

We complete the prayer together as a tear streaks my cheek and lodges itself in my mustache. "'Just hit your knees and start to pray.'"

"That's right," she says looking deep into my eyes and trying her best to smile again. Her hand, like a mother's hand wipes the tear trail from my face. "You do remember."

"I remember," I say fighting it back but my voice starts to break.

"I was there... every time."

"I know you were," I whisper to her. "I... could *feel* that you were. Thank you. For being there."

"I loved watching over you," she says. "Your young voice was... so sweet. And now I can be there again... when I heal... But you have to listen to me, Amarillo."

"Yes."

"Do not forget that prayer... Soon you will need it more than you can ever imagine. Sometimes even right decisions hold difficult consequences... And to follow God is often to suffer. At the moment of your greatest suffering, you will need to pray, and you will need to listen."

"I promise. I will," I say as her grip loosens and her fingers slip away from my arm.

Sensenya's eyelids fall. I look up to the great angel that holds her. Michael's eyes tell me she'll be fine in time, that she's just weak and resting. I nod, and just before he walks off, he speaks.

"You should not have come here, Amarillo Rust. By doing so, you have abandoned your post and in your absence have given evil the opportunity to slip through the cracks. You must go now. Go home and be wary of all around you. The little girl needs you. Elijah the prophet of Tishbe needs you. The road before you is most perilous, and wickedness is closer than you think. Remember what Sensenya has told you, it may prove your only chance for survival."

Chapter 57

IN THE 1930'S, a plane or two crashed in the Guadalupe Mountains of Texas. The FAA promptly opened up a series of what they called "intermediate air fields" all across the country, so planes could land in atmospheric or fuel related emergencies. Situated in markedly rural areas away from anything, or anyone else, they generally consisted of a moderately maintained airstrip or two, maybe a hangar for the plane to escape the elements, and a VOR tower. Most of them have been shut down since the mid seventies. ARC, or the Angel Recovery Corps, as some of the boys have been cheekily calling our present affiliation at large, have put these abandoned and neglected "intermediate airfields" back into play. They're perfect for our purposes, and one in particular, Salt Flat Intermediate Field, a couple hours east of El Paso, was a perfect place for Taber and Narikesh to set down the C-17 without any prying eyes. Taber was nice enough to house an old Vietnam era Huey helicopter in one of the hangers for Narikesh to chopper us back to Tahoka HQ

I've had a bad feeling ever since we left Africa; I think all of us do. The trip back is quiet and reflective. This whole thing about Bock and Evangeline returns to me. Even if he's right, even if I don't really know Red like he does, that doesn't excuse what Yakubu told me. None of it excuses the beatings, or the drinking. Of course, who am I to pry into people's personal lives when they're off the clock, but this? I know Bock can be one sick puppy, but punching each other before making love in the middle of the living room while there's a little girl asleep in the next room is just wrong any way you cut it. Of course, since my little baptism at the Yak's farmhouse, I see myself a little differently too. I am a killer. We all are. We did it for money. Some of us did it for fun. Should I be shocked that some of their personal behaviors might stray into dark territories? That would be naïve. But I've learned we can change our hearts if we just offer them up. I'm ashamed of many things I've done in the past, things I rationalized away before now. I came to this realization in my own time. Some of us like Henry Knapp and Yakubu came to their crossroads much earlier than me. Who am I to force Bock and Evangeline into theirs? But can I allow it to continue, to just play out on its own? Is it faith or lunacy not to stop it once and for all. I mean, she's moved out of the main house, so I assume they aren't sleeping together anymore. She told me not to hurt him. I heard her say it almost under her breath when I left McDonald's. I'm confused by my new perspective, and I'm not sure what to do but keep mulling it over, that is until I see the fires.

The second I saw the black smoke hanging on the horizon over the town of Tahoka, eight-hundred vulnerable feet beneath us, I knew bad things were already underway. Tahoka is under siege, and it's because of us. As we fly over, the town is dotted with fires, some in single family homes, a few in open lots, thick smoke rises from a couple of long-standing businesses, and the biggest one I strain my eyes to see seems to be some strange bon fire on the steps of that church Henry Knapp's been so involved in. There are people in the streets, some running, some just standing from what I can tell, probably wondering just what the hell is happening to their town. Fire trucks, ambulances, and police cruisers with, red, yellow, blue and white lights swirling below like a hundred barber shop poles. There aren't enough of the lights to deal with all the chaos down there, not by a long shot. I turn around from the hot seat and notice that only a couple of them are even looking out the windows. Bock for one has his eyes closed, not asleep, but thinking about something. Yakubu, Knapp, and Horrace are talking and joking, oblivious to what's going on. Then I lock eyes with Everly. He sees, and he's terrified at the scope of it. A layman might think terrorism, a cell got activated and they're causing a bunch of ruckus in town. Crazed, drug-fueled teenagers have taken to the streets. A jailbreak had occurred and now the inmates are wilding through town. But Everly and I know what's really going on, and it's worse than all of those things combined. We hold each other's stare for a moment, and suddenly I know what the president must have felt in that classroom while reading to those kids on 9/11. Now Hell has come to us. Beelzebub warned me of this as *Sharkey's* burned around us, and by going to Africa I've given him the perfect opportunity to do it. We left, and he took over. Ellison was right, you don't go looking for trouble when it will eventually make its way to you. What is happening beneath us is my fault, and now the people of this little farming town are paying for it.

And now I'm just pissed. Everly sees the change in my face. I nod to him and he leans over to unlatch one of the side doors. He throws his weight to one side and slides the casters down their rusty tracks as air rushes in, and complete view of the carnage below unveils itself. The rest of the men's attention turns to the riotous unrest below. Whatever levity remained vanishes. All eyes are on the smoke, on the lights, and on malevolence we all feel responsible for unleashing upon the frantic people below, the places we call home. It doesn't take a second to recognize what the two smoke pillars on the southeast end of town are. They found my house. They found the HQ under Teasel's, and they're both on fire. Without provocation, the men spring into action checking weapons, consolidating whatever ammunition for both human and demonic targets, and suit up for yet another round with the Devil's armies.

The closer and lower we get, the worse it looks. Soon the town is behind us and we're over my house, now just a smoldering pile of ash and kindling. I brace myself for the worst. I take for granted that Teasel's house looks no different than mine, burnt to cinders, with the steel door to the HQ in the living room torn open and vomiting flames like a buried dragon. As we approach, I am thankful to be only half correct. Teasel's place has been reduced to smoldering coals, but surprisingly, the steel door seems untouched. This could be an indication of the attackers and their resources. The HQ is our lifeline. The enemy not only knows that, but they know where it is too. If they didn't, there wouldn't have been any reason to burn Teasels old ramshackle farmhouse. All this suggests human targets since a small number of demons could rip open that steel door anytime they pleased. But it wasn't, so not only are we dealing with human tangos, but typical ignorant ones. A couple of heavy gauge chains and tractors could probably rip open the door to our HQ. They must not have thought to try. They *did* torch our vehicles though—that was smart—so we've got no transport outside of Narikesh and his Huey.

All of this points toward the somewhat safe assumption that we're dealing with a fairly large group of Satanic loyalists, not unlike those that shot up my home only weeks earlier and led me to Beelzebub at the bar. These types we can handle. But if there are demons lurking around, and I'm sure there are, we need to keep brimstone out of the fight as not to bring them into our plane and cause real trouble. In fact I'm sure the demons are counting on it. The Satanists obviously don't have brimstone because we're only feet from touchdown next to the farmhouse and the place looks completely unoccupied. Wait, that's not entirely true.

Just in front, a male body hangs in an excruciating upside down crucifix position by what used to be a ceiling beam running down his back, his arms outstretched on a charred plank to complete the cross. He's bleeding profusely from his wrists and ankles. The flesh of his chest is opened up, exposing the pink ribcage underneath. All the blood running down his face collects at the top of his head and drips down to a red-soaked patch of earth like a faucet dripping to a heartbeat's fading cadence.

I ask Horrace if he's still got that new Ford Expedition parked in front of his apartment on the square. He says that he does, so I tell Narikesh to fly him over to pick it up and drive back pronto. Then I ask if Narikesh will fight with us, that we could use his help. He flatly abstains, saying that Taber's still back waiting at Salt Flat Field with the C-17. It's just us, just the team. Maybe that's for the best. We got our-selves into this, so I guess we're going to get ourselves out. A part of me wonders how my men will fight when there's not a paycheck on the line. But then I guess the second best reason to fight is for your own life.

Everly tosses my SCAR-H over to me, locked and loaded. The boys have alternated rounds, salt and live lead, not only because we don't yet know what we're up against, but also because we've got little ammunition left at all. I pray when we crack open that HQ door we find everything intact, with guns and rounds-a-plenty.

Yakubu slides open the door on the other side of the chopper. We're a yard or so from touchdown, but we decide to bail anyway. Narikesh and Horrace are already up and away toward the town square before we're even upright, the Huey chopping the dry air in deep, rhythmic thuds. We form a perimeter around the fiery farmhouse, and since it's flat and wide open with no real place for enemy cover, each of us ticks down the all clear. Whoever lit the place is long gone.

I walk up to the man hanging upside down, still alive and moaning, dripping what has got to be his final pint of blood down his face. I instantly know who it is. Pastor Ellison's arms have been stretched down the plank and tied, but also crudely and repeatedly punched through with a nail gun at the wrists. Heavy, deep colored bruises erupt from beneath the nail-heads. One or two have snipped the arteries and pulse his remaining blood. His legs are nearly colorless from the blood loss of being hung upside down, but the same bruises appear where the ankles were laid one over the other on the post and then drilled through haphazardly with several more nails. But, Ellison's chest is the worst. Cut right down the middle, down the sternum with some kind of dull knife. The flaps of skin and fat hang helplessly to the sides, the lungs just beneath his exposed ribcage pulsating and struggling for breath. The scene is abhorrent to all of us. Even mercs don't die like this. I motion for the men to cut him down.

"Nn—No," Ellison says so softly I have to crouch down to listen. He tries to clear the blood from his lips to no real effect.

"We're going to get you down from there," I say as the men get closer.

"I-I ss... I said no... jus-just turn me the... hell over."

Yakubu looks at me like I've got an answer for him.

"Do it—" Ellison says faintly.

I don't know what else to do, so we uproot the post and flip him over. Droplets of blood pepper our faces as we right the cross, but Ellison, obviously in the shock from pain as bad as any man could possibly endure groans as we set the other end of the post back into the hole.

"Let us get you down, Ellison," I plead with him. He appears lifeless but for his eyes that look down to me, covered in blood.

"I'm going to… die anyway."

"Yes, but—"

"So… let me—let me at least… die like Him. Give—give me that."

Blood bubbles in his lungs. I ask him who did this, but he doesn't answer. Ellison's eyes move from mine to the sky. "It took *this*…" he says. "It took this."

"Where are Evangeline and Brigita?" I ask.

"At the mansion. They… locked the gates… People are dying…"

"The church," Henry Knapp says as it finally strikes him that the people in this small town have become more than bodies. They've become friends, family even, and most have little or no protection. Except him. "I have to get to the church. They need me at the church."

"No," I say. "We have to stick together. Evangeline and the girl need us more. Brigita is the objective, soldier."

"No. No she isn't. Those people at church are my family, Rust, and they need my help," Knapp says. "I'm going. I'm going with or without you."

"Can you," Ellison whispers, what little life left is carried away gently on his breath. "Can you even imagine what *He* must have felt?"

"Let us cut you down, Ellison!" I turn my attention, but just as I do, I know he's already gone. I check for a pulse at the neck. Nothing. Pastor Ellison, our Text is gone. He never got that letter from Tishbe's angel. Guess he'll have to collect in person. We all stand silently for a moment as we hear an explosion in the distance that jars us back to action.

"Everly, you and Yakubu get down into the HQ and bring up whatever ammunition is left. Bock and Knapp will grab the guns. Looks like we're splitting up just as soon as Horrace gets back with the SUV. I'm going to cut down Ellison and try to get Horrace on the cell. See how far away he is."

The men waste no time. Everly trips the HQ door that raises open just as usual. That's what I call craftsmanship. Each of my men hops over a patch of fire and hastily disappears down the stairwell.

I'm alone with Ellison. I look up at his face, still covered in blood. I take a handkerchief from my back pocket and wipe what hasn't coagulated away, then I hunch down, grab good hold of the post and use all my strength to raise it from the post hole. I'm almost surprised that I manage to do it. I step a few paces with it braced against my shoulder and lay it down flat on the ground. Ellison's body is at rest, his expression more peaceful than I had ever seen it in life. I wish there were time to pry the nails from his wrists and ankles, but he'll have to remain for the time being. At least he isn't upside down anymore. At least he's got something to lie down on until we can do right by him.

I take the cell phone from my pocket and try to ring Evangeline. No answer. I try once more but get the same result. I look toward Tahoka and see only rising black smoke, so I place a call to Horrace.

The line scratches open after only half a ring, "I'm hurt. They were already there for me."

"Horrace, where are you, buddy?"

"On my way to you. Two or so clicks. I'm bleeding. They had the place—"

The phone cuts out. I say his name once, then twice. Nothing but static. I curse the phone and wring it in my hand, then back to my ear. "You got the truck? Horrace? You there, Horrace? They got what?"

His voice emerges again through the static. "They were there, Rust. Waiting. I barely got out with the truck."

"Who was there? Who's the enemy? Humans or demons? Who are we up against?"

"Both," he says and I can hear his tires barreling toward us. I can see the trail of dust kicking up the road. "Brimstone all over my place. Looked shoveled out from one of those government trucks like when the roads are icy. I took out a couple of loyalists I think, but a demon caught me. Looked human for the most part, but. But no hands. Just like sharp bones from the elbow down. Smashed through the driver's window and clawed me. Took a couple of rounds until I got to a salt one. That put him down though, but the town, Rust. Everybody's crazy. It's chaos."

I snap the phone shut as Horrace locks up the Expedition's brakes and pulls a J-turn in front of me so we can load up and head back toward town. He hops out. I can see the gash in his left shoulder. He's still mobile, but it looks painful. He grabs at the wound for a moment before I run over and help him swing open the back cargo doors.

"You hear that explosion?" Horrace asks, grimacing.

"What was it?" I ask.

"Narikesh and the chopper are toast. Brought down by a rocket. Didn't see from where. That town is screwed, Rust."

"They're better armed than I thought."

"It's not just the Satanists, the loyalists, there's plenty of them, sure, but the townspeople are acting really strange too. They're in the streets screaming and crying and smashing windows. It's like they've lost their minds. It's like they've lost control of themselves but don't exactly know why. Strangest thing. The cops are trying to do what they can, but many of them are dead it looks like, and I don't see any backup from other towns here. Not yet at least."

"Let's hope somebody got a line out and that they're on their way. What about the demons and brimstone?" I ask as the men stream up with crates of guns and ammo. They load them into the truck like the pros they are.

"The brimstone seems localized around my place. It was like they knew I'd be coming. I don't know. If I had to guess, the loyalists have been organized. If I was a betting man, I'd say they've set brimstone down anywhere they think we'll be."

"At our houses."

"Yeah, and probably at the church from the look of things. There's definitely activity over there. A giant fire. You could see it from the square. Things seem to be congregating there."

"The church?" Knapp walks up. "What did you say about the church?"

"Looks to be the center of everything. I can't be sure but—"

"We have to get over there, Rust."

"I know," I say. "I know, Knapp. I'm working on it."

"There's no time!" Knapp says.

I turn back to Horrace, "If your theory is right and the loyalists have strategically placed brimstone at locations we'd be interested in, then the mansion's got to be one of them. That's where Ellison told us Brigita and Evangeline are holed up. That mansion's going to be covered in demons."

"Maybe not, mate," Bock says, walking up. "I anticipated something like this, yeah? It'll take more than a sodding punk with a scattergun and neck tattoos to get through that gate. Red knows that. That's why she and the girl are there. Me mansion's got defenses. Right proper defenses. What do you think I've been spending all that green on anyway?"

"What kind of defenses?" and just as I say it, I start putting the pieces together. Yakubu suspects that Bock's been meeting with Elijah some nights in the dark, but there wasn't ever anything nefarious about it. It was because they both knew this would happen. Bock is strong-willed like no other, this I know without question, and he can keep a secret. I trust Elijah completely, even if he has been MIA. Maybe Elijah told him about this. Maybe this siege has been in the planning for a long time, but Tishbe didn't want to bother me with it because he knew it would rattle my cage too much and wouldn't focus on our primary directive of recovering angels. Yes, of course. Bock has been distant because he's been stuck at that mansion rigging it up like a castle ready for a last stand. He's been doing more work than anyone, and I couldn't even see it. How could I not trust a man who's been with me from nearly the beginning? How could I have thought the worst right off the bat? I'm ashamed that my loyalty could be so easily assuaged.

"I've got hoses like the ones you see those Japanese whaling ships spraying Greenpeace in the Antarctic with. Mine are fully automated with motion sensors hooked up to massive tanks of Dead Sea salt water that shoot seventy yards without even trying. I've got mine fields of the same behind those hoses all about the grounds. But the best? The best is, I've got a feckin' rail gun, mate. You know what a rail gun is, yeah? Takes an awful lot of salt to make a round that size, let me tell you."

"No way," Everly says. "A rail gun? A real one? Rust, a rail gun uses electro magnetism to lob a round up to, like, 30 feet long at Mach 8 speeds nearly 250 miles away in something like five minutes. You don't have that, Bock. Nobody does. That tech is just a myth."

"I bloody well do, Everly, but try a fifteen foot long copper encased salt projectile traveling at Mach 2 up to fifteen miles. That's the one I've got. Let's see how well a demon gets to his feet without a feckin' head, yes?"

"You never *did* get rid of your half of the salt and brimstone Elijah gave us," I say, a sly smile creeping over my face. "You cheeky Scottish bastard."

"I'm right full of surprises, mate."

"Alright, boys, let's load up. This is it. This is the time. Yakubu, you're going to want that gauntlet on and ready to dance. Everly, You got anymore of that salt powder in the arm tanks of your EOD suit? If so, you might want to strap on the chest and arms, but you'll need to be mobile, so leave off the helmet and leg protectors. What're you working with, Knapp?"

"Got a street sweeper automatic shotgun here. USAS-12. Full drum on the bottom. Two .44 semi-auto Sigs. High capacity clips. Close combat all."

"Okay, I want at least two guns strapped to every man and as much ammo as you can carry, both lead and salt. Horrace, how are we on that M32 launcher?"

"No dice, boss. Jammed up with African sand. But we do have hand grenades. Both kinds, and flash bangs too if we need them."

"Everybody load up on those too, even if you need a munitions belt or bandolier. We're not gonna have a chance to come back here for more, so what you take is what you've got. Let's move."

Horrace said he's still good to drive, but I don't trust that wound. We dress it as best we can with a kit we've got in the HQ. I put Bock in the driver's seat instead. The plan is to drop Henry Knapp, Horrace and me at the back of the church. I know that's not where the real problem is. Beelzebub and his demons want the girl. They take out the girl and our operation's over. Sure, he'll take me too, but I'm not buying the "vengeance is mine" dung. If he wanted to kill me because of my grandfather's doings, he could have done it years ago. No, this is bigger than me. He's after our work, and if we don't have a Herald, if we don't keep Brigita safe, we might as well fold up shop and go home. Since Ellison told us in his dying breath that Red and Brigita are behind the gates of Bock's mansion, the place we now know Elijah and he have fortified for us, I'll send Yakubu and Everly along with Bock while Horrace, Knapp and I protect the church congregation that Knapp seems all too sure is there.

Henry Knapp hasn't been wrong yet, so we'll head for that church all right, but just before I hop in the passenger seat, I hear a voice way off in the distance. It's female and it's familiar. The voice guides me back to the HQ, down the steps. The men call after me but I don't abide them, I follow that voice I'm sure is Sensenya's. I descend the steps and turn the corner into the weapons vault.

The boys ransacked the armory just like I asked them too, but the voice tells me there's still something in there we need. I look up and see the crosses, their jewels glistening under the lights. I'm compelled to take them down and wrap them in a duffle. I count only six crosses. Bock must have taken the other six with him back to the mansion. I feel good about that. Maybe he heard a voice too. Maybe he's seen the light just like I have, like most of us have now. We may have come along kicking and screaming, each of us in our own way, but I know one thing, when you come to a point that you not only hear the voice but follow it too: That's when you know you're supposed to be. I throw the strap over my shoulder and heft up the duffle. The weight of the crosses rests heavy against my legs as I march up the steps and out of the HQ. I open the cargo doors and see the boys staring at me.

"Forgot something," I say, and lay the duffle bag on the floor of the SUV. "Let's roll," I say, returning to the passenger seat. Bock slams down the gas and we head toward the culmination of everything we've ever done and everything we've ever been, not toward Hell itself, but something perhaps worse—toward Hell brought to Earth's plane in all its splendid ferocity.

Chapter 58

IT'S WORSE THAN Horrace said. The town has lost its collective mind, and the police are offering little to quell it. They've mostly fallen back to their department building, circling their remaining wagons as it were, and just holding off the lunacy that quakes around them in three-hundred-and-sixty-degrees of insanity. There are locals tearing up buildings and pulling people from cars, but sometimes even tearing each other apart too. The ones who aren't fighting or setting fires are either looting or just running wild. I even saw a woman getting pounced upon by both satanic loyalists and a couple of mad locals. If we stopped for every single person, we'd save none of them. We would be overrun. We had to continue with our missions and hope that Evangeline, Brigita, and even the members of Henry Knapp's congregation still held on.

Beelzebub would want us to stop and try to help. He'd want us distracted. All of the madness surrounding us is only proof of the massive demonic forces that must be in the area. See, when humanity does something against God, demons show up, and angels move to fight them. That we already know. But it seems when this many demons show up in one place, the opposite effect can happen. *Their* influence bleeds into *our* world. I guess those that are going crazy out on the streets are under that influence. Everyone seems confused, everyone except those dark loyalists who serve as catalysts, urging along, and guiding the crazed and confused. Sometimes all a wayward ship needs is a lighthouse to guide them, but that lighthouse in the distance doesn't always lead to safety. I'm just hoping the God fearing ones aren't affected, that their minds are still right and alert, and that they've made themselves strong, collectively, in that church. I remember my Grandfather reading to me from Psalms I think it was: "Some trust in chariots and some in horses, but we trust in the name of the Lord our God. They are brought to their knees and fall, but we rise up and stand firm." I just hope there are still some of those left in Tahoka, Texas, and if there are, I hope we make it to them in time.

As we nearly go up on two wheels around the corner of Flushing Street to avoid two vehicle pile-ups, we finally see the bonfire near the church steps. All the looters are collecting out front, tossing whatever they can find into the flames, stoking it, making them burn hotter, bigger. They shout and cry and scream at the church, throwing some fiery items at its walls. Every so often one or two in the crowd storm the steps and make it up to the doors, pulling with all their strength to get in, but just as the doors pry open, we see a collection of hands pulling feverishly to close them again from inside. Knapp was right, there are people in there. Good people, and as the crowd amasses, the crowd I'm sure would be double the size and teeming with demons had there been any brimstone in the area, so does its savage intensity. We've got to get inside to help, but the people aren't stupid, they know there's another entrance to the church, and so certainly we would see another group, albeit hopefully not as large trying to pry open the back doors as well.

Our fears are justified as Bock, without regard, revs the engine at the end of the alleyway behind the church. He drops the Ford into drive. The tires squelch against the pavement as we race down the narrow alley toward the smaller mob. Bock's foot hovers over the brake pedal, but he's got no intention of using it. The Expedition smashes into the invading crowd sending bodies of dark loyalist and citizen alike feet into the air across the scene.

Bock slams on the brakes right in front of the rear door area that's now been cleared by 310 horses of Ford Motor Company grill.

"Go!" Bock says.

Henry Knapp and Horrace leap from the SUV and hold off the stunned crowd that litter the alley in various states of consciousness. I don't exactly know why, but I sling the duffle with the crosses around my neck to bring it along with my SCAR and sidearm before I follow. Knapp pounds on the church doors.

"It's Henry Knapp! Let us in! It's Henry Knapp. Hurry."

"They're getting up," Horrace screams. "Should we fire on them?"

"I don't know," I say back, not knowing if these people are really enemies. We can't tell them apart from the dark loyalists. Everyone's blended into the same rabid cluster. I look back at Bock and motion for him to go ahead and back out of the alleyway.

"We'll see you at the mansion," He calls out of the smashed window. "Make it to the mansion, Rust."

I give him the thumbs up as he, Yakubu and Everly accelerate backwards, and plow mid-panel into a unfortunate passing sedan. There's a short pause as in any car crash while the occupants struggle to regain their senses. Men in the smashed up sedan, four of them jump out, firing pistols at Bock's SUV. These four aren't lunatic townsfolk. These are loyalists. Bock throws the Expedition into drive and speeds away down the street, and out of my vision. The loyalists turn their attention to us in the alley. Their trunk latch got popped open in the crash. Each man plunges a hand into the trunk bringing up a fistful of powder each.

"Knapp, get them to open the damn door," I say.

"Brimstone," is all Horrace can get out before I turn again to see the loyalists throw the powder in their fists like baseballs of sand down the alleyway. None of them go far, but they don't need to. When they're finished, they raise their firearms and start cracking off pistol rounds at us.

Knapp continues to beat on the door, pleading with the frightened people holding them shut. "It's me! Help us!"

"How do we know? Henry, what is happening?" comes muffled through the door.

"Minister Barnhill, please. It *is* me. It's Henry. I know what's going on and we're here to help you. Please open the door! Please... have faith, minister."

I look up, dropping to one knee to dodge fire from the loyalists when both Horrace and myself see the air above the powder shimmy a little.

"Uh oh," Horrace says, dropping his lead-rounded .50 cal and swinging the salt-rounded Steyr TMP 9mm automatic pistol into his waiting hands. He racks it and waits the split second it takes four demons to leap into existence.

They're rampaging toward us on all fours with bulging, black, almost purple muscles like panthers. Their elongated skulls are nearly devoid of meat or skin highlighted with long, thick horns curving to their jaws like rams. Heavy claws scuttle and click on the pavement as they rush toward us letting out violent feline shrieks.

"Knapp," I scream.

All of the sudden, the church doors part. I pivot on my heels and break for the door as salt rounds from Horrace's Steyr and loyalist lead rounds whiz past my head and torso in both directions. Several 9mm salt slugs sink into one demon's body. They sizzle as the wounded demon wails and tumbles in a ball, its brackish horns grinding against the pavement. There's no time to confront the others. I tackle Horrace and push him and Henry Knapp inside the open church doors. Without looking back, I let loose a few rounds of salt or lead or both—I'm too panicked to distinguish—at the demons and the loyalists while the congregation members pull us safely into the church. They fold around our bodies to grab the doors and hoist them shut with every bit of waning strength against the mounting evil outside.

Chapter 59

IT'S FAIRLY QUIET inside the church, save for the low rumble of the crowd and the occasional clatter of objects being hurled at the walls outside. There are women inside, and children. Some are crying, and some in shock. That goes for the men too, but small town Texans are nothing if not resilient, so Horrace and I had plenty of help tearing one of the pews from the floor and using pieces of its metal under-frame to wedge into the handles of all the doors. Should keep the throngs outside at least until Minister Barnhill, a tall, pock-faced man with a thin band of grey hair encircling his otherwise bare head, gets back from his office with the master keys. Of course, the best choice to jam the doors would have been to separate the beams of the giant wooden cross that hangs over the pulpit, but we decided that the cross needed to stay where right where it was. Henry Knapp went with the minister to the office, certainly trying to explain this impossible situation.

Job one for a professional is to count off the surroundings. Horrace and I agree on the numbers. Fifty-eight people inside the church not counting us or the pastor. Pretty good number for a town this small. Sixteen men. Twenty women. Twenty-two children. Most adults are older or otherwise broken down. We count only nine or ten who could help with much. There are three exits, not just the two we initially thought. There's the front, where most of the hostile activity is congregated, the back, where we came in, and a small utility entrance back behind the baptismal area at the front of the sanctuary. All doors have been jammed or blocked with whatever we could find, but if the throngs outside really wanted to get in, all they'd have to do is break the stained glass. Luckily the panels are set high, thirty-five or forty feet at least. Insurgents would need a helluva ladder or climbing equipment. It doesn't stop them from throwing things at the glass though, possibly just out of frustration. Nothing they've lobbed has managed to crack the glass, but that could change any second.

Most of the women work on calming the young ones. One of them even sits at the piano and starts playing a children's hymn. A few of the kids and older women sing from the beginning, others join in later realizing there's really nothing left to do. Might as well go out singing. I even catch myself mouthing whatever words I can remember until I see Henry Knapp and the minister return to the sanctuary. Knapp throws me a set of keys and Horrace and I go to each entrance engaging the deadbolts. Horrace calls to me from the utility entrance behind the baptismal.

He whispers, ear close to the door. "Somebody's out there."

"Of course there is. A whole lot of 'em. Don't get you."

"Listen," he says, bringing a hushed finger to his lips.

The muffled voice on the other side of the door is playful and animated. It sings along with the music it hears from the piano inside. "*Salute, o Satana. O rebellione, O forza vindice, De la ragione.*"

"Is that singing? What's it saying?"

He holds up his finger again. "Hail Satan," Horrace whispers, listening, translating. "O' rebellion, O' you avenging force of human reason."

"*Sacri a te salgano gl'incensi e ii voti.*"

"Let holy incense and prayers rise to you," Horrace continues.

"*Hai vinto il Geova de ii sacer doti!*" the voice sings.

"You have utterly vanquished the Jehova of the priests."

"Stand back, Horrace," I say. "I'm gonna blast whatever's on the other side of this door back where it came from."

"Oh please, no," a male voice outside mocks. "Oh pretty please, Mr. Rust. Don't shoot your big bad gun at little old me. I might just cry."

Horrace and I look at each other, surprised to get a response at all through a door so thick.

"I know that voice," I say.

"Me too," Horrace says. "Can't place it though."

Now deranged sounding laughter registers through the door. "We're coming in—or maybe not—maybe we'll just hold you in there forever, or at least until we flay the little girl. I'll feed her to them, Rust. And they will eat her slowly."

"Who are you?" I yell, and all the sudden I see that we may have made a crucial error in not using our entire team to secure Brigita first. Maybe we fell into a trap coming here to the church. But then I look to the cross and realize that I've got to have faith not only in God, but in my team. Bock, Yakubu, and Everly are entirely capable, especially with the mansion defenses Bock said he installed. It's us who are in the worst position. We're stuck in a giant room with no transparent windows. We don't know how many are outside. We don't know if they've shoveled brimstone around the perimeter, brimstone that brings all kinds of nasty things that could pop through this door like tin foil. There's so much we don't know, and our only defenses are in our hands, around our waists, and over our shoulders. The voice is right. We are trapped, might as well be in a prison cell, but as I look around at the faces in the room, I know we've got one thing that the hordes outside don't. We've got the truth on our side, and as the old saying goes, the truth has funny way of setting people free.

I lean in close to the door, gritting my teeth. "Don't count us out just yet, son. Anyone comes in goes out in a zipper-bag. Now, that voice of yours seems awful familiar to us. How about you come on in and put a face to it."

"Love to," the voice says, then the sound of rapid footsteps fading away.

Horrace and I step back from the door, muzzles pointed. We wait for ten seconds, then thirty. We trade glances back and forth.

"I don't think he's coming in," Horrace says.

Just then, one of the great stained glass panels at the front face of the church explodes out raining a thousand multi-colored glass shards and thin metal framing into the church. The congregation screams. Children cry. Men and women run to shield them and each other. Horrace and I drop to one knee and swing around to train our rifles at the broken window near the ceiling.

Dresden pops his head into view for a quick check, then disappears below the sill. He does it twice more just to make sure we won't shoot.

"Hi there," his voice echoing voice looks down on us, confident enough to keep his head visible. He smiles wide, then surveys the damage he just rained down on the helpless people inside. "Shut those disgusting kids up down there. Don't you see I'm trying to talk to an old friend?"

I notice Horrace's wrist muscles tighten up on that trigger-finger. I place a hand on his shoulder to calm him down. Dresden's a murderous monster, every bit as bad as the demons that I'm sure are now encircling the church in greater and greater numbers, but he's also not the smartest kid in the room. He's got a short fuse and brains to match, that makes him a good source for intel. With any luck, I'll be able to get it out of him before he knows I'm even trying.

I stand up and lower my rifle in a casual stance, looking up at that fool in the window. "You know," I say with a chuckle, "I'm actually happy to see you."

"That right?"

I nod. "I am. Know why?"

He feigns interest.

"Because now I get to kill you."

Dresden's big, wide smile dwindles. His eyes narrow.

"From in there?" he says. "Alamo don't happen twice, amigo."

"Don't need the Alamo. Just need you. Down here. Now. I'll drop the gun, and you can use those pretty little knives of yours and carve me into Thanksgiving dinner."

"You just don't get it. I take orders from somebody else now, somebody that makes things happen."

"I'll bet he promised you plenty."

"More than you ever did."

"See, now that's what I'm talking about, Dresden. You just don't listen real good do you? Only thing I ever promised was your head permanently separated from the rest of you." I figure he's good and riled up by now. Doesn't take long to see I'm right. He can't even form a sentence. I watch him bubble like a cast iron pot of grits over a campfire. Time for answers.

I drop my gun for effect and extend my arms, beckoning him to come down with a grin that would tempt a captain to plunge headlong into a rocky shore. Of course, I'm in no real danger, at least not from Dresden. There's cover all over the place down here, pews, brick columns, et cetera. And, of course, I've got Horrace beside me, who's aching to fire off a couple in Dresden's forehead like a carnival game. The rest of the congregation has moved to a corner, still calming each other and the children. They're mostly silent and listening to our exchange, I'm sure with their collective heads swimming. Then there's Henry Knapp, of course, standing off to the side with the minister who I'm not sure Dresden's even seen yet.

"Tell me why," I say up to the window. "Why come here with that group of thugs he's put you in charge of?"

"Put me in charge of? No. I'm not in charge of them. I'm one of them."

"Who's in charge then?"

Dresden shrugs. "I'm not stupid, Rust. You'll know soon enough."

"How's that? Figured Beelzebub sent you and the rest to kill us."

"I'm just here to... nudge you in the right direction, compadre."

"And which direction is that?"

"Let me in. Let's be civilized about this. Let me in and I'll tell you where to go. I'll whisper it to your diced up corpse."

I stop with a realization. He can't come in. That's it. He *can't* come in, none of them can, even if they wanted to. This is God's house and I guess even these loyalists, demons, and crazies—even Dresden—they *have* to respect it. They're only outside because they have to be. I look around the room. I see the congregation terrified out of their minds, the minister standing next to Knapp trying so hard to keep it together for the others. They don't have to be afraid. Not in here. In here they're safe. We're safe as long as we believe and trust that we are. We're *not* alone. The Holy Spirit is here, keeping us all alive.

"I have to invite you in, don't I? Like some kind of blood-sucking vampire."

"You can think that if you w—"

"I don't have to think it. I know it's true," I say. I shoot a look to the minister next to Knapp. "Tell them."

The minister looks surprised, so does Henry Knapp.

"Calm them down. Tell them they're safe in here. Those people, those… things outside cannot come in. Your faith has saved you, so use it. You came to God's house when the town tore itself apart. Don't you see? You made the right choice. Don't be afraid."

Henry Knapp gets it too. He nudges the minister, urging him to go to his congregation and calm them. Barnhill moves toward them uncertainly at first, but with each step a realization creeps over. He starts to believe it, and that belief gives him the confidence and authority to take the next step and then the next until soon he's speaking, calming, assuring and laying hands on each of them. He's blessing them, and all the sudden, the light coming through the very same window Dresden blew out seems all the brighter.

"Think they could use some music, minister?" I ask. That should calm them down a little more. It will drown out all the horrible sounds coming from outside, and getting louder by the moment.

He nods and turns back to his congregation. Within seconds the same older woman from before walks over to the organ, sits, hands poised in the ready position, and begins to play. The minister and congregation soon recognize the hymn: *O Holy Night.* One by one and two by two, man, woman, couple, and family move to the pews and take seats, singing all the while, letting the words envelope them in certainty of their safety.

I crane my head up to the blown out window, the sounds of angry hordes seeping through it overthrown by the organ and its accompanying voices. "You come on in now, Dresden," I call up. "Just you. I'm gonna kick your ass while they sing this song."

Incensed, Dresden's face disappears. I move to unbar the oversized sanctuary doors up front. Horrace and Henry Knapp stand behind me, ready to hold off anything other than Dresden who might want to come through. I drop the metal pew undercarriage to the side of the doors. It clangs to the floor and echoes through the sanctuary as everyone else continues to sing the hymn.

"You know what you're doing, Rust?" Horrace asks as we wait.

"Nope," I say, and just then a theatrically measured knock comes from the other side of the door.

"Lower your weapons and get the door," I say to Horrace and Knapp who look at each other like I'm nuts. "We have to believe we'll be okay in here. We *have* to."

They register their disapproval with sighs and huffs, but take hold of one door all the same. When they pull it open, we're greeted with two massive, frothing demons, at least nine feet tall with legs thick as telephone poles, long black robes, tattered like always, and low hanging scraggly beards of black and red pouring down from wide, sharp feline faces, eyes of goats and the heavy breath of the dead.

The demons stand like pit-fighting dogs at the end of chain leashes. They want to strike out at us. They want so badly to enter, but something keeps them from invading, from biting with their jagged teeth like a mess of broken blades. Horrace gets jumpy and falls backward over the pew undercarriage that once held the doors shut as Henry Knapp stares into their faces, much as the defiant angels in Africa. The demons mouths bubble and emit guttural chorts and growls as Dresden emerges, slipping through beneath their monstrously broad shoulders. "Be right back, fellas," he says to them.

I step back a few paces to allow Dresden plenty of room to enter the church before instructing Horrace and Knapp to close the doors. They do so with great apprehension. The demons huff and bark as the doors close inches from their maws. Pretty soon it's just Dresden and me no more than four yards apart, hands at our sides, congregation singing, organ booming its notes that often shake us to the core.

"How we gonna do this?" I ask rhetorically as I strip off my grenade bandolier, my heavy vest, and my ammunition belt weighed down with clips of salt and lead. Each piece clops to the floor and I never once think of breaking eye contact. "Suspect you'll want to go with knives."

"You got one?" he asks, producing his, a butterfly model with twin brass handles. The same kind he used to carve up that woman and her kids back in Chicago, maybe the exact same.

"Always got one," I say, unlatching mine from its green metal scabbard clipped behind my right thigh. "But why have a knife when you can carry this?"

It even takes Dresden by surprise. A drop forged combat tomahawk, a mini axe, light and sharp enough to cut through fifty carats of ice. Same one our boys knee-deep in the rice-patties of Vietnam carried. It's a vicious weapon, both in appearance and execution. Eleven-and-a-half inches of pure meanness.

"Chop, chop," I say, readying my stance, legs a little wider than shoulder width, torso turned to the side making my possible target mass smaller, my right arm rests at a ninety-degree angle with the tomahawk held back behind me at ear level.

Dresden's no slouch with a knife, and I don't blame Horrace for looking nervous. "You two keep us honest," I say to he and Knapp, "but don't jump in. I want him to know how it ends."

Knapp and Horrace give an uneasy nod with the focus of the minister and his congregation thankfully still at the singing toward the front of the sanctuary. I don't want any of the kids to see me cutting this bastard up.

Dresden licks at his teeth. "I'm ready, you old heap of—"

"Let's do this deal," I snarl, and we lunge at each other for first blood.

Dresden swipes. I parry feeling the rush of his blade millimeters from my cheek and counter with a heavy downward arc. He moves in time and sends my tomahawk clinging off the stone church floor. Sparks flash from the blade. I swing around and get met with three short step-and-stabs aiming for my torso. I twist around the first, arching my side, but the next come too quickly and both sink into the fleshy side of my abdomen, just next to the kidney. I wince but think to grab Dresden's wrist with my free hand before he recoils, and as I feel the cold chill of the wound beginning to seize up my side, I step around putting one boot behind Dresden's right leg so when I force out the blade and twist his arm the wrong way, he falls back, meeting my leg, and that sends him tumbling to the ground like a meat puppet. Just as soon as he hits the floor, I bring down the tomahawk in my other hand like a butcher's cleaver and sever his wrist just below where I'm holding it.

I get straight quickly and clasp my side, feeling the warm wet soak as we watch Dresden wail and holler, rolling around as that freshly carved stump of his slaps the floor over and over pumping blood with his heartbeat all over the place.

"Gross," Horrace says, turning away.

"Yeah, well. Afraid I'm not done yet, bub," I say, wincing again as my wound starts to throb. "Get me something, Knapp. Some duct tape or something. Anything to close this up."

Knapp jogs off down the center aisle between pews and leans down to the minister's ear. Barnhill turns to look behind him, still singing. The look on his face when he sees me hunched over gives him an appalled start. My blood has just started to creep through the threads of my shirt like one of those stain commercials and Dresden's is all over the walls and floor. The minister is understandably upset. His head must be swirling with the possible outcomes of this not only to him but his congregation. I bet when he took the oath to protect his flock, he didn't have any idea how far that oath would have to go. And that's when Minister Barnhill takes a deep breath. He closes his eyes as his mouth moves not to lyrics of *O Holy Night*, but something else, a small prayer I suspect. He takes hold of the armrest of the pew and rises. He stands in the middle of the aisle and takes another deep breath. Henry Knapp stands with him and whispers something else. Minister Barnhill takes another deep breath as the organ music curls around the room. His back strengthens and with Knapp's hand on his shoulder they walk together toward us, toward a new involvement in the danger we've brought to his doorstep.

"I want to help. What do you need?" Barnhill says, and I can tell he is afraid, but also sincere, and making the toughest decision of all, one he's been charged with even if he didn't know it.

"Could use something to plug up this wound, Pastor," I say.

"The commissary is at the opposite end of the church. I'll go and get some rags."

"And some tape. Duct tape if you got it. First aid kit would be best."

"I'll see what we have." The minister looks back to his nervous congregation over his shoulder, then to me. "If you have a gun to spare, I'd like to help."

"Ever been in the service? Ever discharged a handgun?"

"Reserves... But that was a long time ago."

I stand up straight as I can. "A veteran, huh? You know what happens when you become an enlisted man, right? Your heart may belong to God—"

"But your ass belongs to the United States Army," Pastor Barnhill finishes.

"That's right. That's good. Sergeant Major Amarillo Rust of the United States Army retired. Pleasure to formally meet you. Consider yourself enlisted. We need all the trigger fingers we can get. Knapp, go with the pastor to the commissary. Brief him on the way. Don't leave a thing out either. Minister Barnhill's one of us now. No secrets." Before they walk off, I pass our new conscript my sidearm. I quickly illustrate the racking procedure and the safety functionality before handing it over. "The metal bullets are for people like that," I say pointing to Dresden. "The white bullets are for, well, the other ones."

"Other ones?" Minister Barnhill asks, checking his magazine. He's definitely held a firearm before. Looks a lot more comfortable with it than a reservist too, but I don't have time for a job interview.

I walk to the sanctuary doors, kicking Dresden in the ribs as I pass. "Be right with you," I say to him as he rolls over, his screams down to groans, spurts of blood down to trickles. I take hold of the handles, ignoring the pangs in my side and swing open the doors, revealing the same two demonic behemoths from before. Those leashed dogs of Hell, rabid and wild, thrashing snot and streams of thick, ravenous saliva on the walls, on me, and onto the church floor fight and lurch to break whatever invisible seal bars them from entering the church. Now that I know the deal, I don't fear them, not while we're in here at least, and so I turn my back to them, an act my better judgment fights against. We would never do this in the field, but I know that if these demons had the power, they could eviscerate me with a single flick of a claw. But not in here. Not in here.

I face Minister Barnhill, and I'm a little ashamed at how funny I find him staring into the eyes of the real enemy, the one they taught him all about at seminary, the one he was afraid of as a child, the monster under his bed that shrank little by little as he aged until it was nonexistent, a figment of a child's imagination. Sure, they taught him of the existence of real fallen angels, of Lucifer and his demonic armies, but it all seemed so figurative. A little piece of the human brain always holds out for the possibility that none of it is real, that it was all written by man. Demons are *us*, they are our natural selves, some say our *id*. We mutually affirm each other at church and our likeminded workmates and friends that yes, we believe in God, in angels and in the devil, but even then, a tiny little sliver of us still doesn't really believe it. These things cannot exist, we tell ourselves. And then, just as Pastor Barnhill is now, when faced with the real embodiment of what we knew to be real as children, what we trembled at the thought of, but were told could be warded off with a simple slice of light from a cracked closet door, we become children again, scared, defenseless children. We want to pull the covers over our heads and beg for sleep. And now, with proof that sleep won't come, that the monsters really do exist, and that they do really hate us, and that they really are every bit as bad—no, worse—than we ever could have imagined, we, just like the minister now, are faced with a choice. Are we gonna take the easy road and aide evil in evil's work, or are we gonna do the hard thing and fight the sons of bitches until our legs and limbs and minds fail us.

These things wear heavily on Minister Barnhill's face, and in it I see each man on my team, and their struggle. Even me. We were all there, and we will all in some way be there again. Then I see his face tighten. The slight tilt of his head straightens, and before I know it he's racked and raised the pistol. I don't know whether he's going to shoot me, or that snarling miscreant I'm in front of until I feel the bullet whiz past my temple and thud between the eyes of the beast. The demon screams with such power I have to lean into the wind it generates as if I'm standing before a jet engine.

I grab hold of one of the doors, Horrace rushes to the other and we quickly close them up again. We soon realize that the demon's scream has halted all procession in the sanctuary. The organist has stopped playing, and the men, women, and children in the pews have stopped singing. They understandably seem to be so shocked by it all that you could have heard a leaf fall on the roof.

"It's alright everyone," Barnhill says to them, taking immediate control. "I was just... employing the sword of the Spirit. We all must don the armor of God. Just as Ephesians six instructs us, yes?" He motions the organist to begin another hymn.

"I'm gonna need that first aid," I say.

"Yes, of course," he says. Henry Knapp and he walk off down the darkened hall away from the sanctuary.

"Quite the spitfire," I say to Horrace who only nods, half shaking his head.

"What about him?" he points to Dresden on the floor whose either playing dead or passed out from shock.

I crouch over him with my legs on either side of his body. His hair is wet with sweat and blood as I grab it with one hand and lay a healthy smack to his cheek with the other. "Wakey, wakey."

His pupils roll back from the top of his head and blearily bring me into focus. I slap him again. He comes to and tries to squirm away from my grasp, but he's weak from blood loss.

"Now's the time for answers. Tell me what your side has planned. Where are the angels? Where's Brigita? What is your boss up to?"

Dresden tries to smile through the blood thickening between his teeth, so I clock him again, this time with a closed fist. "I could do this all day long, Dresden."

His bloodless pallor suggests he couldn't. "Okay, okay. Stop. Just. Just stop it. I'll tell you." He licks his lips and instead paints them red. He looks like a concubine. "You might think you're safe, but you aren't. Eventually you have to leave. You know he's after the girl, and the girl isn't here, so the time will come when you have to leave the church. And when you do," he smiles, "and when you do."

"We've been against the odds before. We'll make it to Bock's mansion. We'll regroup. You idiots have painted the town with brimstone, so you know as well as I do that angels will come, if they aren't here already, and they'll start slicing through demons like government cheese. I've seen it. Your side doesn't have a chance."

"Ask yourself why the angels aren't here already. Why haven't they come to save you or the girl? Why are there still demons at the door?"

"You tell me, that or I'll send your remaining hand to the opposite side of the church."

"The Devil plans his attacks better than you ever could," Dresden says spitting. "Better than any man ever could or has. He's the ultimate strategist, and when need be, the ultimate tactician. Who knows war best, but the original opponent? The original rebel. He's just like me, and I pledge my life to him."

"You're gonna have to," I say, raising my combat tomahawk into the air.

Dresden smiles. He knows he's about to die, but it's like he knows he's going somewhere else afterwards, to be something else and to do something else. He likes it. He's almost begging for it, and in this instant his eyes ignite as I've seen them only once before standing over the dismembered bodies he proudly dispatched in Chicago. He was in league with the Devil far before he even gave it a name. Whatever evils Dresden perpetrated here on Earth, it seemed like nothing compared to what he would do after death.

"The forces of your God are being held at the gates. None will get into this city. None will survive their siege. It has been planned from the beginning and your God has been taken off guard. You are alone in here and we are legion. The girl will not be saved, and none of your pathetic rescue team will survive this night. Now, bring down that axe and send me home to Hell where I can be what I was always meant to."

I'm all too happy to do it. I raise the Tomahawk even higher. My eyes blaze down not only at the evil beneath me but the evil surrounding this church, the insurmountable odds that we've only begun to face, and the enemy forces that hold off our ethereal cohorts at all edges of town. We are not alone, and now is the time to be strong and sure. Now is the time to be without fault. Now is the time to be perfect. None of us could do it without Him, but as I bring down the Tomahawk with a swiftness and certainly I've never experienced, I let out a cry, a call to arms so deep and powerful that the walls of the church shake, and the hordes outside take notice. Once again my blade strikes the cold stone below, beheading this human monster Dresden once and for all, sending a splinter of sparks into the air.

I stand and realize that I no longer feel the wound at my side. The congregation looks to me for direction, so does Horrace, so do Henry Knapp and Minister Barnhill who have just returned with a half-used roll of grey duct tape and some fresh rags.

"We have to get to the mansion. The ones outside are trying to keep us here. We might be safe inside the church, but as long as we're separated from the team, we're off the board. Four less things for Beelzebub to worry about. We need to get back into play."

"But what about the demons outside, the loyalists?" Horrace asks. "You heard Dresden, there's got to be hundreds of them now."

"We've got to try. There's got to be a way," I say.

"They've seen us at the front, and they saw us come in the back. I'm sure Dresden had the side utility door occupied too," Knapp says. "All the exits are blocked. We're stuck."

"What about the stained glass behind the balcony?" Minister Barnhill says. "We could break out the windows and jump across to those tall oak trees and slide down. Make a run for it. It'll take a leap of faith, but—"

"That's just about all we've got. We do it. Everyone to the balcony."

Barnhill instructs the organist to play on, and to play louder. He tells the congregation the same thing. They are to create a wall of sound like nothing that church had ever heard before, and plenty of high notes, whatever they could do to mask the sounds of breaking glass high up in the balcony. When he returns, I give Knapp and Horrace the all clear to toss a couple of flash bangs at the stained glass. They track each other in the air and explode white hot just before reaching the glass. We take quick cover behind the pews just long enough to feel glass raining down on us.

"Go!" I yell out. Horrace is first, wasting no time. He runs up the balcony steps, down the short, flat aisle, hops up on the sill and one collective motion launches himself out the balcony window, hurling and grabbing for the great oak tree branches near the church walls. Horrace's hand grabs hold of one, but gravity and the bowing branch cause him to quickly slip from his hold. He flips over backwards, arms outstretched trying to find something, anything to grab onto. One of the larger branches nearly breaks him in half, but Horrace rolls and bear hugs it just before he falls to what probably would have resulted in paralysis at the least. When he rights himself, we get a thumbs up.

Knapp has better luck. It's always harder for the first guy, but pretty soon, both he and Horrace are below readying their weapons for the big push. A small group of loyalist stragglers have noticed them. At first, they pay no attention, assuming we're with them. Then they look up to the smashed windows, and seeing me standing there, they know we're making a break. They rush the wrought iron church fence and begin making a commotion. Soon a crowd forms, spreading more brimstone from pockets and baggies and shovels from buckets they got from who knows where. Not long after, demons take form—lots of them. Some familiar configurations and others I had not yet seen, like the skinny white ones who look as if their skin were made of tooth enamel. There are so many, I don't think we have much of a chance to make it far.

Just before I take the big leap, I slip the duffle of Sepulcher crosses over my shoulder and hand over my SCAR-H to Minister Barnhill. "You aren't going with us, Barnhill."

"What? I thought—"

"Listen, I don't have time. The demons might not be able to get in, but the humans, like the one I killed downstairs, they *can*, and if they do, somebody's got to be here to protect those people. You're the shepherd. They're the sheep, and something tells me you already know how to use one of these," I say looking down at the assault rifle.

"Maybe so," Barnhill says like a man just spotted cheating at cards. "You take care of yourself, Sergeant."

"Okay. We will be back for you, but if we do our job right, I don't think you'll need us."

"Go, we'll be fine, and thank you," he says placing a hand on my shoulder. "God be with you. May He protect you and your men."

Not a second later I'm flying through the air in slow motion. I see the trees waving me toward them. I feel the shower of leaves and twigs falling with me, and the duffle's heavy contents sliding against each other inside. I flip and see the sky growing more overcast. I smell rain, but this rain smells acrid. I note flashes and rumbles in the distance. The last thing we need is a storm. My fingers sway back and forth, up and down to grab a branch and when I do I finally feel the jolt of a large* branch straining under my weight, it gives way sending me crashing to the ground in a clump.

Knapp and Horrace pull me up with their free hands, and when they do, I get a better view of our odds. They aren't good. We're surrounded, the only thing keeping anyone back is the churchyard fence about forty yards out.

"What's the plan?" Knapp asks, still righting me with one arm and pointing his gun at the crowd with the other.

"We run. Mansion gates are a little more than mile away. We have to make it."

"Good luck. Rust, there's too many of them. We'll never outrun them all," Horrace says, a lit cigarette hanging from his lips and the assault rifle at his shoulder overwhelmed with possible targets.

"We're not in charge anymore. We're just gonna have to hope."

"Where are your guns?" Horrace asks frantically. "What have you got in the satchel? Whatever it is I hope it fires live rounds."

"I left my guns with Barnhill. The loyalists will break down those doors once they know we aren't in there to protect the people. The demons can't get in, but regular people can. Barnhill needs the guns more than I do."

The thunder above glides closer and erupts more frequently. This isn't going to be easy, and I'm really starting to question bringing these crosses with me and not the guns. But it was either sacrifice the guns, or sacrifice those people inside that church. I have to believe I made the right decision.

"The crosses Elijah gave us in Albania are in here. I—I don't know what they're for or why but I had to bring them. They mean something."

"Yeah? Guess Bock thought so too," Horrace says. "He took half of them to the mansion while you were in New Mexico visiting Ellison. I hope you're right cause now we're down a gunman."

"We just need to run. You fire lead rounds, Horrace, keep any loyalists away at distance. Knapp, you use salt load. Shotgun blasts seem to hurt the demons much more than solid bullets. I've got a few grenades left. I'll run and toss as need be, but we've got to go now. Triangle formation. Let's move. The gate's over there."

The hostile crowd presses in. The fencing buckles. Demons of all type scream and bark like wild animals. We're not going to make it to the gate. Not even to the gate. Our eyes fall to the ground when each one of us realizes this. My shoulders slump. There is a wall of hellfire being held back by wood and wire, and soon it will break open like a wave of death over a shattered levy. I say a hurried prayer for Bock and his team, and for little Brigita as the thudding thunder grows louder and the fencing cracks, finally giving way and allowing marauding evil to spill into the churchyard. I drop the duffle of crosses and take a grenade from my belt, flicking the pin into the grass and holding the safety fuse until the wall of demons get close enough. I look to my friends once more. I want them to be the last thing I see. My Anointed. My Interpreter.

Henry Knapp looks to the sky as the wall of demons and loyalists rush toward us. I look to Horrace who does the same. My eyes go back to the soldiering multitudes before us, and just before I decide they're within range to let go of the grenade, silently issuing Bock's team a final prayer of confidence in protecting Brigita, I realize that it isn't thunder I hear above me disrupting the trees and sending debris swirling about us, flattening swathes of green grass to the dirt. It's the thud of blades, helicopter blades, and just as I recognize them and look up to another familiar sound, that of a mounted Gatling gun. Not one but two. They buzz like a brigade of killer bees ten thousand deep. They cut through the impending hordes like an invisible hand of protection, several feet tall and wide, slapping each and all back with ultra-rapid munitions blasts.

Bodies fly, both human and demon, hundreds of bodies, creating a wide bubble of safety around us, mounted guns buzzing, flashing thousands of salt rounds per second down as the chopper hovers above us. I strain to see our protectors as four drop-lines fall from the chopper's interior. Four soldiers with crosses emblazoned on their chest-armor clip onto the lines and hop out, repelling down the lines and firing along with the Gatling guns that continue to punish the thinning crowd. When they reach the ground, Knapp and Horrace move up to help them finish the job. I stand in awe and pick up the duffle of crosses, slinging it back over my shoulder and hurling the live grenade at one of the last charging demons. It explodes, tearing a considerable hole in the demon's chest as it crumples to a heap.

I walk up to one of the men from the chopper and hold out my hand. Knapp and Horrace are understandably confused. The one I stand before reaches out and takes my hand, giving it a good shake.

"Seem to always get here in the nick of time," I say.

"Never thought I'd spend so much time saving your neck in Tahoka, Texas," he says back, grabbing the chin of the black GPX-II Soviet combat mask all four wear and lift it up to reveal his face. Horrace's jaw drops to the grass.

"Good to see you again, Park, and thanks," I say.

"Well I'm in trouble just by being here. We all are," he says for his team. "But I'm not just going to let my old team get chopped up by a bunch of hell-dogs either."

"P—Park?" Horrace stammers.

"Much thanks, again. I mean that sincerely," I say.

Park nods.

"P—Park?" Horrace says again, this time throwing his arms around his old friend and squeezing hard. "It's really you, isn't it? You were dead. I mean, we thought you were dead. You died. But, here you are. My friend is alive. Park how? What is this?"

"Park got away that day in Oklahoma," I say. "A team of Catholics shadowing us did something I failed to do. They found Park. Kept him safe."

"How did you figure it out? Our respective factions don't necessarily have the best working relationship."

"I know. Our old intel man told me about your ops. I think we both know more about each other than we believed. Be better if we banded together. Strength in numbers, I reckon. We're both on the same side, fight for the same cause," I say.

"Well, not exactly. Close, but not exactly. In fact, we're not going to be able to help you any further, Rust. We've got to get back. Like I said, we'll be facing heavy sanctions when we return to base. I did this out of care for old friendships." Park looks at Horrace when he says this. "But my allegiance lies with VSOD now."

"VSOD What's that?" Horrace asks.

"Vatican Spiritual Operations Division. I owe them my life, and they have taken good care of me ever since. I hope you'll understand.

We're prepared to chopper you to the mansion; I assume that's where you're headed to meet with the rest of your team."

"Much appreciated," I say.

Chapter 60

THE FIRES ARE worse from the air, but there aren't nearly as
many people or demons on the streets. The sky is dark from storm
clouds. Lightning cracks in the distance, and the smell of rain hangs in
the atmosphere. There's some mean storms toward Lubbock, and I have
a feeling they'll be on us directly. The chopper ride is quiet, and as we
approach the mansion I expect to see just as much activity at its gates as
there was at the church, but I'm wrong. There's no sign of Bock or the
team on the grounds, no demons either, but also none of the defenses
Bock mentioned. The place is dead and cold but for a few windows
glowing orange at the main house. Something's going on here. No way
Park's team took out the main force. Like Dresden said, evil is after the
girl, not us. We're just gravy. Maybe Bock and the others succeeded;
maybe they took out the bad guys and Brigita's safe inside. We won't
know for sure. Not till we're on the ground.

Seems like the VSODs figured out the whole Dead Sea salt bullet
thing before we did. Theirs look better, look mass-produced, and they've
got plenty. Park offers us as much ammo as we can carry and even pre-
sents me with a Glock 9mm sidearm, saying that's all he can do. Just
before we hit the ground, Park gives Horrace a parting hug and shakes
hands with Knapp. He does the same with me, but clasps tight and pulls
close.

"You don't realize what you've got in that duffle bag, Rust. My people would kill for it, and have several times in the past two-thousand years. In fact, that's why they sent me. I'm not going to take them this time. Just know that what you have, everybody wants, on both sides. I can't promise they won't send me or others to take them later, by force if necessary. *Laus Deo*, my friend."

"Well, I guess we've all got our orders, Park. God bless, and thanks," I say, hopping down to the mansion grounds.

Park's chopper rises, kicking up all kinds of nastiness into the air as it pulls away. Soon we can't even hear it. In fact, we can't hear anything at all except distant thunder. The grounds remain completely quiet, so much so that I suspect there's some kind of trap afoot, just don't know what.

The three of us proceed with caution. We check the bunkhouse first. Dark and empty. Then we move to the stables, our surroundings so silent as those storm clouds turn the scene into a recording studio. Our steps are as loud as rim-shots, no matter how we try to mask them. The stables are without activity as well. We can see Yakubu's farmhouse from here. We see no movement, so we decide to press across the grounds, through the small wooded cemetery, which must have been there long before the mansion ever was. Some of the sand-stripped tombstones read mid-to-late-nineteenth century through years of rain and dirt laden wind. The storms are even closer now. A cold front blows in, chilling our skin. It will rain soon.

Horrace says he sees a light on one of the cemetery trees to the left. He moves to investigate. I think it's a lightning bug, but he's intent on seeing for himself. He walks toward the tree, but a few meters before he reaches the small light, we hear a snap, like a clip of fishing line breaking under the strain of a powerful fish. I know that sound, but before I can call out "trip-wire," a small sphere the light was attached to drops from the trees and breaks open on one of the tombstones below. I smell sulfur.

"Down!" I yell. Too late.

Henry Knapp and I go prone, guns ready. Horrace doesn't make it. The demon reveals itself, a big one much like those held back by the sanctuary doors. Its long and tattered black robe ripples back, and before Horrace can leap away, a massive forearm, sharpened bone like a broken sword blade swipes up, taking Horrace's left arm off like wheat from chaff in a combine. The wound doesn't even have a chance to bleed before the beast howls, its robe flips up on the other side taking a wide lash with the opposite razored arm. Horrace tries to jump up to avoid the strike mostly out of instinct. His left leg makes it, but the right is sliced off just below the knee. It tumbles away down a row of gravestones. Horrace's torn body crashes back to Earth. His intact leg hits first, not yet realizing that the right one is gone. He screams and falls to the right, trying to brace the fall with his remaining arm.

Knapp and I pop up screaming, devoid of concern for ourselves. We rush the demon, Knapp's shotgun fires salt as fast as the slide will allow. My 9mm's muzzle steams with combustive shots until the clip has nothing left to give. The demon screams and wails. The bullets and buckshot plunge into the mammoth severing bone from ligament, casting black fluid, rotted teeth, and hair into the air. The demon falls to one knee, its dark blood cascading from its body like rainwater down a gutter. It chortles and uses some horrific guttural voice to call on something worse than itself for strength but it's all for naught. I've already thrown the 9mm away and traded it for my combat tomahawk. Before either one of us knows, I'm in the air, wrapping my arm in a sleeper from behind the kneeling demon.

"You filthy mother—" I yell and I hack away at its skull. It writhes and grabs for me as I ride it like a rodeo bull, swinging my weight in all directions, and slicing, hacking, and tearing.

Knapp gets to Horrace's side, reloading the shotgun. He blasts away at the knees of the beast. Shards of bone, meat, and cartilage splatter off with each strike of salt until the giant demon has nothing left to support itself. It grieves and moans its dismemberment, using the last bit of strength to hurl me away, several feet in the air. I slam down flat on my stomach as Knapp moves back to Horrace, who continues to bleed out on the ground. I get back up and see the great demon prostrate and whimpering, covered in his own guts. At once I'm surprised at what we've done, but the thought leaves me as soon as I get back to Horrace, but he's dying. Horrace is dying. I won't leave him like I left Park.

Over the bestial moanings, we hear something in the distance. A voice, toward the house. A female voice. I pop up and strain to see. It's Evangeline, in the lighted mansion doorway, like a beacon, a lighthouse on the chopping seas. She's waving.

"Amarillo! Bring him here! Bring him inside!" she calls out, still waving.

"They booby-trapped the cemetery!" I call back, not exactly knowing why. All I know is that a part of me is so relieved to see her again and alive, even as one of my oldest friends lies dying on the ground.

"Rust," Knapp says, his arms already under the pit of Horrace's remaining one. "Help me get him to the house. Grab his leg. He's bleeding."

Horrace's blood soaks us both as we lift him and carry him battle-field extraction style the remaining distance from Bock's mansion. Evangeline stays at the open door, the entire time waving. Even as we reach her, trying frantically to pass through the door and get Horrace's seemingly lifeless body inside, all she does is smile wide as if greeting old friends for a dinner party.

The mansion's interior is a complete mess of rabbled things, of broken and smashed things. It is a battlefield all its own. By the way Red's smiling, I assume Bock, Yakubu, and Everly got here in time to secure the girl. Looks like a fight happened, but at least Brigita's safe from Beelzebub. Maybe that demon out in the cemetery was just a straggler. Maybe didn't realize the war was over like some of those boys in the 'Nam, fighting for years without any knowledge that there was a winning side at all.

Knapp and I clear off a sofa and set Horrace down. I expect to see the rest of the boys running in to assist, but no one comes. Red just stands smiling at the door, and it's then I notice that she's wearing some sort of nightgown. Her feet are bare. It's almost like we woke her up. There is no urgency in her eyes. She just stands at the door with that aloof expression.

"Red, Horrace is hurt. We need ropes or belts for tourniquets," I say. "Please. Hurry."

Evangeline closes her eyes, like I've just told her she was the most radiant and beautiful thing I'd ever seen, something romantic like that. She glides over to me, the nightgown rippling by some unknown breeze. We're face to face. Her soft blue eyes peer up at mine. She leans in, her silken hands cup each of my cheeks and she kisses me.

I push her away, "Evangel—Now's not the time. Horrace is dying. We have to—"

She steps back, wiping her lip and giggling. "Now is the time. Now is the time, Amarillo."

Knapp has already improvised as much as he can, shoving throw pillows against Horrace's severed limbs and tying them off tight with curtain cord. It's a temporary fix.

"Red, what is this? Where's Bock?"

"I'm right here, mate," comes from behind us, and I turn just in time to see Bock fire a round from that .45 of his point blank into the back of Henry Knapp's skull. Knapp's body drops like a robot with the switch flicked off.

I am paralyzed.

"Surprised?" Bock says coldly. Evangeline giggles and prances across the room like a schoolgirl. "What do you think of the place? Got a certain charm, yeah?"

Evangeline laughs and skips up behind me. I feel her warm breath on the back of my neck. She runs her hand softly down the length of my arm. I feel her tongue touch my neck ever slightly and run up and down. She whispers something.

"Lix—lix...Lix—lix—lix...," she drones, as her hand reaches the 9mm in mine. I feel strangely powerless to act as she gently strips it from my weakened grasp. Her other hand moves to my posterior, grazing my buttocks and not only unhitches my combat tomahawk, but my grenade belt around the front as well. I stand completely disarmed with not one, but two devastating revelations. Not only is Evangeline still under the influence of the Lix Tetrax, Brigita's original captor, but also my oldest friend, my best friend, Thomas Bock has betrayed me, chosen sides, and chosen to be in league with the Devil. After all we've seen together these many months, I cannot for the life of me understand how he could do it.

"Bock."

"Don't," he says as quietly as I say his name. "If you were smarter you would've seen it coming, boyo. Don't you know? Amarillo Rust runs this outfit, he does. And old Bock, old Tom Bock, well, he's good on himself too. Quite good indeed. No, but that Rust. He's the *real* deal. That right, mate? That about the size of it?"

"No."

"That's an affirmative on that, old friend. Not anymore. Besides, I told you that bitch wasn't right in the head, didn't I?" he says pointing that .45 of his lackadaisically at Evangeline who moves over to a hutch, and grabs a half-empty bottle of brown liquor. She tips it up, taking a ridiculously libidinous drink. "Knew that from the beginning, didn't I?" he says. "You were right about one thing. I never did get rid of any salt or brimstone from that old pufter's Albania job. As you can see I needed as much as I could get my hands on for the little show today. The little Trojan siege. Good thing too. Of course, I still don't know how you managed to get out of Knapp's church. Only thing I was sure about was that he'd break his own neck to get back and make sure his havering born-agains lived on. All the cage I needed for you."

I shake my head in disbelief.

"You see Dresden by the way? He was supposed to keep you all nice and tidy in church while we wore you down and secured the rest. But you're here so... Send a psychopath to do a man's job, I guess. Serves me right, maybe. Never liked the man myself. Admired his work ethic. He was passionate, that he was, but always thought him a bit of a bagger. Oh well, you're here, I'm here. Everybody's here. Except Knapp of course—he's not here anymore—but hey, you should be happy about that. You believe all the shite Tishbe always peddled, yeah? Well," he says pretending to look at his watch. "Good old Henry Knapp should be meeting up with his dead family right about now at the pearly gates. Maybe we should all have a drink to the auld boy."

"That man fought alongside you, Bock. He was part of your team too."

"My team? My team. *Your* team. It was always your team, Rust. We were just cogs, daft cogs. I switched teams, and a right good decision as well from the look of things. Don't like your odds, mate. Don't like your odds. And by the state of this one here," he looks down at Horrace. "I'd say you're about to be the last one standing. I say standing. That's such a relative term, you know. You hear that storm outside, yeah? It's coming, and it's coming for you, and when it gets here, well, I'll just say it'll be a right shame to be one Amarillo Rust."

"Yakubu was right about you meeting with someone at night," I say. "And he was right about you and Evangeline. The Yak found you out, and here I thought you were meeting with Elijah."

"Interesting you should bring up those two names," Bock says as Evangeline dances around the room with her bottle. "Aye, there she goes. Would you look at that? How you wanted that, mate. Dance, my darling baby. Dance away. Would you like to show Rust what I've been having every night?"

Evangeline twirls about the room like some ballerina, not so care-fully avoiding debris that litters the giant living room and bits of Henry Knapp's head. She stops only to drink and to pull down her nightgown, exposing herself only to continue dancing to her silent music.

"Distracting isn't she? I'll be the first to agree: She's not what she used to be. The drink will do that. Takes some of the pallor from the face, but I can vouch, she's still a ride. Got a lot of spunk that one. In fact, you could say I like her better... like this."

I turn my head away from her in disgust when she gets close. I don't know whether to pity her or to break her legs. Anything to stop that infernal dancing. Bock's got me just as fumed. Whatever we used to have by way of a friendship is long gone now. Now he's just an enemy, albeit a strong and resourceful one who knows all my moves just about as well as his own. He's got a gun, Evangeline, and no telling what else. I've got nothing but this duffle bag on the floor.

"I know," Bock says. "You'd like to tear my head off right about now. I know. But you haven't the means. You haven't the means, Rust. Isn't that a pisher? But I know how you feel, auld boy. I do. I didn't have the means once. But you know what I did? I found someone to *give* me the means. And that man is coming. If you listen really well, you can hear him too."

"All I hear is the storm, that and the trash pouring out of your filthy Scottish mouth."

"Let's stay focused on the storm, shall we? He's in the storm, and he's coming to take you to Oz, mate."

"Bock, you think you've been meeting with the Devil, but you haven't. He's lied to you. That's what he does. It's not the devil that promised you whatever it is he promised you, it's—"

"Who? Beelzebub? Who? Who've I been meeting with? Tell me," Bock says stomping over, pressing the muzzle of his gun to my temple. "You know every fecking thing, don't you, Rust? Who've I been meeting at night in the stables? Who? The auld man from Russia? That one? The auld man from that chavy bar in town that Park, that Korean bastard saved you from? Who?"

"Okay, Bock. You're one step ahead of everybody. I get it."

"Try several steps. Several. Do you think for a moment that the other side doesn't have their own intel? Shite, they're the underdogs. They're the ones on their backs, Rust. It's the Devil who needs his ear to the ground, not God. Your God is everywhere, isn't that what that bloody book says? Everywhere, can see everything. All powerful. All knowing. All that prattling garbage. I take a pish on it all. He's not the one who needs help. He's not the one facing extinction. It's us. We're the ones who want man to be what he likes. To do whatever he likes. Your bastard is the one who took that away from us. Any urge we have, no matter how small, any natural fecking urge is to be what? It's to be vanquished! Suppressed! 'You feel one way, puny little human prat? Guess what, I command you to do the other. Do what doesn't feel natural. Do what I tell you to do, by God, or I'll send an aneurism to your mother's brain. I'll send a drunk toward your daughter on the highway. I'll stop your beating heart in its tracks.' Benevolent God. Good. Great. Kind, loving, God. Toss off. He doesn't care about you. He cares for himself, and what you can do for him. He's the greatest narcissist since Narcissus himself. A giant baby in the sky with muscles."

"That is not true, Bock, that's the lie he—"

"Oh it's true, mate. It's right truth, and I'm not playing. Why, he didn't even tell you, nobody would."

"Tell me what?"

"That what you've got there is what it's all about. It's not the girl, mate. It's not Brigita. It's certainly not you."

"Brigita," Evangeline says with a drawn out rolling tongue. She's grown tired of dancing and has finished the bottle of booze. She sits cross-legged on the floor, drooling and blubbering. She isn't smiling anymore. "Lix," she says like a hissing cat when she spots me glancing at her.

I think I hear a train outside. Way off, mixed in with the rain that's started to pelt the windows with all the wind that carries it. Bock points at the duffle bag on the floor. "Those?" I ask.

"That's right, Rust. All that salt and brimstone? The crates? Child's play. Toys. The Sepulchers are the real prize, and they were given to us for a reason. Not every team gets them."

"I know. Ellison told me. You had him killed too."

"But God doesn't want you to know why because he doesn't care about you. He doesn't even care about his own prophet enough to tell him what they're about even when it could save you both. You both, bloody hell, even though it could set all of mankind free from this oppression that Satan supposedly holds over the human race. What's in that duffle bag could do all of that, and yet, he leaves you and his prophet and all the others here to die with no idea how to use them. All this while, *my* god? No, my god is on his way, and oh the things he's promised me. You think this one is worth a toss?" he says spitting at Evangeline on the floor. "I'll have twenty mansions full of the likes of her. Full of women and cars and guns and money, and anything else I want. You know what they say: Rather be a king in Hell than a pauper in heaven. And Ellison? Are you seriously upset about Ellison? That auld drunk deserved worse and you know it."

"You don't know what you're saying, Bock. Forever is a very long time and he's not going to give you anything he's promised. He is a liar and he will say and do anything, you've got to know this."

"Ah, but listen, mate. Listen. I've stared in his eyes. I've looked on the auld man. He's straight. He'll do as I've asked because I'm going to turn that duffle bag over to him, but not before you show me how to use them."

"Are you saying these are weapons?"

"Bright boy."

"How should I know how they work?"

"Because your dear auld grandfather did. You know he killed a demon even when people aren't allowed to kill demons. Of course, if something can kill a demon, then I've been assured that it can kill an angel too. Imagine the power, Rust. Heaven nor Hell would hold any sway upon the one who wields it. I've been promised that too."

"I already told you about your promises."

"That you did. And you've got a right to your own opinion, I suppose, but it doesn't change the facts, mate. I'm in charge now."

"What did you do with Everly, with Yak? They had your back and you turned on them. How could you have done that, Bock? We had a—"

"A what? We had a what? A code? Don't get grandiose, boyo. It's business. That was one of your favorite phrases as I remember, wasn't it? 'Don't get involved, it's business?' Well, so was this. We were mercs once, Rust. Still are in most respects. Don't be getting sentimental on me. There was a time when you would have sold your own mother for a tasty job with perfect margins. Don't forget that."

"People change."

"No, Rust. People *never* change."

"I want to see them."

"Who, the team? Of course. A father must check up on his children. That is how you fancy yourself now, yes? Wouldn't want to offend you, father."

Bock leads me up a darkened stairway, it's opulent and wide, but sullied from filth. Lots of dust and the smell of neglect invades my nostrils. The stairs open up to a hallway much the same, dark and musty with a row of doors all the way down. Bock's bravado is on full display. He walks in front of me with a hubris rivaling the best of them, or the worst of them. He isn't even entertaining the thought that I'd attack from behind. Maybe that's how well he knows me. I wouldn't do that to him. My attacks come from the front. Bock opens one of the doors a couple down from the stairs. It's Everly. He's passed out, beaten to splinters and hanging from his limbs by chains attached to four points on the ceiling with disturbing care. Somebody's gone and been cruel, changing out the only light bulb in the room with a red one. The light might make him look worse off than he is, at least that's what I'm hoping.

"Always a weak little twit, that Everly. Never should have allowed him on the team, but who ever asked for my two cents, yeah?" Bock says, closing the door and opening up the next one. "And here's your mighty African. Hey there. How you getting along, brother Yakubu? Bring you anything?"

The Yak shakes against his chains. The bones of the room shudder against his thrashing. He's bolted to the floor. Looks like Bock had him suspended from the ceiling just like Everly but from the condition of the dry wall, he must have broken free at some point. Perhaps as some kind of joke, his gauntlet lies on the floor just out of reach. Yakubu cranes up his head and I see the worst of it. They've taken his eyes. Streaks of dried blood crust to his cheeks like black tears below cavernous holes where they used to be set. I almost can't take it, but I've got to choose my battles. I've got to be smart if I'm going to get any of them out alive.

Before I can even think about it: "I'm here, Toure'."

"Boss?"

"I'm here."

"I'm sorry I could not protect the girl."

"I know you did your best," I say, trying hard to choke back the lump in my throat. Now I hate Bock. He took something pure and strong and ruined it. The man in those chains saved me, even saved him countless times. He brought me back to God. Set my life straight, and now I have to see him like this and do nothing. What did he get for being good and faithful? Punished. That's what he got. He got punished for being good, and that by someone he called a friend.

"Teach him to spy on me. Can't spy if you've no eyes to do it with, yeah?" Bock says.

"Toure', I'm so sorry," I say, trying with everything in me not to rip Bock's carotid artery from his neck with my teeth.

Yakubu breathes deeply, I suspect to ward off crying. He collects himself and stops struggling. His head lowers to the floor as if ashamed for me to see him like this. That man should never feel ashamed. He's better than the lot of us. "It is okay, boss," he says. "I don't need them anymore."

"You son of a bitch," I say to Bock, my eyes searing holes in him.

"He was a threat, Rust. You always taught us to minimize threats, didn't you?"

He isn't completely wrong. I did preach that to my team. I was ruthless. I was calculating, and in the coldest fashion possible. But Bock is wrong about one thing. People *can* change. Do change. Happens all the time. You just have to want to, and have a good reason. At once, I am overcome with guilt at who I used to be, and the things I used to do. How many alive and dead have I let down? How many apologies do I have to give? Then the training rushes back. I can apologize later. Now's the time to figure out how to get my boys out of here.

Bock shuts the door on Yakubu. "See? Gang's all here, mate. Nice and tidy indeed. Now, about those crosses, the Sepulchers as Tishbe called them."

"Called them?"

"Oh, he won't be showing up to sully the proceedings. I've made sure of that. See, Rust? I wouldn't have been so poor a leader. You could have trusted me."

"I trusted you like no other, Bock. I trusted you with my life. I always did. You were my best friend."

"Well, Mr. holy boy, Tishbe didn't think so. Suppose he was right in the end as it turns out, but I couldn't have him tipping you off to my little side bet. Just good business I'm afraid. It isn't personal, Rust. Except, who am I kidding? It's very personal. It stung being under your thumb. Always did. I know how you look at me. You think I've been unstable, that I let my emotions get the best of me."

"What ever would give you that idea?"

"You called me partner, but the truth is, you managed me. You handled me, and I always knew it. But I knew something else too, mate. I knew that one day the tables would turn around to my favor. Well, it's finally happened, hasn't it? I've one last thing to show you. Something great. Something no man has been able to do before me."

Bock stops in front of the last door in the shadowed hallway, the storm outside is so strong I can almost feel the house vibrating. A low rumble blankets everything as Bock opens that last door. Sitting on a lone twin mattress against the back wall, chained like the rest, another red light bulb making it all worse is Elijah Tishbe, the prophet, our mentor, my leader, and my friend.

Elijah doesn't look up. His tangled, greasy grey hair covers his face. "Mr. Rust. I see you've finally met the real Mr. Bock."

"How long have you kept him here?" I ask.

"Well, let me see," Bock says, feigning thought, tapping his chin. "How long has it been, Tishbe, you whinging auld nyaff?"

"I've lost track, I'm afraid, but know this, Thomas Bock: I could rest in shackles for millennia before you ever have a hope of breaking my faith. My capture only signals your undoing, boy. I remain an ambassador of the one true God and His son Jesus Christ as well as the Holy Spirit that surrounds us all, even now. Even here. I will not be forgotten, and I *will* be avenged."

"Heard it. Not impressed. Let's go back downstairs, Rust, we've a touch of business to execute."

"What about the girl?"

"He is powerless against Brigita, Mr. Rust, or did he tell you that already?" Elijah says, finally raising his head and staring into Bock's face defiantly. "She is a Herald. She speaks the holy language of the an-gels. He can do nothing to the girl."

"That will be enough of you, thank you very much," Bock says, slamming the door shut in frustration. I hear Elijah let out a weak chuckle from inside the room. Then a muffled promise. "You've sealed your own fate, Mr. Bock. You've chosen your own undoing, only that. All he has promised you is vapor in the end, you foolish man."

"He goes on," Bock says.

"He's right."

"We'll see."

"What about his angels? No way you've got them too in your little horror show."

"Oh Rust, I'm the greatest show on earth, don't you know. They're just across the hall, but you probably don't want to see them any more than they want to see you. Angels aren't sympathetic to our plight as you may have noticed. Funny isn't it? As kids, we were told angels were our friends, but in reality, they're just jealous slaves who'd slit our throats for a farthing if they only had that little thing they covet. Free will. We've got it, they don't. And that fact makes them...agitated."

"Angels serve God because they know who he is, Bock. It's us who don't."

"Well, I know I don't. Screw him and screw you. They don't like us and I don't like them. As a matter of fact," Bock says, leading me back down the stairwell, "you've no idea how cathartic it is to simply open up a door and crack a couple of salt rounds into an angel once or twice a day. Keeps them humble. A shovel of brimstone and a clip of salt. All it takes to keep Bock a healthy boy."

"That how you kept Elijah here so long?" I ask as we reach the bottom of the stairs. I see Brigita sitting on the floor with Evangeline who's still got her blouse open like any other mess you'd see in some inner city drug den. Brigita's eyes cry to me for help, but I know now's not the time. I turn away so as not to tip her off. I look to the sofa Knapp and I set Horrace on. I see Henry Knapp's body still crumpled on the floor like a heap of dirty laundry, but Horrace is gone. Vanished. I can tell by the way the others are acting that I'm the only one who's noticed.

"Tishbe's no angel, that we know, and I think he can die, so I don't shoot him all that often, but salt works on him, just not as well as with the angels. I force-feed him a glass of Dead Sea water every night. Keeps him quiet for the most part. Keeps him weak."

"I don't think you realize how much trouble you're inviting on yourself, Bock."

"Maybe," he says, picking up the duffle bag. Then he looks over to the sofa and sees what I already did, that Horrace's body is gone. "Shite! He moves, you kill the girl," he says to Evangeline who fingers an old straight razor as she hums with Brigita sitting in front of her. Evangeline stares up at me, grinning as Bock runs outside to find Horrace. No way he got up and walked out, I think to myself. He was on his way to the big sleep. Horrace is tough, but that tough? I watch Evangeline cut her finger and marvel at her own blood bubbling up and sliding down her finger. She raises her hand over Brigita's head and lets it drip onto the little girl's scalp. Brigita is so broken she doesn't even move. It's not the greatest opportunity, but it's the only one I've got.

I run over to Evangeline, sliding on the floor next to her. I cup her face and pull her close. "This is not you," I say, squeezing her face tight. She doesn't react. "Red, you're in there somewhere and you've got to come out and help me stop him."

Brigita clutches me around the neck.

"It's okay, baby. We're going to get you out of here, but I need you to do something."

I hear a crash outside from the gates. Sounds of twisted metal being torn from the ground. I pop up and look out the window. I see Bock staring dumbfounded at the Ford F250 that just smashed through the mansion gates and continues to sling mud away from its whirling tires as it races toward the stables. But it's not the truck that concerns me. It's what's behind it. Tahoka, Texas is being dismantled by a surging, heaving, wrathful tornado the likes I've never seen either in breadth or infliction. This part of the state is no stranger to twisters, but this, this is something else and it's taking it out on a town that can't absorb it. The absolutely colossal debris field surrounding the thick brown funnel alone is a third the size of Tahoka itself, and it shows no sign of leaving town. I focus my eyes back to the foreground, to Bock who reaches into his coat and produces a corked vial of brimstone and smashes it on the ground. Three demons appear. These look human but for their horribly burned skin and elongated legs below the knee. The demons' faces are obscured by smooth metal-plated masks. Bock sends one after the truck that has almost reached the stables. The demon launches itself into the air several yards away and sprints away to the stables when it hits the ground.

I dip my head back and grab Evangeline again. "Listen to me, Red. You're in there. I need your help. We're all going to die if you don't come back. We need you. I need you, Evangeline. For God's sake, wake up. Fight!"

"Lix—lix. Rust. Lix."

"No, Red. Fight it. Come up. You can beat this. You're strong."

Evangeline's eyes—her eyes, not the demon's—finally emerge. She coughs and vomits down her nightgown. "Amarillo," she struggles out.

"I'm here, Red. I need the Thumper. Where is it? Is it here?"

"Yes. In—in the guesthouse. In the back."

"I'm going to get you out of here. I'm going to get you all out of here." I turn my focus to Brigita who is so frightened she seems as if she's on another planet, her eyes glassy like sleepy Texas ponds. "Brigita, honey. I'm so sorry, but I have to ask you do something else. Please. I should have been here. I should have seen it, but I was weak and stupid and focused on everything else when I should have been here for you. Do you hear me? I'm sorry, but you've got to help us."

The way she looks at me, there's a strength I just don't have, and may never. God gives us what we can handle, and this little girl knows pain and abandonment like no one else. It has made her strong, but not a strength that kills the soul, a strength that stokes its fire, a strength that resonates and consumes everything around it in its brilliance. I don't have to ask her to be strong. She's already stronger than any of us could ever be. Brigita was chosen, chosen because she can take it, because she can endure.

Two careless bobby pins hold Evangeline's disheveled hair in some sort of place like an afterthought. I pluck the pins from her auburn hair. "Honey, take these," I say to Brigita. "You take these to Everly. You wake him up and he'll tell you how to pick the locks on his chains. Get the others free and meet me outside. You can do this. We *have* to do this. Go, there isn't much time left."

Brigita grabs the pins and runs upstairs as Bock bursts back through the front door with the two remaining demons behind him. He looks at Evangeline and spits in her face. I glare up at him and stand nose to nose. "Don't do that, Bock," I say.

He grins. "Take him outside," he says to the demons as he lifts the duffle bag and follows us out.

When we're outside, the demons release and force me on my knees in front of Bock who unzips the duffle and takes out one of the Sepulcher crosses. "Right. Okay. Do your magic, Rust. The big man will be here any moment," Bock says referring to the tornado continuing to rip up town.

Just then we hear a few gunshots and a shriek. The demon Bock sent after the truck explodes through the stable wall and falls on its back. Pastor Barnhill emerges with Horrace over his shoulder. I have to squint to see it, but he loads Horrace into the F250 and drives hard across the field, bursting through the barbed wire fence heading toward Yakubu's farm on the next parcel.

"Shite. What's he on about?" Bock says sighing. "Doesn't matter. We're almost finished here. Let him stand up. Activate the fecking weapon, Rust."

The demons stand back. The tornado makes a turn toward us. Wind picks up, dirt loose and clodded swirls around us.

"Do it," I hear behind me. I turn to see Evangeline behind us carrying Brigita with one hand and holding the straight razor at the girl's neck with the other. "Do it or we'll lix her. We'll lix—lix. We'll kill the girl. We'll lix and kill and kill-kill-kill," she says in a voice not her own, still approaching. The colossal tornado now churns less than half a gridiron away.

Brigita obviously didn't make it upstairs in time to get to Everly. There's nothing else to do. I can't let the girl die. I won't. She's seen enough pain. If I've got to take her place then so be it, but that little girl has seen and felt enough. I will die for her if need be. He can have the crosses. Besides, maybe they don't do anything. Maybe Bock's wrong. Either way, I've at least got to pretend that I know what I'm doing. The tornado's nearly upon us anyway. We might all be meeting the maker soon enough.

Just then a forceful whir and grind, like a freight train slamming on the brakes. The ground beneath us tremors and rattles. There are flies in the funnel, thousands of them. Millions. First they swirl along with the great wind's current, but just as soon stop as a great indomitable pillar of insects a thousand feet tall only to reverse on themselves and spin the other way. The tremors deepen and quake with greater fervency as the flies multiply until populating the entire vortex. The Herculean pillar of black buzzing, undulating, insects detaches from the sky and lifts off the ground, compressing down and impossibly compacting its mass further into a perfect cube suspended at eye level no more than a few feet wide and just as tall. Then a rolling rumble, the deepest groaning like a star's collapse booms, traversing the expanse as the cube explodes into the form of man. It torturously elongates and painfully stretches into being until before us stands the old Russian, the chief demon Beelzebub.

"The Lix Tetrax's whore is wrong," he says, adjusting the tie beneath his overcoat. "I'll not allow the child to be killed. Not merely killed, no. I'll make a promise to you," he says walking up to me. The demons behind and the one from the stables having joined them all bow as if compelled by an unseen hierarchy. When we finally come face to face, I see Hell emblazoned in his eyes. The rot and death and hopeless stagnation of a million souls burn proudly inside his pupils. "No, I'll not make a promise to you, seed of Franklin Rust, to you I will seal a covenant. The little girl, Brigita will be used as a rag and footstool in our court for the rest of eternity. I will personally send her to murder and eat the children of the damned souls as she smells the flavors of her charred feet. Brigita as of yet has known no suffering, and only you have the ability to save her from it. Do as your friend says. Activate the weapon. Show us what your God has decided to keep from my agents. Show us how your grandfather gained the exclusive powers of the divine. Show us how to kill an angel."

I look to the Sepulcher in my hands. If the cross I hold is some kind of weapon, it certainly doesn't look it. It's just a cross, a stone, jeweled cross, with a short wooden handle, something for a priest to carry down a church aisle. Something to look official. Artifice. A symbol. A symbol of God. Something that invites people to pray, to remember themselves, to remember Him and what He did for man. And all of the sudden it's something else entirely. That's when I remember. I remember my grandfather. I remember my childhood and the words of my guardian angel. She told me to remember the prayer he used to say at night as he tucked me in so many years ago. Back in the times I've missed so much. Back in the days I lived in the light.

"When the Devil comes to steal your day," my grandfather would say as I try to remember, as I try to stay focused. "When the Devil comes to steal your day, just hit your knees and start to pray." That was the prayer. I hear my grandfather speak the words. I feel his hand on my forehead. I note that comforting smell. The words of the prayer wash over me. When the Devil comes. When the Devil comes to steal your day. When the Devil comes to steal your day, just hit your knees and start to pray. Start to pray. Hit your knees and start to pray. Start to pray. Hit your knees... *Hit your knees!*

I grab hold of the wooden handle with both hands. I lift it over my head. I bow and take a deep breath. As Bock, Evangeline, Brigita, the demons and their horrific lord of flies watch on, I clinch my teeth so hard they might burst and fall to my knees, the only thing in my mind the power of God and His righteousness, something I've worked most of my life to stamp away. It all returns to me with a blistering fervency. Goodness burns hotter than flames when turned in the right direction, and as humans, God's children, we have access to that power, but like me, we choose too often to run from it, not toward. But not anymore. Now I will choose to follow Him. Now I choose to have faith. My knees hit the ground and I bring the cross in my grasp down, slamming the hilt to the floor. The Sepulcher trembles in my hands, it clicks and whirs and rattles as the gears inside spring to life. The edge of the cross facing east recedes in on itself like a trap door and a great, collapsible curved blade like an axe slides out. It locks into place upon its extension. Another trap door flicks open at the top of the cross and another blade, this time a sharp, pointed one like the end of a spear, like a bayonet snaps up with the force of a switchblade. The wooden handle pops and telescopes out in segments, rising several feet above as I continue to kneel. I let the staff extend through my grasp before using it to brace myself and stand. The cross *is* the weapon. That which sets all men free has the power to overcome those who's might dwarfs our own. We can do nothing without the cross, but a righteous heart can slay any evil with it. The great demon before me knows that, and it is not I, but he who now stands afraid.

Beelzebub jumps back at the sight of the weapon. I take it in my grasp with authority and bring the sharpened tip of the staff millimeters from Beelzebub's throat. The demons behind me shudder at its glow. Evangeline screams and drops Brigita who runs back inside the house before anyone can stop her. Bock steps up and I feel the muzzle of that .45 at my right temple.

"I was made a promise, mate. And I intend to collect."

"Right you are, Mr. Bock," Elijah says emerging from the front door with Yakubu in his gauntlet and Everly strapped up in Red's pneumatic Thumper, ready to cause all kinds of trouble. "But if it isn't your old friend who puts an end to your madness, it will be them," he says pointing to the horizon and the same giant orb of cloud and lightning that carried the archangel Michael and his magnificent angels to our gracious assistance in the Sudan. It glides toward us, albeit a little too slowly for my liking.

"Oh shite," Bock says.

"Oh shite indeed, Mr. Bock. It is finished," Elijah says, now accompanied by his two angel guardians I once foolishly regarded as European goons. "Mr. Everly, Mr. Yakubu, would you kindly assist our friend and dispose of this rabble?"

"With pleasure," the Yak says, his blindness in no way hindering his movement or focus. He sees with different eyes now. Better eyes, just like Samson before him, the greatest judge, he is no longer guided by sight, but by faith.

The three demons turn toward them and separate. They quiver and shudder at what I first believe is fear, but soon we see them vibrate so fast they ghost themselves and multiply. Where once there were three now are six, then nine, then twelve, fifteen and so on. Everly sets the pneumatic Thumper to auto and charges forth, Yakubu follows, his physical blindness now guided by the eyes of the Spirit. He rears back his great arm and heaves his metal fist at the first demon he can reach. It's metallic mask crushes like a soda can as it careens off several yards like paper in wind. Everly perforates his first demon with the Thumper's fluttering pistons so quickly it doesn't even have time to react. Elijah's angels shed their earthly forms and tackle a demon each as more light-ning and thunder cracks inside the glowing orb gliding overhead.

I feel Bock begin to squeeze the trigger and I drop back to my knees, swinging the end of the staff around, sweeping Bock's legs out from under him as a shot rings out and travels into nothingness. With Beelzebub's attention now on the orb in the sky and Bock on his back, I leap on my old friend and use the long wooden handle of the Sepulcher as a choking bar across his neck. I press down as his face swells red and I press some more until the capillaries in his eyes strain and pop spilling their red ink into his white irises.

"Why did you do it, Bock? Why did you do this?" I glare down at him. And as I feel the life slowly drain out of him, I am knocked away several yards by one of the demons. My head rings and the pain in my side where Dresden stabbed me returns.

The demon snarls above me. Strings of its feculent saliva slap my face and run down my cheeks. I see Evangeline off to the side scramble to pick up Bock's .45. She trembles, fighting the evil inside her just long enough to let off a single salt round at the demon hunching over me. The bullet strikes it in the shoulder and sizzles in, a thin curl of smoke rises from the wound. The demon screams, turning its attention to Evangeline just long enough for me roll away, grab the sepulcher and stand. Evangeline drops the gun to the floor and falls to the ground crying. The demon seems to laugh.

"Hey," I say to it, getting its attention back on me and when it turns I lean back and throw all of my might from way down behind the Sepulcher, sending its axe blade first through air, then further until the curved blade kisses the demon's charred stomach and slips inside effortlessly. I continue to push. The Sepulcher's blade slides deeper inside the belly of the demon and upwards, severing its sternum, slicing through its dead organs and up, splitting its esophagus, ultimately carving fluently through the center of its chin, then its teeth and soft palate, up through the nasal passages, the lobes of its brain, and finally the demon's skull until two distinct halves of the beast's body butterfly open flushing all the black blood from each half until they separate and flop to the ground at two places beside one another.

All action ceases. No one even takes a breath. The fighting stops. Everyone's attention is on me and what the Sepulcher cross in my hand has just done as the orb hums overhead. Even the great demon Beelzebub seems speechless. It is true. Frank Rust *did* kill a demon. Now everyone knows how he did it, and now they know his grandson can do it too. The development is cause for much alarm. For the old Russian, the order of the known universe has been turned on its head, and he has to do something.

Beelzebub fans out his arms and he lifts off the ground and inverts like he did at the bar. He turns black with swirling flies all about him. The wind picks up again. The flies roar and number in the millions until the towering tornado threatens to return again. But just as we all think it will, a terrible booming sounds. The flies scatter to reveal a new shape, the greater demon's true form. Several stories tall, the body of an oily serpent rises, the head and manifold legs of a titanic fly replete with thick and sharp batches of black hair each several coarse inches in diameter burst from open sores and eyes bulbous, bulging grids of acrimonious revulsion. The demon rears up like a cobra in striking position—so mammoth and monstrous the ground shakes with its violently carnal exhalations.

"See me!" Its prodigious voice reverberates beneath us.

Then the exalted horn sounds from the heavenly orb above, instantly bursting all windows of the mansion behind us. The orb cracks with thunder again just above the beast's head. Blistering fire-bolts of silver lightning explode onto the grounds, each resulting in a masterful soldier of God's great army, their magnificent swords burning orange and enkindled with the fires of truth. The final bolt is Michael's, and he emerges from the emanation even more glorious and sublime than before. He stands at attention surveying the battlefield without a hint of fear, or doubt, or weakness. All attention turns to him as he unleashes the order that sends his angels into illustrious combat.

"Now!"

The angels chop and slash their way through the demon hordes that now seem to have multiplied all over again. They fight the angels with renewed vitriol at the sight of their general taking his true massive, horrific form. Beelzebub uses his great legs to swat any impending angels away, knocking each one that attacks him hundreds of yards into the distance.

Yakubu, Everly, and Elijah's angels fight on tirelessly as the demons show no signs of weakening. For each they put down two take its place. The battle rages, both demon and angel falling on the sword. The fight is far from over, and neither side can yet claim victory.

"Murder these lapdogs of God," Beelzebub orders, the bass in his voice causing the ground to quake. "Tear them apart. Send them to me!"

I survey the battlefield for Bock. He's gone. I only see Evangeline stumbling back toward the mansion and Brigita standing in the open doorway. Red's still under the influence of the Lix Tetrax. I make a break for her, but just as I push my way through the battle line, using the Sepulcher to hack away any demon limbs that try to stop me, a hand slams against my chest and holds me still.

"First things first," the archangel Michael says. He rips the Sepulcher from my hands. It shudders and shrinks as the gears snap its blades back inside. Segments of the staff collapse on themselves until the mighty weapon returns to its dormant form. "This has served its purpose. The Sepulcher crosses are far too dangerous for humans to wield."

"But the fight isn't over," I say.

"It is for you," he says to me, then turns his attention to Evangeline. "Woman," Michael calls after her. As if by some unseen force she turns toward the archangel. "Come to me now."

She walks toward us absently. Michael places a hand on her shoulder, peering deep into her eyes.

"Carry this burden no more," he says. "You were lost, then found, and now lost again. Your heavenly father anxiously awaits your heart's return. Do so now, and be rid of this evil lurking inside you once and for all. Your soul shall never again be compromised for it belongs to the Almighty, and the little girl deserves a guardian. Take her up, protect her, and never again leave her side. There are still difficult days ahead for you all, face them with the blessed assurance that He is always with you. Now go."

Tears streak Evangeline's cheeks as the battle rages all around us. But for her it might as well be the most tranquil spot on earth. Her eyes thank the archangel though her mouth cannot. She looks at me and smiles like the one I used to know and admire. Evangeline turns and walks toward Brigita with her arms outstretched. The little girl knows she has returned and runs to meet her in a warm embrace.

"Now, Amarillo Rust, steadfast soldier of the Almighty, watch as I send this demon back to Hell where it will roast in its own decay for a long time."

Michael marches toward the great demon, standing so close he must crane his head to view its monumental head. Though he appears miniscule by comparison, there is no fear in him.

"Demon!" he shouts.

Beelzebub glares down and makes a wide swipe with one of his enormous legs. Michael raises his smoldering sword and digs his heels into the dirt, using the monster's own inertia to sever the limb. It falls steaming to the ground with a great thud.

"Unclean devil!" Michael shouts again, and again Beelzebub sends another immense leg toward him like a battering ram. This time Michael lands an overhead strike to sizzle and slice through it, dispatching the leg with another hefty thunk.

"You have insulted the Lord and yet again fail to thwart His will. He has sent me to punish you once again, and just as in the past, I will do my work perfectly in He who protects and strengthens those who choose to follow Him. In the Lord, the weak are strong, and in Him the strong are invincible. Nothing you do will stop it."

"Pompous slave," the demon says. "Even as I tower above your pathetic soldiers, still you bark orders. What can you possibly do from down at my feet?"

"I don't have to do anything... yet," Michael says.

"What do you mean?" the demon taunts.

But, I know what he means. Yakubu's farm tractor sweeps across the field behind Beelzebub with Horrace at the helm, gaining every ounce of momentum it can with the jackhammer implement raised high on the tractor's arm. Before Beelzebub can take action, Horrace initiates the jackhammer throttle and cranks it to the maximum, the immense chrome spear pistons in and out with blinding speed, exhaust billows from the exposed pipes before the gleaming bolt pierces deep into the scaled flesh of the towering demon. Horrace feeds the tractor's engine even more gasoline as heavy black exhaust again flushes from its pipe. The tractor shudders as the jackhammer pulses deeper into Beelzebub's back, working the hydraulics forward and reverse, forward and reverse. Horrace fights for control, the machine's front wheels lift off the ground, hammering the stake in even deeper until the tip splits through the creature's chest. Black blood ripples and cascades down each side of the wound.

"It is good to have friends," Michael says as Beelzebub lurches forward and lets out a howl that threatens to burst our eardrums. Its pungent blood paints the sky and ground.

I turn to notice the tide has gone decidedly in the angels' favor. Few if any demons are left standing, or even in a single piece for that matter. Minister Barnhill plows toward us in the F250. He stops at the listing tractor that holds the demon in place and helps Horrace out and into the safety of the truck while the tractor's jackhammer continues stab relentlessly through the demon's back.

"Gather you friends now and go," Michael calls to me. "When the trumpets sound, your work is finished and ours begins. Go and let none of you look back. Human eyes are not meant to see what follows. You have done well. The prophet was correct in searching you out for his employ. But as I have taken up your Sepulchers to their rightful place in Heaven, know that your former friend has scattered his across the earth for evil's safe keeping. It will be up to you and your team to find them and bring them back."

The angelic orb crackles as the horn booms again from above. Most of us cover our ears for fear of our eardrums rupturing.

"Go now, Amarillo Rust, mighty servant of God. Be well. Be safe. We will call on you again in time. You have only to listen for the trumpets."

I nod and see Barnhill and Horrace pull up in the truck.

"Fancy seeing you two here," I say as Barnhill rolls down the window. I peek my head in to see Horrace grimacing in the back.

"We need to get you to a hospital ASAP. I could use a doctor too," I say, checking the stab wounds in my side again. "Good work though, Horrace. Excellent work, soldier."

He nods, floating in and out of consciousness.

"I just gotta know though," I say turning my attention to Barnhill. "How did you know to leave the church and pick up Horrace? How did you know he escaped, and that Yakubu had that tractor with the jackhammer implement? Just doesn't make sense."

Minister Barnhill laughs like I just made a joke, but I'm not joining him. Pretty soon it dwindles and he realizes that I'm sincere.

"It was Knapp. You sent Henry Knapp back to the church to warn us, to tell us it was okay to come out, that Horrace needed my help."

"Look, Henry is—" and my throat closes up. I can't finish.

"But, he was there, he—he was with two little girls. He stood right in front of me and told me. He said, 'The team needs you. It's safe for you to go. Get in your truck and take Horrace to Yakubu's farm. He'll know what to do.' I asked him who the little girls were, but he didn't answer. I assumed he found them alone out there in all the craziness on his way from the mansion. Soon as he came, he walked out. That was it. Where is he? I want to thank him."

"He's—um—He's gone, Minister, he… He was shot. Long before he appeared to you he was shot." We both know what that means, and we both know what that proves. This is not the end, and maybe if we live right, we'll get to see those that left before us. We might even have a little more work to do from the other side.

I go to collect my team. I take the heroic Judge Yakubu by the hand and lead him like Samson from the collapsed temple. I embrace Everly and smile. He is the Meek, but he has proven himself far braver than most twice in stature. Lastly I greet Evangeline back to the team and the little Brigita, our Herald, the faithful one who talks to God. I seat her next to me. The prophet Elijah only waves to me from distance and nods his approval, both of which I return. I have no doubt we will see him again, and so goodbyes are meaningless as he gently and sincerely mouths the words, "thank you." I return his words in kind.

Though I grieve the loss of Henry Knapp as I watch the angels carry his body out over their shoulders like pallbearers in a deep respect for he, the Anointed, the one who brings them back to God, I also mourn the loss of my friend, Bock, and while he may have taken a different path, still I pray for him, and wish that he would return someday and choose to walk beside us, steadfast in the light. Until then, as the ethereal horn sounds and we drive from it to futures uncertain with the firm knowledge that faith will guide our direction, I now know that we will continue. I know that we will fight. I know we *will* endure. Until the day our Herald hears the language of angels once again, until the day our charge of recovery is renewed, until the forces of Satan must again be met with a resolute might of our own through the Cross, I say *Laus Deo* to you, my friends. Praise be to God, indeed.

The End

www.ingramcontent.com/pod-product-compliance
Lightning Source LLC
Chambersburg PA
CBHW030012180626
46810CB00001B/1